Praise for Patrick Swenson's
The Ultra Big Sleep

"Swenson's future-noir story of alien invasion is deep, vast, and fast. Full of high stakes, unexpected twists, and a truly evil force or two, *The Ultra Big Sleep* is a great read."
—Brenda Cooper, author of *Edge of Dark*

"*The Ultra Big Sleep* combines ultra big worldbuilding with an ultra fast plot. Sleep will be the last thing on your mind. An impressive sequel."
—Ted Kosmatka, author of *The Flicker Men*

"Science-fiction mysteries are hardly new (Isaac Asimov was writing them years ago), nor are detective stories set in exotic earthly locales all that rare anymore either. But Patrick Swenson's interplanetary Ultra novels with their eight worlds, their alien Helks and Memors, and their vast cataclysmic stakes in the hands, here, of a fallible human-Helk duo raise the ante in the long SF mystery story in astonishing, fully satisfying ways. Pick up *The Ultra Big Sleep* and hold on to your molecules; they're about to be shaken *and* stirred in ways you can never imagine: a light-speed, stand-alone noir follow-up to Swenson's admirable debut novel, *The Ultra Thin Man*."
—Michael Bishop, author of *Brittle Innings*

"Swenson's thrilling sequel blends future sci-fi with the grit of a noir detective tale. Lost love, fine whiskey, quantum travel, alien conspiracies—*The Ultra Big Sleep* has it all."
—Beth Cato, author of The Clockwork Dagger series

"Patrick Swenson's deft touch with complex themes of interstellar noir resonate in *The Ultra Big Sleep*. With mystery, danger, and intrigue on every shore, detective Dave Crowell is back and faced with new challenges. *The Ultra Big Sleep* again showcases Swenson's skills with pacing that reveal those dark corners that exist when everyone thinks they're safe. A great ride!"
—Fran Wilde, author of *Updraft*

"The nightmare of the Ultras who threaten the Union of Worlds has returned ... Private detective Dave Crowell and his partner are drawn into a convoluted underworld of the drug RuBy and its connection to the Ultras, and their lives are quickly put in jeopardy. If you enjoyed *The Ultra Thin Man*, you'll really like this one."
—James C. Glass, author of *Shanji*

"This splendidly lively SF debut alternates between the narrations of Alan Brindos and Dave Crowell, two irreverent gumshoes who work for the Network Intelligence Organization of the eight-world Union in the year 2113. Swenson provides Shakespearean riffs on identity as Brindos is transformed and becomes a target for the NIO ... Pig Latin, an exotic drug, a comic strip, and a retractable penis add colorful detail to a showdown that puts love and sacrifice at the heart of the self."
—*Publishers Weekly*, starred review

"The thriller pacing carries the story along until the structure of the conspiracy becomes clear. By the epic finale, the universe is fleshed out enough to make the ultimate question—Who is behind this chain of events?—one worth answering. All in all, an entertaining piece of storytelling."   —*Booklist*

"*The Ultra Thin Man* races like a bullet train from one adrenalin-arousing development to the next. It has everything—aliens, murders, interstellar conflicts, conspiracies—and none of them are what they first seem. Exciting, inventive, and explosive."
—Nancy Kress, author of *Yesterday's Kin*

"Patrick Swenson keeps the pages turning in this slick, clever noir novel. Wonderful world-building, a terrific read, and an auspicious debut: truly the stuff that dreams are made of."
—Robert J. Sawyer, Hugo Award-winning author of *Quantum Night*

"Patrick Swenson charts a twisty journey through a futuristic landscape of aliens, detectives, murder, political intrigue, grand space opera, and unforgettable characters. It's great fun. Turn the first page and you'll forget where you are."
—Jack Skillingstead, author of *Life on the Preservation*

"Blending elements of noir crime and science fiction isn't a new thing, but Patrick Swenson tackles the mashup with enormous talent and verve ... [It's] informed by a Chandlerersque sensibility, with its short, crisp sentences and snappy one-liners. It's truly a terrific read."
—John Dodds, *Adventures in Sci-Fi Publishing*

"A sprightly SF thriller ... fans of future noir should enjoy the ride."
—*The Hamilton Spectator*

"Action, mystery, and furry aliens . . . what more could I ask for in a book? Swenson's tone and pacing are perfect—I swear I could hear Harrison Ford's *Blade Runner* voice narrating as I read—and more than one twist caught me completely by surprise . . . I burned through *The Ultra Thin Man* at light speed and can't wait for the next installment. This SF noir thriller is storytelling at its best."

 —Kristene Perron, co-author of *Warp World*

"A decently told mystery and a lot of fun getting to the solution."
 —*Critical Mass*

"An entertaining and worthwhile read . . . Swenson uses the tropes well and creates a compelling story with an interesting setting."
 —*Seattle Geekly*

"Interstellar conspiracy, enigmatic aliens, bizarre drugs, body-morphing technology, 'Thin Men,' and the fate of the Union . . . just a few of the elements that make *The Ultra Thin Man* awesomeyay. I just love this stuff."
 —Patrick Heffernan, *Mysterious Galaxy*

"Very clever and intriguing take on science fiction noir. Loved the Helks and especially the Crowell character. Excellent job by the author bringing his 'verse to life."
 —Dave Bara, author of *Impulse*

Praise for *Slightly RuBy*:

"A richly realized near-future noir tale . . . a potent cocktail of genre homage: equal parts bodies murdered and missing, corporate intrigue and synth-drug addiction, finished with a dash of aliens and interstellar politics, and a twist of corruption."
 —Stephen Susco, writer of *The Grudge* and *Flatliners*

"From within Patrick Swenson's Ultra universe, *Slightly Ruby* offers a tempting glimpse at the mysterious, dark underbelly of a human and alien conspiracy. A dangerous and compelling story!"
 —Fran Wilde, Andre Norton and Compton Crook Award-winning author of *Updraft*

Also by Patrick Swenson

The Ultra Thin Man
Slightly Ruby

The
Ultra
Big
Sleep

Patrick
Swenson

FAIRWOOD PRESS
Bonney Lake, WA

The Ultra Big Sleep

A Fairwood Press Book
August 2016
Copyright © 2016 Patrick Swenson

Fairwood Press
21528 104th Street Court East
Bonney Lake, WA   98391
www.fairwoodpress.com

Cover by Kuldar Leement

First Edition

ISBN: 978-1-933846-60-6 [Hardcover]

First Fairwood Press Edition: August 2016
Printed in the United States of America

For my sister Melanie, my number one fan.

The

Ultra

Big

Sleep

One

WATCHED WITH SOME AMUSEMENT AS ALEX RICHARDS HURRIEDLY put on his pants, barely staying vertical, while the girl he'd been having sex with took her time. In her late twenties, the girl had to be fifteen years younger than Richards. She had a markedly different attitude about the whole adultery thing, simply draping her blouse strategically on her upper torso as she lay on a heavy blanket on the concrete floor.

I looked away. It was hard to see in the low light anyway, although my antique digital camera still had an excellent low-light sensor and an extremely high ISO rating. The old digitals had about reached their peak in the late 2030s. I was lucky to find this one.

The hour was very late, one o'clock in the morning, and I was anxious to get this over with. The abandoned warehouse on Seattle's waterfront smelled of stale fish and salt, and for all its space, I felt claustrophobic amidst the crates, concrete columns, and scattered debris. My head hurt, and it might have been from the smell, or it might have been because it had been a while since I'd had a good shot of Temonus whiskey.

I dangled my camera from its strap, swinging it slightly, as if to remind Richards I had the goods on him, that his wife would finally get the answers she'd hired me to find. He looked at it as if he thought my antique digital camera was a joke.

Asshole Alex, his wife called him.

Easy duty, really. I got to stay on Earth, I didn't have to deal with aliens, good or bad, I didn't have to answer to the Network Intelligence Office, and I didn't have to come into contact with imposters and body doubles.

Richards cinched up his jeans. Thin, almost scrawny, he looked down at the girl on the blanket, who still made no move to get dressed. Well, I hadn't been investigating *her*, and Liz Richards hadn't wanted any names. Just high-resolution photos and a confrontation with him. Yes, a confrontation. She assured me he was not only an asshole, but someone who avoided conflict. Weak and wimpy, she said.

"So Liz hired you?"

"Slapped the cash right down on my desk," I said.

"Paid you in full, said bait the son of a bitch and rub it in his face, didn't she?"

"Son of a bitch wasn't exactly what she said."

"Yeah, I can just imagine. When?"

"Just yesterday, near the Eighth Avenue Apartments, where you two live. It didn't take me long to find you because she knew about this warehouse."

Richards had just pulled on his green T-shirt. "We used to come here back before—"

He broke off, and I knew he'd been about to say before most everything moved off world, to the other colonies in the Union. She'd filled me in about his dreams to move to Helkunntanas, of all places, and start his own business. It had never happened, and he'd become disgruntled and sullen.

"Not very smart," I said, "coming back here with your girl."

He pointed at my camera. "You get good pictures with that piece of crap?"

"You wouldn't understand the importance of a good antique. Don't worry. It caught you and lover girl right in the act."

The girl on the carpet moved a bit, up on one elbow, her blouse slipping a little. She pulled at the fabric and repositioned it, releasing a slight odor of lilac perfume.

"So you're a private detective," Richards said.

It was almost a question, with quaver of surprise in his voice. As if he expected me to be something else. I didn't like him one bit. "Private as they get around here."

I was who I was. Dave Crowell, man of intrigue and mystery, part-time savior of the Union, and still no big cover story on the flashroll mags.

"It's fun keeping an eye on people, isn't it?"

I shrugged. "Pays the bills."

"You must get bored, if this is what you have to do to make a buck."

"My clients keep me company."

"And your secretary, no doubt."

He was fishing for something, but I couldn't imagine what. "Can't afford one. If I don't have clients, I talk to myself. Or my mom."

He picked his belt off the concrete. When he straightened, he had a faraway gaze. Then he raised an eyebrow, and his pupils did this quick darting to and fro thing. An odd tic that seemed almost familiar.

"Your mother," he said. "Really."

The stupid shit. "She lives in Montana, but I can still talk to her." I really didn't like this guy, and not just because of what his wife had told me. He was slick. And condescending. And, yes, he *was* an asshole.

I did have a partner, and I *did* talk to him. Tonight, I'd left him standing guard at the warehouse exit. But I didn't mention him to Richards.

I spent a moment thinking about my backup. Given that his wife had called him weak and wimpy, I let my guard down and played with him. "I can assure you the camera's good. Seriously, look at it." I held it out to him and he glanced at it a moment. It's not like he knew how to use an old antique. He wouldn't know how to delete the files, and he couldn't escape the warehouse, so the hell with it. In the space of a breath, however, he grabbed it and ran into the darkened warehouse.

"God *damn* it." I headed after him. "Richards, where the hell you going?"

He'd run the wrong way, toward the back of the giant warehouse, so I'd be able to reel him in like a big fish. A slippery but stupid fish. He *was* fast, though. Now a shadow in the distance, he disappeared behind some large cargo containers, his footsteps echoing as he ran.

When I reached the containers, he had totally vanished. Running, I heard nothing but my own steps and breaths. He must have stopped and hidden behind the containers to wait me out.

I leaned against a graffiti-marked concrete column. Only one overhead florescent light worked, but it flickered like a strobe. I squinted in the direction I'd seen Richards go. The only exit was behind me, guarded, so at length I would corner him and retrieve both my camera and my proof. It would be lovely not to have to give Liz Richards her money back.

I almost always chose the cheating spouse cases. They beat missing-persons cases, which were nearly impossible to solve. These days, missing persons were missing because they'd fled to one of the other seven worlds of the Union, totally out of my jurisdiction. These days, I didn't deal with Union-threatening plots from aliens conspiring from places unknown. I avoided all mention of the Ultras, the aliens who, a year ago, had threatened the Union of Worlds.

Well, there *was* a special cocktail created in their honor. For a short time, I had ordered nothing but *Ultras*. They came in a special glass. You got two drinks in that glass, separated in the middle by a thin membrane that dissolved after you'd quaffed the first half. Novelty shit. A sort of self-imposed punishment, maybe.

Oh, and I *worked* with an alien, but that was different.

Now when I had my camera back, things would be better. Even better if I had that whiskey.

Movement caught my eye. A flash of something—a chance glint of light off my camera?—near the high back windows, close to more stacked cargo containers. I jogged forward, nonchalantly. He was an unfaithful husband—I didn't need stealth, and I didn't fear for my life.

"Come on, Richards," I said. "You're not getting out of here with my camera."

Asshole Alex was not in front of the containers, so I whipped around behind them, hoping to surprise him, and I ran headlong into a wall.

The giant formidable wall barely grunted as I rebounded from it and landed hard on the concrete floor. A massive torso and an angular head bent down and looked at me with a menacing grin.

He couldn't help the menacing grin, owing to the fact that he *always* looked menacing.

"Forno," I said, shaking my head.

"Crowell," my alien partner growled.

I ignored the Helk's offered hand and unsteadily rose. As a Second Clan Helk, Tem Forno wasn't the biggest, but the difference between First and Second Clan didn't matter much to humans. Many humans, whose attitudes toward the aliens were less than favorable, liked to call them Hulks.

Forno wore a gray overcoat that had once belonged to my old partner Alan Brindos. The Helk version of him anyway.

"You're supposed to be guarding the front door," I said. "What're you doing back here?"

"I got lonely." Forno towered over me.

"Hulks don't get lonely."

"No?" He scratched his head, the only part of him free of fur. "Okay, so, the girl? She left the warehouse—no clothes on, I might add—and I got scared."

I sighed. He was shitting me; he wasn't afraid of most things. "Where's Mr. Richards, Forno?"

"Not in this warehouse anymore."

I really would have to give Liz Richards her money back—minus the retainer—if I couldn't produce a visual of what I'd seen her husband do.

"How'd he get by you?" I asked.

Forno looked hurt. "You really think he could get by me?"

"Through the only door," I said, pointing that way.

"If you don't count the side door."

"What side door?"

"The one on the side."

I stared up at him, not sure I wanted to hurt myself trying to slap him. I'd practically have to jump to reach his face anyway. "Please just tell me."

"Relax, I scooped it out earlier. It's a separate room attached to the warehouse."

Maybe my eyes were adjusting to the light. I could see the side door now, not too far away. "*Scoped*, Forno. You scoped it out."

"I'm just messing with you. No other exit from that small room. Nothing but some crates in there. He went in a few minutes ago, and can't have come back out without going by me. I can understand how you missed it."

I looked back the way I'd been chasing Richards earlier and frowned. "You sure he went that way? I'd been following him *this* way."

"Saw him clear as morning."

"You didn't just go in there and drag him out?"

"What for? Figured you had all the photos you needed."

"He has my camera."

"How'd that happen?"

I glanced away. "Never mind."

"So Network Intelligence gave you those nice shock capacitors in your fingers, but they didn't give you a retinal camera? I thought those were standard-issue for agents. I wouldn't trust those old digitals, myself."

"No retinal cameras for borrowed hounds," I said. "And I didn't want the caps. They made me install them."

"And now you don't even charge them up."

I glared at him. "I don't work for the NIO anymore."

"I know."

I was happy doing private jobs now, even if I had to do them without my old partner: the one I'd killed—out of necessity—to stop an alien invasion.

I was going to say that *someone* had to pay the bills. Working on our own without the NIO tracking us did that—when work was steady. But Forno didn't really need the money I paid him. He had plenty of credits from his life on Helkunntanas, thanks to a short undercover career with their intelligence agency—the Kenn—and from his often suspect dealings with underworld contacts.

Forno cocked his head toward the side door. "Asshole Alex is still in there."

So, Forno leading the way in that old overcoat, we walked past a few shipping containers and pallets. I hadn't thought about Alan Brindos for a long while, not wanting to remember the details of his death. The Ultras had been altering humans, Brindos himself transformed into an exact copy of the Helk terrorist, Terl Plenko.

Long story.

"Mr. Richards!" Forno called into the side room.

I had to stop, unable to peek around my own personal Helk. "Move through the door," I said. "So I can get through?"

He moved, and I entered a room a quarter of the size of the main warehouse. High windows and high ceilings also dominated these premises. "Stay at *this* door, please? So you can see the main warehouse."

"You know, it's nice to walk around in these buildings without ducking my head," Forno said, raising his arms high. "Ceilings almost as tall as my old place on Helkunntanas. Maybe you should've opened an office in one of these instead of that old artist studio."

I ignored him and scanned the room. Not as many florescent lights worked in here, making the room darker, but I could literally see most of the room at a glance. To be honest, I was surprised any of the lights worked at all, or that electricity still flowed. Dozens of clustered rectangular crates, stacked about five high, occupied the middle of the room. Nothing else was in here.

"Those don't look anything like the containers in the main room," Forno said from his place at the door.

"Mr. Richards?" I said impatiently. "There's no need to draw this out any longer. Pictures or no, your wife will be contacting you." More likely, her *lawyer* would be contacting him.

No answer. The silence unnerved me, and I looked back and found Forno's shadow.

"You have your blaster?" he asked.

In answer, I pulled it from my coat pocket and stepped nearer the boxes. "Forget the door and come in here. If he's gone, he's gone. We'll figure that out later."

Forno came to me, concern wrinkling the leathery skin of his face. Then he lumbered to the first stack and knocked on it. "Wooden."

I knocked on a crate too. "They sound hollow—could be empty, but I don't know."

"You don't think—"

I no longer cared about Mr. Richards. "Top one. You can reach it."

He nodded, turned, and easily lifted the top crate from the nearest stack.

He didn't even grunt, either lifting it or setting it on the floor. Pausing, he squinted back at me.

I waved my blaster at the crate, giving him the go-ahead.

Forno wrenched off the lid, which clattered to the floor. He looked up, relief in his eyes.

"Empty?" I guessed.

"Empty."

"Okay." I swallowed, mouth dry, my head still pounding. "The rest of the stack."

Soon, Forno had all five containers opened, and all of them were empty. I frowned, but in the overall scheme of things, a cache of empty crates in a warehouse didn't mean something was amiss. Most of the large cargo containers in the main warehouse were probably empty too, or filled with things forgotten, useless to a city port that had long ago closed up shop. The remaining ports now housed drop shuttles that ferried humans up to Egret Station to make connections to the colony worlds through the jump slots.

Worlds Apart, and Committed to Union. But a little less committed to Earth.

With the stack torn down, the other stacks clearly formed an uneven circle, as if to call some demon to the center. Except there were no candles, no chalked-in diagrams. I eased into the circle, and there, in the middle of the stacks, was a single crate.

Forno had come in behind me, and when I turned toward him, I stepped on one of his clubbed feet. Not that he noticed.

"Like the others?" he said, in what passed for a Helk whisper.

I braced myself, raised my blaster, and waited for Forno to lift the lid.

I had expected a body to be in this one, and indeed a body *was* in there. Forno slipped to the right to allow me a better look. Although dark, I easily made out some of the details of the body inside. It was definitely dead. A human male with short black hair, clad in jeans and a green T-shirt.

"Alex Richards," I said.

Forno snorted in my ear. "There's no way, Dave. I saw him go in here. The dark's messing with you."

I reached in my pants pocket, found my mini pen light, turned it on, and shined it inside the crate at the corpse's face. "It's Richards, all right." The hairs on the back of my neck bristled.

But there was something not right about him.

At the collar of the T-shirt, the pen light showed something dark. I leaned in, putting my face closer to Alex Richards.

"There's writing," I said.

Forno, who couldn't see, nudged me. "What's it say?"

I used the pen light to pull down the collar of the T-shirt. The message was crisp and bold, a single word neatly written along his collar bone. It looked like blood.

I really hadn't expected it. I'd hoped to avoid anything more like this for as long as I lived. There was an instant when I expected Asshole Alex to open his eyes, laugh, and call me the most gullible person who'd ever lived, but I'd seen enough during the past few years to know better.

"Damn it," Forno said, "what's it say?"

The single word on Alex Richard's collar bone really pissed me off.

"Ultra," I said.

Two

IT TOOK THE COPS ALMOST AN HOUR TO ARRIVE AT THE WAREHOUSE. Figured. Not high on their priority list. They made me wait another hour before Earth Authority officer Lieutenant Jaymes Freelund interrogated me about Alex Richards. They didn't find my digital camera. I spilled everything I knew about Richards, giving Freelund a detailed description of what had happened in the warehouse.

Then they made me wait some more. It had to be closing in on morning. I glanced at my Rolex. Except—it wasn't there. *What?* "My watch," I mumbled. I'd received it as an award from the NIO and the government for my efforts against the Ultras and Terl Plenko.

Had I even put it on? Yes of course I had. I rarely went anywhere without it. Antique that it was, having it with me always seemed safer.

I stood, ready to go look for it. Had Asshole Alex taken it somehow? I couldn't think of any other way it would've just slipped from my wrist.

"Lieutenant Freelund will be here soon," a uniformed Authority officer said to me. She smiled reassuringly. Her hair had a hard time looking natural under her cap. "Please remain here."

"I've lost my watch. It's very valuable."

"Yes, Mr. Crowell. We'll keep an eye out for it."

"And my camera."

"Yes, sir."

I sat back down. I fretted about the watch, but considering what had just happened, it meant little. I tried to put it out of my mind.

Instead, I mulled over what I'd seen written on Alex Richards' body. Filled with dread about the prospect of dealing with the whole mess again, I hoped it had all been some kind of prank. I really didn't want to know why the word Ultra was written in blood on a man I'd been chasing minutes before he turned up dead.

Tem Forno had snuck out long before. His absence spared me from having Earth Authority hounds pitch me a bunch of shit about his involvement with anything related to the Ultras, even if he *was* my partner. This pervasive and misguided attitude—the same one that let the derogatory name "Hulk" proliferate—found its stride with Terl Plenko, the Helk leader of the defunct Movement of Worlds. Plenko was now dead—three times over. The NIO had vindicated the original Plenko, but humans' distrust and fear of Helks tempered the positive reception Plenko had received on the other colony planets. This was particularly true on Ribon, the damaged planet slowly coming back to life after the Coral Moon disaster. Several habitation domes now existed in the ruins of Venasaille, where Plenko had lived.

Plenko was dead. Brindos was dead. All the known Ultras were dead. Even the alien copy of my old flame Cara Landry had self-destructed in an antimatter explosion on Heron Station above Aryell. The Ultra had vanished completely, no trace of her after the detonation.

I had a notion, while sitting on an empty wooden crate, to call Dorie Senall, a friend deeply involved in the resettlement project. Although human, she'd been the wife of the original Terl Plenko. She'd worked on Ribon for the past year at the project headquarters. Dorie's deep connection to Plenko had caused her great suffering, for she had lost her husband and her home, as well as nearly losing her life because of her RuBy addiction. She was clean now, and I wanted to see her, but money was tight. When I'd told her goodbye in my new Seattle office, I'd promised her I'd get to Ribon.

I was good at making promises. Not so good at keeping them. I thought of Cara Landry then, whose image often flashed into my head like an unwanted Net pop-up holo, reminding me of my own loss. My own stupidity. I had promised Cara I'd return to see her and, after a long absence, when I finally did . . . Well.

My guilt summoned the image of her neck, nearly severed, her head lolling to her chest as I held her. Perhaps she had been the woman I loved. Perhaps—

Cara Landry had been my enemy.

Perhaps seeing Dorie Senall now would chase away some of the physicalness of those memories. Drinking sure wasn't doing it, but what the hell.

Like I said about all this: long story.

Lieutenant Freelund appeared before me. He held out a cup of coffee.

"Don't suppose you have a bit of the blue poison," I muttered, rubbing the stubble on my jaw.

I really shouldn't. Promised Forno I'd cut way back, after hitting the bottle hard after Brindos's funeral and setting up shop in Seattle.

"Do I look like I can afford Temonus whiskey?" Freelund said, regret in his voice. "I'd do better going out on my own like you did."

I took the coffee, even though I dislike the strong odor and don't much care for the stuff. "At least your paydays are regular."

He glanced over at the untended crate with Richards' body still in it. Freelund was a big man, tall and stocky, his hair buzz cut, his ears big for his head. He had a thin moustache, and he'd just stuffed his hands in the pockets of his long blue coat.

"You know how long he's been dead?" I asked.

"Not me. Seems relatively fresh, though. The coroner's looked at him, but I don't know if she knows yet. They'll be taking him to the county morgue soon."

I nodded. "Can I go home?"

"NIO's coming in on this one," Freelund said quickly, without looking at me. I stared up at him until he did look. His eyes narrowed. "You expected it, right?"

"Can I go home?"

"You can, but you have to stay there."

"The NIO will come to me," I guessed.

"Lucky you."

The word stabbed me. *Lucky*—it's what my mom called my dad when I was a kid. I'd rarely heard her call him Lawrence. Once, I asked her how he'd got the nickname, but all she'd ever said was that it was just a handle that stuck. She couldn't remember, or didn't offer, the specifics. My mom, now on her own in Montana; my mom, who'd dealt with the aftermath of his disappearance alone, and who continued to ignore my pleas to join me in Seattle. Or to move somewhere less remote. Warmer. I needed to see her soon and talk about Dad.

Lucky Lawrence, not so lucky. Unless he counted disappearing on us when I was sixteen a lucky thing, victim of a drowning accident, body never found.

"Tell me something," Freelund said. He waited while I forced some coffee down. He fixed me with his brown eyes, which looked almost black in the warehouse's low light. "You got up close with few of the Ultras. What're they like?"

"You never saw one?"

As earlier, when I'd heard the regret in his voice, I sensed a similar melancholy in the way he shook his head. "Naw. Just the copies. The Thin Men, you know."

I knew. The Thin Men had become directionless without the guidance of the Ultras. Most of them—men and women—had peacefully given themselves up to Authority personnel, and most had suffered through a long, arduous process of comfortable incarceration, followed by relocation to designated settlements scattered among the planets of the Union. I was reminded of the tent city on Aryell, where we'd found the army of RuBy addicts waiting to be copied for the secret Ultra army. I shuddered, remembering how many of those poor souls had perished after we'd discovered the takeover plot and they'd had to come off the drug.

"Still rounding them up?" I asked.

"Wait. Who's asking the questions here?"

I shrugged and gave him his answer. "They're like us." Freelund narrowed his dark eyes, and I added, "In body, anyway. But they moved—slower. More deliberately. Like they weren't used to the form. Like they were trying out their new bodies, not really comfortable, maybe even hating it."

Oh yeah: and the coldness.

The dead, glassy eyes, the emotionless looks, and the silence. The silence of Cara's expression had frightened me, as if I were alone in the dark; the silence roared now in my memory, a deafening presence.

"But," Freelund said, "you never saw their true form."

It was a statement; as an officer of the Authority, he knew that much. We had no knowledge of the Ultras' true form. No knowledge of where they'd come from. We knew only about the Thin Men—the copies—and their alien human handlers.

"To answer your question," Freelund said, "we've found about a dozen of the copies who didn't turn themselves in. I've heard that overall, including those that came peacefully, fewer than a hundred, Union-wide, mostly found on Temonus, did so. A third eventually died from the process. No doubt, many Thin Men have chosen to stay hidden. No one knows how many may remain."

"They can't do any harm—not without the Ultras," I said, but I wasn't sure I believed it. Not with that word on Richards's collar bone. Freelund knew it too.

"For now." The Lieutenant stood up, stretching, hands at the small of his back. After another glance at the crate, he sighed. "Okay, you're done. Straight home, and stay put."

"Yeah." I also stood, the coffee cup still slightly warm in my hand.

"She'll be contacting you."

"She?"

"Special Ops. She's taking this one herself."

"Jennifer Lisle?"

"Special Ops *Director* Lisle," Freelund said.

I'd worked with Lisle, when she'd been an NIO field agent, helping uncover the aliens. Discovery of Ultras in the upper echelon of the National Intelligence Organization, including its director, Timothy Nguyen, had given Jennifer Lisle and other agents a giant leap forward in their careers.

Lisle had been copied, too. In fact, my partner, Tem Forno, had killed her—the copy, I mean. Lisle had also been the agent who'd taken a stunner beam in the leg before witnessing Dorie Senall's copy plummet from a hundred-story building.

"Oh." Freelund dug in the pocket of his blue coat and pulled out my Rolex.

My heart jumped in a good way. "*Damn.* Thank you."

"Found it outside the warehouse. On the ground."

"Outside? But Richards never ended up outside."

Freelund shrugged.

It must've pulled off somehow when Richards yanked the camera from me. And I hadn't noticed it. Freelund handed it to me, and I glanced at the time. Nearing five o'clock in the morning.

Freelund said, "Antique?"

Lifting my arm, I gave him a better look. "Hobby of mine. I'm a collector, old stuff, when I can find it. Or afford it."

From his pocket, Freelund pulled his comm card, a slim piece of lightweight black metal covered with a flash membrane that connected him to Earth Authority: communication, time, news, Net. As an NIO agent, I'd had a code card, the fancy equivalent, juiced up with more features and ties to the Union than imaginable, but I no longer had it.

"I've never seen a timepiece like that." Freelund fumbled with his comm card. "This seems almost inelegant compared to that beauty. You have to wind it?"

"Self-winding," I said.

He shook his head, unfamiliar with the idea.

"Rolex invented the first self-winding mechanism in the early 1930s."

Freelund said, "Huh," as I put it on. "Worth a bunch?"

"A bunch." I couldn't afford half the antiques and memorabilia I wanted, but occasionally the price was right. In this case, as a gift, the watch had been right.

"Sometimes it's hard to trust the tech," Freelund said.

"I'm with you." Although many improvements have occurred in the Union, Earth's declining status and the newness of the colony planets somewhat counteracted those advances.

"No luck finding my camera?"

"Nope." Freelund redirected his gaze to the coffin yet again. "Damnedest thing."

"I hope Lisle waits until tomorrow," I said, "because I'm going to bed."

"Sure," Freelund said. "She'll stop here first, anyway." One of the uniformed Authority cops walked up, and Freelund asked for more coffee. "How's the perimeter?"

"Secure." The cop was young, probably just out of training. "We've swept a two-mile radius on land and out into Puget Sound. Nothing unusual."

"Expand your search another mile," Freelund said. He looked back at me. "As I said, you're free to go."

I exited the side room of the warehouse, sending Forno a ping to let him know I was leaving. I thought about contacting him more directly, but he couldn't help with anything now, and I just wanted to get away from the police lights, the warehouse smells, this reminder of all that was bad with the Union. Well, no—all that was bad with me.

Ultra. Just a single word.

It shouldn't have affected me so strongly, but as I walked the pier toward Alaskan Way, intent on getting home fast, I could think of nothing else. That single world and all the shit associated with it downloaded into my brain like a DataNet update.

Still dark. Rain threatened as I headed south along the waterfront toward the old ferry terminal. From the terminal I'd have a short walk up the hill toward Western Avenue and my studio and office, a nightcap, and bed.

Only a few people stumbled around at that early hour, most homeless, but a few early risers were hoping to score some RuBy, or the nasty human version of it, AmBer. Not that RuBy wasn't nasty in its own way, but AmBer had blasted onto the market when the Union government outlawed RuBy last year on every world except Helkunntanas, where it was manufactured. AmBer lacked some of the essential ingredients RuBy had, found only on the Helk planet, particularly because of the hotter climate. Getting those ingredients to Earth was hard, if not impossible. AmBer mimicked the high of RuBy, but it was short-lived. AmBer was non-addictive, but had a worse physical effect on its user. Rot gut.

The world fuzzed out, and those night people dwindled to empty shells, like animals shuffling along aimlessly. I heard none of the city's sounds, scented none of the salt water's odor, and felt nothing in my trudging feet. But, inside, a plea for attention scoured me, warning me: *This is wrong.*

Was it my imagination, or did my ticking Rolex sound unnaturally loud? I stopped. I might've believed Freelund had put a tail on me to make sure I made it home, but the prickling of my nape did not stem from a sense of being watched.

I turned in a tight circle, peering into the dark. Nothing out there. The ticking of my watch had me completely discombobulated. Its metronomic sound reminded me of . . . a timer—a timer for something about to detonate near me. That was all the prompting I needed. I darted down Alaskan Way toward the abandoned ferry terminal, heading for Columbia Street, where I could turn up the hill to Western, and my studio. Shortly, the brown brick building of artist studios and offices came into sight. Now on a street that I knew well, I found myself slowing, secure in the relative safety of this familiar neighborhood. Walking fast, I focused on the front door of my building half a block away.

The ticking continued—if anything, even more loudly.

"Shit."

I looked about and foraged through my pockets again. Just say it, Dave: *Bomb.* This possibility rattled around in my head, although I couldn't figure out how a bomb could have followed me down the waterfront and up the hill.

Then it sent me spinning.

My head felt as light as a balloon. I could not concentrate, even on the front of my building. I tried to turn its door into a point of reference, a jump-slot beacon beckoning, but I began losing consciousness, even as my vision blurred. My whole body relaxed, as if I'd crawled into bed and let sleep overtake me. Sounds washed away into a muffled, unintelligible drone.

Even the ticking lost its rhythm and volume, until I thought maybe I no longer heard it. What the hell was going on? Was this what Alan Brindos had felt? Cara, Jennifer Lisle, and Joseph? Before they woke up to report having missed almost a full day of consciousness? Was all that weirdness starting again?

Dizzy, I lurched toward my building, but I didn't get far. My eyes ached, my heart raced, my muscles relaxed, and I fell to the pavement, flat on my back.

I lay there, looking at the overcast sky, colored and textured like yellowed tinfoil. It seemed as if a nightmarish eternity stretched out before me. Thunder rumbled as I fought to remain conscious, then a dark shape appeared above me, peering down, blocking my view of the sky.

More thunder. A shadow hand reached for me, long fingers outstretched. In the spaces between those fingers, I tried to make out a face, something distinguishing.

Instead, in my ear, I heard a soft, low whisper: *Terga-gla. Doik arumta.*

The rain came down.

I slept.

Three

YOU HAD TO WONDER ABOUT HUMANS, TEM FORNO THOUGHT AS HE looked down at the unmoving body of his partner Dave Crowell, now flat on his back outside the agency office building, in the early morning, at the top of the three steps leading up to the main entrance. Sun barely up. Not that he could actually *see* the sun.

Humans. They rarely heeded their surroundings. Took more sleep than they needed. Passed out so easily. In the morning air, Forno shivered. The planet was too cold for him. Why had humans been cast onto this planet? Into this galaxy? This universe?

Perhaps he should've been concerned for Crowell's current state of consciousness, particularly after seeing Alex Richards dead in a warehouse not far from here. Richards, with an Ultra stamp of approval.

How long had Crowell been out cold? Couldn't have been that long. Crowell had pinged Forno after he left the warehouse, done with his talk with Authority.

Maybe Crowell had been drinking again. Humans didn't handle ingestible substances well: alcohol, drugs, Helk foods. Forno's stomach grumbled at the thought of his favorites, for he truly missed the fragrant spices and the hearty meals he hadn't eaten in a long time. Yeah, Forno knew humans well. Better than most Helks. He spoke the language, understood many of its subtleties, and didn't care what other Helks thought about him.

Crowell looked inconsequential, stretched out, arms and legs seeming to reach for something. Crowell exercised, was a big human, in his thirties, relatively young, but still. Humans *were* small. Fragile. Incredibly slow. Even First Clan Helks, with all their bulk, could run circles around the fastest human.

Crowell was one of the most interesting humans he knew. Forno wouldn't be working for him otherwise. Smart enough, if a bit naïve. Crowell wasn't one to take drugs, but getting loaded? Lately? At least he kept in shape.

So, yeah. Maybe Forno should worry about finding Crowell on his back in an unnatural pose like roadkill, wet from the evening's rain. Didn't expect to see this on his daily walk to the Crowell Agency offices. Well, *office*. Okay, *half* an office, stuck in front of Crowell's living quarters, still separated by a stupid plywood wall.

He nudged Crowell with his foot. That's all he meant to do, anyway. Crowell grunted as the kick nearly turned him over onto his stomach.

A car turned onto Western Avenue from Columbia. Unusual enough for an actual car to come down the road, but then it slowed down when the driver saw Forno. Forno glared at the driver's side window, and the car sped off.

Crowell groaned. Flattened himself on his back again, one arm over his eyes.

"You taking an early morning nap?" Forno said. "Getting some fresh air?"

Still covering his eyes, Crowell mumbled, "My beauty sleep."

"You better keep resting then."

Crowell peeked through the crook in his elbow. Then he moved his arm and stared up into the gray sky. It was, of course, almost always a gray sky. And cold. Always cold. Forno pulled his overcoat tighter.

"I was lying here thinking about advertising for a partner who can protect me from evil bad things," Crowell said.

Forno grinned. "Let me know if you find one. It's too damn cold on this planet anyway."

"And too damn hot on your planet, so we're even."

With some more grumbling and groaning, Crowell managed to rise to a sitting position, his back against the door. "What time is it?"

"Six." Forno glared down at him. "So what happened?"

Crowell shook his head. "A ticking that seemed to be my Rolex, except that it was all around me. Then lightheadedness."

"Then you passed out. Drinking again."

"Not this time."

"You didn't see anyone? No one smacked your lights out?"

"Punched my lights out," Crowell said.

Got him again. "Yeah, I know."

"I did see something," Crowell said.

"Besides gray sky from on your back."

He nodded. "Someone. After I fell, looking down at me, real close. Said something."

"What?"

"It wasn't in English."

"Typical." Forno reached out to help Crowell up.

Crowell eyed the long, furry arm with distrust. "I like my arms in their sockets."

"Helk's breath, Crowell," Forno said. "I won't pull. Grab it for leverage."

Getting his legs under him, Crowell seized the arm, and Forno left his arm outstretched like a chin-up bar.

"Thanks." Crowell got to his feet and brushed himself off.

"You recognize the language?" Forno asked him.

"Memorese."

"A Memor?"

"Maybe, but I couldn't make out the actual body."

"Male? Female?"

"Couldn't tell. It was whispered."

"You speak Memorese?"

"No, but a Memor called me *doik* on my trip to the Flaming Sea Tavern on Aryell, so I recognized that word."

"Doik. It means idiot."

"Thanks for the translation. I think I recognized their word for Earth, too. *Terga.* Or close to it. Terga-gla."

"Yeah. Earth-man."

"So basically, Earthmen are idiots, or something like it."

Forno tried to give Crowell a look of pity. "Poor humans."

"Shut up, Forno."

Who had done this to Crowell? Left him lying there. Didn't even steal the Rolex. Turning his head to the street, Forno checked for cars parked nearby to see if anyone was staked out in one of them. As usual, just a couple of rusted, worthless vehicles occupied spaces on Western Avenue.

When Forno looked up, Crowell had already slipped through the building's entrance.

Humans might be weak, but they could move with stealth and purpose. Forno considered following him inside—maybe the assailant was waiting. Maybe it *was* a Memor hoping to insult his partner again. It would be warmer inside, but it might be better to guard the front of the building. Crowell could handle any trouble on the inside with his quick wit. And stealth.

Yes. Good guy, Crowell—for a human. That's why Forno had signed on with Crowell's agency.

Moments passed as he stood with his back against the building. He daydreamed about Helk foods and spices. On some days, when deprived, a Helk's brain could conjure up all seven senses and experience them as if they were really happening. It didn't happen very often with Forno these days, because he was always too damn cold. Who could sense-dream a hot and juicy gabobilek when the brain cells were frozen?

No other cars approached. The gray sky got grayer. The buildings got older. A sign half off its chain creaked, announcing "Public Parking" in red-white-and-blue. The building across the street was the same number of stories as Crowell's building—six—but looked a little better kept. Neither seemed a good choice for humans to live in.

Forno felt almost guilty living a few blocks down on Madison, in a decent brick office building. It had a round entrance hall that stretched upward for three floors before a ceiling capped it off. No one ever entered it. No one bothered him. For a bed, he'd set up four mattresses in a rectangle, and another four on top of those. It was close enough—his feet hardly overlapped the edge.

It was morning, but Crowell had kept him out too damn late. After an hour, Forno gave up and headed home to sleep some more. Later, barely comfortable on his bed, a ping returned him to his senses. He reached for his comm card. Cheap tech, but effective. He looked at the screen, rubbed some gunk off it, and read the message:

Get here. Now.

Crowell's message surprised him. His partner should be asleep, so a ping now meant a new development. Forno was out the door and to Crowell's in a few minutes. He picked his way up the stairwell's steps until he reached the top floor. All the hallways smelled of old paint—unrecognizable solutions and chemicals—from the days when it had been a haven for artists. He felt his fur tighten at the thought of all those caustic liquids.

A Memor stood by Crowell's desk, long orange hair cascading down her back. A flowing blue and white garment, a robe-cum-kimono, covered her from neck to toes.

Crowell waved me forward.

"What do *you* want?" Forno said, much too gruffly. He'd promised Crowell he'd do better at that sort of thing.

"My name is Terree." Her voice had a soft warble that most Memors had when they spoke casually. He wondered if she were a client. That would make Crowell happy.

Sitting very still at his desk, his face a little pale, Crowell nodded at the Memor, who sat in the chair reserved for clients.

And she was a *female* Memor. More rare than Helk women, only because most Memors, when they morphed—when nature haphazardly chose their intersexual assignment—usually became males during reproductive mating periods. Females were allowed only one name, not a surname, for they did not belong to any family or to any one male. A female Memor often had a tough life, bound in some cases to a host of male Memors.

Not having morphed male, this Terree had just one name. She seemed young enough, for a Memor, so perhaps, lacking the need to procreate, she had not yet had the chance to intersexually assign.

He thought of Lorway, the Memor from the Science Consortium who'd helped the Ultras with the tech needed to build the Transcontinental Conduit.

"Jeha-la," she said. "Hello, Mr. Crowell." She turned to Forno. "Mr. Forno."

"Just Forno. Not to be rude or anything, but you're a Memor."

Terree looked confused. "Yes?"

"Sitting in this office the morning after my partner was accosted and rendered unconscious by someone speaking Memorese."

"Forno," Crowell said.

"It wasn't me," Terree said.

"Do you know why a Memor would attack my partner?"

"Forno, stop," Crowell said. "We're not certain it was a Memor, just someone speaking the language."

"Calling Earthmen idiots," Forno added.

"In answer to your question," she said, "I *can* think of why a Memor would attack Mr. Crowell."

Forno gave Terree his best ugly look, what Crowell said was always ugly.

"I'd like to explain my problem," Terree said, "and why I want to hire you."

"So explain," Forno said.

"I will hire you both, and pay double the rate," Terree said, her voice soft and barely audible through her thick, pale lips.

"We *are* a team." Crowell eased back in his chair.

"That's us," Forno said, still wary of the Memor.

Terree sat back down, and Forno sidestepped to the plywood wall and leaned back carefully, ignoring the huge chair he'd created from old lumber, mattresses, and pipes.

"I want you to find someone," she said.

Crowell said, "I'm not big on missing-persons cases."

"But he *is* big on getting paid work," Forno said, in case Crowell had forgotten. "No luck on the official level? Nothing Authority could do to help?"

"No." She looked at her lap for a second.

"Still," Crowell said. "Why us? Plenty of experts in the Seattle area could help you. I mean, how do you lose track of a Memor here?"

"You stand out almost as much as I do," Forno told her, hoping to offend her because he could not trust her, whatever she said.

Terree smiled, pulling her orange hair in front of her, perhaps a nervous gesture. She then stared at Forno so hard, for so long, he felt she might be reading his thoughts.

"Do you want the job or not?" she asked.

Forno looked to Crowell, unsure.

"The missing person isn't a Memor, is it?" Crowell asked.

"It *is* a Memor," she said.

"Another female?" Forno said.

"Male," she said.

"Bigger than a bun basket?" Forno asked.

Terree frowned at him. Wrong again.

Crowell, smirking at Forno, said, "He's only doing that to make you think he's an ignorant Hulk, when he's more human than some humans."

"I am, therefore I think," Forno said.

Crowell shook his head. "See what I mean?"

Forno gave Crowell his most intense *Watch it!* look.

"This Memor you're looking for," Crowell said. "He isn't on Earth, is he?"

The last thing Crowell wanted, Forno knew, was to go off planet, having put most of that Union and alien stuff behind him. Double U, Union and Ultra. With the discovery of Alex Richards' body, and Crowell's sleepy time on the street, Crowell might not have a choice.

"You're right," Terree said. "He's not on Earth."

Forno soon knew the truth; he knew because of the way she had stared at him so intently earlier. "He's on Helkunntanas."

"Yes." Her voice barely a whisper, she continued to stare at Forno. "Or maybe he isn't."

"I love a good mystery," Forno said.

"Yeah, well," Crowell said. "I'm not going to Helkunntanas. Excuse me." He left the office area, walking through the makeshift door in the plywood to the living space behind it.

Clearly surprised by Crowell's departure, Terree frowned at Forno.

"He *really* doesn't like my planet," Forno told her, smiling. "It's the heat."

Four

INSIDE MY STUDIO, I FLOPPED ONTO THE KING-SIZED BED I'D ACQUIRED from an empty room in the building. I stared at the stained, misshapen ceiling tiles, counting the little holes, expecting to hear the muted voices of Forno and the Memor discussing me. I half-expected Forno to barge in and ask me what the hell I was doing walking away from the possibility of good money.

Or a good drink. I'd left a bottle in my desk.

No money that the Memor offered would be worth slotting off planet, nor was any incentive in the known Union bright enough to make me even *think* about going to the mysterious Helks' inhospitable planet. Memors be damned. Helks be damned.

Ultras be damned.

And yet: Recent events could not be explained, and every body part felt pulled in a direction away from Earth. Once Forno had kicked me awake on the entryway to my building, I'd felt fine. No ill effects from the—well, whatever it was that had been done to me. Only soreness from sleeping on the hard steps outside. In reality, I had plenty of energy and craved a big plate of bacon, eggs, and toast.

I'd missed a workout, and I didn't like missing my workout. Whenever I did, bad things happened.

What *had* happened to me? Going all fuzzy in my senses, especially my hearing. A loud ticking in my ears. A person who might or might not have been a Memor rendering me unconscious. Or had he just happened upon the scene as I was passing out? Terree had said it wasn't her. Really?

Then there was the warehouse. How had Alex Richards gone from alive to dead in a matter of minutes with the offensive word Ultra spelled out on his body? Because of it, I now had to talk to Jennifer Lisle. Jennifer served only to remind me of Cara Landry's Ultra persona, and my own Cara dead, killed by a copy of my dead partner.

Images again. The Brindos double on Aryell had said something about Alan Brindos in the buffer. A viable copy. But the copy itself had turned out to be a lost soul turned on itself, warped mercilessly toward an insidious purpose I had supposedly helped quell.

The Brindos copy had been genuinely angry. During those tense moments at the ski resort, it had not occurred to me to ponder the resentment he'd felt. Resentment was what I knew. The copy's resentment was just what had seeped into me over the past year, and I'd tried living with it even as it pissed off my own soul. Immersing myself in the business, drowning myself in the blue poison, I'd tried to escape the memories tying me to the Ultras like a thin, strong wire I could not break.

Through the high window of my room, the sun inched toward noon. No sounds came from the office half, and I wondered what Forno and the Memor were doing, if not talking. The plywood wall was hardly soundproof. Perhaps sometime during my reverie, Forno had led her outside into the hallway. Maybe she had just left.

Part of me relished the prospect of Terree giving up and walking out. I grumbled about Memors sucking all the memories from my head, even though no one believed they could actually do so, and forced myself out of the bed. At the door I listened, and yes, they were still there, talking in such hushed tones that I felt I was missing something important and should just open the door and go in.

Closing my eyes, I waited for a wave of vertigo to wash away—some belated side effects from my sidewalk sleep. My dizziness was brief, though.

When I opened the door, they stopped talking.

Forno hovered near my desk. Terree still sat in my client chair. Some of my earlier vertigo threatened.

"You okay?" Forno asked. "You change your mind?"

I rubbed my eyes. The confusion seeping into my head did not sit well with me. Then my legs muscles faltered.

"Okay, that thing from last night is messing with you." Forno reached me in three steps and guided me back to my desk chair.

A silence ensued. I stared at Terree, cursing myself for displaying weakness before her. Or Forno for that matter. Too much had happened since the warehouse. I couldn't keep up. Terree's face remained impassive, her lips clamped together, although a tic rippled above one cheekbone.

"Sorry," I said.

Her eyes boring into mine, she lifted a hand to her blue robe's collar and gently tugged it. A pleaseant scent came from her, and I wondered if it was Memor aromatherapy at work. The aliens were known to use these scents to calm those in close proximity to them. Terree seemed aware of my notice and smiled widely, those wide lips shivering with an almost sensual movement. "It's okay," she said. "I know you've been through a lot."

I nodded mechanically. Forno didn't look at me, studying Terree instead, and he held his head cocked tensely to one side. He inched back to the plywood wall, his massive bulk looking more intimidating than usual. He didn't trust the Memor, and I didn't blame him. Stumbling upon a corpse, falling into a deep sleep, and a female Memor suspiciously hiring us to go to Helkunntanas to find another Memor. The word Ultra colored all of it, everything skewed. But somewhere, out among the Union's planets, it must all come together. Or else go all to hell, fast.

"Tell yourself whatever you want," Terree said, "but the details of this job—details I've not yet given—should matter very much to you."

"Why? Because I passed out? Because someone called me an idiot? Because—" I paused, then managed with difficulty to say, "because of Ultras?"

"Yes," she said. "All of it. Or—maybe none of it."

I waited. Waited for her to get to the details that mattered.

But she only said, "Will you take the job?"

"What about the part where you were going to give me details?"

"You won't agree first?"

I laughed, and Forno did, too.

"Agree first?" Forno said, chuckling. "It's business, Miss Terree—"

I waved him off. "Why would I take a job not knowing all the details?"

Terree leaned toward me, her orange hair spilling forward, her green eyes hard upon me. "All right. Once you hear the details, including what might have happened to you outside, there's no going back. You'll take the job."

A chill snaked down my back as she produced a large, colorful card from her robe and placed it on my desk.

"What's that?" I scanned the card quickly. It pictured a knight in a chariot. Two horses pulling it. The knight holding something, a mirror or wand.

"It's a Tarot card, Mr. Crowell. The only thing I have from my father. A souvenir from Earth that he gave me before his last trip. Before he disappeared."

"This is supposed to mean something to me?"

Terree looked uncertain. "Hard to say. That card is called the Chariot."

"Sorry," I said. "I don't know anything about Tarot cards."

"I'll leave it with you when you take the job."

I laughed. I already had all the details necessary to say no. One: a missing-persons case that would take me off Earth. Two: Helkunntanas.

"Going to Helkunntanas," I said. "It's not automatic."

"No."

"A big planet, mostly unknowable, and even Memors don't go there unless they have to."

"That will make it easier to spot the Memor I need you to find."

"Restrictions make travel there for humans difficult."

"I know."

"There's paperwork and Union customs. I may have to bribe a few officials."

"Well," she said, "it's a good thing Tem Forno's on your side."

"Oh, so I'm an ignorant Hulk *and* a briber," Forno said.

"You should feel important," I told him. "Is briber a word?"

"You're asking me?"

Terree flipped her hair behind her. Tugged at her robe again. "I already said I'd pay double."

More aromatherapy, probably. I felt an almost unnatural desire to accept her money. I eased back in the chair and sighed. Forno took up a lot of space next to the desk.

"You *will* take it," Terree said.

I chuckled inwardly at her certainty. "You know what, Terree? You believe I won't say no, but I can't think of any reason to say yes."

"My father," she said.

"Father?"

"My father is missing."

"Why should I hassle with the Helk planet to find him?"

"Because he's been gone for nineteen Memory cycles."

"I'm guessing that's a long time for someone living on Memory," I said. "And you're just now deciding to hire someone to find him?"

"Yes."

"Because?"

"Because I've only now figured out a vital connection to his disappearance."

I waited. Forno took up even more space.

"My father, Greist Sahl-kla, disappeared the same day your father, Lawrence Crowell, disappeared."

A rock dropped into the pit of my stomach. "He did?"

"My father was an Envoy. A mediator. Because of his exceptional memory, he was a favorite among mediation hearings throughout the Union."

I blinked. My dad had been an Envoy for a short time. Before he'd given it up and bought the Hammond Marina. Before he drowned on the lake, body never recovered.

"He was on Earth," Terree said. "After several weeks of hearings, including an important conference in Chicago, he gained a few days' leave, and a group of Envoys took some time to get away."

"To Montana," I guessed.

"Montana. That's what I was told. He never came back to the Chicago conference. He disappeared the same year, on the same day, that your father disappeared."

"But why—?"

"Do you not know what your father did?" she asked, surprise in her voice.

I managed to say, "He owned a marina. The Hammond Marina on Flathead Lake. He worked there nearly every day. He was boating one day, and there was an accident on the north end of the lake, and he drowned. He was never found, but parts of that lake are so deep that—"

"He was an *Envoy*," she interrupted me, craning her neck, as if trying to better see into my soul.

"I know. He *was*, but he gave it up. Mom said all the traveling around the Union was too much. He bought the marina."

"He was an Envoy when he disappeared."

"What?"

"He knew my father." She leaned forward and laid her hand on my arm. "Mr. Crowell, your father and mine were friends."

Five

T HE WAY I FIGURE IT," VANDERBERG PARR said to the HELK SITTING
across from him in The Mirror, a RuBy bar in Khrem, "you've got
two choices. You're not going to like either of them."

"Vander, hey now," said the Helk dressed in a black slicker so light it kept
falling off his broad shoulders. He had a tumbler of Helk ale in hand, and he'd
already sucked down half of it. Nervous, taking the edge off.

Parr didn't care for Shyler Frock, a snot-for-brains Fourth Clan who rarely did what he was told. It was going to cost the Helk, no getting around it.

"Don't hey now me, Fuck," Parr said.

"It's Frock."

"Not at the moment, it's not. What the hell kind of name is Frock anyway? Or Shyler? I've always meant to ask."

Frock shrugged, an annoying gesture the Helk threw Parr's way whenever
he wanted to change the subject. As Fourth Clan, Frock wasn't much taller
than Parr, but he was bulky, and strong, and not to be taken for granted. Still,
a good blaster would make just as big a hole in a Fourth Clan as a First, and
Parr's hand twitched with the possibility of it.

"You didn't take a human name for business purposes," Parr said, "and
maybe you should have."

Parr was coming down a little from the RuBy he'd rolled earlier, a dull
ache centered behind his eyes. Signaling Juke, a Second Clan Helk, over at
the bar for a refill on his Temonus whiskey, he snicked two credits into the
slot on the metal paystick in the middle of the table, and after a palm reader
confirmed his identity, two squares of RuBy dispensed into his palm, glistening with the drug's signature red dye.

"Why you paying for that stuff, Vander?" Frock asked. "It's your own district."

Parr rolled the squares so that the RuBy didn't hit all the taste buds and papillae on his tongue right away, and dropped both into his mouth, the cinnamon odor strong in his nose. Saliva interacted with the Helk chemical compounds, fueling the reactivity of the drug. In humans, it resulted in a high that hit hard and stayed long. Extremely addictive, it also overtook the nervous system and alleviated pain. A Helk, on the other hand, found the drug soothing in small doses, and in larger does, felt some of the same euphoria and pain relief, but without having to fear its addictive qualities.

Parr took it for the pain.

"Don't worry about it, I'll do what I want," he told the Helk. "It all comes back to me anyway." It hadn't been coming back from Shyler Frock, however, who'd been holding out on him with his district tithes.

Juke might be only Second Clan, but he was still the biggest Second Clan Helk Parr knew, and maybe the scariest. The Helk dropped off the whiskey and asked if Frock wanted more Helk ale.

Frock shook his head and, once Juke left, said, "You're not getting any younger, Vander. You don't want to go down that RuBy mine. How old are you? Forty?"

"Thereabouts."

"My new mate, Qerral, she's hooked on the stuff, you get it?

"When did this happen?"

"What?"

"Getting a new mate."

Frock smiled. "A few weeks ago. Crazy, huh? Anyway, she says to me why don't I ask you for a better cut."

"Because you don't set the tithe."

Nodding his head. "You do, yeah, I know—"

"Not me."

"The Boss. Yeah. But you monitor, you adjust. You're down in the district, doing favors. You see it. You see where we're at and what we need. Protect us, right?" He smiled with effort, picked up his tumbler and threw back the rest of the ale. "It's hard enough for humans to get around here—you're not so good with the heat, not so chummy with the Hulks, but you *do* it, Vander. You live here, love it here—"

He couldn't say he loved it. Khrem was a shit-hole, and this bar was too dark, and attracted too many Rubes wanting to get high and suck at the Boss's paysticks for as little as possible. He lifted a foot off the concrete floor and felt the telltale tackiness of dried RuBy dust on the sole of his shoe.

"Right upstairs, for Helk's sake," Frock said. "Crash pad in the heart of the district, tight with the Boss and sniffers." He waved at Parr's simple black buttoned-down shirt, sleeves rolled up. "You look good out there doing it. Monitor and adjust. We get too crazy about the RuBy, you work things out."

"Helks don't get hooked on RuBy, Fuck." He was loving playing with the name, making Frock even more nervous. "Not even Helkettes can get addicted." The warm glow of RuBy had started to take the edge off his pain, and now he was just playing with the Helk.

"See, Qerral's got this groomer," Frock was saying, "she hits the RuBy even harder."

"A groomer. She in Khrem? Inside the district?"

"Yeah, in the district. Best at what she does, I tell you."

"My dog needs a trim."

"Not funny, Vander."

Just keep playing with him. Keep him off balance. "How often you groom? You let the fur grow in the winter—which is still hotter than anything on Earth, *ever*—get a big clip as summer rolls around. Then what—weekly? Maintain appearances?"

Frock shrugged again. "Depends. But look, Qerral's groomer—"

"What I don't understand is how you stay cool with all that fur. Like right now, middle of the day. I take a walk to the corner to grab food from the gabobileck vendor, I'm sweating oceans if I don't have a skin cooler."

"Plenko's Stick, man, you like gabobilecks? Humans find those meat sausages too intense."

"I handle them okay."

"Like I said, you're out there, not hiding like other humans, right? You know what we need."

"Qerral tell you all this about her RuBy? About her groomer?"

"She never seemed the type to hit the Red, you know? I think maybe she started after her last mating. Before she found me. Just got to the point she needed to have it."

Parr sneered. "How many times I have to tell you? Helks don't—"

"Okay, so she's not hooked," Frock said, "but she goes through it, sure enough, and she's not feeling so well. I don't know if she got some bad stuff, or it's just not playing fair with her system. She looks awful. The RuBy seems to calm her, you know? But it's expensive, even with my cut."

"She could try some AmBer. Some of it works its way into Khrem."

"That fake Earth shit?"

"Have you tried it?"

"AmBer? Completely flawed, not worth the price, expensive by the time it gets here."

Parr didn't care about it and got back to the point. "You have two choices," he said.

"Back to choices again? Really, Vander? Look—"

"You've skimped on the tithes for a while now. Think I wouldn't notice?"

"Hey now—"

Vanderberg Parr lost patience and let Frock see the blaster he'd had in his lap, now resting it on the table, his hand around the grip. "I said no 'hey now.'"

Shyler Frock leaned back, visibly shaken. Hard to tell with his dark, leathery face, but Parr imagined if the Hulk could turn pale, he'd be as white as the rarest snow on Helkunntanas.

"Okay, Vander."

"Two choices." He waved the blaster as if it were his index finger, ticking off the points. "One. You give me what you owe me now. The agreed upon tithe, prorated back six months—"

"Six months!"

"—When you started skimming from the district. You said it, stupid Fuck. You said it yourself, I'm out there. Monitor and adjust. You should've known."

"Listen, Vander. I don't—"

"Payable in credit or RuBy, if the exchange works out."

"Now?"

Parr nodded, cradling the blaster in the crook of his arm, the barrel pointed toward the ceiling, which was black and barely visible, even with the recessed lighting. "Now."

"But I don't have it." He scratched his shoulder, at his fur, pulling it some, a nervous habit. "Qerral, she just kept asking for more, and what could I do?"

"There's more missing than could've possibly been given to Qerral."

"Well, a little, maybe."

"A lot."

Parr wished the RuBy's effects lasted longer. They used to, but the longer he'd used, the longer he kept it in his system—which was most of the time, these days—the shorter the high. He threw more credits at the paystick for two more squares.

"Speaking of a lot," Frock said. "That stuff is pretty tough on humans, and you go through it like water."

"Did I tell you to worry about it?"

"No, but it seems excessive, even for a human."

"Don't worry about it."

Frock fiddled with his empty glass, looking apprehensive, as if doubtful about asking Parr something.

"What?" Parr asked.

Frock forced a nervous smile. "Out on the street, the other jewel sniffers, they wonder." He pointed at the RuBy Parr had just rolled. "The rumor is you *have* to have it. That you're a trademark."

Parr squeezed the grip on his blaster, narrowing his eyes as he stared hard at Frock. "Trademark." The Hulk didn't back down like Parr thought he would. In fact he leaned closer.

"Yeah. Trademark. TM. You know what it means, Vander."

"A Thin Man."

"That's the rumor." Frock leaned back, acting almost too casual now, at a time when the Hulk should be sweating snot about the whole skimming thing. "Is it true?"

It was true, but the fact that Shyler Frock thought so—the fact that the other *sniffers* thought so—was not good at all. Everything Vanderberg Parr had been before the Ultra scare—not that he knew what that was—everything he was now, depended on the utmost secrecy. Many Thin Men had died from the process, but Parr had gone from human to a copy of a human, which didn't lead to death for most. But it still hurt like hell, because the Boss had told him they'd made some adjustments in the way he'd trademarked. Improvements overall, but with some undesirable, if necessary side effects. The RuBy helped.

"Of course I'm not a trademark," Parr lied. He smacked the paystick and it wobbled a little. At closing, the paysticks would telescope down, out of sight. Get locked up. "The sniffers tell you this?"

Frock shrugged. "We've figured—"

"Maybe it's too much. Maybe I need to cut back. But that's not your problem. Skimming money from me is the problem."

"You get to have all the RuBy you want, whether your own stock, or you buy it. But I can't have some extra to get Qerral through a tough spot?"

"I *told* you. Qerral couldn't possibly have gone through that much. What my book says is missing doesn't stack up with what you say. I need what's owed me. You think I don't have to account for everything? That the Boss can let this shit slide?"

Frock lost his earlier confidence, even slumping in his seat.

Parr said, "You owe it, you pay it, or give me the equivalent in stock."

Actual sweat beaded on Frock's forehead, his dark, leathery skin glistening. "It'll take some time. I just need some time. You can give me some time, can't you, Vander?"

"Now, or never."

"Hey n—"

Parr shot him a look, and Frock shut up. You could see how hard it was for the Hulk to do, not to say his stupid "hey now," wanting to get the words in. "You don't have it? You can't have it brought over here to The Mirror in the next few minutes?"

Frock pulled on his fur again, harder this time, shaking his head. "No. No, I don't. I can't."

Leaning back calmly, Parr gave the Hulk his best sad, disappointed look. Frock said, "Two choices. You said two. What's the other choice?"

Parr raised the blaster and aimed it at Frock's head. "I shoot you."

Shyler Frock stood up so quickly, it almost took Parr by surprise. Damn Helks were fast. But Frock didn't try to run, he just stood frozen in place by his chair. A couple of patrons took notice, as did Juke behind the bar, but no one made any sign of leaving, or panicking, or accessing their comm cards to call for help. And why would they? A RuBy bar in a district with humans everywhere, in the city of Khrem of all places—no one gave a snotty Helk what happened.

The thought of Frock standing there now, in utter fear for his life, brought a smile to Parr's face. Let the Helk see that, wonder what's up. Hell, he *should* shoot him. He'd been asked on more than one occasion to do just that to human and Helk alike, and for infractions lighter than Frock's.

He was going to let Frock stew, maybe even beg for his life, before giving him a few more options, show his kindness. Just being the human *out there* in the district, adjusting, doing him a favor. That moment, though, The Mirror's back door opened.

Shyler Frock saw him first, behind Parr, his eyes widening, but Parr knew without looking it was the Boss walking in. A moment later, he came into Parr's view, standing so close to Frock that Parr thought they might embrace.

But Frock didn't know Baren Rieser that well; the Boss wasn't here to comfort the sniffer.

The Boss was a mountain of a man, and equally as tall as the small Fourth Clan Helk. Baren Rieser, who looked even taller with his signature tailored pinstripe suits, this one bright white, was an imposing figure, a human who didn't take shit from anyone, certainly not a delinquent Helk trying to squirm his way out of debt. A slim black tie rested on a dark red collared shirt. His head was bald, but covered in tattoos of numbers in various sizes, one through nine. Parr knew nothing about what they meant, but right now, they looked like a countdown of the miserable Helk's time running out.

Baren Rieser, notorious data forger on Earth, had holed out on Helkunntanas, relatively safe from the NIO, the hounds trying for years to grab him. Of course, the man no longer waded in data cycles, having worn out his welcome, but he had become an even better jeweler.

The King of Khrem.

RuBy shone in every corner of Khrem, the biggest human settlement on Helkunntanas; Rieser owned most of the Red, and worked miracles in his attempts to obtain the rest.

Rieser made a barely perceptible motion with his head, and Shyler Frock sat down. He also nodded to Juke behind the bar, and within moments, Juke had given a silent signal to the three others in The Mirror to get the hell out.

Serious, when the Boss did that, and no one argued with Juke.

"What's our status here, Vanderberg?" Rieser asked, his voice not matching his stature at all, resonating with a slight twang, a high-pitched what-do-I-care nonchalance to it, drawn out and slow.

Parr gestured with his blaster toward Frock, who nervously picked up his tumbler and stared at it. It was still empty. "Frock doesn't have it," he said.

Rieser cocked his head a little, at the same time looking down at the Helk, disappointment evident on his round face. "Oh, Shyler."

Shyler Frock looked at him, and his eyes, the dark of his leathery skin surrounding them, pleaded with the Boss. Parr stewed a bit too, knowing he'd come up short, not getting the money from the Helk.

Frock had another play, though, for he spoke up, loud and clear: "I'll get your money, and sniff out some extra RuBy, in a couple of days—"

"I don't think you'll pay it," Parr interrupted. "And that wasn't the agreement."

"Vanderberg, please," Rieser said. He grabbed Frock's shoulder firmly. A sign that the Helk could relax. Friends, is what we are. Relax. "We're settling up. I'm here to make sure it gets done."

"What do you mean?" Frock said, shying away from Rieser's outstretched arm. "Settling up? Get what done?"

"What do you think?"

"Let me have those days. I'll pay you. Haven't I always paid? I'm warning you—"

Baren Rieser's eyes became slits. "Warning me?"

"Give me the time or I'll tell the other sniffers—I'll confirm what they already suspect—let it slip to the Kenn, even, that your man here—" and he pointed to Parr "—is one of them. A Thin Man."

Parr kept looking at Frock, not wanting to see his Boss's accusing eyes, but said to Rieser, "He told me it was a rumor."

Rieser shook his head. "Well, now, isn't that interesting?"

Shyler said, "It's true, isn't it?"

Rieser said, "Oh, it's absolutely, positively true, Shyler." He snatched Parr's blaster out of his hand. "May I?"

Shyler Frock panicked. "Hey now—"

Apparently Rieser didn't like Frock's signature "hey now" any better, for the Boss lifted the blaster and fired it point blank at Frock's black slicker when he tried to stand. Rieser fired again, and again, Frock stumbling forward, grabbing at the table on his way down. He landed hard, inched forward on his elbows. Rieser popped him twice more, and Frock lay still.

Rieser rubbed his tattooed head with one hand, the blaster still in the other. He didn't even look at the bar, but said, "Juke, you got this?"

Juke mumbled something, good enough for a yes.

Parr now looked at Rieser, who seemed to be trying to read Parr's own expression. "Sorry."

"You should've shot him twenty minutes ago, Vanderberg."

"I guess."

"That news can't get out. You know what'll happen if the Kenn or, God forbid, the NIO find out about you."

"I know."

"You'll spend the rest of your life in a detention camp somewhere, poked, prodded, and humiliated. Sensitive information could come out."

"I know."

"That's what it means to be a Thin Man. On the run if you're not under someone's protection."

"I *know*, Baren."

"And I can't protect you if this district thinks you're somebody else. You have to be who you are. Vanderberg Parr. You understand, don't you?"

Parr nodded, then gazed out the front window of The Mirror, at the thoroughfare baking in the afternoon heat. "What about the rumors Frock mentioned?"

Rieser gave Parr's blaster a spin on his index finger, then flipped it, grabbed it by the barrel and handed it to him.

"It's a nice piece. Wesson particle?"

"Yeah." He dropped it into his side pocket.

"Hang onto it, be careful with it. Worth a bunch now, a helluva lot more to collectors down the road if you decide to give it up. Sentimental piece. Maybe not the best when it comes to reliability."

"But good enough for the jobs I need it for."

Rieser nodded, rubbed his head again, then nudged Frock's body with his foot. "Stupid Hulk."

Not too smart of Frock, Parr thought, trying to threaten the Boss. Juke had disappeared, already getting some help to disappear Frock's body, in itself not an easy thing to do on Helkunntanas, even in a human district. No worries about Juke; the Second Clan Helk belonged to Rieser.

"Rumors are gone, Vanderberg. Frock disappeared because he held out on his tithe. That's the only message the other sniffers need to hear."

"Okay. What about Frock's mate?"

"He had a mate?

"Recent. Named Qerral."

Rieser sighed, but Parr saw tension in the Boss's face. The Boss didn't like loose ends.

"I'll have Juke take care of her after she's had some time to wonder where Shyler is. Not much else I can do about it."

"I don't imagine she knew much—"

"Can't assume," Rieser said, glaring at Parr. "Never."

Parr nodded.

Rieser clapped Parr's shoulder, an accustomed gesture from his years dealing with Helks on the street. "I have some work for you tonight, Vanderberg."

"Sure."

"There's a shipment going out from Crossbill Station and I need to make sure it's secure. I don't want Abby Graff getting wind of it."

"I can do that."

"Take a few sniffers. Shouldn't be any problems, but bring along some locals with you, in case things get dicey."

He meant some Helks, of course. Muscle mass. "No problem."

Rieser nodded, then said, "After that, I need you at the House."

At the House. Parr's stomach cramped, the physical pain a reminder that he needed more RuBy, and a reminder that he hated the House. Although Rieser might think it disrespectful, Parr pulled some RuBy squares from the paystick and quickly popped both. The tips of his fingers, almost permanently stained red from the drug's dye, twitched slightly.

Seeing his discomfort, Rieser laughed, stroking his black tie. His voice pitched up in his excitement. "Company, Vanderberg, a small gathering. A little fun."

Parr almost missed it. Missed what the Boss meant. "Fun?"

Baren Rieser laughed again, even louder. He pointed to his bald head, at the numbers tattooed there. "Your number's come up. I have a big announcement to make. We're going to have an Ultra good time, sniffer."

Inside, he felt a rush that had nothing to do with the RuBy, and it was not at all pleasant. It was a need. A desire he couldn't hope to fulfill. It was a question. *You have to be who you are. Vanderberg Parr.*

"You've earned it, despite your hesitation today," Rieser said. "I see a lot of Red in your future, and this is a new step."

"Yes, sir. I can't believe it."

Rieser patted Parr's cheek. "Welcome, Vanderberg, to the galaxy of belief."

Six

THERE WAS SOMETHING I'D FORGOTTEN. SOMETHING ON THE periphery of my memory that had to be important.

In the filtered sunshine of midday, as I walked along the waterfront with the Memor woman, Terree, the thought niggled at me enough that she glanced my way, concern on her face. Her orange hair was now tied back in the typical ponytail.

"Are you okay?" she asked.

We had come to the abandoned ferry terminal where I'd been when I made my dash to my office from the night before, and now we were headed north, Puget Sound on our left, the various piers and buildings looking old and worn. I kept thinking I might fall prey to lightheadedness again, to heightened hearing picking up the ticking of my watch, but as usual on the waterfront, all was quiet. No one else walked along the piers, no ships or boats sat at the terminals or docks, no one manned the dilapidated shops and store fronts. I didn't feel too bad for having gone more than a day without a drink, which was more than strange.

"I keep thinking I'm forgetting something," I said.

She smiled. "Nothing too important, I hope. Or maybe it's something *very* important, about what's happening to you."

Then something clicked. It brought me up short, and I looked back over my shoulder. "Forno's not here."

Terree's smile widened. "Is that what you're forgetting?"

I shook my head. This time the odor coming from her was like fresh berries. "Not that. He stayed back at my place. In case—"

"—In case the NIO agent came by."

That must've been it. Jennifer Lisle was coming sometime soon, and Freelund had asked me to stay put at home.

I nodded slowly, the realization like an alarm reminding me of an important task. We continued to walk, but remembering the upcoming talk with Jennifer had not eased my conscience.

Perhaps this was a result of the spring sunshine, rare these days, and surprising after the unrelenting cloud cover of the past few weeks. The waterfront had a surreal quality to it, the surface of the water glinting unnaturally. My surroundings took on an almost virtual feel, like something manufactured or fake. Not very much seemed right with the world as it was, and my walk with Terree did not make me at all comfortable, for all her attempts to calm me. I wondered again if the strange experience of the previous night had jarred something lose in me.

"Forno will let you know, and you can be back there quickly," the Memor said.

"I know."

"Then let's talk as we agreed to do."

"My dad."

"And mine."

My gaze flicked to her face a moment. Her thick lips, almost blue in the dreamlike sunshine, were clamped in distress.

"Look, I'm sorry," I said earnestly, because to a degree I knew what she felt; I'd been without my own dad for a long time too. Now, with the events of last year's Ultra scare still fresh, and the mysteries of last night immediate and disturbing, he played on my mind more than ever. "Tell me more about him. Tell me about his friendship with my dad."

She folded her arms across her chest, as if cold, and searched the Sound. An old barge was there, not far out from the pier, half submerged, the aft end completely hidden. It had never moved during the time I'd been here. Terree must have been surprised to see how far Earth had let itself go. I'd never been to Memory, but seen enough holovids to know her planet had some of the most beautiful cities in the Union, with grand structures of glass and stone, with jewel-cobbled streets and unpolluted waters that flowed through impeccably engineered watercourses of stone and polished metals. I'm sure the pictures and holovids I'd seen did not do these wonders justice.

"My father," she said, her eyes moist with memory, "was Greist Sahl-kla, my mother's third bondmate. I like to believe he loved her most of all, that he loved me most of all, among his fourteen children. I was one of only two females born to my mother. I never knew the other female, my sister, but I heard she morphed male after her first mating."

As much as my old partner Brindos had tried to explain the intersexual oddities of Memors, I had never understood it. I said, "So, like me, you were young when he disappeared."

"Yes. I have many memories of my father before that time, including trips with him around the Union, accompanied by a guardian, or once in a while, my mother. Or sometimes, one of his other mates."

"He must have had a soft spot for you then, to take you along. He didn't do this with his other children?"

"Yes, he did, once in a while. But not as often. At least from what I remember. And of course I didn't know my mother very well, as is the custom. She either maled, or became bondmate to someone else."

I nodded, feeling deprived, for I remembered no trips with my dad. He had always talked the big talk, though. *Your lucky day is coming, David*, he'd said. His life as an Envoy barely registered with me. I really only remembered the marina. One day he had come home from the marina, bragging about a couple Memors that had visited his tackle shop to buy bait for a fishing trip.

Terree was a Memor. Her memories, her ability to recall every important fact, was inherent in her genetic makeup. Of *course* she would remember everything from her youth.

"You don't remember, do you?" she asked.

"What part?" I kicked a rusted metal container out of our path, and it clanked down the cracked concrete as we worked our way to the next pier.

"About everything."

"Only bits and pieces." *Your lucky day is coming, David.* "Barely there, some of them." *Lucky Lawrence.*

"What about the marina?" she asked. "What do you remember about it?"

Even coming up with specifics about the place my dad had supposedly worked proved difficult. "There was a tackle shop. And boats. Dozens of boats." I smiled, glad to summon the image of boats of all kinds lined up at the various docks.

"Did your father own the marina?"

"Yes. Everything we had came from what he made running it. My mom didn't work, although she gardened, and often sold some produce, herbs, flowers and plants. We had a little greenhouse."

"Did you ever do work there for him?"

I thought a moment. "No."

"Did you ever visit the marina?"

"Did I ever ... What kind of question is that? Of course I did. I remember the boats—"

"And your mom didn't work there."

"No. But she often took my dad hot meals, because it wasn't far from where we lived on the lake."

"Did she tell you a lot about the marina? About how her day went, or about your father's day?"

I grabbed her shoulder and made her stop. "Where are you going with this?"

She uncrossed her arms and stared up at me. "Your memories of the marina come from your mom. She told you about it. She may have even taken you to a marina. What was it called?"

"The Hammond Marina."

"Hammond?"

"Yeah. Do you know that name?"

She narrowed her eyes. "I don't know. It seems familiar, but I don't know why. I mean, why Hammond? Why not name it the Crowell Marina if your dad owned it? Did he always own it, always run it?"

"Terree, you obviously know more than I do. Why the barrage of questions? You said my dad was an Envoy and knew your father. Tell me. Did my dad own a marina or not?"

She shook her head. "He didn't."

"So you're saying it was a cover story."

"You don't remember."

"I don't remember. I was sixteen when he disappeared. But damn it, that's old enough to remember my life before. And if he was that important as an Envoy, even if he went missing, there'd be records at the Emirates. People who knew him and remembered him. I'd know about it just like you know about your own father."

"Yes, there are records of Lawrence Crowell working for the Emirates."

"And about the marina?"

"Deed of purchase. Deed of sale."

"Yes, my mom sold it after his death."

She sighed. "Greist Sahl-kla and Lawrence Crowell were good friends. Both Envoys, both working for their worlds, and for the Envoy Emirates. Sorting out disagreements around the Union, the colonies, city governments, even corporate disputes."

"He was gone a lot, then. Jump-slot travel is fast, but he had to have been gone for days at a time."

"Weeks. Months."

"I just don't remember."

"I know. But I do." She put a slight, long-fingered hand on my chest.

"How do you remember so well?"

"Mr. Crowell. *David.*" Her smile was sad, but hinted at something personal. "I remember *you.* That's how."

I studied her face, her high cheekbones, the pale, perfect skin, a stray strand of her orange hair drifting across her forehead. "This is crazy," I said, "but . . . I think I believe you."

She looked away, then walked out onto the next pier. It creaked ominously under her feet, but she didn't hesitate. She went as far as she could, although not to the very end, because a load of discarded wooden crates and buoys barred her way on one side, and the other side had too many missing planks. My vision fuzzed a bit, and I thought I saw slivers of light gleaming amongst the cracks, as if backlighting the pier. But it was daytime. Middle of the day, with an uncommon spring sunshine.

I let it go and caught up to her, stayed a few steps behind. God, I wanted to know everything she knew, and right now. I could fill a jump slot with the memories and missed chances that had come from not knowing my dad.

"I remember seeing you a few times," she said, her voice tight. "I knew who you were, because my father talked about you. Said you were Lawrence Crowell's son. You were often accompanied by one of the Emirates' pages, tending you while meetings were going on."

"You saw me, but did you talk to me?"

She briefly showed me her profile before returning her gaze to the Sound. "Yes," she said. "Once. We were younger, about four years before our fathers disappeared."

I turned my hands palms up, a gesture she couldn't see. "What did we say? What did we talk about?"

She faced me, finally, her arms crossed again. "We exchanged names, even though I already knew yours." She smiled, remembering. "You said you were Lucky's lad. You said it might be your lucky day."

I shivered, hearing the very words my dad said to me after coming home from the marina.

My senses crackled with the intense feelings those words kindled in me, and I moved a step back from her. She moved too, following me. She touched my chest again—I remembered something about Memors doing that as a gesture of trust—and warmth spread through me.

"Do you want to know, David?"

I stayed mute, my skin tingling.

"Because if you do, I can help you."

"Help me?"

"You have to trust me."

There was a bench on the pier, a rusty metal one big enough to seat three. She led me to it and we sat. The bench felt fragile, as if rust were the only thing keeping it from disintegrating. The slight breeze on my face felt warmer than it should. My nose might've been plugged, since I could hardly smell the sea air.

"Something happened to you on the day your father and mine disappeared," she said.

"You saw me that day? You said they went on leave. The Envoys went to Montana. Were you there?"

"I was there, but I don't remember much, and that's why I need to hire *you*, to find out the truth. But you need to find out what happened, and for that, *I* can help."

I shook my head, not understanding how the person who couldn't remember anything could help *me* remember. Still, I seized her slim hands, wanting her to understand that I was interested.

She smiled reassuringly. "If you trust me, I will attempt the next phase of memory."

Oh, so there *was* some kind of Memor brain control. "Next phase? It sounds like mad-scientist stuff."

"Was what happened to your partner and the other Thin Men mad-scientist stuff? No one could've believed the Ultras' conduit could create copies of humans, even change outward mass and form. This *is* connected to the Ultras, and I know that's a topic you'd rather not think about. But I'm afraid you'll have to."

I looked at the sky, roughly toward the rest of the known Union. "We're on the edge of something here, aren't we?"

She worked a hand free of mine and pointed at me. "You're important. You were important even before the events leading up to Plenko and the Ultras. Have you wondered why you were singled out? Why you were set up to take the blame, and why you were watched by any number of Ultras along the way?"

"I've thought about it," I said.

"Think harder. And I'll help you if you let me."

"So what do I have to do?"

"The process has already started." She must have seen the surprise in my eyes, for she immediately spoke again: "Your sleep on the pavement. It wasn't me, as I said, but someone, either a Memor or someone with the knowledge, tried to phase you into Memory."

"My memory?"

She shook her head. "The phase connects you to something that Memors *call* the Memory."

I nodded, remembering the difference. Their planet was named after the concept. I was aware of the Memors' idea of—for lack of a better term—group consciousness, but I didn't know how to explain the idea of it. Humans tried to relate it to the concept of quantum theory. Quantum memory, frozen light, the ether.

"Our genetic blueprints are never quite connected as they should be, and sometimes we need our DNA realigned," Terree said. She touched my forehead with her finger. "Consciousness is not strictly about your brain on its own. It's a brain that has communicated with other brains. *Someone* knows what happened to you; you just need to pull it from the Memory. It might be disconcerting seeing things from someone else's perspective, and sometimes objects and words are little more than symbols for some larger picture."

I frowned, not understanding. "Why can't you see your own memories?"

"I've tried. I'm blocked, probably because I'm his daughter. Because of the way Memors sexually assign, it's likely that my genetic blueprint doesn't permit me to connect with him. I'm sure something was done to him to keep this from me."

"But you found some memories of me, and through me, you were able to piece together the information you have about my father."

"Yes," she said. "What little I know is from you."

"Have you tried the Emirates Headquarters right here in Seattle?"

"I'll be going there soon, but I don't know that they'll be able to tell me anything different about my dad than they have for years."

This all made little sense. "Someone's hiding something."

"Maybe. Or they really don't know."

"Someone tried to phase me into the Memory specifically to get that same information from me, didn't they?"

"Maybe they gleaned something, but they would've needed more time to get anything of worth. I'm guessing your partner came along at just the right time, scaring off whoever was trying. If it's not an Ultra, it could be someone working in some capacity for Ultra goals."

Again, I wanted to say bullshit about the technology, which seemed more surreal fantasy than science, but Terree was right. All I had to do was think of the Transcontinental Conduit, of Alan Brindos transformed into a Helk, of the human copy of Alan himself, to know that anything was possible in the deeper mystery of the Ultras.

Beyond scrutiny, Plenko had said about the aliens, during that fateful showdown on Ribon. They were beyond understanding, and yet Plenko had said they were learning from us. *Rebuilding themselves by tearing us down and recreating us.*

I thought of Alex Richards. Fucking some young girl his wife had known about one moment, running with my camera the next, and stone cold dead the next, *Ultra* stamped on him like an expiration date.

Or maybe he was lost in the sweet mother of quantum Memory somewhere.

Soul mates from an alternate reality. It was a small universe. Very small. *I could be bounded in a nutshell, and count myself a king of infinite space.*

Terree's voice pulled me from my own memories. "David?"

"We can never understand them," I said, remembering Plenko's words. "They can only understand us." The words were hollow, almost lost between two people alone on a dilapidated pier on a nearly forgotten world.

"All there is, is memory," she said. "You can forget it. You can hide it. You can destroy it. But in the end, you have to own it."

"Even if the memories come from someone else."

"Exactly," Terree said, and with a touch of her hand to my forehead, she put me to sleep.

Seven

THERE WAS SOMETHING I'D FORGOTTEN.

If not forgotten, then I had completely messed up my dad's instructions about where to meet him. He'd screamed at me. Screamed to get out of the building: *Get away from here. Stay away from us. We'll meet later. Run!*

I remembered running from the conference room, past my unconscious Emirates page, looking for the front doors. I was pretty good at getting away from pages and escorts when I wanted to. Mom had been pretty upset a few days earlier when I'd skipped past my escort at home.

Something had kept me from going out the door. Suddenly nervous, suddenly scared for my father, I turned around and headed for the main foyer. Maybe Dad *hadn't* told me a place to meet him.

Now I searched frantically from the crystal balcony overlooking the vast foyer of the conference center, hoping to catch sight of him, or his aide, or even my assigned Emirates page I was supposed to elude.

I was still panting, my heart beating too fast, as I peered into the foyer. Some Envoys were there, as were several aides, ambassadors, interpreters, pages and vendors, whether human, Memor, or Helk, and they all seemed to be in the foyer at the same time. But Dad was not there.

The Emirates conference had gone on for days in the Knightley Tower, the tallest building east of the Continental Divide, in the heart of downtown Chicago. Some of the most important ambassadors from all Union worlds had converged on this spot, and although I didn't know the specifics of the conferences and the ongoing talks, I knew—because my dad knew—that it was the most important meeting he'd ever attended. The Envoys had lost plenty of sleep over it, and skipped many a meal, and the tension had thickened as the week had progressed.

I'd wished Dad had never dragged me to this. Let me stay home with Mom. I worried about her being alone at the lake house for so long, even though she had the family escort, Tilson, to watch over her. She had fussed over me more than usual as I reluctantly packed for the trip, and she did that thing she did, rubbing my shoulder. Some day, I told her, she'd wear me down to my shoulder blade.

"You're just sixteen," she had said to me as I climbed into the small shuttle that would take me to Chicago, where Dad had already gone.

"Tell that to Dad," I said, my assigned Emirates page smirking in his seat beside me.

Mom smiled sadly, rubbed my shoulder one last time, kissed my cheek, and walked back inside the lake house.

Now, as I tried to spot my dad in the flurry of activity below, I wished I was back home, with Mom rubbing my shoulder again.

"I'm going to guess you're looking for Lucky," said a voice behind me.

I turned, breathing hard, and found one of the Memor Envoys studying me, his hair tied back into its ponytail, but so long that it was wrapped in four places from top to bottom, so that it nearly resembled an orange spike. The tip of the hair was dyed white, a symbol of a dignitary of Memory.

For a moment, I hadn't recognized him.

"Oh," I said, "hello, Greist." In my mind, I sometimes called him Grease, especially when he'd just oiled his ponytail for an important session. Memor names were almost impossible to remember, even when I wasn't frantic. I could never remember his last name, much less how to pronounce it correctly.

He was old for a Memor. Meaning I'd rarely seen older Memors. Lines creased his face almost unnaturally. Did the hair of the Memors gray as they aged? I wondered if he dyed the orange of his hair, too.

"You've been running," Greist said.

"Yeah. I guess."

He wore a sort of blue silk blazer, short-waisted, but long-sleeved, the fabric extending well past his hands when his arms hung at his sides.

"I think he might have left, Lucky Lad," he said, those big puffy lips quivering. He seemed amused by the nickname, but also a little sad.

"My dad calls me that."

"Indeed he does. Is it okay if I call you that?"

I shrugged. "It's okay."

"Or I could just call you David. Young Crowell."

"Did you say my dad left?"

"How old are you again?"

"Sixteen."

His eyes glazed in an effort to calculate the difference between Earth's calendar and Memory's.

"Ah yes. About the same age as my daughter."

"Terree."

The Memor smiled a forced smile. "Yes. You've met her before, have you?"

"A few times. We've only talked once."

He looked at the space behind me, beyond the balcony. "She's probably down there somewhere, too. It's not surprising you've missed each other. Such a scene. Like Memor rats scurrying along, all with places to go, thoughts tucked in their heads." He frowned. "They just have no idea. No idea."

I fought the urge to turn and look, keeping my focus on his face. Behind him, a maze of mostly empty hallways led nowhere and everywhere. An impressive crystal chandelier hung in one of the intersections, the lights bright enough to wash out the hallway entrances, like a lantern at the mouth of a tunnel. On either side of the entrances, hugging the balcony, escalators led to the foyer, one coming up, one going down.

"Sahlkla," I said, his last name coming to me just then.

"Sahl-*kla*. Accent always on the second syllable, lad."

"Sahl-kla. Yes, sir."

"'Sir?' We don't believe in that honorific." He managed a nervous laugh, a gurgly noise that sounded like a smoker's cough. "There are just too many of us, and we don't always *start* as sirs."

"Of course," I said, briefly looking down. "Sorry."

The Memor walked to the railing, and as he looked over the crowd, I stared up at him. He turned and stared at me with his glassy eyes, his pupils large and very dark, like black holes swirling with all the memories of the past week trapped in them. Very serious.

"Do you know what the conference is about?" he asked.

I shook my head.

"It's nothing, David. Nothing. It's all a ruse."

The sadness returned to his eyes, and he looked at me for an eternity while the buzz of the Union's representatives below became almost unreal and the click-clack of shoe heels echoed like firecrackers.

I didn't understand his remark. "How's my mom?" I asked when I realized he would say no more about it. Apparently he was content that I didn't know, or didn't care, about the conference. "I worry about her being on her own for so long."

"She's fine, as always. Tilson watches her. You know that." He pulled his ponytail in front of his shoulder, fluffing the white-dyed tip. "You can believe me when I say she'll be fine."

I found the way he said it odd, but I got past that and asked him about his own wives. Or his mates, rather.

The gurgling laugh again. "Well, see now, that's confusing, isn't it? I am Terree's mother's third bondmate. And I have seven bondmates, of various ages and sizes." He leaned in. "One of them even likes to dye her hair *black*."

"Seems like it would be difficult to remember everyone."

"Oh, lad, it's like anyone you meet and become friends with. You never forget who they are, or why you love them so much. That many other male Memors love them too is part of our species' way to propagate. Sadly, one of my bondmates is not doing so well. When you're that close to death, you're thankful just to be taken care of. Death isn't truly death, if the connections to our shared bondmates are strong. It's only a brief interruption in our waking life. She's not minding too much, but it is difficult for me. If I could give my life for her, for the sake of her children, I would. Alas, I cannot. I am myself. I am male, and can not change that."

"Sir—I mean, Greist—I really don't understand at all what you mean."

He waved me off. "Not important. Not now. But please remember something."

"Remember what?"

He paused a moment, then said, "Something about your dad."

"Dad. Yes. Are you sure he's left? Where would he have gone?"

He stooped, put his hand on my chest, and when he spoke, his voice took on a tone I'd not yet heard from him—low, cautious, almost conspiratorial.

"Look at me, lad, right here," and he pointed with two fingers of his other hand to those dark, glistening eyes. Memors have only four fingers, each of them long, each of them thick and ridged with hard calluses. The long sleeve had inched up showing something on his wrist—some kind of tattoo. A word. It said—

"*Look* at me," Greist said.

"What—?"

"You won't remember any of this," he said.

"Any of what?"

"Not until you can see the Memory. Then, and only then, will you be able to retrieve what I see and know. You can see it as I saw it, and perhaps some of what you saw." He shook his head. "I don't know that I can get this exactly right."

I tried to back away. "Greist—"

His fingers seemed to dig into my chest. "No, stay!"

A noise from below caught my attention, and amidst the persistent earlier buzz, this noise did not belong. My gaze shifted away from Greist.

"Eyes here!" he yelled at me.

"What's going on?" I suddenly felt more afraid than I had been for Dad. My fear grew as the noise that did not belong became many noises, many screams, high-pitched and strident. *Oh God*—

"I'm sorry, lad. Today is *not* your lucky day. I had to do this; I had no choice. But they won't be here long, and when they have what they want, they'll leave."

"You're scaring me."

He ignored my complaint. "David, listen. Find Terree if you can, you hear? If she can't find you, you'll have to find her. She'll help you with the Memory. You'll know what happened from *me*. It'll be you witnessing it. At least for the few minutes I can give you. After that, you might be able to access other memories from those you know best. You'll have to take what you know and go from there."

"My dad—"

"I know, I'm sorry. He's really gone."

"Gone where?"

"And the others. I've given them away, but you have to understand I had no choice." He concentrated on keeping his attention on me, but he was having trouble. "I had no choice. The choice was made for me. This may all be too late. You'll be alive, but you might discover the Memory too late to stop them."

"Them?"

"The Ultras."

I trembled, barely staying upright. It was the word on his wrist. Somehow, I recognized the word. Why? With one arm, I gripped the railing of the balcony. "Who are the Ultras?"

He shook off my question. "I had no choice."

"What about Mom?"

"I told you, she'll be okay. That I can guarantee. Tilson will watch her. Just keep looking at me!"

The screams below morphed into a nameless howl, nothing I'd heard before, an alien sound. "What is that?" I asked the Memor, but he had stopped talking for now, only searching my eyes, his hand on my chest. My head felt heavy, then light, then heavy again, as if it couldn't decide if I should be dealing with any of this.

The foreign howl, the screams of everyone below, intensified, and now I heard the distinct whine of blaster fire.

Dizzy.

Light-headed. My head had made its decision, obviously.

Greist Sahl-kla nodded. "Okay."

I barely heard him. "Okay?"

He took his hand from my chest, but kept his eyes locked on me. "Are you ready?"

"For what?"

He leaned in close, the dark pools of his irises sucking me in past the margin of reality. "If you can, look for one of us. Otherwise, we'll try and find you."

"Greist, I'm scared."

"One of them is going to come and take your memories. But we'll be *linked*, David. There are always holes. It won't mean anything now. Trust the memories when they come to you. When you break through. Even if they aren't yours. Even if they're *mine*."

The noise redoubled below, followed by a thudding noise, and the natural quality of the light seemed to change, brighter, flickering, as if thousands of candles had simultaneously lit up. Greist tensed. "I have to go. Travel well, and trust yourself."

He touched me on my forehead, and I fell asleep.

There was something I'd forgotten.

Somehow the whole scene moved in slow motion. Except for the body of the boy David Crowell slumped against the balcony railing, out cold, I was alone, which didn't seem right, considering all the chaos downstairs. Short staccato cries, sounding like commands, grew louder, and heavy feet stamped on the escalator coming up from the foyer.

I headed down the other escalator, realizing as I did that it wasn't the smartest idea I'd had, heading down to where the conference's attendees happened to be screaming and running.

Like Memor rats, I thought, thoughts tucked in their heads.

Where was Terree?

I stayed in a low crouch as I ran down, keeping my head below the escalator's hand rail. Peeking quickly over the side, I was surprised to see the foyer nearly empty. Hadn't I just heard screaming? Hadn't there been shooting? A discharge of weapons familiar and alien?

I slowed to a stop. A few people wandered the polished floor, all of them human, but none of them in a hurry, all of them exiting the foyer. No one seemed to care about me coming down the escalator. I looked up to the balcony, and the voices and footsteps I'd thought I'd heard coming up the other escalator had lessened in volume, as if they'd all reversed direction.

I searched frantically for signs of people I knew in the foyer, but no, they were gone.

Where was Terree? *Where was my daughter?*

At the bottom of the escalator I stood straight, confused. Why was I worried about Terree? Shouldn't I be worried about someone else?

Yes, Lucky Crowell. Was it true? Had they taken him? Taken him with the other Envoys? *Leaving me behind. Leaving me to travel elsewhere, to a place unimaginable.*

Emboldened, I walked to the middle of the foyer, where a large, sophisticated-looking gentleman in a fine suit stood with his back to me, hands clasped behind his back. His full head of dark brown hair seemed to flutter, as if a slight breeze disturbed it. I couldn't tell if he was smiling or frowning, and he made no move to turn and face me.

In my mind, a vision emerged of a dark passage, a hallway with tall, black walls on either side forcing me down, down, toward a pale light. I blinked it away.

"Are you done?" I asked. "Am I done?"

His shoulders moved in what might have been a shrug. "They'll come for you soon, and that will be that," the man said to the space in front of him.

I craned my neck, willing myself to see him. "But am I done?"

The gentleman reached in the pocket of his suit jacket and pulled out some squares of red paper. He held them out behind him, still facing away from me, and I stretched and took them. "You will never be done," he answered, his voice mildly melodious, then walked away without another word.

I rolled one of the squares, placed it on my tongue, and waited.

I awoke, my body against the railing of the balcony. I started, now wide awake, and stood. I remembered what I'd forgotten.

Griest was gone. A man stood before me, his hair patchy across the top of his head, a mix of gray and black. He gave me a hint of a smile. He closed his eyes and mouth and touched his face almost lovingly.

An image formed in my mind of my dad, whose smile warmed my heart, for I could also see, behind him, my mom saying something, her hands laying out a hot meal on the small table in the tackle shop: fried chicken, a biscuit, two cobs of corn. I could almost smell it, there, with the sails from the docks outside snapping in the breeze.

This is your life.

The old man nodded, letting me know that the soothing words I'd heard in my head were his.

We will meet again, his voice intoned, *on another day.*

Who are you? my own inner voice asked.

The man's hand shone instantly white.

He spread the fingers of his hand and a glow sparked between them all just as he reached for me.

I woke up on the bench beside Terree. We were still alone on the pier, and the sunshine still seemed fake, the reflection off the Sound making me squint. I remembered what I'd forgotten.

She looked at me inquisitively.

"What the hell?" I mumbled.

She touched my chest with her hand, and said: "One more."

I awoke up on the floor of my office, and remembered what I'd forgotten. It wasn't about Tem Forno not being with us on our walk along the waterfront. Terree had explained what had likely happened to me when I'd passed out the night before, and she'd agreed to check out her theory about whether I'd been phased into the Memory.

Terree and Forno looked at me from above, but without any serious concern.

My head pounded and hurt like hell.

Terree reached for me. "David—"

I fended her off with an upraised arm. "Don't touch me."

"You looked so peaceful," Forno said. "Kind of boring watching you sleep, though."

"That is creepy," I told him, but I frowned up at Terree.

"Hey, twice in one day," Forno said. "Creepy shit or not, you've got some explaining to do."

"I think Terree has some explaining to do." Ignoring their outstretched arms, I picked myself off the floor. "The whole walk on the waterfront was part of the Memory. Things weren't quite right. The quality of light. The unfinished feel to everything. Why the walk? The bench."

"It was necessary to prepare you," she answered, "not have you come into the Memory cold, as happened the first time. Plus, I could, while you were out, explain some things more thoroughly."

Still woozy, I leaned up against my desk. Why hadn't she warned me in advance about the levels of memory? The whole schmear came rushing back at me, the real memories, the borrowed ones. . .

"Well?" Forno asked. "What did the Memory tell you?"

Terree shifted uneasily as I continued to regard her, now with a new set of facts that changed everything.

Everything.

"We'll take the case," I said.

Terree's eyes brightened, her lips trembling slightly.

I couldn't stop staring at Terree. Taking the case to find her father was only a small part of the task ahead of me. My own dad could be out there somewhere. The mention of Ultras back then, when I was sixteen, came as unwelcome news.

One of us has already gone beyond the mirror. We are damaged. A short while ago now, the Ultras had come, and Plenko had come, and Joseph had come. And while all of them had seemingly died, or surrendered, or retreated, I could not imagine any scenario making the Union safe from them. I couldn't imagine it because I partially understood what Greist Sahl-kla had done in Chicago.

Terree became wary. She smoothed out her ponytail with a shaky hand. Fear came into her eyes as she started toward me, her arm outstretched.

I put up my hand. I didn't want her near me, knowing she might send me spinning back into my past.

She stopped. "David, what—?"

"I'll look for your father in order to find out what happened to my own dad," I said, "but you're asking me to do much more than you thought." I gave Forno a quick glance before telling her, "There's no amount of money in the Union that could pay for this."

"I *will* pay you. Double, as I said."

"I said we'd do it. I'm talking about a different cost."

"Okay."

"Nothing's sacred. This is bigger than all of us, and I won't leave any possibility unchecked. Assuming I can even get to Helkunntanas."

"Okay." She nodded forcefully. "David, what did you see? Why are you so upset?"

"The Ultras were there in Chicago when I was sixteen. During the conference. Your father saw me, and he told me."

She waited.

"He's not worth saving," I said.

"You're so wrong, David. I didn't come here to—"

"It was a setup." As I gripped the edge of my desk, her eyes flashed with a reddish-orange tint like the spark of a struck match.

"Maybe I'll wait outside," Forno said. He eased toward the door.

"You will not," I said.

"*What* was a setup?" Terree asked.

I shook my head, remembering how Griest had said he had given the Envoys and my father to them. *To the Ultras.* I let it all come out: "Your father is a traitor to the Union."

Eight

VANDERBERG PARR FIDDLED WITH THE LEVELS ON HIS SKIN COOLER, adjusting it as he stood there at the Khrem port's loading dock, the private drop shuttle steaming on its pad, the pallet with the shipment of RuBy in front of him. His two human sniffers, Tate and Mendez, to his left and right. A couple Second Clan Helks from his district on the perimeter, visible enough to warn off trouble, but far enough away as to make this party seem legit.

Nervous as he was, standing in the dying light, Parr found the evening heat oppressive, and he couldn't dial in the coolant to his satisfaction. The cooler tendril wrapped twice around his neck and snaked down under his loose shirt to his lower back. The bulky Helk-designed control box, clipped to his belt, pulled at his side.

He had heard that the coolant, which was toxic, was enhanced by nano-fluids to help with the heat transfer, but it was all chemically inert, and apparently low cost. Not that he cared. Baren Rieser paid for it. Nothing but comfort for the Boss's sniffers.

His blaster, its presence reassuring, was tucked in his pants, his shirttail covering it. Frock had liked his outfit, but really, the light buttondowns and pants he wore, he wore because they were comfortable, and cooler. A little more difficult to hide a blaster, but then again, few people much minded about weapons in plain sight in Khrem.

Rieser didn't expect trouble at this little job, but these days you never knew. The Boss wouldn't have suggested the Helk escort otherwise.

RuBy, outlawed on all the other planets of the Union, could not be transported off Helkunntanas.

Yeah, well, according to the official *manifest*, the steel, DNA-locked, hermetically sealed crate on the pallet contained only Helk spices. RuBy? Oh no, oh no, just transporting those strong spices that made his nose run when he smelled them, everything fine, according to the Port Authority administrator Rieser had in his back pocket, and the carefully assigned but superfluous fees and taxes levied by the commissioner. The crate would soon be on the shuttle to Crossbill Station, and at that point, Parr's job would be done, thank God, the outgoing RuBy fairly safe until it reached the next port. In this case, Barnard's World. With the manifest approved on this side, and the DNA-lock keyed to Rieser's associate on Barnard's, the crates could slide in without much trouble. Most of the Union governments had reservations about the new ban on the drug, and rightly so, as far as Parr was concerned. Blind eyes often missed the fine details and approved shipments even without DNA failsafes.

Get this done, head to the House.

One last Port Authority inspector stepped up on the pallet just then, Third Clan insignias on the collar of his uniform, his digipad held tight in one hand.

"What's this about?" Max Tate whispered to Parr, the sniffer leaning toward him discretely.

Parr clicked his cooler up a notch. This couldn't be a problem, not with a private shuttle, in a public area of the port, and the inspector looking like the only authoritative figure around. "Relax, Tate." He held out his hand to Mendez, the other sniffer, for the manifest. The sniffer's first name escaped him at the moment. A district greenie.

Mendez handed the bound papers to Parr just as the inspector turned toward them. All the wonders of the DataNet and news tubes, and most ports still required paper documents.

As the inspector walked up to Parr for the manifest, the shuttle, with a hiss, released some coolant of its own.

"Already approved and double-checked," Parr said to the Helk, handing it over.

The inspector flipped through the top pages, then tucked the manifest under his arm. He rested the digipad in his palm and snapped in what he wanted to say. Parr wondered if he was entering words in Helk, the digipad translating. Goddamn digipads. Making them wait those extra, tense beats while the RuBy sat there like a treasure chest. Worth *more* than a chest of jewels. A shitload of those red paper squares could be packed into one of these cases.

But a small percentage of the Helk population was mute, so the digipad was a necessity. The digipad said, in English, *Then it'll be triple-checked.* Followed by: *Is your name on the manifest?*

"No no," Parr said. He wasn't sure this Helk—it said "Officer Kash Neviya" on the digipad—was in on Baren Rieser's understanding with the Port

Authority. "The shuttle's gonna be missing its connection at Crossbill. If we can just get this on board we'll be on our way."

Officer Kash Neviya waved at the crate, making obvious gestures to have Parr open it up.

Parr eased forward, his eyes locked on the Helk. He suspected his own Helks on the perimeter had edged closer to the shuttle, curious about the exchange, but he didn't look away from Neviya. Even if the inspector had no weapon, he must stay alert. "No. See, we're checked through. Signed off by the Comish." He nodded at the manifest. "Last page, you can see it. The crate's DNA-locked. I can't open it."

Kash Neviya's motions to open the crate became more insistent.

Parr shook his head, uneasily, and fished in his pocket for a square of RuBy.

Neviya took a few more minutes with his digipad.

Parr rolled the RuBy and set it on his tongue. The cinnamon made his nostrils flare, the paper dissolving and releasing.

Open the crate, the digipad said when Neviya showed it to him.

"Is he serious?" Mendez said. "You just told him."

Parr stepped to the crate as if giving in, but gave an imperceptible nod to his perimeter Helks to close the distance.

"You're forgetting," Parr said to Neviya, "that this is my crate, it's spoken for, and do you know the hell whose district this is?"

Parr snatched the digipad from Neviya with one hand and drew his blaster with the other. In a moment—because the Helk could outmaneuver him quicker than shit if he had the chance—Parr raised the barrel high and pointed it at the alien's temple.

Neviya made some guttural noises in his throat. His hands, coming instinctively to his face, dropped the manifest. Well then, Parr thought, the inspector could at least grunt a bit. He had to be thinking that Parr could shoot him to keep him from notifying Crossbill. Keeping the shipment from being seized up top, at the station.

Parr's own Helks had Kash Neviya now, their stunners at either side of his head. Backing up, Parr put away his blaster, picked up the manifest, and slipped it under his own arm. He tried to type on the digipad.

"Shit," he said, making mistakes. Wiping the screen, starting over. "How the fuck do they use these things?"

"It's a mystery," Tate said.

Mendez chuckled.

Parr looked up from the digipad, ready to make his point to Neviya. "Not sure what the delay is about. Do you? No need for hostilities. No need for this to happen."

Neviya nodded.

Parr held up the digipad to Neviya, waited while the inspector read it. If this went bad now, he'd never make it to the House in time, having to clean up the mess here. Never meet with Rieser and his only opportunity to ask him the question he'd had on his mind for months.

It was the very same question he'd typed onto the digipad:

Do you know who I am?

Kash Neviya frowned as he looked up from the screen, cocking his head at Parr.

Parr raised an eyebrow. A restatement: Do you know?

Neviya shook his head, and it was obvious from the look on his face that he had no clue who Vanderberg Parr was.

That makes two of us, Parr thought.

The manifest didn't need another sign-off. Kash Neviya had simply decided to play the hotshot inspector, hoping to get lucky with something and make a name for himself. Yeah, hooray for names.

"I'm keeping this," he said, raising the digipad.

The Helk's leathery face looked tight, like the skin of a drum, and Parr saw the change in him, an acceptance of his fate. Probably thinking this was it, that Parr would shoot him to keep him from transmitting to Crossbill Station.

Parr leaned in closer, staring into his eyes. "You idiot, I'm not going to kill you." He tapped the Helk on the forehead with the digipad. "Snot-for-brains. Your words are here, your report. Log entry about this shuttle."

Neviya barely nodded.

"You have a weapon?"

He shook his head no.

"Comm card?"

No again.

"You have a family?"

Yes.

"You've got enough personal information on this digipad for me to find them, officer Neviya. If this evening's misunderstanding somehow gets pegged to me in any way? Well, I think maybe we have an understanding, do we not?"

Kash Neviya nodded vigorously.

Parr, satisfied, motioned to the Helks beside Neviya. "Take him somewhere and hold him. Wait until the shipment's cleared Crossbill. Then let him go."

Both Helks fell in tight behind the inspector.

"Good evening, inspector." Parr nodded at his crew to remove Neviya from the loading dock.

Mendez came to Parr's side as the three Helks walked away from the shuttle. Tate sat on the crate of RuBy. His hair damp with perspiration, Parr clicked his cooler up another notch, and the fresh coolness down his neck and back felt good.

"You shoulda killed him," Mendez said.

The thought had crossed Parr's mind, particularly since he hadn't shot Shyler Frock earlier in the day, as the Boss thought he should have. Plus, there shouldn't have been any trouble with the inspector in the first place, no questioning of the cargo.

"True," Tate echoed. "He could still make trouble for you."

"He won't. Not with his family on the hook, and me with his digipad."

The sun had sunk below the buildings around the port, and their shadows, and those of the crate and shuttle, disappeared.

"Should we tell the Boss?" Tate asked.

"What do you think?" Parr said.

"Guess not, then."

Parr tossed the manifest to Tate, who caught it as he stood up from the crate. "Load and secure the shipment for me, and find your own ways home. I'm late for a meeting with the Boss."

He left them there, not caring whether they had to take a ground bus, hire a car, hitch a ride, or call the Boss himself. They wouldn't say anything to Rieser about letting Neviya go. He didn't care if they thought that his leniency signaled something off about him. If, like Frock, they suspected Parr was a trademark, they'd be stupid to bring it up. And if they knew nothing about it . . . well. Parr had an in with Rieser, and Parr had access to the House. In the long run, Mendez and Tate both wanted their own invitations to the House one day.

Not that they knew what *he* knew about the House.

Tonight was different, though, with the question on his mind. He stared at Kash Neviya's digipad.

Do you know who I am?

Shyler Frock had wondered a little about Parr being a Thin Man, and

Rieser had taken him out. Frock and his mate, Qerral. One dead, the other as good as dead.

When he got to his flier, Parr took off his cooler, sped away from the port, and headed out of Khrem. He didn't care about Neviya's shuttle log. No way would Neviya put his family at risk and say anything.

Parr really didn't care who they were.

He waited until he was outside the city limits before throwing the digipad out the window.

Nine

TERREE DID AS ASKED AND PAID A RETAINER FOR MY SERVICES. THE overall cost would be exorbitant, so I was surprised she gave up the credits so quickly, particularly because she didn't like my identifying her father as a traitor. It was a lot of cash, and only a fraction of the final bill. I offered her a drink, but she refused. I drank hers.

She *had* said from the start she'd pay double, and that meant double on the expenses as well, since Forno would tag along.

I told her more about my time in the Memory, and although she refused to believe her father was a traitor, she didn't back down from her desire to find him.

Part of my life was a lie, if the memories were true. Terree's father had given something to the Ultras. Told me sorry, my dad was gone.

This part of the Memory I didn't tell Terree. It seemed prudent to hold some of it back.

But *was* my dad gone? Every credit I earned from Terree I hoped to use to find him, if he was still alive. Damn it, she had *known* I'd take the case upon hearing the information about my dad.

Terree figured she'd remain on Earth for a few weeks at the local Emirates office, unless I came up with something that required her to travel to us, or if I found nothing and she had to slot back home to Memor. She left the tarot card of the Chariot on my desk. I hadn't expected her to actually leave it. What good was it going to do me?

She had been gone about ten minutes when my comm card pinged with a call from NIO agent Jennifer Lisle. Instead of answering, I picked up Terree's Chariot card and looked it over without comprehension. The comm card kept ringing.

"Miss Lisle?" Forno asked, leaning against our plywood wall. He gave me so much shit about my divider wall, but he sure loved to lean against it.

I nodded.

"Didn't you say she was coming here?" he asked.

"Warning me ahead of time, I guess."

"You answering?"

"Eventually."

The comm card kept pulsing, and I couldn't bring myself to answer it. I didn't want to find out what she knew.

"Eventually, as in before it stops ringing," Forno said, "or eventually as in the next time she calls?"

I kept turning the tarot card over and over. But eventually I answered the comm card, putting it to my ear.

"Crowell?" came Jennifer Lisle's voice.

"Yeah."

"Yeah? That's it?"

"What else am I supposed to say?"

"How about 'Sorry I'm late' or 'I'm on my way.'"

"How about you tell me what you're talking about?"

Lisle sighed. "You're supposed to be here, at the county morgue." Her voice loud, almost accusing me.

"I thought you were coming here."

"Who told you that?"

"Freelund."

Another sigh. "Goddamn it, Crowell, why would I come there? The body's down here."

"Just telling you what Freelund said, at the warehouse."

"He tell you I was coming in on this one?"

"He did."

"He didn't tell you to meet me here this afternoon?"

"He didn't."

"Well, get here. You know where I am? County? They moved it a year ago, you know. You know how to get here?"

"I know where County is. I'll see you in twenty minutes. You want Forno, too?"

"No. He'll scare the workers."

County was a group of mismatched buildings up on Capitol Hill, far from the downtown district where the original offices had stood. In the early days of the Movement, some of Plenko's followers had hijacked an assault plane and leveled a chunk of several city blocks. The remaining County services struggled on for a while, until forced to move north and up the hill into an old elementary school and a neighboring Catholic church, where the morgue was housed. Somehow fitting, considering.

The Capitol Hill area made me think of controlled chaos. The street, Broadway, and many of the side streets, were mostly clear of abandoned cars and refuse, owing to the efforts of County employees still plugging away to make the place appear operational. Many of the adjacent buildings were in disrepair and a little out of alignment, as if shoved off to the side to make room for more important structures.

What front yards there were had no grass, just dirt, and the cracked driveways sported a mix of old and new vehicles. Dogs, skinny and sickly, sniffed at trash cans. A few folks had actually ventured into the late afternoon. Most wore coats, some too threadbare to offer much warmth.

Closer to the church, the elementary school and surrounding buildings boasted a coat of fresh paint, and signs out front identified the various departments inside. The church itself was the color of Puget Sound, grayish green, mold blackening some of the stone and mortar. A wide oak door, painted green, stood half open. A concrete monument originally made for the church now sported a plaque that read *Morgue. Medical Examiner. Pathology Lab.*

I parked my ground car in front of the church next to a moss-encrusted fire hydrant.

Inside the green door, the outer foyer of the church had been converted into a reception area. A middle-aged man sat at an old wooden banquet table, his shirt buttoned up all the way to his neck. His nametag said "James Passmore." A modest DataNet terminal sat on the table. When I told him my name and that I had a meeting with Special Ops Director Lisle, he guided me into the nave—formerly, the worship area—now the heart of the morgue, where the deceased were brought in. A large cart and scale apparatus sat near the front, and a body lift hung from the ceiling. I was surprised to see a state-of-the-art low-dose radiation scanner—I recalled seeing one in the security offices of the NIO. In a few seconds, it could create a holographic image of a body perfect in every detail.

We crossed past the north and south wings, to a wall and steel door that now separated the nave from the area I assumed had once been the sanctuary. Another sign on the door said "Autopsy Suite." I probably wouldn't need to make the sign of the cross before entering.

"Gloves, please," James Passmore said. A box of disposable gloves sat in a file holder by the door.

I put on a pair and Passmore opened the door and motioned me in. The sanctuary had none of the trappings of a religious ceremonial space. It had all been cleared out, and I'd have never known this was a church by the traditional but small autopsy room now in front of me. Some other doors led out of the sanctuary, probably to rooms housing the coolers, the medical examiner's office, and perhaps a homicide room or a room designed for containing contagious diseases.

Near the back of the room, on an autopsy table, lay a body covered by a pale blue cloth. I guessed it was probably Alex Richards. His very white feet poked out from one end.

"She'll be here shortly," James Passmore said, and slipped out.

I walked over to the table and glanced side to side, sizing up the shrouded body. The feet looked fake, like part of a clown's trick, stuck on wooden slats or something. I should have waited for Jennifer, but I grabbed the cloth covering the head and pulled it down to the corpse's shoulders.

Richards. Paler. Muscles relaxed, looking a little less *worn*. Cooler, the death chill settling in. His green T-shirt had been removed. It had been less than a day, so Richards didn't smell bad yet. Or, really, not at all. Probably, he'd spent some time in the morgue's cooler.

The word Ultra seemed darker against the white of his skin over the collarbone.

"What happened to you, Alex?" I whispered.

He'd been having an affair. I'd found him with the girl, and I'd chased him through the warehouse. Then he was dead. Unless this was a different Alex Richards. Had he been a Thin Man? I shivered, the room feeling as cold as the blood in Richards' body.

It took me a few moments to work up the nerve, but I took off the glove on my right hand, and with my index finger slowly traced the word Ultra, the skin cold to the touch. The word wasn't written in blood, that was for sure.

I looked Alex Richards in the face, oddly peaceful in death, his eyes shut, and said, "How long has it been since your last confession?"

Ten

YOU HAD TO WONDER ABOUT MEMORS, TEM FORNO THOUGHT, AFTER deciding to learn more about Terree No-Last-Name, who had left for the comfort of the Emirates office in the posh Seattle Center district.

Memors made his fur curl. Orange hair? Lips big enough you could wet them and stick them on blackrock and they'd make a nice seal. Almost all of them skinny as gabobilecks. And that Memory stuff. Helk's breath, that just wasn't right, and it made him nervous as human hell. He would never have allowed Terree to do that memory thing to him that she'd inflicted on Crowell. He didn't trust her, simple as that. He had decided fairly early on to see if she even made it back to the Emirates Tower.

Crowell had headed to County in one of his appropriated cars, but Forno wouldn't have fit in one. He wasn't sure how Terree had traveled to Crowell's office, but Forno could walk or run just about anywhere in the greater Seattle area without breaking much of a sweat. In fact, it *would* warm him up some. He figured he could, with his speed, arrive at Seattle Center before Terree and wait near the Emirates Tower for her to show.

If she did. He was more than a little doubtful.

No more than two miles to Seattle Center. He jogged north along Western Avenue before heading up the hill at Broad Street, which took him right by the Space Needle, an old landmark that still stood, but no longer allowed tourists. Not that there were many tourists these days. Crowell had filled him in about much of the city's past. The Needle was now flanked by two buildings taller than itself by almost double. Both towers sat in spots where museums had once been. The taller of the two was the Emirates Tower, occupying the space just northeast of the Needle.

It took him just ten minutes to jog from Crowell's place to Seattle Center. Pedestrians gave him plenty of room when he came near, and one young couple uttered shrieks of surprise when he rounded the corner of Western and

Broad. It didn't bother him; he was used to it.

A flaw in his plan—which was *always* a flaw in his plan when it involved surveillance on Earth—was his size. Hard to remain inconspicuous. He couldn't simply lean against a light pole in his overcoat and pretend to read a newstube. Luckily, even a place such as the Emirates Tower did not attract a lot of traffic. Scanning the area around the Tower, he soon found a relatively new air van across the street in a parking stall. The van, resting on its extended rubber pads, would be big enough for him to crawl into and keep low. The advent of dusk would help too.

He waited until the street seemed most clear of both pedestrians and vehicles, and walked as casually as he could to the van. It was not an abandoned vehicle, and it was locked, so after a last look around, he broke the passenger window with a firm elbow. The tempered glass shattered almost silently into cubes. He quickly cleared away enough of them it to disable the lock and fold himself inside.

Not very comfortable, but he had a good view of the double glass doors leading into the lobby of the Tower. He wondered why he'd gone to the trouble. Terree probably was who she said she was and had no ulterior motives beyond having Crowell find her father, Greist Sahl-kla. But trust was huge in Helk culture, in the offering and the earning of it. Maybe Terree had won Crowell's trust, but she had done nothing to satisfy Forno.

So he waited.

At some point, the owner of the vehicle might appear. Then what? Forno could growl at him and say "go away," but the owner would likely report him. Forno could resolve the problem with a good swat to the owner's head, but that would stir trouble he didn't need. No, if the owner showed up, Forno would end his surveillance and call it a day. Make up a story as he towered over whoever it was. He could imagine the owner nodding briskly, hoping the giant Hulk beast would go away.

Terree showed up ten minutes later in a ground bus that pulled into the circular drive in front of the main entrance. That explained the delay, as most ground buses, rare these days, had longer routes to complete.

Nothing out of the ordinary. The fact that she showed up at all confirmed some of her story. She walked into the Emirates Tower casually, and alone. Now what? He couldn't just walk into the Tower and ask to look around, or to use the bathroom. Not that human restrooms could accommodate his size or his anatomy when it came to relieving himself.

Forno frowned. Disappointing, but he didn't consider it a waste of his time. Terree, earning a little trust. And hell, he'd at least managed to get a nice jog out of it.

He waited until darkness fell, and was ready to work his way out of the van, when someone leaving the Tower caught his attention. Not Terree. Not a Memor woman, but an older human woman.

Forno knew her, though. Oh, did he know her.

Abigail Graff, a heavy, imposing woman whose undeniable presence could make a Fourth Clan Helk nervous. She wore a dark green jumpsuit of heavy cloth embroidered with geometric shapes, and a black leather corset belt cinched her waist. Her graying hair was thick and pulled back into multiple braids, with some of them swirled atop her head. Two First Clan Helks in their head-to-toe traditional leathers followed her.

What the *snot*?

During his years on Helkunntanas working with the Kenn, Forno had delved into the underworld, gaining knowledge of both humans and Helks with questionable behaviors and morals. A driving ambition and a greed for power and credits motivated them, with RuBy at the heart of it all these days. Abby Graff was one of those people, a human who commanded respect not only in the underworld but also in the surface streets of her district, and, in fact, in all of Helkunntanas. Someone the Kenn had not been able to touch.

In Graff's city of Swain, she was the Boss, controlling the RuBy trade in every district there, even putting a strong hand into other towns, particularly the few human ones, always expanding her empire of the Red. The sheer fact that Graff controlled Swain, a mostly *Helk* city, kept a lot of other players at a distance.

Abigail Graff had been Forno's Boss in the underworld. Back when he'd lived in Swain undercover as a jeweler, he cut deals with other districts and cemented ties with their own negotiators and their sniffers while personally trying to avoid the Red. His Boss even farther back than that, before the undercover work with the Kenn, had been a human simply known as Thurston. Before—

He squelched the thought. Graff now stood on the sidewalk outside the Emirates Tower, a place Forno would never have expected her to be, looking back and forth down the street, her Helk bodyguards not seeming to care how much they stood out.

Forno slumped lower in the van. What the hell was she doing at the Emirates Tower?

After a few minutes, another human came out the door and joined her with a casual air denoting a comfortable relationship. The man was bundled in a heavy coat and sported dark glasses and, of all things, an old fedora. Quaint.

Forno thought he should know the man. Likely a sniffer from Graff's camp. Perhaps he wasn't a Swain sniffer. Perhaps he was a Khrem sniffer and belonged to Khrem's Boss, Baren Rieser.

Rieser was one of Abby Graff's biggest enemies, Boss of one of the largest human cities on Helkunntanas, one of the few she'd been unable to slip into. If Graff was talking to one of Rieser's people, she might be planning a heist of Baren Rieser's Red. A heist, or even a takeover.

Graff and the man spoke a while, and their exchange became heated, the man's hands gesturing vehemently, Graff crossing her arms low over the corset belt, glaring. Finally, Graff leaned in, said something to him, then moved to the street. The man shook his head, and, a beat later, an intercity shuttle slid to the curb. That alone should've clued Forno into . . . something. Abby Graff on a Seattle shuttle? The flash marquee atop the shuttle announced its destination: the Seattle port. Graff and her bodyguards climbed on, and the vehicle sped north.

Forno repositioned himself a little higher while the man took a few steps in the direction Graff had gone, gazing at the shuttle as it moved away. He removed his hat and ran his hand through his hair, and Forno thought he *did* know him. He looked a little like . . . Richards? Alex Richards? Hard to tell at this distance. But no, this man was older. A little hunched, some gray in his hair.

Really, what did this have to do with Crowell's present case? Underworld contacts were good when the information they imparted was useful to a case, but Forno had left all the day-to-day dealings of that life far behind. Seriously. Why must he worry about any of Abigail Graff's shit?

An instant later, his question was answered.

Terree, the Memor woman who'd hired them to find her father, came out the front doors, paused to get her bearings, and approached the man in the hat. They exchanged a few words.

Just before reentering the Tower, as Terree started to pull away, the man grabbed the back of her neck and kissed her hard on the mouth.

Eleven

IO Special Ops Director Jennifer Lisle found me waiting in the morgue ten minutes after I'd entered. During that time, I'd searched Alex Richards' body as best I could without doing anything to piss off Lisle or the medical examiner. Likely, the ME had done some of the preliminary reports, but the full autopsy had not yet happened.

I put the glove back on my hand just as Lisle walked in. She limped a little, still favoring her left leg, due to being shot by Dorie Senall's copy during the early days of the Ultra scare. She'd also been shot in the same leg by a Helk stunner on Heron Station during our assault on the Ultras. I hadn't seen her since, and she'd been promoted as well. I wondered if she and I could still talk to each other as easily as we had during last year's craziness.

Jennifer Lisle wore a long, tan double-breasted trench coat over her blue denims and a red patterned sweater. She liked sweaters. I had considered getting some specially made for Tem Forno, who was always cold.

"Crowell, thanks for coming." She threw a friendly smile my way. She already had her disposable gloves on. "Sorry about the mix up with Freelund."

Her long blonde hair, normally straight, had some curl in it, and I thought she might have grown it out some since I'd last seen her. She shook my hand then, but looked at Richards' body instead of me.

I said, "I'm a bit freaked out by this, as you can imagine."

Lisle smiled again. "I can imagine."

For the time being, I decided not to tell her anything about losing consciousness the night before. Nothing about Terree hiring me, showing me the Memory, about the Ultras making a suspicious deal with her father, and perhaps others. Not until I understood more about Alex Richards.

"Do we know what's going on yet?" I asked.

"A little." Lisle circled to the other side of the table and faced me across the body. "Examiner's doing the full autopsy when she can get to it, and to be honest, I don't know when that will be. She shuttled down to Portland yesterday to help with some work backed up there. But she did figure a few things out before she left."

"Yeah?"

"Enough to know what we're dealing with."

I drew out my next sentence to match both my curiosity about the truth and my reluctance to hear it: "What exactly *are* we dealing with?" Her face darkened. "Because Alex Richards was supposed to be a simple case, and suddenly he was dead, with that fucking word written on his body."

"We're dealing with that fucking word."

"Ultra."

She nodded. "Ultra."

I waved a hand, not wanting her to go on. "Okay, let's back up. Let me ask some normal questions first. Cause of death? I mean, he *is* dead, isn't he?" With the Ultras involved, anything was possible when it came to unusual bodies.

"Seems so, doesn't he? We won't know the actual cause until the autopsy. Or maybe not even then. At this point, nothing tells us how he died."

"That figures. How about time of death?" I was thinking about the interval between chasing him and finding him in his coffin.

"The examiner said rigor mortis had both set in and then relapsed by the time the body was found and examined."

"That means he was dead before I got there. It takes up to thirty-six hours for rigor mortis to disappear."

"That should tell you something about who you were chasing. Lividity suggests he was in that crate without being moved. There's discoloration where we'd expect it from a body on its back, blood pooling naturally in the lower portion of the body."

"Shouldn't I be smelling him by now, then?"

"The more pinkish discoloration suggests extreme cold caused the death, or he'd been insulated or refrigerated beforehand. And then we've had him in the coolers until an hour ago."

Cold death. Or, more likely, something very alien.

I pointed at the word Ultra on Alex's collarbone. "That's not blood. The color's right, but the letters are too precise."

Now it was Lisle's turn to rub at the word, her gloved finger whispering across the skin. "Nothing like blood came up in any initial testing. It's likely a tattoo, some kind of ink, but the examiner thinks it's deeper into the skin than normal."

"Tattoo," I mumbled.

"You didn't notice the tattoo when you found him with the girl?"

I shook my head. "The last clothing he put back on was his shirt, but I didn't see anything. I wasn't trying to stare. Anyway, the light in there was bad."

She pulled back from the body. "What about Liz Richards?"

"What about her?"

"She hired you to find him."

I took a deep breath. "Liz Richards hired me to catch her husband in the act, so she knew he was having an affair. She thought she knew where I'd find him, and there he was, with his girlfriend."

"Convenient."

"Have you talked to the girlfriend?"

"We don't know who she is," she said. "Neither does Mrs. Richards. That's why she hired you."

"She *hired* me, Jennifer, to take dirty pictures of them in the act and rub his face in it. She really didn't care who it was, and I never had the chance—or need—to find out."

"Okay." She reached into her coat pocket and pulled out a slim hard-copy photograph. "Liz Richards gave this to me earlier today when I went by their place on Madison."

"I know where it is. Hard-copy picture of what?" I asked, even as she handed it to me.

"Alex Richards."

I brought it close and stared at it.

She grew more serious. "Did you get a photo like this from her before you started looking for him?"

"Yeah," I said, but I soon understood why she was asking. "It's not Richards." I looked back and forth between the photo and the body on the table. "It doesn't match the photo she gave me, and certainly wouldn't match the ones I took at the warehouse, if anyone ever finds my camera."

"It's not Richards?"

"There's an uncanny similarity. Differences though—hair, weight, wrinkles, even age."

After a moment, she lifted the blue cloth from her side of the table and pulled up his arm, showing me his palm. "Scanned fingerprints say he's Alex Richards." She pointed at his head. "Holo-imaging of his skull and teeth say he's Alex Richards." She dropped the arm unceremoniously, and it flopped

THE ULTRA BIG SLEEP

onto the table and slipped back toward her. "His wife unequivocally identified the body."

I rubbed my forehead, hoping to coax some sense out of my brain. "The photo she gave me is back at my place—"

"Forget the photo, David," she said. "I've seen the same photo at her apartment. It's him, and Liz Richards and science confirms it."

"He's younger," I said. I gazed at the body on the table and saw it clearly. "I thought he just looked a bit different in death. This is Alex Richards as a younger man."

She wiped at Richards' forehead with her palm for no reason I could tell, then leaned to get a closer look at the dead man's face. "His wife guesses it's him somewhere between ten and fifteen years ago."

It put the younger Richards around age twenty.

"How is it possible?" I asked, but what I knew about the Ultras made it inherently possible, even if unknowable. "If this is a younger Richards, dead in that crate before I got there—"

"Then what happened to the older one? The one you were chasing?"

"Jennifer, there can't be two of them, different *ages*, one of them dead, appearing at the same time in the same fucking warehouse."

"Why not?"

"You saying he's a Thin Man?"

"He's a dead man, and younger somehow, but that doesn't mean he wasn't a copy. Or the guy you were chasing could've been the copy."

"Seriously?"

"You're some kind of copy magnet, aren't you, Dave? They just keep coming after you."

"Damn it, *no*. I was talking to him. He was oblivious to anything other than his girlfriend. I didn't get any sense that he had knowledge of that younger version of him in the crate."

"Then where is he? Why didn't he go back home? You said he didn't get by Forno, and he didn't show up at that side warehouse. At worst he'd have to face the wrath of his wife at some point, if he thought you had the evidence against him."

I didn't answer. I knew nothing. Typical.

"I'll tell you why," she said. "He was taken. He was going to be replaced."

"Replaced by a dead body?"

She pointed at Richards. "Have you considered he might not be dead? It's the Ultras after all."

"If he's not really dead, then maybe it was a mistake to bring him in here."

"It's a risk, maybe, but then again, this isn't NIO Central, either."

"Well, he can't be an Ultra. You'd have discovered the antimatter core. Or he would've blown to bits already."

"Sure. But do we know for sure all the Ultras are gone? The Conduits may be destroyed, the metal to make them gone, but there are a bunch of Thin Men, some known, and many unknown." She paused a moment, letting that sink in. "I do think there's an Ultra around."

"You do?"

Jennifer Lisle circled back around the table until she stood a few feet from me. "We've had reports about her, alive."

I blinked, not believing, hoping she was kidding me. Funny, funny Jennifer, playing with the ignorant detective.

She said, "Cara."

Cara? Cara was dead. My Cara dead on Aryell, the Ultra not-Cara version dead on Heron Station. But missing.

"We have to assume she's a copy, unaccounted for."

I stared at her. Jesus, not Cara. *Not Cara.*

I tried to give her the photo of Alex Richards, but she waved me off. "Keep it. You might need it." She inclined her head toward the exit. "Let's get out of here, and I'll bring you up to speed. I'm tired of looking at Richards. Unless you think you can get something more from that."

"No," I said, "that's it." I had other work to do.

She led me out of the autopsy suite, back to the nave, our footsteps echoing in the larger space of the morgue. She walked to a desk full of file folders and books, pushed a few of the books aside, and sat on the tabletop.

"Who reported Cara?" I asked.

She produced her code card and held it out to me. "Don't know who. But he works for this guy."

I stared at the code card longingly. It was larger than the standard comm card, but so much more: the finest flash membranes, super responsive, connection to the DataNet, access to NIO databases, communication capabilities beyond anything known by the masses, capable of receiving and sending signals anywhere, even through the jump slots. My own NIO-issued code card had long ago been ruined, ironically enough, by an Ultra copy of Jennifer Lisle. I'd not been given another, now that I was no longer a borrowed hound.

"Jesus, Dave, take it and look."

I took her code card and stared at a man's image, data scrolling across the bottom of the membrane.

"You know him?" she asked.

I flexed the membrane and pulled the holo-window away from the card, expanding it with a twist of the corners. "You're kidding," I said, staring at the mugshot of a bald human, his head tattooed with numerals. "Is that Baren Rieser?"

She nodded. "You know him."

"Brindos and I chased him a full year across the Union."

"Four years ago, before your NIO commission."

"That's right. A slippery data forger Seattle Authority couldn't corner, and we got in on it."

"Remind me of the details."

I told her. The trail had gone cold at Aryell. We suspected Rieser had fled to Barnard's World, doubled back despite our best efforts to corner him. We'd been to Barnard's earlier in the process, flushed him, but hell, it was a big colony, easy for him to hide if he got back there. Seattle took us off the case, and we stuck around on Aryell a while longer, debating our next paychecks, and that's when Brindos and I met Cara, at the Flaming Sea Tavern. We stayed several months, knowing we'd soon be saying goodbye to our private-detective business. It was sheer luck the NIO hired us to help spearhead the Movement investigation. Of course, we soon found out the reason why, with NIO director Timothy James already compromised by the Ultras, setting us up big time.

"So you know where he is?" I asked, returning the code card. "He still in data?"

"He's mostly pushing Red."

"RuBy? I'd heard something about that."

"He's running a huge network of sniffers and vendors, and he's trying to extend his influence among the jewel thieves."

I stared at her. "So he's on Helkunntanas."

"Untouchable."

"Unless he's selling elsewhere in the Union."

"You've got it."

I knew what she was going to ask of me. A day ago I would've said no. But half a day ago, my life had turned again, and I had taken on a client who needed me to find her father, who might lead me to my own dad.

On Helkunntanas.

I'd been wondering how to conjure official clearance to the Helk planet, and here was my chance. I should probably mention Terree and Greist Sahl-kla and Lucky Lawrence.

She touched my arm. "I need your help."

Then again, I shouldn't appear too eager. "Got my own business to run."

"You were the last person to see her up close." Talking about Cara the Ultra.

"If it's really Cara."

"You're familiar with Baren Rieser."

"I'm familiar with Alex Richards," I pointed out, "but I don't know anything about him, turns out."

"What else is new?"

I let that sit there, let her wonder.

"Anything you need," she said. "We'll take care of the protocols and travel visas. You'll be on Helkunntanas on official NIO business."

"I hate the idea of going there."

"That's the destination, regardless."

"So I'd have to check in with the Kenn."

"Helk planet, Helk intelligence people, so yeah."

"Expenses?"

"Everything."

"For both of us."

"I'm not going."

"I mean Forno. He'll be an asset, Helk that he is. He still has a place there, or so he tells me, and he knows as much as I do about Rieser. He used to be involved in the underworld, when he was undercover, negotiating RuBy for one of the districts there."

"Which one?"

"Swain."

"Could be Forno's familiar with whatever districts Rieser has infiltrated."

"Could be."

"Forno, too, then. Whatever you want."

"Maybe a third, but I don't know yet."

"A third person? Jesus, Crowell, that's pushing it."

"Whatever I want."

She sighed, hands on hips. "I'll need a name at some point."

"You'll have it," I said, still holding back Terree's name. She'd be the third if I needed her. "You can get the travel visas going without the name for now?"

"Sure." She indicated the cluttered desk. "I've got a temporary office set up here, and I can access NIO files through the DataNet and keep in contact with Assistant Director Hardy."

We stood there silently then, the gap between us less than a Helk's width. The silence lengthened, and Jennifer looked away.

"Anything else?" I asked, dread weighing me down as I considered doing more work for the NIO, when all I wanted to do was search for my dad. I *really* should tell her about Terree.

She dug into her pocket for another code card and held it out to me. "Here."

I took it and smiled. "Aww, a present for me?"

"A *loaner*. I'll need to keep in touch. Don't lose this one."

"I didn't lose the last one. Your copy broke it."

"Just hang onto it." She extended her pointer finger and revealed a tiny ear stud for private conversations resting on the tip. "Adheres nicely to the porch of your ear and stays there. Good enough sound."

"*Now* I get the upgrades."

"You resisted the finger-caps upgrade the last time, so don't get smart with me, hound."

"Yes, ma'am. No love for Forno?"

"You can configure his comm card so he can patch in to you. I know you know how to do it, and I'm not going to ask questions about it, but he doesn't need to have a direct line to NIO business. Particularly now that you bring up his underworld past."

"Good point."

She pushed a strand of her hair back behind her ear. "I suspect he knew about Rieser being in Khrem. Do you trust him?"

"Is that a serious question? Really? Do you remember everything that happened—"

"Okay, okay. But what do you really know about his past?"

"Enough to know he's on my side." Where was she going with this? Trying to make me second guess Forno's trustworthiness?

She said, "Stop beating yourself up over it."

"What?"

"Brindos. His death is still eating at you."

"What's that have to do with Forno?"

"Forno was with you."

"Yeah, and he saw me kill my partner."

"Dave, you saved Brindos."

"Bullshit, Jennifer."

"Call it bullshit if you like, but you're ignoring what Brindos wanted."

Anger rose to my face, its heat burning my cheeks. "Like you know."

"Have you forgotten you told me all this? He was dying, he was in pain. Shooting Brindos was a mercy, and it gave you the opening you needed to kill Plenko."

"Dorie was there too, and she was copied. You have any trouble with her?"

"I don't know."

I didn't care for her line of questioning. "Do you have something specific on Forno?"

"What do you mean?"

"Something I don't know? Something related to an NIO investigation, or some tie to the Ultras?"

"You just told me about his underworld involvement. He won't talk to us about anything leading up to the end game."

"Such as?"

"The Kenn."

Forno had called himself Gray when he first told me about the NIO traces on Brindos and me. That had forced me to Aryell, where I found out Forno had belonged to the Kenn, Helkunntanas's intelligence agency. They had found themselves compromised just like the NIO, infiltrated by the Ultras during their silent, sideways attack.

"He's not told me much about his undercover work with them, if that's what you're wondering," I said.

"Yeah. I have my doubts."

"You don't trust him because of the Kenn? Or because of the underworld?"

"He told you he belonged to the Kenn first, correct? Before he went undercover?"

"He put himself in the Ultras' way—"

"I think he might have been underworld *before* that. He lived in one of the most troubled districts on Helkunntanas."

"Stop, Jennifer. The Kenn verified him. He's a goddamn hero, so stop already."

She lifted both hands. "Okay, I'm stopping. He's a hero, I know. And it'll be good to have him with you on this."

At that point, the nave was unnaturally quiet, even for a morgue, a place as dead as the world we kept trying to hang on to.

Death in an old church. If only we had bread and wine, and a priest to consecrate it, we'd have something, right? I recalled Alex Richards' body in the autopsy room: dead, cold, but off somehow. Younger than the Alex Richards I'd chased.

Time to get off this wheel of suffering, I thought. Karma. What goes around comes around. Come back a new person in hours, let aliens squeeze your essence through a thin wire because no one knew who the hell anyone was these days, evidently.

Whatever the Ultras had started by stirring the Union into a froth, it was nothing holy. There was something deeper the Ultras were going for. Terree's father had opened some kind of door in the past, and Plenko had gone through it, and Cara had gone through it, and Joseph had gone through it, and they'd all knocked at the gate of an even darker, more sinful world abutting ours.

I have my doubts.

Jennifer nudged my shoulder. "Crowell?"

I'd been staring at Jennifer Lisle, but not seeing her, eyes sore from not blinking. When I spoke, my words came out as the ultimate understatement: "Sorry. I guess I'm having my *own* moment of doubt."

"Yeah, well," she said, "so did Christ, at the crucifixion."

"Our doubts are traitors."

She raised an eyebrow. "Shakespeare again?"

"Measure for Measure."

A door opened and closed somewhere nearby. Only silence followed.

A year after the Ultra scare, it wasn't possible to reach deep and see inside her, unlock those fears she had buried. She'd pushed at my own fears, wanting to understand me, understand Forno, but she wasn't immune to what it meant for herself. She'd been involved, too.

Jennifer Lisle cocked her head. Eventually, her mouth quivered into a smile. "It's good to see you, Dave."

I smiled back. "And you."

She pushed away from the desk and surprised me with a hug. Then she limped toward the exit, saying over her shoulder, "I'll start on the visas, which should track through fine. Not much longer on that third name, okay? You'll be ready to go by tomorrow."

I was impressed. "That quickly?"

"We need to move fast. I'll be in touch."

Her footsteps echoed in the nave, clicking steady, like the ticking of my Rolex. I stood and watched her, mesmerized by the sound. When she reached the door into the foyer I called out to her.

"I need something else," I said.

She turned and looked at me. "There's more?"

"I have to visit someone, and I'd appreciate a ride."

"Jesus. Visit who?"

I needed to talk to the one person who might know more than anyone else about my dad's disappearance. "Joan Crowell."

She frowned, confused. "Joan?"

"My mom," I said. "I'm going to Montana."

Twelve

Vanderberg Parr hated the House for many reasons. Coming to Baren Rieser's place—built like a fortress into the hard blackrock to the far west of Khrem—signaled an experience. If the Boss invited you to the House, you came upon it not by chance, but because of specific detailed directions, instructions, previously signed affidavits, promises, and warnings. You crashed through the dense jungle-like screen, and there it was, brooding in the rock like a beast lunging from a cave mouth, its own rock face brutally sharp, its spires and crenellations the beast's own natural protection from predators in the wild.

Neither private nor public vehicles just stumbled upon the House, owing to the virtual datascreen surrounding the area, a disturbing light show of bright white light and swirling colors of blue and green, flecked with gray and shot through with infinite variations of seemingly random patterns. He'd never heard of datascreens until Rieser told him about the one on Aryell protecting the Ultras' tent city of New Venasaille, where the RuBy-subdued refugees from Ribon had lived, awaiting their destiny as an army against the Union.

Parr remembered asking the Boss, "How did you get one?"

Rieser rubbed his bald head and winked. "Friends in high places."

Friends. High places. Well, Parr knew who the Boss was talking about for sure. Rieser's patron was Cara Landry, and although no one had ever said it aloud, other than the Boss slipping in the word like an adjective here and there, she was an Ultra. Rumors swirled about her. Some of the sniffers said she was a copy. Some said she had died and come back to life, but changed, more human than before, her original Cara Landry shell somehow upgraded.

It didn't take a genius to know where all the RuBy the Ultras used at New Venasaille had come from. All bought and paid for. Baren Rieser's claim to fame among the jewel thieves. It must have irked Abigail Graff no end and sent her fuming back to her vendors in the Swain district.

Abby Graff had nothing as awesome, or intimidating, as the House. Jealous of Rieser's success, indeed. Graff had once sworn that one day she would bury him in so much RuBy it would make what they found at New Venasaille look like free samples.

As an official in charge of a Helk City, Graff was not to be taken lightly. Her fingers reached deep into districts in other cities. No one believed she would long sit idly by and let Baren Rieser rest secure in Khrem. But Graff didn't know about Rieser's friends in high places who shielded him with datascreens and helped finance the Red.

Parr's flier approached the datascreen, the preprogrammed course now kicking in and angling him toward the arranged insertion point. For a few minutes, a virtual breach would open, though it would still look similar to and as daunting as the rest of the datascreen. Checking the time, little twinges of pain accompanying his movements in the flier, he notified the House of his position and speed, and let the autopilot take over. Hitting the datascreen at the wrong place would not necessarily end in disaster, but most drivers would panic and turn back, the nonstop attack of color and illusion—along with the buffeting from the magnetic repulsors and the screams of white noise—too much for them.

Parr scrambled for some RuBy, rolled it and put it on his tongue, then closed his eyes and tried not to think about his other reasons for hating the House. He took deep breaths, preferring not to stare at the approaching screen. The flier bumped like his mind struggling with this visit. For one thing, the House had been built Helk-size. It was even furnished for Helks. What the hell for? The huge rooms made humans feel like small indoor pets hanging around without a clue of the bigger world outside. Baren Rieser was a big human, and intimidating, but even he lost some stature inside the House.

Eyes still closed, RuBy buzzing him, Parr sensed the varying light as the flier entered the breach of the datascreen. The hint of a screaming wail outside, the noise suppressors working. Another few bumps as the flier scraped the boundaries of the breach, and then Parr had cleared the screen, thankfully. He opened his eyes, and the rock face of the House yawned, the distressed rock walls and the spikes out front—also carved from the blackrock—looming over the flier.

The damn countdown was already in his head. More of Rieser's obsession with secrecy, not wanting anyone to know where to find the docking area, the entrance to the House, or the means to find one's way inside. *Here we go*, Parr thought.

The fuzziness spread quickly from his forehead to his eyes. Then muscles letting go, body limp, chin coming forward against his chest as whatever neural destabilizing field Rieser had procured from his friends took over and dropped him into a brief, semi-conscious purgatory.

As usual, he would have a hell of a headache when he awoke. When the House's security system took control of his flier, sleep grabbed him and didn't let go.

When Parr woke, he groaned, opening his eyes slowly, knowing he wouldn't be in his flier. Jesus, there had to be a better way to visit the House.

The Pool Room came into focus. It was Baren Rieser's own joke for a glorified waiting room, where everyone "queued" up for entrance to the House. Parr had tried once to explain to the Boss that *queue* was different from *cue*, but he wouldn't hear it. Rieser didn't even own a pool table. Not that any were even available on Helkunntanas.

The Pool Room had blackrock walls and a high ceiling, with nothing inside it but five cushioned cots. A single steel door provided the only exit. On most visits to the House, Parr woke up alone in the room, but tonight humans occupied all the other cots, and two Helks, both large First Clan giants, sat on the floor, their backs against the walls. More tolerant of the effects, they had graciously given up the cots to the humans.

Well, wasn't that polite of them.

Parr's head throbbed. RuBy would counteract the ache, of course. The ultimate irony was waking up and not finding a single paper of the drug in the Pool Room. Visitors weren't allowed to bring any into the House, although the Boss made an exception for him. An exception for the Thin Man.

His RuBy haze prior to the datascreen seemed to help, though. He usually woke earlier than most in the Pool Room. That habit might come in handy some day.

Why were so many visitors here? It didn't make sense; Baren Rieser didn't hand out invitations to the House lightly.

The room was cool, and smelled too much of Helk fur for his taste. But at least it was preferable to the ubiquitous smell of RuBy inside the House. Ruby, its own boss, the laws of the Union unable to touch it. No amount of foreknowledge could prepare someone for the availability of the drug at the House. Parr tolerated the heavy cinnamon odor of RuBy, out of necessity, but just barely. Another reason he hated the House.

Parr rolled to his side as one of the Helks stood, stretched, and punched the buzzer at the steel door with his fist, ready to exit. A sensor for a DNA lock, inset underneath the buzzer, was useless to all but Rieser. Maybe Juke? He wasn't entirely sure. While the Helk waited, a few humans unfolded from their cots and lined up behind the Hulk.

Parr recognized no one in the Pool Room but the Helk still on the floor. Beyer Jander, a sniffer. Parr knew a lot of Rieser's people, but the Boss's RuBy empire already stretched beyond Khrem, threatening to engulf other Bosses. It wasn't surprising he didn't know some of them. And he was late due to the job at the port, so maybe the sniffers or vendors he knew had arrived earlier. These might be first-timers, or middle-grade fucks invited to help fill out the Boss's guest list, although he couldn't imagine why. It seemed an awfully big risk.

The door opened and the guests left the Pool Room. Beyer Jander got up off the floor too, and followed the others out. The steel door clanked shut and Parr stretched out on his back again and stared at the high ceiling.

Not ready yet. Hell if he was going to rush it, not with the ordeal ahead. The ordeal, cut through by the RuBy-like rush and anticipation of the House. Maybe crossing that thin line between his humanity and the unanswered question on his lips.

Who he was, inside the House, was nobody, and he hated it.

The rock walls threatened to topple onto him, the ceiling's height frightening. It protected the House from the outside, but it was unreachable, unfathomable, almost a paradox, as it was also seemingly composed of rock.

Parr cowered beneath it as he entered the Quarry—the main room—a space larger than The Mirror bar. In fact, Parr imagined a couple of the bars could've fit inside the Quarry. Air from the House's coolers whispered across his face, and soon the cinnamon odor struck him, strong and pungent.

The House was black and red, and he despised the pervasiveness of those two colors, but at least he didn't have to sweat, or wear his own cooler.

His hands shook, and he shoved them in his pockets, eyeing the guests, eight in all. The last two humans on the cots had left the Pool Room with him, so this looked to be the evening's whole guest list. The guests mingled and talked, their voices amplified inside the cavernous space. The Helk furniture, sturdy chairs and couches of black leather and heavy distressed wood three times the size of what Parr would sit in, were mostly taken up by

Helks, because humans avoided them.

The sickly cinnamon odor nearly gagged him when he ventured deeper into the room. He rubbed his nose and face casually, not wanting the others to see his discomfort, but he imagined many others were also struggling with the smell.

As devoid of RuBy as the Pool Room had been, the Quarry had so much of the drug that it took up more space than the invited guests. Piles of red paper—stacked haphazardly on the floor of the room, leaning against the couches and chairs, covering the shiny black tables and spilling even onto the food trays—threatened to inundate the room. No fancy dispensers here. RuBy everywhere, free for the taking, and its cloying cinnamon odor pervasive.

It stopped Parr from taking any, though. The Quarry overwhelmed him, as always, and he never came here but that he made up his mind to stay on edge, dealing with the pain, afraid to dull his senses and his thoughts. Rieser made much fuss about the fact that the Quarry held some kind of freakish focusing ability. It was bullshit, he was sure, but it didn't take away from the room's power.

Parr took a deep breath through his mouth, straightened, and eased into the center of the room where the main table dominated. Two Second Clan Helks on one of the couches were complaining about how cold the House was. Good thing they did that now, before the Boss showed up, ripped the fur from their bodies, and sent them back to the Pool Room. Stupid Hulks.

Another Second Clan, towering over the human he was talking to, Parr recognized as Zantz Marko, Rieser's liason with the mayor of Khrem. Marko also had a taste of just about every gabobileck sold on the streets, for he owned most of the vendor carts. He took a cut of sales as deep as the traditional slices buyers knifed into the meat casings so they could fill them with fresh onions and sauces. Supposedly, Marko hated the things himself, and never went near the street vendors. Parr hoped Rieser had kept gabobilecks off the party menu. Marko did seem to be munching on something though, perhaps a Helk red rice ball, or a spicy mustard egg. Parr's stomach grumbled at his thought of mustard eggs here. He'd worked up a good tolerance for them because he now appreciated their flavor and texture.

The human, appearing disconnected and somewhat confused as he looked up at Marko, was Alex Richards, one of the Boss's head sniffers from Khrem's east district. A formidable guy on the street, but here, with Zantz Marko and his less-than-traditional red leathers looming over him, Richards looked ready at any moment to make an early exit.

Perfectly fine with Parr. He was surprised Richards was even here. Hadn't he had business off planet?

He didn't trust Richards.

Zantz Marko still talked down to Richards, something about the mayor's office beginning to suspect that a good deal of RuBy was leaving Helkunnta-nas illegally.

"There's a breach, somewhere," Marko grumbled, pointing a stubby, gabo-bilek-sized finger at Richards. As usual, most Helks closest to Rieser, and in fact most Helks involved in the RuBy trade, spoke English well, and actually preferred it during business and social situations with the Boss.

Parr walked up, stood on his tiptoes, and grabbed Marko's shoulder. Now, Zantz Marko he *liked*.

"Hey, Vander," Marko said, still glaring at Richards. He took a moment to throw back into his mouth the last of what he'd been eating.

Oh yeah, mustard egg. Parr would need a plate and some utensils to eat one of those monsters.

"Didn't you know?" Parr said. "Richards here has a soft spot for the mayor."

"You think, Vander?" Richards said, sneering. "Because I'm over there ev-ery day, offering him RuBy he can get for free? Oh wait, no. That's Zantzie's job."

"Don't call me that," Marko growled, and Richards paled a little.

Alex Richards stood taller than Parr, but his thin frame was well-muscled. His dark hair was streaked with gray, and his deep brown eyes darted to and fro, a habitual trait of his. That alone detracted from Richards' physical pres-ence, knocking him down a notch or two. He wore a blue jacket with wide lapels over a black T-shirt.

"What're you doing here?" Parr said. "I thought you were on a job off planet."

"For your continued well-being," Marko went on, ignoring Parr for the moment, "you better watch what you say around me, Richards. And consider this, next time you accuse me of being cozy with the mayor: I have a business, and I have a right to be there on that account alone."

"That doesn't make you—"

Marko somehow seemed taller when he drew nearer to Richards. "The Boss *made* me, sniffer. Besides keeping on top of my own vendors, I've a job to do, and that includes keeping tabs on the mayor's office. I don't have time to worry about you."

Richards grimaced. Helk and human stared each other down for a moment, Richards's eyes flicking endlessly.

Before long, Richards redirected his dark gaze to Parr. "I was gone, but I'm back, okay?" he said.

"Quick trip," Parr answered.

"Leave me the fuck alone," the sniffer said, and he ducked away without another word, weaving between a few other guests while Parr watched him.

"That snot-for-brains is a lead sniffer?" Zantz Marko said. "Couldn't find a stack of RuBy unless someone shoved it up his nose."

Parr grinned, but the talk of RuBy brought him back, the pain seeping into him from the inescapable cinnamon scent. He put a hand to his temple and massaged it.

"Okay?" Marko asked, his leathery face wrinkling in concern.

"I'm fine. Thanks."

Marko probably noticed Parr's red-stained fingertips, for he said, "You need some Red? I'm thinking you might be able to find some here." He laughed heartily.

Marko seemed proud of his joke, so Parr laughed a little. "Good one," he said.

"Rumor has it the Boss's stockpile here is huge. Bigger than any the jewelers have stashed in the refineries."

"It's true, though I've never seen it."

"Well, outside the Quarry, the House is a mystery."

Early on, during his first few weeks working for Rieser, the Boss had taken him on a tour of the Khrem refinery, a gigantic building near the Wending Causeway, made of red brick and stone. The manufacture of RuBy had long been legal, and still was, even though the Union had outlawed its export to the other planets, so the Helk made no apologies for their refineries' showy prominence.

The trip was memorable for more reasons than one. Parr had never seen so much RuBy in one place at the same time. It was also the first time he'd heard about refineries in the other cities on Helkunntanas. Moreover, he learned of the other Bosses, including Abby Graff, from Swain. There in the vault, with so much RuBy gleaming in its various piles, some packaged in silvery, shrink-wrapped cubes, some and stacked precariously high in all corners, Baren Rieser first told him about the Thin Men. No one had yet discovered the true purpose of Aryell's Transcontinental Conduit. The Union still wept over the horrifying news of the cataclysm on Ribon, the unfortunate refugees secretly ferried away to New Venasaille.

In seeing the RuBy, Parr saw red in the blood of thousands, and soon understood that the presence of the alien plot against the Union included allies on this side.

"You are a Thin Man now," Baren Rieser had said to him during his tour. "You are a special creature, Vanderberg."

Parr hadn't understood, of course. He didn't understand even now.

The visit to the refinery was also the first time he'd recognized the full extent of Rieser's ruthlessness, the Boss taking care of a spy from Graff in brutal fashion. A First Clan Helk, nightmarish to most humans, seemed to shrink in Rieser's presence. Rieser restrained him with clamps to the bottom of an open vat. The Helk didn't give Rieser anything about Graff's operation, and refused to say a word about his purpose.

Rieser blasted him six times, all wounds meant to kill him slowly. He then buried the spy in thousands of squares of RuBy, the Helk breathing in the drug, swallowing and choking on it, Red comingling with red, his shrieks audbile to everyone working at the refinery that day.

On the street, that amount of RuBy would've made the poorest street dweller a rich, powerful player. In the refinery, Rieser had looked on expressionless as the Hulk suffocated and bled out. Then he told the surprised foreman to pulp the vat with the body in there, drain the swill to the Wending Causeway, and keep every worker in the building until the following day, by which time they would have replenished the lost RuBy squares.

By remote flier, Rieser sent what was left of the dead Helk's body, completely reddened and sticky with old, useless RuBy, to Graff's refinery in Swain, making sure the flier crashed conveniently into the fresh water tanks outside the main building.

Oh yeah, a memorable trip, that one.

Now, with stacks of RuBy all about him, Parr wondered at Marko's statement, at the maddeningly simple idea of it. *It is a mystery indeed.*

Parr swallowed, some of his pain now working up toward nuisance status. He made a show of glancing around the room. "Where is the Boss anyway?"

Marko glanced around too. "I don't know."

Baren Rieser had asked Parr to be here, but Parr hadn't planned on encountering so many guests. The Boss thought Parr was a special creature, someone above and beyond the Thin Men eking out an existence in hiding. Someone above and beyond those Thin Men detained by the Union and forced to live lives devoid of any worth. If the Boss felt him ready for something big, then perhaps tonight he truly would find out the answer to his question.

Do you know who I am? He seemed to be on the verge of something, looking through the glass, ready to break it and emerge as someone Baren Rieser could trust.

Marko blocked the way of one of the House's servers, a petite young girl who barely came up to Marko's thighs, and studied the plate a moment. He snagged another mustard egg from her tray, as well as a metal toothpick that might be big and sharp enough for a human shish kabob. She walked away quickly and Marko took a big bite. Then he pointed with the last bit of his egg behind Parr.

Vanderberg Parr turned and watched Baren Rieser work his way to the middle of the room. He spoke to a couple of his guests, but Alex Richards gave him a wide berth.

Rieser stepped up onto the main table—barefooted, for some reason—scattering the piles of RuBy and knocking over someone's glass of Helk ale, the red squares becoming instantly worthless as they soaked up the red-brown liquid. The value of the ruined drug would've amounted to a year's wages for most Helks. For Baren Rieser, it was just a mess for the servants to clean up later.

The Boss was dressed in a long, blood-red pinstripe suit jacket that hung past his knees, a white buttoned shirt, and his usual thin black tie. But no shoes, as if he'd run out of time and so come without them.

Fuck, but the Boss knew how to make an entrance.

Rieser held a black cloth in one hand, a drink of his own in the other, from which blue Temonus whiskey repeatedly sloshed over the rim. His bald head glistened with sweat, as if he'd just come in from exercise, and he took a moment and wiped it down with the black cloth in an intricate pattern. The numbers tattooed along his bald head might have meant something cryptic, if anyone could understand what they meant.

Conversations died down, and the King of Khrem threw back the last of his glass of the blue poison. A Helk on the couch, maybe Third Clan, continued to talk—Parr couldn't tell who he was talking to—and Rieser threw his tumbler hard, striking the Helk in the forehead. The Quarry hushed completely, everyone understanding what had happened.

Everyone except the Helk, that is. Oblivious of his peril, he stood up and screamed, "Plenko's *ass!*" He put his giant hand to his forehead and yelled "You fuck!" a moment before he saw the man he'd insulted, too late to remedy his mistake.

Oh, yeah. There was another reason why Parr hated the House. A visit did not necessarily mean you'd leave the place alive. Or in one piece.

The Helk's eyes widened, and he backed up a step, instinctively turning to protect his right-hand side and his heart. "Oh, Boss," he mumbled, "oh, I'm sorry, I'm sorry—"

Baren Rieser already had his blaster drawn and leveled. No one else could bring weapons inside the House of course. He said nothing. He neither smiled nor frowned. He simply fired, just as he had shot Shyler Frock in The Mirror. The blast from his weapon caught the Helk in the head near the spot that the glass tumbler had struck him. Textbook perfect, naturally. The Helk dropped, dead before he hit the floor.

"Okay, now," Rieser said, aiming the blaster at the Helk like a pointer, "who the hell was that?"

No one answered. In the continuing hush, Parr kept his eyes locked on Rieser, who turned a full circle, his bare feet squeaking on the table. He made eye contact with everyone, and all the guests returned it, not wanting to show any weakness before their Boss. Eventually, his harsh gaze settled on Parr.

Parr didn't look away, and didn't move.

The Boss nodded, gave Parr a smile, then took a moment to straighten his tie. His eyes—glazed with RuBy, Parr saw now—were slits, barely open. He raised his blaster, looked at the barrel a moment, then put it to his head and scratched at an itch, right on the number 6 tattooed there—or maybe it was a 9. Parr fought the urge to tilt his head for a better look.

"He's not important," Rieser said about the dead Helk. He swept the blaster in an arc over everybody in the Quarry. "You know most of these people, Vanderberg, don't you?"

Parr took in as many of the guests as he could in a brief second or two. He knew Zantz Marko. He knew Alex Richards. And Beyer Jander.

"A few," Parr said.

Rieser said, "They're all here for a reason."

"What reason?"

"They're all here to see you."

Parr tensed, stunned as the Boss's words rolled through his head. At the same time he caught the whispers and murmurs of the others in the Quarry. Clearly, they had expected someone else.

"Me," Parr said. "Here to see me." He stared at Rieser. "I'm sorry, but what?"

Rieser raised his voice, talking to the room now. "I promised all of you that tonight you'd get a glimpse of the future of Helkunntanas. I said you'd see the one who would change everything."

"Vander?" Zantz Marko said. "Not Plenko?"

"A copy of Plenko in the Union?" Rieser scoffed. "Oh please, Marko."

Richards, in his dark blue jacket, had backed up some more, inching toward the main entry that would lead back to the Pool Room; others in the room stirred restlessly.

Baren Rieser came down at last from the table, took three steps toward Marko, and inclined his head. Marko took a step back. Rieser's eyes softened, and his face seemed utterly calm. The bottom half of the number 5 looked like a hook on Rieser's upper forehead.

"Vanderberg Parr *is* our Plenko," Rieser said, looking back at Parr.

Chills froze Parr, and he couldn't say a thing. He was ... their *Plenko*? Did that have something to do with who he was? He felt oddly disjointed. Jesus, but he needed to understand this information rushing at him.

"You're a special creature, Vanderberg."

Parr glanced quickly at the blaster hanging at the Boss's side. "So you keep telling me."

"You are meeting Cara Landry tonight, Vanderberg." Rieser approached, put his free hand behind Parr's neck, and said, "You hear? Cara."

More whispers and mutterings from the other guests. They knew the name *Cara Landry*.

From the corner of his eye, Parr watched Alex Richards open the door to the Pool Room and slip out. Maybe Parr should say something about that. But it was a dead end. No other way out of there. So why go in? A moment later, though, Parr felt a burnng sensation on the back of his neck. For a moment he thought the pain of going without RuBy for so long would now come back strong, taking him over, but Rieser started humming something.

A bizarre sensation overcame him, as if he were being pulled in two directions at once. A split second later, all the guests in the Quarry slumped to the floor and no longer moved. All the guests except for Vanderberg Parr, who stood in shocked silence, staring at his Boss. What the *fuck*?

As if a switch had been clicked off, Rieser, too, fell—blaster still clutched in his left hand—and lay still. The room was as silent as a graveyard.

Parr put a hand to his chest, unsure why he still breathed when no one else seemed to be breathing. But ... a woman, having suddenly appeared out of nowhere, stood next to Rieser's body. Long, auburn hair cascaded over her shoulders. Not a shred of emotion showed on her face. Her eyes, almost gray in the light of the Quarry, dead as stones, scarcely moved as she studied Parr.

Parr fought for breath, his pulse in his ears. How was this possible? You didn't just suddenly turn up—Well, yes. Maybe you could. If you were an Ul-tra. That was how it was possible.

A dozen questions came to Parr, but the first one really didn't need to be asked. He knew who this was. He'd seen enough holovids and pictures in newstubes to recognize Cara Landry, the Ultra everyone in the Union be-lieved to be dead, victim of her own anti-matter detonation.

Parr stared at the guests scattered on the floor. Stared at the Boss. "What did you do to them?" he asked.

She did not answer. Not at first. Instead, an image formed in his mind, a vivid image of someone he did not know. A Memor dressed in a silk tunic the color of water and sky. Cara Landry had projected the image, willing him to see it, but he had no idea who it was.

They are asleep, her silent voice informed him.

Parr jumped at the sudden and otherworldly presence in his brain. He would not have believed anything like that could happen. But again: Ultra.

Parr peeked at the Boss's body. "Asleep? I don't understand."

You will.

"Who is that you showed in my head?"

"The Donor."

Parr had no idea what that meant.

Cara Landry glanced away from him for the first time, and Parr watched in confusion as she frowned and focused, seemingly trying to dredge up some-thing. When she looked at him again, she moved her lips unnaturally, as if testing the motion, but no sound emerged. Parr shivered.

Ultra fucking freaky.

Air escaped her mouth, little better than a sigh, followed by a faint mur-mur. Then she pointed at him with two fingers close together, her other fingers and thumb at a right angle to them, a very alien gesture. A moment later she spoke in a long breath. "Parr."

He tensed, losing himself in the mystery of Cara Landry trying to speak; he realized she must never have spoken this way before. When she did speak aloud again, the words were weak and unsure, their syllables spaced apart.

"You are the only Thin Man who matters," came her voice.

Parr sucked in a deep breath.

"I will be your One," she said.

Thirteen

THE NEXT MORNING SAW THE RETURN OF A BIT OF SUN TO SEATTLE, and instead of sleeping in, I skipped my morning drink and went on a run through Pioneer Square—what was left of Pioneer Square, anyway—my talk with Jennifer Lisle gallivanting through my head like a jump-slot backlash.

Lots of rundown buildings and graffiti and garbage. I had to watch my step zigzagging through the streets, but I was now familiar enough with the area and its obstacles to navigate the maze without mishap. A few blocks from my place on Western, I stopped in at an abandoned gym and did some lifting. I'd found the place shortly after opening my business. It hadn't taken too long to carve out a decent workout space with some decent weights and barbells, and a relatively clean floor mat meant I could get in some situps and pushups without worrying about the less than stellar condition of the rotting wooden floor. Even a few of the fancy exercise machines, including a virtual boxing simulator, still worked when the power didn't fluctuate too wildly.

Jennifer had found a private shuttle I could take to Montana in the early afternoon, so I'd called my mom in the morning before heading out on my run, and let her know to expect me. She might not know much more than me—her own memory of the real life we'd lived before the coming of the Ultras could be gone as well—but I had to try. She'd been at home when the Chicago conference happened, but if she had once known the truth about Dad, something had caused her to forget it. Or she *did* know, and had kept silent all these years for a reason.

Jennifer also sent the Helkunntanas protocols to my new code card, including travel visas, special government authorizations, NIO contract-status verifications, Union immunization records, and pre-administered holo-body-scan approvals. I was more impressed with her ability to find immunization records than anything, but I did appreciate her efficiency. Without her, I'd have waded through red tape and waited weeks to get the paperwork, with no guarantee of success.

When I returned from my workout, I found Tem Forno sitting in the office. I felt better, having managed some exercise, but I should have known my improved mood would not last long. And the moment I saw my partner lounging in his Helk-sized chair, a frown creasing his leathery face, I did know. I thought Helks were ugly at the best of times, but Forno's scowl, although I had often seen it, never failed to startle me.

"What?" I asked, peeling off my damp sweatshirt. I threw it to the left of Forno, at the door leading to my back room.

"I was going to tell you the worst news yet," he said. "Instead, that sweatshirt you threw past my ear may qualify."

"Thought about aiming for your head—to improve your face."

"Twigs and bones will never damage me."

I rolled my eyes, but didn't give in to his I'm-a-stupid-Helk routine. I pulled up my T-shirt and wiped my forehead with a dry spot.

"Anything on Alex Richards?" Forno asked.

"He's dead, and not dead."

"What?"

"I was chasing an older version of him. The Alex Richards in the crate was younger."

"Plenko's balls."

"Yeah. I'll fill you in later. The next wrinkle, I guess."

"Next wrinkle's coming from me, actually."

"I knew that scowl meant something."

Forno scowled deeper. "Terree might be as dirty as her father."

"Terree? Not likely. How do you figure?"

"I followed her."

"You what?"

"Acually, I ran ahead of her, staked out the Emirates Tower."

"You don't trust her."

"Didn't I already tell you that?"

"Nope."

"I don't trust her."

I put my hands against the wall at shoulder-height, stepped back with one leg, and pushed to loosen my hamstrings. Miraculously, the plywood held. I pressed my heels to the floor. "So? What did you see?"

"A kiss."

I looked around and met Forno's eyes. "A kiss? She knows someone here well enough to kiss him? It *was* a *him*, wasn't it?" Usually you never knew with Memors, considering the whole gender-morphing thing.

"Yeah, a *him*."

"Shit, not her *father*."

Forno gave me a look informing me I wasn't even close.

"Okay, not her father." I sat down, back against the wall, and reached for my toes, stretching some more. "Who?"

Forno leaned back and stretched out his tree-stump legs. "Don't know. He was covered up with coat and hat."

"Underworld?"

"Likely, I'd say."

"Whoever he is, I imagine he's off the grid. Nothing crucial about him on the DataNet."

"You imagine right. For a while, though, I thought it might be Alex Richards. But it didn't seem possible. But now you're talking about a younger one and an older one. So maybe . . ."

"She really kissed him?"

"Actually, he kissed her. Grabbed her neck and pulled her to him. I don't think she expected him to do it. She seemed surprised. Frowned and backed up a step, then disappeared into the Tower. After that, I slipped out of there."

"Interesting."

Forno shifted in his chair. "You know Abigail Graff?"

Sure, I knew. A RuBy Boss on Helkunntanas. I'd first heard of her before my NIO commission, when Brindos and I had our old private detective agency. After Tem Forno agreed to be my new partner, I looked her up, to see what she'd been up to. I'd been researching the underworld to understand Forno better. To corroborate some of the info he'd given me, and some of the Kenn background on his undercover work.

I nodded. "You worked for Graff."

"Scary human, let me tell you. She wants to sweep away the RuBy competition on Helkunntanas. But—" He pointed at the ceiling, readying me for his big revelation. "—she's still second flute to the newest, baddest Boss."

I waited a few ticks, pissed off that I had "fiddle" in my head, but I'd already had some of this conversation earlier at the morgue. "Our old friend Baren Rieser."

"That's right. He ripped the old Boss Thurston out of there so fast it wasn't even funny. Bloody business."

"Thurston?"

"That's all he went by. Just Thurston. Did Jennifer fill you in on Rieser?"

"A little."

"Get this. A few minutes before Terree strolled out of the Emirates Tower, this guy who kissed her was out front talking to Abby Graff."

The Mother of all RuBy dealers, far from her comfort zone. "Graff is *here?* On Earth?"

"Surprised me, too. But she left with her bodyguards on a shuttle. Maybe to the port. Probably trying to get home. No doubt her passage will be invisible—if she manages it. Could have bought off Transworld Transport somehow."

"Maybe. So this guy was talking to Graff. Consider the possibility that it *was* Richards. The older copy of him."

"My thought was that if Rieser's involved in this, maybe Richards, or whoever this is, is playing more than one hand."

"Giving Graff the inside slot on Rieser," I said, nodding. "Take down the competition."

"And Terree there with them. What does that tell you?"

I wasn't sure. Forno's leathery black face, besides being ugly, gave me no answer. I reached for my toes again, stretching some more.

"I'll tell you what I think," Forno said. "She's playing us. She knows where her father is. And if he's the traitor you say he is, she may be helping him perpetuate the mystery of the Ultras by playing the two biggest Bosses of Helkunntanas against each other."

I shook my head, unconvinced by Forno's theory. "She doesn't *know* where her father is. But she's learned something—something about one of these Bosses. A connection, however flimsy, to her father. Rieser or Graff knows something about her father's disappearance, and sliding close to whoever this guy is you saw gives her easy access to both of them."

"Big risk, letting her in like that."

"Maybe."

"What does a sniffer get out of a relationship with a Memor woman who doesn't have ties with the underground?"

"No ties we know about."

"What's he get out of it?"

"Memorable sex?"

Forno grinned. "Memory. Sometimes you're almost clever."

"I hear interspecies sex, although not without its challenges, particularly with you Helks, stimulates more erogenous zones than a hyper-frenetic virtual adventure."

"If you're not crushed in the process," Forno said.

I thought about Dorie Sennal and her Helk husband Terl Plenko and found it difficult to imagine the intricacies of Helk/human lovemaking.

"What would bring Graff to the Emirates Tower?" Forno asked, taking another track.

"I don't know."

But a moment later, as I regained my feet and shuffled over to the desk, I understood that Greist Sahl-kla, as an Envoy, had access to many inside secrets of the Emirates. And now here was Graff, at the Seattle Emirates Tower. How did someone as notorious as Graff step in and earn the trust of an organization whose purpose is to help solve disputes, not encourage unrest? Unless things were not quite right with the Emirates.

Terree believed someone had started to phase me into the Memory, and it had definitely been someone who spoke Memorese. She'd denied it was her, but maybe, through someone like Richards—and had no other name to go on but his—she *had* attempted to phase me there. Maybe that had made it easier to send me deeper into the Memory last night and see if from my memories she could learn where Greist Sahl-kla had disappeared to.

Still, she'd genuinely been shocked when I'd called her father a traitor. I couldn't figure this one out.

I told Forno my thoughts about the Emirates connection and forwarded the NIO travel protocols to his comm card.

Seeing my new code card, he complained, "Where's mine?"

I threw him a look that said, *Really?*

"Tash," he swore: a crude Helk word for excrement.

"Give me your comm card. I've got some tricks and some . . . intriguing basement progs that will configure it so you can get messages to me through the slot, all neatly coded. A little."

Forno shrugged, then tossed me his comm card. "Jennifer know about those progs?"

"She's looking the other way." I started fiddling with the nodes on Forno's comm card, which were far and few between. Also, the flash membranes felt wrong. Where had Forno picked up *this* thing? I prepped the card to tether to my code card and sank into the DataNet basement to pull up the progs I'd need to configure his card. Tricky.

Forno asked, "When do we leave?"

"Today. But you're heading to Helkunntanas on your own, and I'll meet up with you later."

"Alone? Where you going?"

"Montana."

"Your mom? A visit now?"

I spent a few minutes explaining to Forno the information I'd kept from Terree about my dad. About the lie that my life had been after my dad had *supposedly* left the Emirates. He was my partner; he deserved to know. He listened intently, taking it all in, and when I finished, he nodded, and for a moment even seemed to show a little sympathy.

"You never told me he was in the Emirates," Forno said.

"I barely remember it. I remembered the marina more."

"But apparently that's a false memory."

"Apparently."

"You told Terree you hoped to find your dad by taking on her case," he said.

"It's a good possibility. I have to find out what Mom knows, if anything."

He remained silent, but I saw agreement in his eyes.

"After that," I continued, "I'll find you on Helkunntanas."

"Okay, so what's my connection from Crossbill Station? Swain?"

"No. You didn't live there, Forno."

He glared at me from his big chair, and I sank into my own seat a little more. He said, "You want me to go to Khrem."

"You lived there, you know Helks. Of course I want you to go there."

More glaring. How could he continue looking bigger and bigger sitting in that damn chair? I took my code card from the table to give my hands something to do.

"I have a problem going back there," he said.

"Jesus, Forno, you told me you have a place, didn't you?"

"It's complicated. I'd just as soon forget—"

"You've got underworld contacts. In fact, *you* brought them up as a valuable asset when we started working together."

"Contacts are one thing. Khrem is another."

"Look, I know you've distanced yourself from that life, but this is the job, okay? I have an added interest in this, and I'm taking a few side trips, but it's my agency, Forno, and you work for me. Get to Khrem and find out what you can."

Forno stood now and came to the desk, where, gazing down, he towered over me. I really hated it when he did that. I kept cool, though, and refused to let his physical appearance intimidate me.

"You want me to go back into my district? Do some subtle advertising to Graff's sniffers?"

"Subtle would be good. But for now, stay away from Graff. Away from Swain."

"I can do that. What about Terree?"

"She's still at the Emirates Tower. I called her a while ago and she confirmed her plans to stay a couple weeks."

"Easily said."

I'd done some searching before my run. "I downloaded a smart cobweb from the DataNet and hid an NIO protocol there."

"So?"

"It gave me a look at TWT's manifests for the day. No record of Terree's passage."

"If Graff left undetected, couldn't she?"

"Less pull than Graff, even though she's the daughter of a known Envoy."

"A *missing* Envoy," Forno said.

If I'd dredged up the nerve to tell Jennifer Lisle about Terree, I could've asked for help keeping an eye on the Memor. I figured I could spill everything later. "If it comes down to it, I'll get in touch with Jennifer and put her on Terree's trail."

"She'll be happy to hear that news."

"We'll be somewhat hard to reach at that point."

"Only a jump slot away."

"She'll need time to get a Helkunntanas travel visa, even for herself. So work fast when you get there. Stay low. I'll get there when I get there."

"You'll stay in touch?"

I threw his comm card back at him. "Best I can do. We can do some scattered pings with your card now. Make sure you swipe the access node first, or you'll end up broadcasting to every NIO and Kenn agent in the Union."

"It sure would be nice if I just had an actual *code* card, don't you think?"

"Shut it, Forno. We're lucky we got what we got."

"I'll try to remember that when I'm fighting for my life."

"At least you'll be warm."

"There is that."

"Helk food, rich meats, pungent spices. You'll be in Helk heaven."

He smiled. "Then I'll be on my way." He searched his comm card for the forwarded data. "My whole itinerary here?"

"Seattle Shuttle port to Egret Station, then Transworld Transport to Crossbill."

"Need to stop at my place here first."

"Good. Put together what you need that you don't have in Khrem. You need a ride to the port? It's twenty miles from here."

"I know where it is."

"I can call an intercity shuttle. They're large enough to fit you and still fly straight."

He grimaced. "You're a chuckle a second, Crowell. No, I'll run there. It'll be faster, and fewer stops."

"And less conspicuous."

"You wanted inconspicuous, you should've hired a different partner." The thin line of a smile crossed his face.

Nope, still ugly.

Helks could be irritating, but Tem Forno had his moments. Those moments had grown on me, begrudgingly, like Helk's fur. Humans had been distrustful of Helks from the start, and some held even stronger grudges against them now, our fears slow to dissipate in the aftermath of the Ultra scare and Plenko's Movement—which really had nothing to do with Helkunntanas—but I'd come to understand Helks more through my growing friendship with Forno.

"I hope you shower before you fly out," Forno said, bringing me out of my thoughts. "You stink like a ten-day-old gabobileck."

Irritating. What was it I'd just been thinking? Something about understanding Helks?

Fourteen

CARA LANDRY SAID NOTHING ELSE.

She'd told Parr she'd be his One, then she simply stopped project-ing her thoughts into his mind. Parr had tried to get her to say more, he really had. But she only stared at him with indifference, eyes barely open. Then she stopped moving. Unnerving.

Once, during a delicate job for the Boss, teaching a lesson to a human vendor who'd missed his tithes, Parr had turned his Helk bodyguards loose. Roughed the guy up bad. Parr had said, "You want to tell me again why you're holding out?" and the guy stood there like a statue, blinking at him, barely able to comprehend the beating he'd received, mute. Parr had said, "I need an answer." No answer. "I can turn my Helks on you again." At which point the vendor came to his senses, his body literally unlocking and flailing as he pleaded for more time. At least it had ended better for him than it had for Shyler Frock.

But Cara Landry? She hadn't done anything, said anything, or thought anything for five minutes. What did all this mean, her coming here and put-ting on this act? It made Parr want to pull a Richards and slip out of the Quarry, out of the House. He wondered if he even could, considering the Boss was down. Would the automated security measures allow him to leave? He wondered if Richards had actually been able to get out. He wondered if Richards, given his early exit, had maybe *known* something about all this.

The Quarry seemed darker now that he was in the middle of it. Now that he was the only one who seemed to be breathing.

A room that focused power, Rieser had said.

There were so many RuBy squares on the floor that it looked as if an old, threadbare carpet had been thrown down. The bodies of the guests, when they'd fallen, had knocked over many piles of the squares. Until this moment, Parr had forgotten about the strong odor, the lack of the drug in his system, and the numbing pain. He rubbed his nose, then stared at his shaking, red-stained fingertips—nearly the only movement in the room.

The bodies around Parr: asleep.

Cara's silent treatment prompted him to circle the Quarry, checking for pulses. Beyer Jander. Zantz Marko. He checked the Helk the Boss had shot earlier, just to make sure. Even the young girl serving mustard eggs. All alive, all breathing shallow.

Baren Rieser, too, his bare feet sticking up, fanned out, almost comically.

Cara wasn't actually *doing* anything, but she'd certainly surprised everyone with her entrance. And then, for Christ's sake, Rieser's goddamn fingers had started *glowing*.

Parr succumbed to his body's aches and picked up a few squares of RuBy from the table next to Rieser's body. He rolled them, stared at them, and popped them.

He closed his eyes, head back, and waited.

Always a letdown. He didn't get the skin-tightening, brain-numbing smash of the first wave any more, not with his continual use. At best, his incipient high calmed his nerves and dulled the pain. Sometimes, ten minutes later, he needed more, certain the earlier pop had done nothing for him.

Feeling brave, Parr put his face only inches from Cara Landry's. She didn't blink. Didn't even seem to breathe. Hello? Anyone there? Okay, the next level of brave: He poked her shoulder with his finger. Nothing. He poked her sternum. Nothing. It was as if she were Rubed out herself.

He touched her cheek.

Cold. He studied her nostrils. Put a hand in front of her nose. Was she breathing? He couldn't say one way or another, but he didn't think he felt air coming from her. Definitely air had come from her earlier, her words emerging out in breathy whispers.

RuBy freaking hell.

"If this is what you mean about being my One, I'm not impressed," he said aloud.

Cara remained silent on the matter.

"Do you know who I am?" he asked for the second time that night.

She didn't offer any opinions.

"According to you, I'm the only Thin Man who matters. Is that why everyone else is napping?"

He thought about tipping her over. That would show her. She was an Ultra, after all, right? Ultras had nearly taken control of the Union, ready to squeeze it, even though no one knew why. The bad guys. The bad aliens.

Baren Rieser was no saint either. The Boss had sidled up to the Ultras somehow, ready to do some business. The alien threat had come to an end, but he'd found a way to do a little more damage for profit. He was going to let Parr in on it. Bring him into the fold, meeting Cara Landry, the unlikely Ultra back from the dead.

Or was she? This Cara wasn't the same as the one that detonated and destroyed half a space station. So was it another copy of her?

Parr was working for Rieser, so he guessed that made him a bad ass, too. Hey—he *was* a bad ass. He'd done his fair share of questionable things under the Boss's rule, and done them with panache and a cold, calculating impartiality. Except for his moment of weakness with Shyler Fuck.

Maybe he should cut his losses and escape this mess. Leave Rieser and Cara and the room behind him forever.

But no. He eyed the RuBy squares surrounding him like a magic circle. RuBy was his barrier, his way to protect himself from his "One." Whatever the hell that meant.

Without Rieser, he couldn't get RuBy in the amounts he needed. RuBy was the only thing keeping this Thin Man from going crazy. Half the time he did feel crazy, unable to make sense of the mixed signals in his brain. About who he'd been, who he'd become, and, according to Rieser, who he was yet to be.

Now might be the time to get out of the House. If nothing else, he should find out where Richards had got to. He might be stuck inside the Pool Room.

At least he could arm himself. No weapons inside the House, but Baren Rieser had shot the Helk in the head with his, and Rieser had fallen to the floor cluching it. The blaster remained in the Boss's grip. Parr wondered if he'd have any trouble wresting it from him. He fell to his knees, the RuBy squares cushioning him, and put his hand on the blaster. Before he pulled at it, however, he caught sight of Rieser's bald head, like a white stone, mysterious as a tablet inscribed with ancient runes. The nine numbers tattooed on the skin were dark in contrast with his skin.

Your number's come up, Rieser had told him earlier in the day, after Shyler Frock had discovered the price for disappointing his Boss.

The blaster twitched. Parr wouldn't have realized it if he hadn't had his hand over it. But it *had* moved slightly. Was the Boss awake? A light appeared on Rieser's head. A sad, not-quite-formed halo. Parr's eyes widened when he realized the light came from one of the tattooed numbers. It pulsed, growing brighter, and Parr fought the urge to scramble away. Instead, he inched closer for a better look.

The number 8 above the right ear, one of the larger numbers on the Boss's head, glowed with an intensity that made Parr squint, the light pulsing at goddamn near the rate of a heartbeat. The Boss's heartbeat.

Cara Landry unfroze and took in a breath of air, a sound more like a squeak than a breath, and turned toward Rieser.

Parr yanked the blaster from Rieser's hand and stood. He backed up, the weapon pointed at Cara, or at Rieser, back and forth between them. *What the fuck?* Maybe one of them would blow the House up. Send shards of blackrock out to impale anyone within their range.

Then he had a feeling.

A sensation of motionless movement. He closed his eyes, suddenly queasy, and fell to his knees. What a weird sensation. Like a moment between life and death. A breath of power moving among them. Cara. Rieser. Himself.

Rieser coughed. Then he squirmed. Then he sat up, the 8 still lit, still pulsing, seemingly giving life. He glanced at Parr on his knees, and Parr fought to keep his hand steady and his grip on the blaster firm. Rieser saw the weapon.

"Put it down, Vanderberg," he said softly, managing a slight smile.

Cara, anticlimactically, sat on the oversized couch, suddenly looking small and timid as Rieser slowly arose from the floor. The 8 stopped glowing.

Unsure, Parr lowered the weapon a notch at a time. "Fucking hell," he said. "What the hell did you—?"

"Hoo-boy," Rieser said. "That is *always* a rush."

"What *was* all that?"

Rieser scratched at the 8 above his right ear while Cara continued to sit passively, her hands in her lap, her eyes looking past Parr at nothing.

"Number eight," Rieser said. "Nice trick, huh?"

"*Trick?*"

Rieser winked. "Almost like having nine lives, Vanderberg. That was number eight."

Parr stared, unbelieving.

"What's wrong?" Rieser said. "You should be happy to be alive and well."

"Um, thanks, I think."

Rieser looked at Parr with the eyes of an artist worrying over a new creation. He seemed satisfied and nodded. "Oh yes, you look very, very good. How delightful. The test was a phenomenal success."

This was a test?

"You're a special creature, Vanderberg," Rieser said. "No one else can claim your place now."

At that point, Parr looked away from the Boss and realized that, except for Rieser, Cara Landry, and himself, the bodies of the other guests had disappeared from the Quarry, and so had all the RuBy. He stood and gawked.

Rieser came up next to him. "I told you your number had come up," he said. He calmly took the blaster from Parr's hand.

"I don't understand."

"Number eight. That was your number."

Fifteen

THE SHUTTLE WOULD TAKE ONLY HALF AN HOUR TO REACH MONTANA and the small port at Lakeside, a bustling resort town tucked along Flathead Lake's west shore. I chose to opaque my window, content to stare at the back of the seat in front of me while the engines warmed up and the automated take-off instructions droned on over crackly speakers that cut in and out like someone gasping for a last breath.

The ticking of my watch, faint and steady in the silence of the shuttle, brought up a quick wave of panic—but no, nothing to worry about. I took the watch from my wrist and stared at the second hand as it ticked jerkily around the face. The numbers, ordered and geometrically perfect, stood out dark and bold. They seemed to float freely in my vision, but out of order now, as if someone had purposely rearranged them.

The disturbing sight reminded me of the incident near the Seattle waterfront, after finding Alex Richards. I had no clue what had happened to Richards, and that really pissed me off. I tried to untangle the threads: take the cheating husband I'd been assigned to watch, figure out the connections to the Ultras. The unfathomable aliens and their younger version of Richards, dead or not-dead, stamped with the Ultra brand, 100% Grade A Asshole Alex.

I was missing something, but hell if I knew what it was. Well, besides a stiff shot of blue poison.

I put my watch back on and stilled my thoughts, willing to relegate its metronomic rhythm to white noise, but instead, I thought back to a fateful, previous trip to a small, out-of-the-way place. A place like Montana, known for good snow and skiing: Aryell. I felt that I should be wrestling with some deep, cathartic revelation—Aryell and Montana, Cara and my mom—all of it anchored by the Ultras and their mysterious plans for the Union. I found it increasingly difficult to remember Cara as the human girl I'd once had feelings for. She was now that girl on Snowy Mountain, her head nearly severed from the enemy's blow, a dead, alien presence tucked into a girl's copied shell, totally disrupted by an antimatter blast.

Better not to think about it.

As the shuttle took off, I closed my eyes, glad that the thrusters drowned the ticking of my watch and quieted my unsettling thoughts. In fact, I slept and awoke only on the crackling announcement of our arrival at Lakeside, where I gladly disembarked.

I didn't plan to stay here, and had no overnight bag, or even a coat; the spring weather had a slight chill to it, the afternoon wearing on. I'd need to get back and on my way to Helkunntanas as soon as I could. Mom had answers, or she didn't.

I pinged Jennifer Lisle to tell her I'd arrived safely in Montana. Mom's lake place was just two miles from the port. An access road fronted the highway, and, from it, a rough road cut from bedrock would lead me to her place. She no longer drove, so when she ventured out—which wasn't often—she called ahead for a Lakeside courtesy van. In any case, I decided to walk and, after exiting the shuttle port property, made my way to the lake road without calling Mom. She knew I was coming, and I'd be there soon enough. Besides, I had my blaster, which, thanks to Jennifer's clearance, I'd been been allowed to keep boarding the shuttle.

Night was on its way, dusk settling in faster than expected, shadows of the evergreens lengthening. Halfway down the road I heard something and stopped. My watch kept time, ticking loudly again, as loud as the first time I'd heard it near the warehouse on the waterfront.

It was happening again. I spun but, as before, saw no one. This time, I didn't run. I was still a half mile out from Mom's place.

I pulled my blaster with one hand and fumbled for my code card with the other. I made a call, awkwardly stretching the flashpaper membrane to its largest surface area even as it connected. Mom answered after a couple call tones, but the world spun faster, my watch's ticking louder in my ears. I swept my blaster from side to side, all around, helplessly frantic.

"David?"

I couldn't see her on the membrane. My eyes refused to focus. I shouted, "Mom, I'm on the lake road—"

"David, are you all right?"

I kept my eyes open by an act of will, the spinning and ticking even wilder now.

The muscles of my mouth refused to cooperate, and I had only a moment to slide to the edge of the road before dropping to the ground. My code card slipped from my grip, and I somehow lost the blaster too.

I peered about, expecting to see the dark shape I'd seen in Seattle, but nothing coalesced in the failing light. I heard no Memorese. But I sensed a presence. A presence *behind* me. A shadow hand reaching for my arm.

My mom's voice on the code card, calling my name over and over, was small and otherworldly, but I intuitively knew that I was gone. I had bled out into the Memory.

I was forgetting something important. Mom expected an answer from me, but I had lost my train of thought. I scratched my head, trying to remember.

"Maybe Greist can go in there and dredge up the reason why you're late," she said, looking behind me.

I turned, and the Memor smiled, his wide lips almost gray in the soft light of the lamp by the couch. Greist. Greist somebody. I could never remember his last name.

"Oh, lad, don't look at me. We only use our powers for good." He winked, pulled his orange ponytail forward over his shoulder, and groomed it with four long fingers.

Now it came to me. The bonfire at my friend's house down at Table Bay. This must be an example of what Mom called selective memory. Now, suddenly aware, I smelled woodsmoke on my clothes.

"I lost time."

Mom raised an eyebrow. "Time. Oh really."

"Lost track of time," I said, correcting myself.

"I know you sometimes feel trapped here," she said, her tone that of a professor admonishing a student, "but you're not allowed out without an escort. Imagine how worried Tilson was, losing track of you. Your dad, just like Greist, is an important man—"

Here it comes, I thought.

"—and there are those who would take advantage of him and his skills. He expects you to honor his wishes and stay with your escort."

It was bad enough I had to travel with Dad to the countless sessions the Envoys had to oversee and resolve, always with an Emirates page following me everywhere. But to have to remain under watch even while close to home was too much. It wasn't the first time I'd snuck past the escort to escape the monitored life of an Envoy's kid.

"Give the boy some credit, lass," Greist said. "It takes a little skill to get past the escorts."

Mom's gaze on me softened.

Quietly, I said, "I'm sorry. I won't do it again." *For a few days.*

"Go get cleaned up. You smell like smoke, and dinner's ready."

I nodded, then asked, "Where's Dad?"

She looked behind me again, and asked Greist the same question without words.

"Called away while you were at the bonfire," the Memor said. He walked past me now and stood by Mom.

Light dawned in Mom's eyes. "That's right, a session in Chicago."

"Chicago?" I said. "What's going on in Chicago?"

"Big developments, Lucky Lad," Greist said. "A conference of Union-sized proportions."

"I've called a shuttle," Mom said. "One's picking you up after dinner."

"Wait, I have to go?"

"Your dad's already over there."

"He's expecting you," Greist said quickly.

This wasn't the usual procedure. I almost always left *with* Dad. And why was Greist Whats-His-Name here at the lake house? As an Envoy too, he should be at the conference.

"Are you going with me?" I asked him.

"No, lad, I'm going ahead of you. It'll be just you and your Emirates page."

This was all highly irregular. "What about Mom?"

"I'll be fine." She smiled brightly. "As always."

"I worry about you alone out here."

She rubbed my shoulder. "Unlike you, young man, I don't try to slip past the escorts. Tilson will look in on me. Now. Go get changed for dinner."

Greist's voice, almost too cheerful, rang loud in the living room. "Perhaps you'll meet my daughter, Terree. She'll be there, too."

Terree.

Her name, like a code word, pulled me out of the Memory, and I woke on the lake road on my back.

It was dark.

I turned over, reached all about for my blaster, and couldn't find it. Sensing someone behind me, I shot to my feet, but as I turned, strong hands grabbed my shoulders and pulled me backward. An arm encircled me. I did my best to keep my chin down to prevent the arm from squeezing my neck and windpipe.

I kicked backward with my foot and struck my attacker's shin, eliciting a reassuring grunt. The pressure loosened enough for me to wrench free and separate from my attacker before turning around. In the dark, I could not make out who it was, human or Memor, male or female. It definitely wasn't a Helk, because we were about the same height.

"What do you want?" I wheezed. I didn't expect an answer, and I didn't get one.

So I rushed the shape, slamming into its upper body, which was clad in a dark cloak featuring a cavernous hood. I remembered Forno's report about the hooded figure at the Emirates Tower. Was it Alex Richards? I wrapped my arms around its torso and carried us to the ground. I landed atop my attacker, and all the air went out of me. Stunned, I waited a few heartbeats to get my breath back, and my assailant took that moment to swing an arm at my head. I raised my arm and caught the blow on my shoulder. The force of it pushed me off, and the shape rolled aside.

We both stood and faced off not five feet away from each other.

I heard a whine, the unmistakable powering up of a blaster, and it sounded a hell of a lot like mine.

What followed was like a rewind, a do-over: I ran at the shape, hoping to take my assailant by surprise, and this time, as we collided, I reached for the arm holding the blaster. The blaster fired, and pain sliced through my lower right side as we fell again, grunting. A hefty forehead rushed forward and struck me on the nose, but I had the better position, and when our heads hit, the attacker snapped back and hit the ground hard. Wrapped in a cloak, perhaps to disguise its sex, my attacker remained a mystery, but I was now pretty sure it was human, and fairly strong.

Warm blood trickled down my side, which throbbed with increasing pain. Still dazed by the effects of my entry into the Memory, I fought for control of the weapon before being shot again.

And, before I realized it, the blaster was in my hand and I was primed to fire it. But my mystery attacker's struggling had stopped, and he, she, or it lay motionless beneath me, apparently out cold.

When I rolled off, the wound in my flank reminded me of its presence. I winced at the jabbing pain as I scrabbled to my knees. My cloaked assailant lay an arm's length away, but I could not reach it. I was fading. Falling sideways. Losing consciousness.

Not before I see who this is, I thought. Had I killed my attacker? If not, could I find out who it was and what it wanted?

No. Just no. I passed out.

"David? David?"

A buzz in my ear, faint.

"David?"

I opened my eyes, tried to gather my wits. Apparently, I lay on the couch at the lake house, my mom hovering over me, worry lines adding to the wrinkles on her face.

"Oh, thank God." She put a fluttering hand to her chest and straightened.

I sat up and swore, trying to parse what had happened. My ticking watch. Passing out. Witnessing a memory of my past life, experiencing my family as it should have been, my dad an Envoy, Terree's father at our house.

Awakening to find the cloaked attacker near me. Human, not Memor. Our struggle for the blaster. I remembered, then, and put my hand to my bandaged side.

"I hope I did that right," she said. "I was more than a little rattled by everything."

"How'd I get here?"

"I called the courtesy van. The driver found you and brought you in. I was going to call emergency—"

"What about the other person?" I said.

Mom wore jeans and a heavy green sweatshirt featuring the slogan COME TO THE LAKE in white block letters. Now in her sixties, she kept her graying hair short and had it styled weekly.

"He found only you. There was someone else? The person who shot you?"

I nodded.

"I told the van driver to go," she said, rubbing my shoulder. "When I knew you'd be okay. You're lucky it wasn't worse."

Lucky.

"I'll get you some water."

"Maybe something stronger? Might help clear my head."

She left, and I let my head fall back into the couch cushion, my thoughts whirling madly.

Terree had not initiated this phase into the Memory.

Someone else had phased me into the Memory, presumably the human

I'd fought. Was it the same person who had spoken Memorese in Seattle? The one Terree said had tried to send me the first time? *To get information from me.*

But was it the right information? Had the assailant's hope been to pin-point the time Greist had spoken to him at the conference?

This time, whoever was responsible had succeeded. This time, I'd been attacked in Montana, near my mom's house. I'd been followed, or the attacker had staked out the lake house, waiting for me to show up. The human had escaped and I didn't know a thing. Whoever it was hadn't killed *me*, even after I'd passed out, so that meant something. If the attacker knew about the lake house, why hadn't there been an attempt to put Mom into the Memory?

Mom came back with a glass of water and a small flute of red wine. Well, it was something. I sat up, my side aching, and reached for the wine, but she handed me the water.

Mom said, "Are you going to tell me what happened?"

I took a sip of the water, then patted the couch next to me. "I need to talk to you."

She put the wine glass on the coffee table, sat down, folded her hands in her lap, and waited.

How to approach this matter? My first thought was to ask about Dad, but I feared that if I somehow hit a nerve, Mom would button up and say nothing.

So I simply blurted out the name: "Mom, whatever happened to Greist?"

She frowned. "Grease?"

Grease, the name I'd privately called Greist when younger. "No, Mom, Greist the Memor."

"Oh, goodness, David, how would I know any Memors? They certainly didn't come around here."

"You never met any when Dad was an Envoy?"

"Such ancient history, David. He never brought his business home, and he put all that behind him when he bought the marina."

She saw I'd drunk most of my water and held out her hand. "Would you like some more?" She reached for the wine. "The merlot?"

"No," I said, setting the water glass on the side table. My side twinged as I did. Okay, her first responses rang true, all consistent with a life that had never included an alien Envoy. "Why did you sell the marina?" I asked next, leaping past specific questions about Dad.

Her body tensed, and her lips drew into a pout. "Why did I sell it?" she asked.

"Or, a better question, *when* did you sell it?" If her memory had been altered, if someone had done to her what had been done to me, she would know nothing about Greist Sahl-kla. Nothing about Envoys. The conference in Chicago.

"You know this," she said. "Why are you asking?"

I pressed ahead. "You sold it after Dad disappeared, right?"

"Yes, afterward. But not right away. A few years later. You don't remember?"

"I'm a little fuzzy about it."

I flashed on images of the Hammond Marina, the boats, sails, the loons. The tackle shop. The meals Mom supposedly had taken to Dad when he'd been working.

All lies.

I figured I had my truth: Mom believed the lies. She didn't know what I knew about Dad, didn't know who Greist was or what he had done to betray the Union—and perhaps to betray my dad—and she certainly didn't know I knew the truth about all of this, thanks to Terree's easing me into the Memory.

I didn't actually know the particulars of how the marina had been sold. Had I once known? Had it slipped away because of my trips to the Memory?

I asked, "Do you remember who bought it?" *Do you remember the lie about who bought it?*

Now she stood up. "David, you must've knocked something loose when you fell on the road out there."

"That's probably true. Who bought it?"

"The original owner."

"Who do you mean?"

"Hammond."

My head threatened to spin out of control again, as if about to take another trip into the Memory. Good thing I was already sitting down.

"Hammond," I whispered. *The Hammond Marina.*

She nodded, recalling the memory. "That's right. *Such* a nice man. Your dad and I were quite impressed with him. The way he ran the marina, how he bent over backwards to make sure we understood what we were getting ourselves into when we first bought it from him."

If this Hammond had hypothetically bought the marina, for whatever reason, even a fake reason, had he *truly* owned it before? And was he running it now?

Before leaving Mom's and slotting to Helkunntanas, I'd have to take one more detour and visit the marina.

"You really don't remember him, do you?" Mom said.

"Afraid not. Is Mr. Hammond still working at the marina?"

"Yes. I can't believe you don't remember, David." She paused, maybe waiting for me to catch up. But I didn't. She said, "It's *Tilson*. Tilson Hammond."

Sixteen

PLENKO'S ASS, TEM FORNO THOUGHT, IT FELT GOOD TO BE WARM. To be surrounded by Helks in a world the right size and shape, with the right colors, the right smells, and the right goddamn temperature.

He shed his gray overcoat, slung it over his shoulder, and picked up his bag. He'd stuffed it with everything he could think of to get through the visit. Home.

Strange to think that now. Was it still home? He'd left on the run. Fleeing the Kenn, its hierarchy upset by an Ultra and copies. Infiltrated as effortlessly as the NIO had been.

He hadn't been back since searching for Crowell.

There were worse things about being home than having to deal with the Kenn. He had the underworld to consider. He'd once been a part of it. He'd escaped in a plea deal after he'd tashed a RuBy transfer and got caught. The Kenn trained him, paid him, and sent him back in to work undercover for the information they needed to loosen Abigail Graff's grip on the districts of Swain.

He had a life before then. It wasn't the Kenn, and it wasn't Abby Graff. He'd left it all behind long ago, but now he could no longer avoid it. He was home, and before he threw himself into the turmoil and gloom of the RuBy wars, he would have to gain back his peace in Khrem.

Forno cleared Helkunntanas customs without mishap—it was laughably easy with the NIO clearance, which no one seemed to care about. They didn't even check his bag, or worry about his blaster. He didn't like Helk stunners, knowing what they did to people, so he'd found a specially made blaster designed for a Helk. Customs could've cared less whether it was a blaster, a stunner, or a slingshot.

No matter the time of day, the port was always quiet and nearly empty. Few Helks left the planet, and non-Helks didn't visit unless they had to, and only when they managed to score the travel visas to do so. The arrival atrium spread out before him like a monstrous cavern, the rows of strip lights criss-crossing the high stone ceiling to create the illusion of a gateway, Helkunnta-nas's Emirates symbol.

Forno had some credit vouchers, courtesy of Crowell Investigations, and he stopped at the first gabobileck vendor, a Third Clan operating a cart near the entrance arch just outside the atrium. He ordered four of the meat sausages, slit the casings, and stuffed them with spicy mustard, onions, and an insanely hot green sauce. He devoured them in minutes.

By Ozsc. Forno stood, eyes closed, multiple flavors still banging around in his mouth. He considered buying more, but he would pay for it in flatulence and lost sleep. So he stood a while longer soaking up the warm sun, then followed the signs to the concourse and caught the automated bus to the T-shuttles.

The T-shuttles, labeled by number and destination, boarded their passengers by Clan. First Clan Helks slid over on the inside ring from the concourse; Second Clan had the middle ring; Third Clan walked to the outer ring; Fourth Clan walked the concourse until they could find private taxis willing to take them to their destinations. A caste system all too familiar to Forno.

When Crowell arrived, he'd have to find a private taxi, like all non-Helks.

"Too bad you're not First Clan," Crowell had told him the day they took on their first case together. "I could walk behind you and no one would ever know I was coming. You could just growl a lot."

"Clans are about more than physical stature."

"I know. Social status. But the bigger you are, the more street cred you have."

"Whatever that means."

"Money, Forno."

"No. Power. More power."

"Like I said. Money. Power goes where the money goes. The smart ones always look for the money trail."

"You're not designated a certain Clan by how smart you are."

"A lot of Helks have snot for brains. You said so yourself."

"So do a lot of humans." Forno watched Crowell wince at that. "Humans came up with that stupid saying anyway."

"Right," Crowell said. "Your snot is not offended."

Forno took comfort knowing that Crowell wasn't always right. The fact was, Forno *was* offended when non-Helks suggested social status had something to do with smarts. Most Helks, the ones who could talk at all, for example, could not speak any human language. Did that make Forno smarter than most?

Scrambling now into the T-shuttle on the second ring, he didn't feel any smarter than Helks waiting on the first ring, or any dumber than those on the third ring. Glancing back at the first ring, he saw a couple First Clans waiting patiently for their T-shuttles.

Street cred? Crowell was right about money equaling power. But Forno didn't need any more power.

It had never done him any good.

A couple hours later, after three T-shuttle transfers, Forno arrived at the Khrem terminal. If Helkunntanas was home, then Khrem was like a mate: a nurturing presence, but one always on the edge of volatility. Khrem was mostly dirty and corrupt; moreover, it also had the largest number of human districts.

Abby Graff had seized the neighboring city of Swain, taking over the one human district embedded there. Then, with more brains than most of the underworld could lay claim to, she engineered the entire city's takeover. RuBy, not snot, powered Graff's brain, and she knew how to use it.

But Khrem? This was now Baren Rieser's town.

Forno slid off his shuttle ring and found his way to the tunnel leading to D1, the largest Helk district. The closer to the terminal, the larger the district.

The tunnel stank of age and decay, of protectorants and coolants, and of stale air whistling in through rusting metal shafts. The walking surface, almost always wet and slimy, demanded a rider's careful attention.

Humans couldn't wrap their brains around the idea of a civilization existing on Helkunntanas for six thousand years. Helks had tried to colonize Temonus hundreds of years ago, before the Memors discovered Earth, and some Helks had decided to stay there. Humans, while erecting their own cities, had found the settlement, and were surprised to learn that the Helk population had lived there over a thousand years.

The Khrem council of First Clans believed in preserving ancient history. Leave things as they were. Helks and technology could grow around the city, but never absorb it.

So the tunnel stank, and the walls and arched ceiling groaned as travelers worked their way through the bricked arch. Coolant dripped from the air shafts, and mold and green rot peppered the crimson walls. Going through the terminal and out through the tunnel was like going backwards in time, to the years before Helks divided themselves into Clans. It was ironic, given that the council—all First Clan—would never abdicate power to lesser Clans.

On the other side of the tunnel, Forno found himself at the Hub, a crisscrossing of thoroughfares, and experienced a brief wave of nostalgia. Here in Khrem, with hundreds, even thousands of Helks roaming the Hub, he felt at home. He lifted his gaze, slitted his eyes, and took in the D1 towers and their surrounding bridges until his gaze alit on the Desci thoroughfare. Desci would get him to D2 and his place near the Square. Not the best of areas, but, then, few areas in Khrem qualified as "better."

When Forno took his next step, a human male rushed across his path and, startled, stopped and looked up. Forno saw a glimmer of some negative emotion in his dark blue eyes—probably distrust or even fear. Forno sighed in exasperation. Still monsters to humans, after all these years.

"Sorry." Tall and skinny, with a full beard and moustache, the man still looked small and out of place near the Hub. His cooler, not in the best repair, coughed and hacked. The tendril had slipped out from his shirt, which was wet with perspiration. The cooler control box spit static. The man started walking again.

"Hey," Forno said, "wait."

The man stopped abruptly, looking very much like a cornered animal.

"Relax. Your cooler's out."

The man stared a moment before discovering the wayward tendril. "Oh—"

"Here, let me." Forno approached the man, who backed up two steps. "Holy snot, relax."

"I'm—I'm sorry."

Forno reached behind the man and grasped the cold tendril. He held out the end so that the man could do the rest.

"Thanks," he mumbled.

"Sure."

The man looked past Forno, toward the tunnel. "Heading to Crossbill."

Rushing to leave the planet of giants. "Take the A-taxi," Forno said. "You'll get a better rate."

The man looked into Forno's eyes again, as if to find the Hulk that wasn't there. "Yes," he said. "Thanks."

"Sure."

The man tried a smile, not quite successfully. "Okay, bye."

And away he went, hurrying toward the tunnel entrance towering over him like a mountain.

"Have fun," Forno said, amused, and walked quickly toward the thoroughfare, more anxious than ever to get to his place. Desci's T-trolley had just finished its loop and turned in place to begin its next pass down the thoroughfare. Forno draped his coat over his bag, hopped onto the platform as the T-trolley finished its spin, and slipped a credit into the closest paystick.

Only a handful of Helks were on the T-trolley to D2. Of course. Bad area. Too many humans. Too much RuBy. Grease coated the handrail, so he leaned carefully against the plastic wall behind him.

The T-trolley picked up speed and whisked him toward the Square. The T-trolleys never really stopped, just slowed at intersections. Pedestrians crossing the thoroughfare and riders on their uni-wheels kept their eyes open, not just for the trolleys, but for the ongoing flow of vendor carts, flash peddlers, data scammers, pickpockets, and RuBy freaks out to buy or sell a few squares. It was no accident that the heart of D2 was called the Square.

Helkunntanas' sun, which had burned hot all day in a cloudless sky, had started sinking in the west, the light dimming. Forno jumped off the T-trolley as it crossed the first major thoroughfare into the Square and decelerated. Suprisingly, he kept his balance, juggling his bag and coat and landing on the synthetic blackrock. Because it hadn't been oiled recently, he didn't fret getting the muck on his feet pads.

Almost immediately, a Fourth Clan hawking some flashware accosted Forno.

"Don't want any," Forno said in English.

The Helk responded in English, surprising Forno. "Good Helky day, eh, my Second?" He wore a black fur cap with leather straps that hung past his shoulders. Otherwise, he showed a hell of a lot of matted and ungroomed fur. "Flash today, flash tomorrow, no?"

"Not interested." Forno moved off the road and scanned the Square for an avenue of escape.

"Ah no, do not ah no a poor Fourth." The Helk waved his head back and forth dramatically, his hat's straps flying. "I'm Bilki, prince of the thoroughfare, and ah—flash I have, readers for your nails, your fingers. Smart shoes, I can get, even." He winked.

"No, Bilki, find someone else to bother," said Forno, irritated by the Fourth Clan's hard sell.

"Ah no, you're slapping me here. Best prices, best in the Square." His palm displayed a flash mod. "This? This is—"

Forno shoved the Helk in the chest.

Bilki fell back flat on his furry ass, losing his hat in the process. "Ah, tasher! Damn Second-rate tasher! Why ya gotta knicker the prince?"

Knowing better than to cause a scene in the Square, Forno set off down the sidewalk, ignoring Bilki's outraged complaints.

He passed a line of legitimate shops selling everything imaginable, from accessories and tech designed for humans or manufactured by humans to items and services local Helk Clans might want: DataNet terminals, comm cards, skin coolers, eye mods, flashbooks, holo-misters, flash *this* and flash *that*. Over here a salon for head waxing; over there a shop for grooming; above the dye-works, a jeweler for Clan ornamental jewelry such as rygsa earrings and calsza rings; down the stairs in the basement of a human diner, a gallery of blackrock sculptures; and across the thoroughfare a clinic specializing in silicon foot pads. Forno's feet *did* feel a bit tired, but the cost for pads would have been more than his share of Terree's retainer.

All of it, though, all the buildings and shops, seemed coated in centuries of grime, ignored for so long by the Council that no one now had a clue how to scrub it down, to repair the brickwork, re-plumb the doorways, or re-sheet the roofs.

Of course, above all else, there was RuBy and its ubiquitous cinnamon odor. Legal as it was on Helkunntanas, it was sold everywhere: RuBy outlets, RuBy boutiques, RuBy chain stores, RuBy apothecaries, RuBy bars. Available by the square, the stack, the cube, or custom-sized to fit any need. All pre-packaged, all neat and tidy, cellophane tied up with gold floss, arranged in designer crystal, or layered in special membrane-covered holo plastics imported from offworld. All sold for retail at five times the unit cost. Of course.

But the shops lacked on customers. Traffic was as discouraging as their unattractive facades, and most of the shops were closed. A Khrem customer was a *street* customer; few had the credits for the slick pretties in the ugly shops. Shops appeared and disappeared in the Square and throughout the commercial districts of Khrem, sometimes all within a month or two. Owners bragged that they could make a go of it, but most ultimately closed to minimize their losses.

Forno slipped past more street hawkers, one selling holocams, another silicon gloves. Two selling RuBy, two looking to buy RuBy. Another trying to pawn some of the drug packaged up in miniature glowtubes. He passed them all by, enduring their aggressive spiels and frustrated name calling. He passed the old RuBy bar he'd frequented in his early underground days, before the Kenn nabbed him and put him to work in Swain. The Mirror had a little more class than most of the RuBy bars. Patrons kept low profiles and also their cool. Assuming he still worked there, the proprietor—a Helk by the name of Juke—ran the place with a heavy hand and a hard head. Underworld, of course. Someone else had paid his bills, though. Thurston. But now that someone was Baren Rieser. RuBy might be plentiful on Helkunntanas, but any of the Red that passed through Khrem or sold in Khrem had Baren Rieser's name on it.

Forno slipped past The Mirror without even a glance through its front window. Around the next bend, he'd be off the main thoroughfare, free of the onslaught of hawkers, and only a couple of intersections away from his old place in the Village Villa Apartment building. Mostly human district, mostly human names. He wondered how they had decided on *Village Villa*.

The synthetic blackrock gave way to gray cobbles, and in the failing light, embedded lights in the buildings started flickering on, illuminating the nearly deserted thoroughfare. Even away from the Square, the smell of RuBy lingered. The apartment building, when it came into view, didn't look too much different. It was run-down, sure, but its painted black brickwork still had a distinctive appeal. On the roof, the oversized metal "V" had an eye-catching blood-red glow day and night.

He'd left almost everything he owned here, the rent paid by the Kenn, even after refusing—like Crowell—the reward of an intelligence-agency post for helping solve the Thin Man plot. Nice perk. Too bad he couldn't transport the apartment and all its roominess to Seattle.

How quiet the district became just a few thoroughfares away from the Square. The block around the Village Villa reminded him of the historic Helk quarter on Temonus, which he'd visited a time or two while working for Abby Graff.

Forno entered the building, lugged his bag up to the fourth floor, and stopped at apartment 4C. The DNA lock clicked as he seized the knob, swung the door open, and walked in.

By Helk standards, the apartment's dimensions were small: two rooms and a toilet. But it was his place, and he could stretch his arms over his head and not touch the ceiling. Smiling, he palmed the light pad and did a quick inventory of the main room, which remained pretty much the way he'd left it, the furniture blocky but cushioned, and too many mismatched pillows scattered about. The place had been closed up a long time, but surprisingly, the air did not smell musty, which surprised him. In fact, he still had the smell of RuBy in his nose, and he really hated it. He never took payment from Graff in RuBy, and he never popped it on his own. Irritated, he rubbed at his nose.

After he tossed his bag and overcoat onto the chair by the door, a fog of uncertainty and fatigue overtook him. The front windows facing the street were shut, their curtains drawn. The wood floor appeared clean, altogether dust-free. He frowned. Deeper in, a light blared like a spotlight over the stove.

What?

A drinking glass on the table in the kitchen area also surprised him. So did the plate with a half-eaten mustard egg. And . . . so did a few RuBy squares scattered near the plate.

He eyed his bag, the blaster hidden in the DNA-sealed inner pocket, and wondered if he could reach it quickly enough if assaulted. No one had jumped out at him, so he retrieved the bag, pulled his weapon, and held it at his side as he approached the darkened bedroom.

Someone was sleeping in his bed.

A Helk. Head barely visible, covers rustling because the Helk underneath seemed to be shaking. Forno stopped in the doorway. Didn't the humans have some kind of kid's story about this? A golden girl and a bear, the latter an unwanted guest that was somehow just right? The Helk under the covers said something unintelligible. A female voice, groggy and raspy. Forno remained mute.

Finally, the Helk rolled toward him and cleared her throat.

"Shyler?"

Forno frowned. He wasn't Shyler, whoever that was. But the voice. *The voice.* "Oh my ozsc," he whispered.

"Who is it?" said the female Helk anxiously, realizing that this wasn't Shyler. Then her breath caught in her throat.

It was a voice he knew, and knew all too well.

"Qerral?" Forno said.

A moment later, her breathing labored, the female Helk in the bed said, "Tem? You're back?"

Forno brought up the lights. Qerral blinked. The skin of her head was chapped and gray. Her hands shook, and her bracelets jangled loosely around her wrists.

"Qerral, what's going on? What're you *doing* here?"

She frowned while swinging her legs over the edge. Then her feet carefully sought out the floor. Much of Qerral's fur was splotchy, skin showing through in places.

"You never changed the lock," she said. "You just—" She stretched a bit, gaining some presence. "—left without a goodbye."

Qerral. *Helk's breath.*

Confusion washed over him. Or maybe it was anger. Or maybe a gut-wrenching, complicated passion he didn't know what to do with. *Qerral.* The Helk he'd lived with and loved for years, until the Kenn took over his life. The Helk he'd left, unceremoniously, putting all that emotional baggage behind him, never believing he'd see her again. The Helk he'd never told Crowell about.

His mate.

Seventeen

The next morning, I paid the Hammond Marina a visit.

The marina was only about five-thousand feet of shoreline from my mom's place, tucked away in an inlet north of Lakeside next to Caroline Point, a knob of land that connected to the main spar like a big toe.

Private property and rugged terrain prevented me from walking around the shore, so I called back the courtesy van and gave the driver a healthy tip to take me to the marina, which meant returning to the main road and, just before reaching Lakeside, taking Caroline Point Road.

Much larger marinas existed on the lake. The Hammond Marina had slips for, at most, two dozen boats. The driver dropped me off on the pavement near the clearing connecting Caroline Point's toe to the spar like vestigial webbing. I asked for about thirty minutes, and he promised to return for me after driving his next few customers to their destinations.

The entrance to the marina consisted of a gap-ridden narrow ramp, its slats all on the diagonal and the spaces between them more than a little disconcerting. Holding onto the white metal handrail, I expected all my memories to come pouring back, but they didn't. The Memory had changed me, and I now knew that this past had not been real. The *marina* was real, but those nurtured images of bobbing boats and flapping sails, those scents of fish and spilled fuel, mold and mildew, along with those memories of Mom's hand-delivered lunches to Dad at the bait shop—well, something had scrubbed all those images clean away.

But for my visits to the Memory and hearing my mom and Greist mention Tilson the escort, Hammond, the name of the marina owner would have meant nothing to me. Apparently, ever since my dad's disappearance, Tilson had been watching over my mother and perpetuating her cover story.

The ramp skirted a cabin that could have been Hammond's place. In front of the cabin, the ramp connected to the main dock. The bait shop sat to this dock's right, and a couple of abandoned gas pumps with red and gray paint peeling like dead skin rose up from the decking near the water's edge. A cheap plastic table and two deck chairs, chained to the wooden slats of the dock, sat before the bait shop. A solitary brown bottle of Moose Drool beer, half empty, stood in the middle of the table. A legendary Montana brew. Astonishing that anyone still sold the stuff. If it's still cold, and no one's here, I thought, I could chug some of that.

Half the boat slips were empty. The few sailboats moored there looked worn and unused for years. No sails flapped above them in the morning's light breeze.

Nothing about the marina seemed familiar. But the lake and the mountains and the other recollected details from my childhood remained both constant and real. You never outgrew the grandeur, or breathed in a surfeit of its power. I sensed that this place could hide me from the Union, and thoroughly calm me. However, blood and marrow lurked beyond the fringes of this longed-for peace.

I looked out at the lake, its surface choppy in the morning wind, and down the shoreline toward my mom's place, now no longer visible behind the jut of the last tip of land within my range of vision.

A haze had settled on the other side of the lake, nearly obscuring the Mission Mountains. Only their tops stood clear, as if severed in a horizontal line and placed to float above the haze. The clouds above the peaks swirled in a pattern not unlike that of the nano-slurry sculpture I remembered in Aaron Bardsley's office at the old NIO building, before Timothy James' antimatter core vaporized it. A few strands of mist also hugged the lake, like smoke. In the bay, flowering rush seemed to choke the surface. Only a few flowers bloomed from the triangular stems above the water line, beautiful with their umbrella-shaped pink and white petals, but the green weed, malignantly invasive, made it next to impossible for boats to maneuver in and out of marinas and home docks. Over the last hundred years, the flowering rush had changed the ecology of the once clearwater lake.

"Help you?" said a low voice behind me.

I jumped, then turned toward a man as big and stocky as me. He was older though, with white in his eyebrows. Age and sun had wrinkled his face, and his skin was rough and deep black. Muscles swelled under a white T-shirt that rippled with his every movement. A bald, no-neck, wide-backed original who looked fit enough to shoulder the weight of the entire world. The marina had seemed unreal to me, but Tilson Hammond had a reality that unlocked my memory, and he was *right*. I had known this man, as he had known me.

A few seconds later, his eyes widened and his shoulders slumped, as if he had seen a ghost.

A ghost. That was me. He knew who I was. He knew I had finally broken the code of his charade, and he wanted to mentally teleport himself elsewhere to escape this confrontation. What would he say to me? Meanwhile, I had no idea what I would say to him.

To regain his composure, he stared out at the lake, as if, like a ghost, I had suddenly disappeared. A moment later he sat in the deck chair at the plastic table and folded his hands on the tabletop. Then he turned his stony face back to me.

"I'd meant to ask about renting a boat," I said, "but on second thought—" I took another look at the boats in the slips "—maybe not."

"Plenty of other marinas if you don't like my boats."

"Actually, I'm here to talk to you."

"You know who I am."

I put my hands on the top of the other chair at the table, but did not sit. "I do."

"Yeah?"

"Tilson."

"That's me," he said. "And who is Tilson?" He picked up the Moose Drool bottle, rubbed his hands over the blue label, and took a sip. He didn't offer me any.

"Tilson Hammond, family escort for a prominent Envoy."

He waited. Took another sip.

I said, "Lawrence Crowell traveled all over the Union as an Envoy, and his son David often went with him. Tilson Hammond stayed here on the lake babysitting the mother. Sometimes he kept her son out of trouble. Then the son's dad went missing, and Tilson Hammond bought the marina as part of a cover story with which he hoodwinked the mom and the son. Am I getting it right?"

Tilson Hammond lowered the beer bottle and rotated it clockwise serveral times between his palms. Still, he waited.

"I'm getting it right," I said.

"So you say."

"You recognize me."

He shook his head. "I've owned this marina a long time. I bought it from a Joan Crowell a long time ago. There was a boy, a teen. You're saying that was you?"

"I'm Dave Crowell and you're Tilson Hammond. You knew me when my dad disappeared. I think you know why he disappeared, and I think you might even know where he is."

Tilson took the bottle again, leaned back in the canvas chair, and waited. He was good at waiting.

It was my turn. I pulled out the chair I'd been leaning on and sat down across from him. Ignoring the throb in my side, I placed my elbows on the table, and studied him intently without blinking. Better that than contemplating his muscular bulk or the undeniable likelihood of his giving me a run for my money in a fight.

"There's no way you can know about *any* of that," he told me. "No way to find the person you'd need to talk to in order to know that."

"Unless?"

He raised his eyebrows. Maybe he hadn't expected an "unless," but he knew there was one.

"And I mean a person other than yourself," I said. "Tilson, you know who I'm talking about."

He said, "Okay, I'll play. *Unless* you talked to the person who could tell you about that person you *need* to talk to."

"I don't suppose it surprises you that I completely understand what you mean by that."

"Then say the name and we can get on with it."

"Who's the person you think I need to talk to? If I don't know the name, the name I tell you will mean nothing."

The skin under his left eye twitched.

"It's only fair," I said. "I'm pretty certain about you, but a name would make me feel a lot better."

He turned away and gazed at the lake. Without looking at me, he said, "Greist."

When he turned back, I said, "Terree."

He nodded, but his eye still twitched. He tried to compensate for his apparent confusion by taking another sip of Moose Drool and rubbing his his bald head. "She came to you, did she?" he asked, his voice distant.

"Hired me. I'm a private detective and—"

"I know what you do. Your mom told me."

"Okay."

"Hired you to do what?"

"To find her father."

He looked genuinely surprised at that. "Her father's dead," he said, shaking his head. "Just like yours. And I don't know why or how it happened, either."

His lie angered me. Why would he be here, now, watching over Mom if my dad and Greist were both dead? She might not get out much, as she'd told me, but Tilson was an escort and knew how to watch inconspicuously, even *if* I had managed to give him the slip a few times in my youth.

"No, he's missing," I said.

"You think Greist is missing." A statement.

"Maybe both Griest and my dad. I took on the case to look for Greist, but hoping I might find my dad."

"He drowned in the lake. Body never found. If he was still alive why would he stay away from you and Joan?"

"Same reason Greist stayed away from Terree."

"It's common for Memors to leave their mates and family—"

"Bullshit, Tilson. Okay, if he's dead, he's dead, and maybe that's what I'll find out. But if he's missing, there's a reason, and I think I know what that reason is. I think you do too."

"I have no idea what you're talking about."

Keeping my elbows on the table, I crossed my arms. "Tell me what you know about the conference."

"The conference?"

"In Chicago. When they both disappeared."

Grudgingly, he nodded. "It's true, they disappeared sometime after Chicago."

"I was told my dad came out to Montana with Greist and a few other Envoys."

"I know nothing about that, I never saw them after they left for Chicago. I never knew the specifics of your dad's schedule other than where he was going and when he'd be back. You were there in Chicago. You should know more than me."

"Except for the cover story. Greist told you to help, didn't he? Told you to watch my mom and me. Told you to buy the marina. He told you my mom and I would never remember the truth about what happened there. That's why I don't know more than you about Chicago."

"I believe you know this, but I'm not sure how just by talking to Terree."

Now we were pulling apart the story like nesting dolls. I wasn't exactly sure how much to tell him, but given everything he'd done—even secretly—to help my mom, he deserved to know some of it. Too much, and I'd put his and my mom's lives in danger. More than they already were, that is.

"She didn't tell me," I said. "Greist Sahl-kla told me."

He looked more confused.

"I know," I said, "you're wondering how I talked to him if I'm looking for him. I've not actually talked to him since I was sixteen."

The truth of this struck him, knowledge flashing in his eyes. "Ah," he said. "You remembered something. The cover's falling apart."

Bingo. "For me, anyway. I've learned some things by remembering what happened at the conference."

"You talked to Greist there the day they disappeared? How about your dad?"

"Yes. I don't know about my dad. That's not clear yet."

"Terree?"

"She was there, but I didn't see her. However, she knew something. Enough to help me now."

"Ah," he said again. "That Memor brain trick."

"Yeah."

I wasn't surprised he knew about the Memory. Tilson had worked closely with my dad, who'd been all over the Union with his friend the Memor, and afterward Greist had given Tilson the cover story, which would have included a plan for something to happen to make me forget everything about that life.

For a moment I was back on that balcony in front of Greist with all the commotion going on downstairs. Greist mentioning the Ultras, and talking about memories, and holes, and then touching me on the forehead. Waking up and seeing the older man, hearing him tell me of my life on the lake, the marina, *this is your life*, and then *until we meet again*, glowing fingers putting me to sleep.

That's when I forgot everything.

"You know nothing about what Greist was up to?" I asked Tilson, who nonchalantly finished his beer. Damn.

The bottle thunked when he sat it on the plastic table. "All I know is that he paid me a lot of money to keep on with the family, as a distant observer."

"And you just said yes."

"It was a *lot* of money."

"He and my dad were good friends."

"Yes."

"Do you believe Greist would have done anything to hurt my dad? Do you believe Greist had anything to do with his disappearance? Or his own disappearance?"

"Not the Greist I knew."

"Unless, maybe, he didn't have a choice."

I'm sorry lad, today is not your lucky day, Greist had said. *The choice was made for me.* When I'd asked about my dad, Greist had said he was gone. He'd given him—and others—away.

"Have you lived here at the marina all this time?"

"Since I bought it."

"With Greist's money."

"Yes. He told me your mom would remember me buying it."

"You've gone nowhere else? No other world?"

"No other worlds, no other cities here on Earth. This has been my home, and since you left, your mom my only family."

"No family of your own?"

"None I care about."

I didn't push that. It reminded me too much of Brindos. "You never saw Greist or my dad again after Chicago?"

He shook his head.

"No one else came to see you? How did you know our memories had changed?"

"No one came to me. Greist told me beforehand to stay away after the conference, then approach your mom to buy the marina. When I came to do that, things with you guys were different."

"He left you no other instructions? Back-up plans? What to do if some-one came after us or asked about the Envoys?"

"Buy the marina, observe from a distance, protect you. And protect your mom after you left."

"You've never had to—protect her?"

"Never."

"No unusual visitors?"

"No."

"Infrequent guests?"

"Just you."

I ignored that and kept going. "Was Greist part of a larger group who might have put all this together?"

"A conspiracy? No. Not that I know of." He glanced toward his cabin, prob-ably wishing he could get another bottle of beer. "Are we almost done?"

"Look," I said, leaning back in the chair. "I'm blind here. I've got some sight back, I'm seeing some things in shadow, but I still can't walk around without slamming into things. I need more light."

"That's pretty, David. What does it mean?"

"It means I have no fucking clue what's going on." I took out a v-card, the transparent surface as thin as cellophane, and placed it in Tilson's palm. "If you think of anything else, you'll let me know?"

Tilson admired the v-card. "These are slick." His finger brushed the surface and a number of tiny nubs appeared like com nodes on a code card.

"You can ping me with a message with any of the left-hand nodes, or leave a query I can answer. The right-hand nodes will send a slotted message to my comm card"—I didn't tell him about my code card— "if you remember something."

"What about the middle nodes?"

"Small electromagnetic shock."

He whipped his head up, frowning, and took his fingers away from the nodes.

"I'm just kidding," I assured him.

I stood to go, and a moment later he got up and followed me as I edged toward the ramp off the dock. He left the empty Moose Drool bottle on the table. Maybe it was his last bottle, which was why he hadn't offered me any.

"Thanks for your help," I said.

"Griest told me one thing. He said if you ever came around, I should tell you something about there always being holes."

"I heard something like that from Griest. What does it mean?"

"I wish I knew. Griest was afraid to tell me anything specific for fear of something happening to your mom. Or you. I'm sorry. I'm not trying to derail your investigation."

"That's okay. I believe you. I believe you even if I don't completely understand it."

"You may not remember me," he said, "but I remember you and everything about you and your mother during the time before your memory alteration. Rest assured, I'll keep watching your mom. I have no reason not to."

"Thanks. I know you will."

Knowing he was looking after Mom eased my mind. But he couldn't be with her always, and, for me, that was a problem. When I got back to the lake house, I would ask another favor of Jennifer Lisle, a request for a 24/7 security detail for Mom and the lake house. I'd think of a reason why.

I'd just started up the ramp when Tilson called out, "Hey, David."

I turned and stared at him.

When he realized I wasn't going to speak, he said, "You know any Memorese?"

"Very little."

"Greist said he named his daughter Terree after having a vision of being with a future bondmate. You know what her name translates to?"

"In English?"

"Yeah."

In that instant, I thought I knew. Alex Richards in the crate, the tattooed word on his collarbone. God no, not *that* word—

Tilson Hammond shrugged, as if her name in English should have been obvious to me.

I shrugged back at him, my way of saying, "Yeah?"

"Sleep," he said. "It means sleep."

The wind gusted, and the flowering rush seemed to hunker down a little against it. And then the lake was calm and quite at peace.

Eighteen

TEM FORNO LEANED OVER AND HELPED QERRAL UP FROM THE BED. She felt thin and fragile. Her bracelets jangled. Unsteady on her feet, she gripped his arm to achieve some balance, but it was no use. She moaned and sat back down on the edge of the bed.

"Qerral," Forno said. "How long have you been here?" He crouched and looked into her eyes. "And who the hell is Shyler?"

She avoided eye contact, but answered in a raspy voice. "Been here a few days." She picked at the dry skin on her arm. "When did you get back?"

"Qerral, who is Shyler?"

Her eyes darted to and fro before looking at him directly. "You were gone," she said. "You left—"

"Qerral."

"He's my mate."

"*Mate?*"

"A couple weeks ago."

He stood and stared down at her, but she kept her head lowered. It wasn't as if she'd found a new mate days after he left Helkunntanas. That was something, anyway. Still, Qerral had been *his* mate, and he'd not broken the declaration. He'd left without warning, without telling her, regretting the decision almost every day since, but he had never believed she would take on another mate.

He saw RuBy on the bedside table, as well as some squares on the floor. Qerral, hitting the RuBy? How had *that* happened?

Forno said, "I assume it's all official? You declared with the district magistrate?"

Now she looked up. "Yes. Qerral and Shyler Frock, declared."

"Frock? Shyler *Frock?* What the hell kind of name is that?"

"Tem, please."

"You're here in my apartment. Why? Where do you and Shyler live?"

"My old place."

"Where is he, and why are you *here*?"

"I don't know where he is."

"Working?"

"He didn't come home."

"Working where?"

"Tem, you mustn't judge him."

"What do you mean?"

"He's a sniffer."

Forno had been a jeweler in his district. Vendor sometimes. But he hated sniffers as much as he hated RuBy. Pushy tashers. And here was Qerral, married to a sniffer, and RuBy in the apartment, and she used the drug more than she should, having an unusually bad reaction to it. She kept scratching her arm, and Forno looked away in disgust. He should ask her about the Red, how that all got started.

"He works in this district? In Khrem?"

She nodded.

"So he works for Baren Rieser." Forno, having just arrived, had already found his underworld connection.

"I think he's in trouble," she said.

"Why do you think that?"

"He was . . . helping me."

"Getting you more RuBy, you mean. Dropping the tithe. Skimming from the Boss."

"I didn't know how, and didn't ask. But I'm guessing so."

If Baren Rieser or one of his leads had found out about it, Shyler Frock had become a liability.

"Where does he meet Rieser? Or the lead sniffer?"

"I don't know."

"Where does he go when he's not working, besides home? Emporium? RuBy bar?"

Her eyes widened a bit. "RuBy bar," she said. She paused, reached for a red square, and rolled and popped it. "The Mirror."

"Snot." *Juke's bar.* Bad news. "If Juke's on the prowl, or worse, if the Boss himself has taken an interest, Shyler is as bad as dead. Dead as a nail." It wasn't nearly as rewarding to play stupid Helk without Crowell here, but it didn't hurt to practice.

"Tem, don't say that! He has to be alive. We've just declared." Her eyes misted. "He *can't* be dead."

"Worse," Forno said, "if they think you know something about it—and you do—then you're in a planet of hurt, too."

Qerral's leathery face wrinkled in confusion. Clearly, this was news to her.

"Shyler knows about my place?" Forno asked.

She nodded. "Something to fall back on if we needed."

"Who else?"

"No one, I swear."

It wasn't likely Rieser's people knew about this apartment, unless they got it out of Shyler Frock. Qerral was probably safe here for the moment. He could check out the Mirror, learn what he could. It was late, but still early enough for it to be open. Juke would remember him, but he wouldn't know Qerral; he'd never met her, and Forno had never talked about her at work. Safe from reprisals if things went bad. Like now. But maybe Forno had used her name. Had Shyler Frock mentioned her name?

"Are you going to look for him?" Qerral rubbed at her nose, her chapped upper lip. She had a RuBy square in her hand, and she inched it toward her mouth, hoping he wouldn't notice. But he did and resisted the urge to scold her.

"I'll try The Mirror," he said, "but I can't just barge in and start spewing questions."

"You have to find him."

"Maybe I will. I'll check your place, too, in case he simply came home late from a job or something."

She told him her address, but Forno knew it, of course. A few blocks off Desci, behind the Mirror. Shyler Frock, staying with Qerral to keep it close. Made sense in a way, but Forno bet the Helk thought it an inconvenience now.

Qerral forced herself to stand and shuffled toward Forno. She slipped an arm around him and, managing a coy smile, placed her other hand over his heart. "Did you come back to see me?"

No, she wasn't even close. "A new case led me out here."

"Oh." Visibly disappointed. "For the Kenn?"

"Kenn? No, not for a long time, Qerral. I've been working on Earth."

"Earth. *That* cold hunk of rock. Whatever for?"

"It's my partner's home world."

She let go of him and sat down hard on the edge of the bed. "Earth Authority?"

"Private."

"What's the case?" she drawled, halfway between wakefulness and Rubed-out stupor.

Best to keep things simple now. "It's a missing-persons case."

"To find Shyler?"

He humored her by nodding, but she had closed her eyes and fallen back onto the bed, mumbling something about finding Shyler. He swung her legs onto the mattress and covered her again.

Once, he had loved this poor, messed up Helk. *Qerral . . . what happened to you?* He'd left her behind, feeling they had no future while he worked in the underworld. He kept the declaration intact and ran, thinking he could make excuses later if he needed to.

He hadn't expected to run into her now. He'd hoped *not* to, having decided long ago to leave this part of his life behind.

Now Qerral's and his lives had intertwined again.

"Whatever you do, please stay here, Qerral."

"Okay. Just find him."

"I will," he whispered, but, deep down, he didn't expect to.

The Mirror emerged from the shadows, an extension of the thoroughfare's synthetic blackrock, with just enough light seeping out the front window to convince Forno it was still open. Nearer the window, he counted a half dozen or so customers inside sitting at tables, nearly motionless, hunkered over their drinks.

This was what Crowell had wanted him to do. Find out what he could about Rieser. Put feelers out, see if anything came up about Terree's dad. Or Crowell's.

But stay away from Abby Graff.

Not that he *wanted* to come face to face with Graff. Talk old times? Not high on his list. Maybe she'd heard something during his absence about the cover the Kenn had provided for him. He hoped he'd extracted himself from Swain without leaving a trail. No one else in the Union had made any connections as he fled Helkunntanas to find Dave Crowell.

But there was Juke.

And Baren Rieser, who Crowell and Brindos had chased across the Union years before.

And maybe Shyler Frock. Alive or dead, finding out what had happened to him could help break the case.

Forno entered slowly, but took in everything at once, re-familiarizing himself with The Mirror. Things seemed no different from the last time he'd been here. The paysticks at the tables the same, the models about two generations behind. The same flashscapes on the wall, depictions of bright thoroughfares, T-shuttles, and the Khrem terminal and tunnel. The air was stale, tainted with cinnamon and sweat.

Behind the bar: not Juke, but a human woman, tall, wide, formidable. Black hair short but scrunched and gelled, spiking wildly from her head. She wore a black collared shirt and a white vest. Glasses clinked as she pulled them from a steaming washer beneath the bar and slid them into the grooves of the overhead racks.

Surprising. Not too many things would keep Juke away from his bar, particularly this late at night as it neared closing time. Nothing like a grumpy, moody Second Clan with a reputation for dispensing violent justice to get unruly patrons out of his establishment.

On his way to the bar, Forno had a moment of panic thinking of Juke gone from The Mirror and Qerral hiding out at his place. Had he made a mistake leaving her alone?

"Ten minutes," the woman said.

It was later than he thought. "No more drinks?"

"Sure." She looked up at him as he loomed over her. "If you can drink it in ten minutes."

"Ale, then."

"Six." She tapped the paystick beside him on the bar.

He scrounged six credits from his overcoat pocket. As he dropped them in, a paystick behind them snicked when another customer bought some RuBy.

"You're new," Forno said.

She shrugged. "If you call a year working here new."

"I've been gone most of that time. What happened to Juke?"

"What do you mean, what happened to Juke?"

"He's not here. He's always here."

"Putting out a fire." She extended her hand. "I'm Mayira."

He took it carefully and shook. "Tem," he said. He decided to hold back the last name, although he didn't expect Mayira the "new" girl to know it.

"Whaddya know, Tem?" she said, pouring his ale. "Juke, obviously."

He kept looking down her, accentuating his size, hoping to make her a little uncomfortable, before realizing she'd seen all the Helk clans here in Khrem, even in a mostly human district.

"Sure, Juke," he said. "Days spent here. District deadbeat, working the streets, running the Red, making trouble."

She placed the ale in front of him. "Ah, that's how you know Juke."

"Maybe you remember Thurston."

"The old Boss. Sure, I know of him. You worked for him?"

Forno sipped his ale. "I was more of—an independent. Under the rug, so to speak, maybe an annoyance, but nothing Thurston would trip over and worry about."

"I see. And what do you do now?"

"Still an independent."

"A nosy one."

"Don't forget annoying," he grumbled. "It's sort of what I do these days."

She nodded, doing something under the bar that clicked and whirred. Paysticks behind him rattled, powering down.

He said, "I'm guessing Juke won't be back in tonight."

"I'm closing up for him."

"Tomorrow?"

"Sure. His mess will undoubtedly be cleaned up by then."

"So who's the mess?"

She eyed him, frowning. "If you know Juke, you know better than to ask that."

No time to delay further, with The Mirror closing in moments. He had to force the issue. "I'm looking for someone."

"That narrows it down."

"Technically, several someones. But let's start with a guy named Shyler Frock."

He expected to see signs of recognition, but she went about the tasks of cleaning the bar and putting washed glasses where they belonged, seemingly unimpressed with the name.

"Doesn't sound familiar," Mayira said.

"Fourth Clan Helk? Might've been in here a day or so ago."

"I wasn't here most of last week."

"He's a sniffer." There, he'd said it. "And we both know who he works for."

She paused mid-wipe. "You probably want to be careful right now," she said, her voice low, her face as dark as her spiked hair.

"Careful about what? Look, when I lived here, Juke worked for Thurston, the old Boss, and now he works for the new Boss. Baren Rieser's the King of Khrem, everyone knows that, and Juke knows a lot of what Rieser knows."

Her pupils dilated as she stared at him, sizing him up. Taking in everything she could about this unfamiliar Second Clan Helk talking big about her employer and the Boss of Khrem. Forno liked putting her there, but knew full well that his forwardness could quickly escalate into something dangerously unexpected.

He turned and again surveilled the room, suddenly aware of the other patrons, who seemed disinterested. None looked capable of walking very far or fast without falling on their faces.

He glanced back at Mayira.

"Closing," she said, still staring at him, but her voice resonated throughout The Mirror. "Time to go."

A couple of patrons behind Forno grumbled.

"No arguments," she said, sidestepping toward the open end of the bar nearest to the main door. Still, she kept her eyes on Forno.

He smiled and started to inch off his stool.

"Stay," she told him. She came around the bar with her rag and picked up some glasses as other patrons obediently moved toward the exit. She wiped down tables and locked and telescoped paysticks into the hollow cores of the hardwood, smiling as she did, until everyone had left . . . except her and Forno.

Mayira locked the door and enabled the bar's security with a flick of her hand against a sensor. A hot zone shield shimmered into existence around the door and main window, light blue for an instant before fading from sight.

After a glance at Forno, she nodded at one of the empty tables and sat down. Forno joined her at a heavy bench beside the table. With the patrons gone and the paysticks out of sight, the cinnamon odor soon dissipated. Fine with him.

Wiping the tabletop that she had cleaned moments earlier, Mayira said, "Shyler Frock was a stupid, ignorant Helk, more concerned about his own well-being than about the bottom line."

Forno said, "The bottom line according to Baren Rieser."

"Business is business."

"So he's dead."

"What?"

"Past tense. You said 'Shyler Frock was a stupid Helk.' Was that Juke's fire to put out tonight?"

"I'm in no position to say anything about what Juke does or doesn't do."

The set of her jaw indicated he high degree of discomfort. She had to worry about Juke, but she also had to fear the Boss. Juke might be a hard, cold tasher, but Rieser was unpredictable. Forno knew that much from what Crowell had told him, and from DataNet profiles.

"Mayira, can we stop with the runaround?"

"Runaround?"

"You know that Shyler Frock is dead. Juke killed him."

Anger in her eyes, she threw her rag at the tabletop. "No."

"No, he's not dead?"

"No, Juke didn't kill him."

"So he's dead."

Mayira said nothing, but Forno had the answer from the way she sat back in her chair, touched her ear with her right hand, and then reached higher and twisted the spikes of her hair. At which point an odd softness claimed her face. Oh yes, Shyler Frock was dead. No doubt in his mind.

Poor Qerral.

"I need a name," he said.

"The other 'somebody' you're looking for?"

"Maybe. Who killed Frock?"

She patted her spikes, not wanting to answer.

"Give me *some*thing."

"Who are you, really? Authority? Kenn?"

"I am who I said I am."

"Tem."

"Yes. I'm on a private case."

"You're a private investigator?"

He nodded. "And I have a sidekick. Somewhere."

"A *sidekick*. Do you even know what that means?"

"My partner's a fool for old antiques, old sayings, obscure references. That one, I know." Crowell would've puked if he'd heard Forno call him a sidekick.

"You can understand my hesitation, Tem. This is all I have. My life and my job."

"No family?"

"No."

A lot of that going around. "Give me a hint," he said.

She managed a smile. "Is that a question they teach you at P.I. school?"

"On the second day, right after 'I need a name' and 'Give me something.'"

Now Mayira laughed, her face visibly lightening. Sometimes, humans were almost pleasant to look at.

A moment later, she sank deeper into her chair, as if trying to hide from him. "I can give you the name of someone you might be able to talk to," she said, "but he didn't kill Shyler Frock. You'll have to believe me on that."

"Okay. Who is he?"

"You have to promise I'm kept clear of this."

"I'll do everything I can."

"Promise me."

"Promise. I've forgotten your name already."

She nodded, apparently satisfied. "He's a lead sniffer for Rieser."

Forno took a guess, figuring it wouldn't hurt to throw his name out there. "Alex Richards."

She blinked. "Richards? No."

"I wouldn't mind talking to Richards as well."

"I don't even think he's on Helkunntanas right now."

That was true, if Forno had actually been right about it having been Richards outside the Emirates Tower in Seattle, kissing Terree. Forcing a kiss, more likely. Cozying up to Abby Graff, Rieser's competition. So did that make it three Alex Richards Thin Men now? The dead one in the morgue, the one on Earth, and one here?

"This sniffer," Mayira said, her voice sounding quite certain, "is the Boss's right hand man. Talk to him and you're pretty close to Rieser. Some say he's destined to take over Khrem, if and when Rieser calls it quits."

"And his name?"

She paused only briefly before answering. "Vanderberg Parr."

Parr. Forno had never heard the name. But now he had it, and now he had something to tell Crowell.

For the time being, he also had Qerral to worry about.

Nineteen

EVEN THOUGH THE NUMBER 8 ON BAREN RIESER'S BALD HEAD HAD stopped glowing, its afterimage imprinted itself onto Vanderberg Parr's retina. He tried to gather his wits and make sense of what he'd just seen.

Rieser apparently coming back from a deep sleep or coma, thanks, perhaps, to his tattooed head. Before that, Cara Landry appearing out of nowhere, then standing immobile for fifteen minutes before awakening and seemingly working with Rieser to do the impossible: make the Boss's guests and thousands of squares of RuBy disappear from the Quarry. Parr licked his lips, suddenly feeling that he hadn't had a square of the Red in days.

Just another wild evening in the House.

At least that's what he kept telling himself. He needed to stay and figure out what was going on, although leaving the House was hardly an option with the Boss and the Ultra staring him down, and the blaster back in Rieser's grip.

Number 8. That was your number.

"Confused, are we?" Rieser said to Parr. "Hard to take in?"

The Ultra fidgeted on the couch, but made no attempt to speak.

"A little."

"Understandable."

"I don't care if the Ultra army is on its way behind Cara Landry," Parr said. "I just want to know, in plain, easy-to-understand terms, what the fuck happened. Tell me 'Careful, Vanderberg' one more time, or call me a special creature one more time without explaining what you mean, I'll head out the door and never come back. And you can decide to shoot me or not as I leave. I don't care."

Rieser smiled sympathetically, letting the blaster hang limp at his side. It was supposed to reassure Parr, he figured, but it didn't. For all his bravado, Parr still expected Rieser to put him in his place, maybe even shoot him right now, decide the Thin Man wasn't worth the trouble, for all the earlier hype about his being the only one who mattered. According to the Ultra.

Parr wanted to go up to Cara Landry and kick her in the head. Take whatever means necessary to kill her during her low-power mode. She could barely talk, had hardly moved, and seemed incapable of doing any serious harm. In many ways, she came off as weak, maybe even inconsequential, at least compared to the Boss.

She hadn't even bombarded his head with her spooky mind talk.

"You want to walk out that door," Rieser said, "you go ahead. I won't shoot you. Let's see how far you get."

Parr fumed, upset that the Boss had casually dismissed his threats. "I'll just follow Richards out, maybe, considering he took off unnoticed during your little circus act."

"Oh, I noticed," Rieser said. "C'mon, walk with me." The blaster still at his side, he led Parr to the steel door of the Pool Room and opened it as easily as Richards had earlier. Not a difficult task from this side.

Parr glanced back at Cara Landry, who still sat on the couch staring at the blackrock of the Quarry. He followed Rieser in, and the stark reality of those five cots, empty, reminded him of the bodies in the Quarry that had disappeared. But a body lay on the floor of the Pool Room like an afterthought.

"He'd have survived in the Quarry," Rieser said. "This room is unique. Not always in phase, so to speak. It's not kind to those who try and hide here. It could kill you, or send you on a very long trip." He smiled. "Depending on your point of view."

Parr had no idea what he meant. So much for the earlier threats to Rieser about needing to know what was going on in easy-to-understand terms.

Rieser turned his attention to the body on the floor and kicked it hard with his bare foot. No movement. "He was working for Graff."

It was indeed Alex Richards; Parr recognized the blue jacket. Using his foot as a lever, Rieser turned the body over.

The jacket flapped open, revealing the sniffer's black T-shirt, which Rieser put his bare foot on, his toes inches from the dead man's face. And he was dead, Parr was sure of it. *Sniff that, you son of a bitch.*

He really hadn't liked Richards, but he was surprised to find him dead. All of this was coming fast. Too fast. Parr's forehead flushed, his hands trembling now, aching for RuBy. How had all the RuBy disappeared like that, at the same time as the bodies of the Boss's guests?

Rieser stuck a hand in front of Parr's face, then twisted his wrist, opened his palm, and revealed a single square of RuBy. Rieser could be giving him the

only square left in the House. An offering of peace? Or was it a simple necessity, keeping the RuBy-freaked Thin Man cogent and manageable?

Parr took the square, rolled it quickly, and popped it in his mouth. No
time to even think about enjoying the experience. Parr glanced again at the
now-dark 8 on Rieser's head.

Rieser noticed. "Number eight was for you, but number nine will be for
me," he said.

"I don't know what that means."

"Your first time *traveling*."

Parr shook his head. "Not helping."

"We traveled somewhere else. It was a test."

"So you said. But where?" *A place where bodies and RuBy disappeared.*

"You will know soon enough. Your education will begin, the waiting complete. You are taking over Khrem."

Parr gulped. *Taking over—*

"Do you understand?"

"Yes, sir."

"For me, it was my last complete round trip."

For once, Parr heard disappointment in Rieser's voice. The Boss was losing something, giving up some kind of power no human had experienced
before. At least as far as Parr knew. Glowing numbers and glowing hands?
Yeah, not a human trick.

"We have work to do on Helkunntanas," Rieser said. "Take down the districts, including Abby Graff and her jewelers and sniffers. And when they fall,
so will the infrastructure of Helkunntanas, and the Union will follow. And
when that falls, the Ultras will be ready."

"How can all that happen any time soon?"

Rieser spread his arms. "The ways of the Ultras."

"So what am I supposed to do?"

"Learn from Cara."

"Now?"

"Later. You have a job to do."

"What's that?"

"Go to Khrem. Find Juke and tell him to help you."

Parr frowned. "Help with what?"

"We have a little problem with a local."

"Shyler's mate?"

Rieser nodded, then took a moment to sit down on the Helk-sized couch, the black material giving only slightly under his weight. He leaned back, and only his head made contact with the cushion.

"Found a message node on my comm, before you woke. Juke didn't find her at her place."

"Just a fucking Helkette," Parr said. "Juke's the best, he'll take care of it. Why does he need my help?"

Rieser sat up straight, still dwarfed by the couch. "Because he returned to the bar and saw a different problem. A Second Clan talking with Mayira."

"Know him?"

"Juke remembers him."

"A sniffer?"

"No. Vendor, I think." He sat straight on the couch, rubbing his neck. "He worked for Thurston. Then he disappeared. We thought he was dead. Maybe gone over to Graff."

"So he's not dead?"

"No." There was a long silence before Rieser continued. "Now we have three problems."

"Three?"

"Mayria, too."

Parr gulped. New girl, not going to make it. Too bad. Parr had liked her well enough.

"No loose ends, Vanderberg. Khrem is yours now. Juke knows this. You have to be who you are, because no one can find out about you and your mission, about what the Ultras are bringing. Not until it's time, when the Union can finally appreciate their peace."

Parr remembered his first days as a sniffer, the secret Trademark working into the good graces of Baren Rieser. Even though the Boss hinted about his special status, Parr spent many nights worrying he might take a wrong step and not wake up the next morning. But he *would* wake up. Wake up drenched in sweat, the not-memories (do you know who I am?) crashing around his RuBy-hazed brain in the already stifling Helk heat, his mouth bone dry, his hands gripping the crash pad so tight he couldn't let go without a concerted effort.

At least it would be quick for Mayira.

"I'll take care of it," he said.

Rieser smiled, but it seemed to Parr that a hint of sadness seeped into it. It wasn't his district anymore. The Boss knew it wasn't up to him to contain these kinds of problems.

"What will Cara do?" Parr asked.

"Bring to a close a situation that has been more than troublesome."

Parr thought he knew what the Boss meant. Or, more accurately, *who*. "That guy who stopped the Ultras. What's-his-name."

"David Crowell." Anger flashing in his eyes, Rieser rubbed his head thoughtfully. "You don't know him. Trust me, he's no one to worry about. Much of who he is was dealt with long ago. You have your own work to do. After you take care of the Helk and Mayira, come back here. I'm adding your automatic passage to the House, and you'll understand at last what is at stake. You'll help Alex Richards with another delicate issue."

Parr stared at the Pool Room door. "But he's dead."

"Yes," Rieser said, "but his copy isn't."

Parr snapped his attention back to Rieser. "He's a Thin Man?"

Rieser inclined his head slightly. "Several copies on Earth, but the one we're concerned with is on his way back."

Parr had wondered why Richards was at the House—that rumor about being off planet. "The copy works for you?"

Rieser nodded. "He'll be here soon enough. He's done a nice job taking care of the competition."

The knowledge came to Parr like a jump-slot beacon morphing in the black of space. "Oh shit. Abby Graff. She's on Earth?"

"Stuck. She'll get caught by Earth Authority or the NIO and that will be that. Before I go for good, Richards will come to the House. He's bringing me a present."

"What present?"

"A Memor." Rieser's earlier anger now fueled his decidedly wicked smile. "Not just any Memor. It's Terree, the daughter of Greist Sahl-kla."

"He's the Donor, isn't he? Cara mentioned the Doner."

Rieser said, "Yes, the Donor who made everything else possible."

"Everything?"

"It's time for you to know the truth about the Donor."

"What truth?"

"The truth about where Greist Sahl-kla is, and why he can never, ever be found."

Parr nodded, fascinated. He glanced over at the couch, but Cara was already standing, sliding toward him. The Ultra's fingers glowed.

"You can do this without us," Rieser said, "on your own. But until you understand more, Cara will help you return."

"Return?"

"Travel home. You'll see what I mean. I'll tell you everything when you come back. Everything I know. The rest will come from Cara." He pointed at Parr. "And you."

Parr would know everything, Rieser assured him. But really, he only needed to know one thing. *Do you know who I am?*

Twenty

THE COURTESY VAN PICKED ME UP AT THE MARINA AND DROPPED ME off safely at Mom's. Shortly afterward, outside the cabin and down by the water, I put a call through to Tem Forno on my code card, the illegal tracker prog bubbling up as a red node that would've sent most of Authority into a tizzy if not buffered.

Unauthorized pings through the jump slot. Good thing Jennifer had agreed to look the other way.

"You've missed me," Forno said, voice scratchy and distant. Hell, he *was* distant.

"On several occasions. One of these days, I won't miss."

"Oh, funny. I jogged right into that one."

I didn't acknowledge his act. "What've you got?"

A pause followed, not slot interference. Forno didn't know how to say something, or he was thinking about holding back.

"Forno?"

"Found a contact," he finally said.

"Anyone I know?"

Pause.

"Forno?"

"My ex-mate, Qerral."

"You had a *mate*? What the hell, Forno?"

"Yeah, I didn't tell you. Sorry, but it was a part of my past I was trying to forget."

"You don't forget something like that."

"I was doing a pretty good job of it until today."

"Anything else?"

"I'm looking. I'm thinking there might be another Alex Richards over here."

"Another?" The Ultras had made more than a few copies of the same person, but why Alex Richards?

"Maybe. I'm at The Mirror, a RuBy bar. It just closed, but I talked to someone and found a name associated with Rieser."

"Who's that?"

"Vanderberg Parr."

"Parr. Don't know him. How tight is he with Rieser?"

"His main guy. Supposedly set to take over Khrem when Rieser's done. I know nothing else about him at this point."

"Be careful."

"Careful as a Helk on a high wire."

"That's doesn't instill me with any confidence."

Forno waited, this time because of actual slot static, before continuing. "Anything on your end?"

"A few things. My mom remembers nothing, and a guy who keeps an eye on her out at the lake likes Moose Drool."

Forno said, "I'm not even going to ask."

"And Terree's name means sleep."

"No rock unturned in your pursuit of the truth."

The slot-tracker prog warbled a warning, most likely because local Authority had got wind of it. Jennifer and the NIO might ignore the ping, but Authority would be another story. Time to terminate the prog.

"Just be careful," I said.

"You told me that already."

"I'll talk to you later."

Forno grunted, and the slot line degraded and threw out static before he could say anything.

I pinged Jennifer Lisle to request the security detail on Mom's lake house. Jennifer was still in Seattle, and the assistant director, Steven Hardy, had joined her. I still wasn't sure I should tell her about Terree and Greist, or about the search for my dad.

"You think your mom's in danger?" Lisle asked. "From Rieser? Why?"

I'd set my code card to show the special ops director in flat mode, an actual holo rendering, and sound transferred to the tiny ear stud she'd given me now snug in my ear. She wore a light sweater featuring navy-blue and sky-blue vertical stripes.

"A hunch," I said. "Isn't that enough considering all the shit going on?"

"Sure."

"There's a guy named Tilson Hammond," I said. "He bought the marina from my mom when my dad disappeared. He's very protective of her and looks after her. Watching, sometimes, without her being aware of it."

"He's okay?"

"He's okay."

"Did you tell him you were adding security?"

"He'll figure it out."

"He won't shoot them, I hope."

"He's smart enough, if your team is smart enough not to shoot *him*. He'll know who they are. Unless you want to make sure and paint N-I-O on their foreheads."

She blurred on the code card, a slight buffering. "Okay. First detail's on route from New York. They'll be in position before the day's through. Learn anything else from your mom?"

"Not much. Just needed to check in, talk to her some about Dad."

"I'm sure there was more to it, but it's good you did that. Don't miss your ride."

"I won't. I'll be on Egret Station by this afternoon, and from there I've got the slot to Crossbill and Helkunntanas, thanks to you. I should meet up with Forno sometime tomorrow."

I closed the conversation and, stuffing code card and my hands into my pants pocket, I trudged up the hill to the house. It was almost noon, and the glare of the early morning sun had vanished from the big picture windows. Mom waved at me through one of them, and I wanted to wave back, but thought twice, my hands comfortably in my pocket . . .

And time slowed.

I heard the ticking of my watch in my ears.

Mom stood framed in the window. I could see her. *See* her. But something had changed. She had turned . . . misty, like a mirage. Had she waved? Or had I imagined she was *about* to wave?

Time slowed some more.

I could still see her, but also, there, in plain sight, was my dad.

My dad?

He wasn't in the window. He occupied a space in front of her, outside the lake house, as if projected in the foreground, a holo-like image, but real enough, even though I could see through it to my mom waving . . . or preparing to wave.

I was in the Memory.

But it was different this time. I was conscious of my surroundings. I hadn't passed out, and as far as I could tell, no one near me had instigated the transition.

But *something* had brought on this experience. Had I somehow entered it on my own? I shivered, uncomfortable that I could do this, especially without knowing how. Was this what Terree had meant by having to *own* my memories? *Even if they come from someone else.*

The sensation was not unlike a waking dream, but the dream included two realities blended like a double exposure from an antique film camera.

This was different, almost as if my body fought a complete immersion into the Memory.

My dad, however, gained prominence in the dream. My dad as I remembered him, from the summer he disappeared. It could've been the Hawaiian shirt—white and pink and blue—and the matching blue trunks that I remembered. The wide smile. The bushy eyebrows and the stubbled cheeks.

He walked down the hill to me. My mother dwindled in the distance until I could no longer make her out, as if she'd walked away from the window, having waved at me already. . . or decided not to wave.

"You're not mad at me?" I said as he came close.

He put his arm around me, pulled me to him. "About what?"

"Tricking my Emirates page at the Temonus Symposium. Sneaking out."

"Yes, I heard about that."

"I thought you might be, you know, mad or something."

He pushed me away quick, held on, and pulled me back, slamming me into his body. He did that when he was in a good mood and wanted me to know that all was well.

"I did far worse things to worry my parents," he said.

"But you're an Envoy, and I put you in a tight spot."

He laughed, and now he did let go of me.

"Why is that funny?"

"You're so apologetic."

"So?"

"It wasn't a big deal because"—He reached over and elbowed me in the ribs—"there was backup."

"Backup?"

"You may have slipped past the page, but another hotel worker saw you and kept you in sight. Kept me updated about your *illicit* trip through Midwest City." He said "illicit" in a sarcastic tone implying I'd done nothing wrong exploring on my own.

"Then you know where I went? Where I ended up?"

"Yes, I do." He smiled again, this time sympathetically. "The historic Helk district. You wandered into it and got lost, but the hotel worker never lost sight of you. He said you were perfectly safe, and you slipped the notice of most Helks on the street. At least until you got to this restaurant, hungry, and stumbled in."

My waking dream faltered at this mention of a restaurant in the Helk district. Some of my current reality asserted itself: The lake house stood by itself, and Dad appeared more and more mist-like and diaphanous.

When he spoke again, he solidified as if nothing had happened. "He said you were in there a half hour. Eating, right?"

I nodded. "Who followed me?"

"You came out," he went on, "and he followed you until you returned to the downtown district. You bought one of those meat sausages from a street vendor, and then slipped back into the Orion Hotel, thinking your little jaunt had gone unnoticed. That about right?"

I nodded, embarrassed he knew about the Helk district. Hell, even about the gabobileck. "Who was it, Dad?"

"No one you knew. He was supposed to be on duty, but he felt it important to follow you, since most Envoy kids aren't allowed out of sight of escorts or pages."

I figured it out. "The concierge."

"That's right," he said. "Joe was his name."

Joe. My non-Memory self understood the implications, but I was still locked in on the Memory and followed it.

Dad walked farther down the hill toward the lake and I fell in behind him, hands in my pockets. He gazed at the lake and sighed, perfectly content, not in the least upset with me. It seemed quite strange that this was the case.

"Joe contacted your page, your page caught up with you, and that was that."

"I don't like my page," I said. "Can't I have a different one?"

"Oh, ho, is that it?" Dad turned back to me.

"He's barely older than I am, and he's annoying."

"Four years older. It's enough."

"I don't like him," I repeated. "He's rude, and he tells me things that aren't true."

"David—"

"He says humans are the weakest species in the Union, that we're territorial and imperialistic and someday we'll all have to die so stronger races can live in peace without us."

"Oh, please, David, you're telling stories."

"He talks crap about the new order of the Union. *Please* don't let me have Alex as a page again."

Abruptly, Dad's smile disappeared, and a stern glare replaced it. He jabbed a finger at me. "That's not your choice to make. Get used to the idea, because not only is he your page for the trip to Chicago, he's escorting you there from here."

"He's going to be *here*?"

"Yes, it was the easiest way. The conference is huge, and pages are hard to come by. He asked for the assignment, and I couldn't refuse a sure thing. I can't be worrying about you while I'm there. Greist says this is the most important conference to come along in decades."

My whole body slumped. "When will he be here?"

"I'm already here," said a snooty voice behind me.

I groaned and turned.

Mom was back in the window, waving at me as the Memory inevitably collapsed. I knew, too, that Dad had already misted away behind me.

My page glared at me, his eyes darting about wildly. Then he winked malevolently and melted away.

I followed Alex Richards out of the Memory and waved back at Mom.

Alex Richards, an Emirates page.

I'd gone back inside the house, and now stared out the window at the lake; Mom was in the kitchen baking up something sweet.

She, of course, had seen nothing unusual during the incident in front of the lake house. I had found my own way into the Memory—somehow—without prompting from anyone, and this time I'd shared it with Dad, with Mom in the background, real-time. I still didn't understand the Memory, and experienced it only as a bystander: a bystander who'd bought into the whole thing. Why not? It had helped me discover my real life before Dad disappeared, and Tilson and Terree had acknowledged much of it.

But now—Alex *Richards*?

Someone from my past. No wonder I'd reacted so negatively to him when I found him in the warehouse. Found him twice, actually. I'd also found him dead . . . in a younger body. He'd affected me the same way in my youth. I wasn't sure yet how he connected to Greist and the coming of the Ultras, or to my dad.

At this point, the disappearance of Richards seemed more important than the *death* of Richards. Someone had put him in my path. I hadn't simply been following an unfaithful husband. It had all been a setup, and it made my blood boil to think I'd been tricked.

I needed to talk to Liz Richards. After all, she had put me on the case.

What bothered me most was that I'd stumbled into the Restaurant in the Helk district as a kid. The one Dorie said she'd worked at, the place where she'd found Brindos.

And I'd been with my dad at the Orion Hotel, and the concierge there had followed me.

Joe.

Jesus. Joseph Sando? The old man I'd gone to a baseball game with in Brindos's honor. The old man—a different Ultra version of him—whose antimatter core detonated at the mortaline vault on Ribon. That Joe?

My heart sank as I let the implications sink in. First Brindos. Now me. I'd been inside a place that Terl Plenko had frequented, and eventually owned.

More and more, I understood why all the events from the past year had come through me, everything landing in my lap. I had pulled Brindos into the whole mess, and look where it had gotten him.

Bile rose to my throat. Goddamn it. They'd been in my way, in my dad's way, for many years, and I'd had no chance to get away from it. I *thought* I had. Thought I'd put those demons—those Ultras—to rest for good.

But I'd known some of this, in my gut, the moment I'd seen the word Ultra painted on Alex Richard's collarbone.

I needed to let Forno know. I also had to call Jennifer and change my travel plans again.

I dug my hands deep into my pockets, breathing deep to calm myself. My left hand felt something slick, and I frowned putting my fingers around it.

When I brought it out, I blinked in surprise at the yellowish square of paper. *AmBer.* How the hell had that ended up in my pocket? I'd never touched that nasty shit before. I remembered the RuBy squares I'd slipped into my pocket in the tent city and shuddered.

And grew dizzy with the disturbing memory. It almost felt like the Memory wanted to pull me back in. I rolled my hands together and turned the AmBer square into a crumbled ball. I flung it at the waste can while heading down the stairs to my old room.

There, I accessed the DataNet with my code card and downloaded software and freesource programs I thought I might need, guided silently by the ghost of Brindos, who'd always loved the fun gadgets, and who reveled in obtaining and hiding them on our code cards. Illegally of course. Remembering old contacts and breaking through a number of underground data-dens, I descended deep into the DataNet basement for some of the more questionable progs, including the old crossword cipher program, as well as an image blender that distorted reality within a ten-foot radius, and an electromagnetic transblocker that could neutralize communications for five hundred feet, even inside an enclosed space. I doubt that I hid them well enough, but it didn't matter now.

Finally, I rummaged around in the double-door closet, pulling aside old clothes, coats, and life vests, until I found the loose panel I knew would be there. I pried it out with a coat hanger. A portable charger, good only for finger capacitors, rested in the cavity. I pulled it out of the opening, withdrew from the closet, and sat on the bed. I blew dust off the charger. I'd placed it in the closet cubby almost four years earlier, when I'd taken on the NIO Movement commission and Director Bardsley had me install my finger caps. I'd never expected to use the thing but, well, it was Mom, after all. Whatever help I might be able to give her while with her, regardless of bureaucratic mandates, I had to give. Insurance.

I'd never used it.

Now I might have need of the electric handshake. I plugged the unit in and hoped it still worked. It hummed promisingly as I flicked the capacitors to charge mode, and when I inserted my fingers into the slots, the suction felt right.

I sat there, silent, until the readouts glowed green under my fingernails.

Twenty-one

As the afternoon slipped away, I showed Mom both the hard copy pictures I had of Alex Richards: the one Liz Richards had given me, and the one from Jennifer, with Alex noticeably older. She had no memory of Richards, although she appeared to study the photos closely, as if she had a dim inkling of a memory, but could not put things together in the parts of her brain Greist had tampered with.

I sent a message to Jennifer about the latest change in my itinerary. She warned me not to wait too long and miss the flight window to Helkunntanas that she'd finagled from the paper pushers. The tracker prog did its best to establish a connection with Forno through the slot, but Earth Authority had likely registered the earlier ping and shut it down.

I took the shuttle out of Lakeside, had a stiff shot of Temonus whiskey on board, charged it to the NIO, and returned to Seattle, a half hour flight. Once away from the port, I commandeered an intercity shuttle to the Emirates Tower.

Depending on what I found out, and assuming Terree hadn't skipped town, I would likely call in that extra seat to Helkunntanas and let Jennifer in on the whole mess. I could've called Terree directly, but something was hincky at the Emirates Tower, and this was my chance to figure out what.

I'd never been inside the Emirates Tower.

I rethought that. I couldn't *remember* having been inside the Emirates Tower. In my youth, had I come in here with my dad? Again, I couldn't remember these trips Terree—and now the Memory—had told me about. This place was both a hostel and a staging area for many Envoys en route to whatever tasks they had across the Union. Still, nothing in my brain connected those childhood times with this mysterious, oversized building.

A security locker near double glass doors beckoned insistently. The instructions etched on its surface prompted the stowing of any and all firearms and hazardous materials inside the locker, for this was the domain of Envoys, where peaceful coexistence allegedly reigned at all times.

There went my blaster.

The glass doors whispered open after I DNA-locked the weapon in the protruding locker. I entered, looked behind me as the doors shut, and checked the street, still visible through their crystal clear glass. Evening was settling in. Would any daylight remain by the time I got out of here?

Inside the Emirates Tower, I quickly familiarized myself with its layout. The foyer was a maze of glass and dull silver beams. Holo windows built into the glass flickered to life at irregular intervals. Nope. No memories of this.

The windows, indistinguishable from regular glass, grew slightly opaque just before holos populated them, showing views of a Union world from orbit, many of the world's attractions and a scrolling bulleted list of its DataNet stats. Then there appeared a graphic of the Emirates symbol, and a smiling actor looking first at you, then sidelong at the data, as if all of it were irresistably entertaining. How much did the Emirates pay their spokespeople? Actors didn't have much work these days, for they had to compete with the U-One government network and a host of virtual amusements.

I watched as these holos rotated through the eight planets of the Union. Earth popped up with virtual immersion star Ted Hartman looking on, our planet's symbol a collection of circles and lines forming a representation of a hearth—"keep the home fires burning," came a famous but mostly forgotten line of poetry—to indicate where everything related to Union started. Sort of. I had no trouble tearing my gaze away from the windows.

Inset into one glass panel, a bubble-like protuberance not unlike a transport lock-out bubble housed a receptionist, a good-looking guy with perfect brown hair who beamed at me after I noticed him looking bored as hell. I swear the smile grew bigger the closer I got to the bubble.

"Worlds Away," he said, stating the company's motto, a bit too brightly, at that. "I'm Nick. How can I help you, sir? A tour of the facility?" He brought it down a notch. "A problem to resolve? An Envoy request?"

"I'm here to see Terree," I said, flashing my code card and its NIO-approved ident setting.

He barely acknowledged it. "A voucher? Forward thinking there, sir, setting up the tour in advance."

Yeah, I could see they were extremely busy. Jesus.

"It's not a voucher, Nick. I'm a private detective. I'm working closely on a case with the National Intelligence Organization. The NIO."

"To see who again?"

I struggled not to let my impatience show. "Terree. A Memor. She's here awaiting results of my investigation. She has protection, special Envoy eminence. She's a daughter of a known Envoy."

A missing Envoy at that.

He stared at me briefly, apparently dumbfounded, before brightening up once more. "Oh! A Memor. Yes, well, we don't get too many Memors here at the Tower."

"That's why I figured it'd be easy for you to remember her, Nick. Orange hair? Pony tail? Puffy lips?"

He laughed. "Oh, very funny, sir. Very funny." He held up a finger. "Give me a moment, please."

I waited, and he waited, smiling at me. Only after I nodded did he nod back and exit via the back of the bubble. As soon as he did, I could not see him anywhere amid the glass panels to the left or right.

He'd vanished just as my memories of this place had vanished.

A good five minutes passed before Nick returned with a less amiable supervisor. As they entered the bubble, she walked stiffly, radiating an air of importance that belied her probable standing within the Emirates Tower. Her one-piece gray suit seemed almost painted on, her black hair unnaturally straight.

"May I see your ident, please, sir?" she said

I showed my code card, nodes deactivated, and she reached through the bubble to scan its surface with her index finger, which was coded, most likely, with a cobweb tracker etched into her prints' grooves and whorls. This quick whisk across the flashpaper brought up my vital information, but because my code card was NIO-issue, nothing truly sensitive.

"Mr. Crowell," the woman said. "I have heard of you, of course."

"Good to be heard of."

"I'm Amanda Hoban, director of Envoy services. How can I help you?"

"Amanda, I'm looking for Terree," I said. I gave Nick the evil eye, and he did his best to keep his smile broad and friendly. But he had trouble, nonetheless, and that was fishy as hell. "I gave her name to Nick, here. Honestly, ma'am, getting her to me should not be a difficult task."

"Mr. Crowell," she said, "no Memors are staying in the Tower at this time."

I frowned at her and said, "Of course she's here. My partner saw her here, called her even—"

"No call came into the Emirates exchange, sir," Nick piped up. Smile almost gone now. "I log in all calls."

"A private number," I said.

"No number is private inside the Tower," Amanda Hoban said. "Surely you're aware of that regulation."

"I've heard of it, but it wouldn't be private outside the Tower."

"Well, then she would not be *in* the Tower."

"Come on, director!" I glared to emphasize my seriousness.

"Well, even if she was here, you're not on NIO official business to talk to this Terree."

"How do you know that?"

"Your itinerary includes transport to Helkunntanas, on a different matter."

"And you know that *how?*" I glanced at my code card, still in my right hand.

"Not your code card," she said, amusement playing at the corners of her mouth. She flicked the side of the bubble. A holo-window in the glass opened and slowly filled with data moving left to right, everything too small for me to read.

Jennifer, I thought, a moment before Amanda Hoban spoke.

"Your NIO contact," she said, her eyes focused on the holo-window, "Jennifer Lisle, first attempted to procure passage for you on an Emirates transport, hoping to save time and avoid Union protocols to obtain your travel visa."

I nodded. "Okay, but that still doesn't explain why I can't see Terree—"

"No Memors are inside the Emirates Tower," she repeated, "including your sought-for Terree."

Nick had stopped smiling. I raised an eyebrow at him, and a wisp of a smile reappeared.

But then I had a strange thought and grasped at a very small straw.

"How about Alex?" I said directly to Nick.

Nick's smile vanished again. "I'm sorry, sir?"

"Did you log any calls for Alex Richards? Is he here?" After all, Richards had been an Emirates page earlier in his life, according to my last trip in the Memory, and Forno might have seen him come out of the building. "Can I talk to him?"

Amanda Hoban cleared her throat. "I suggest that, unless you have a Union clearance you've forgotten about, you leave the Tower."

"Does Alex Richards work here? Do you have a record of him working here a decade and a half ago?"

"Mr. Crowell—"

"I can wait here for him."

"I will soon enable security measures if you do not cease your questioning and exit the premises."

Too late. The light in the room dimmed slightly. The glass double doors were no longer transparent or the street beyond them visible. Security measures had already taken effect.

"Alex Richards," I said. "Where is he?"

"Mr. Crowell, Alex Richards has passed away."

I refused to show any sign of knowledge of that fact. Alex Richards in his crate. One version of him, anyway. Nick averted his gaze from me, and had eyes only for Amanda Hoban.

"Richards is dead?" I feigned surprise.

"An unfortunate accident, I'm afraid," she said, "during a serious incident that occurred at a mediation hearing. Tragic, but not unheard of."

"Really. Off planet?"

"I'm unable to answer that question. The Envoy Privacy Act states—"

"And you decided to leave him in a crate in an abandoned warehouse."

She paled and lightly touched the perfect black hair near her temple. "You're joking, naturally."

"Naturally."

"Then if there's nothing else . . ."

"Is this the only entrance to the Tower?" Of course it wasn't, but nothing felt right here at all, and I'd been getting a deliberate runaround. They knew about Richards, and they knew about Terree.

Nick's eyes flicked nervously, with a slight but noticeable glance past his supervisor.

"May I speak with Vanderberg Parr?" I asked, throwing out the name of the RuBy sniffer Forno had told me about. Amanda Hoban's eyes finally widened in surprise.

That did it. Two guards in full Emirates dress, one male, one female, appeared on either side of me, glass doors I'd not seen earlier sliding shut behind them. I'd rarely seen Emirates uniforms, except on U-One broadcasts. They were light blue with brown piping along the sleeves of a form-fit tunic and on the seams of their matching trousers. The guards' blasters were large and conspicious. They wore snug brown caps and had comm cards attached to their tunics' wide lapels. A third, much bigger guard came through the front doors, but at least none of them had the body mass of a genuine Helk.

Amanda Hoban said, "Mr. Crowell here needs some assistance finding his way."

It wasn't at all about getting me out of there. There'd been a reason for the runaround. A reason for the show of force. It had all been designed, I knew, for a single purpose—to delay me.

"Have a nice day." I started toward the exit. If only I could get to the security locker outside, unlock it, and remove my blaster . . .

The guards moved on me and blocked my passage. I turned back to the bubble.

"As if that's what I meant by finding your way," said Amanda Hoban, smiling at last.

I took Nick's earlier glimpse behind him at face value, as well as Amanda Hoban's earlier perusal of my code card, and before anyone could react, I dove into the bubble.

The air shimmered as I jackknifed through the opening and fell, tucking my head at the last minute and somersaulting. I was on my feet and running out the back of the bubble before either Nick or Amanda could do anything except stumble back in surprise.

Glass gave way to stone and more dull silver metal beams, the light almost blinding as I stopped to get my bearings.

"Get him *now!*" Amanda Hoban yelled. The guards had not come flying into the bubble, so had to leave the foyer through the doors they'd used earlier—which bought me some time.

I glanced at the bubble door, and both Nick and his supervisor came after me, but so what? The backside of the bubble led to a hallway as wide as a Seattle street, slatted with cherry wood. I figured I'd get to its end and find something serviceable for my purposes. So I ran, hoping for the best, but once accustomed to the light, saw that the far side of the hallway ended in a blank wall. So much for *serviceable*. I'd passed three narrow hallways intersecting with this one, and when I spied a fourth just ahead, I put on some speed, hung a left, considered whether the choice behind me looked more promising—it didn't—and plunged forward.

Two guards stepped through a side door in this new corridor as I passed, their blasters drawn. I stopped, and before they could aim, spun and ran headlong between them, knocking them both aside and almost going to my knees myself. One guard fell, his blaster clattering across the wood floor. The other caught himself and turned, but so did I. In that same moment, I reached out and gave him a good strong jolt with my recharged finger caps. He dropped immediately, landing atop his partner and preventing him from rising. I still had a charge left in my finger caps, so I reached out and shocked the other guard into unconsciousness.

I claimed the second guard's blaster, the nearer to hand, and found that it was DNA-locked. Of course. I tossed it aside and barged through the door they'd emerged from into a stairwell down. I was already on the ground floor, and stairs leading down signaled the strong likelihood of entrapment and capture. I might chance upon some sort of emergency exit, but that possibility seemed remote. On the other hand, the guards had come from down there to accost me. Maybe they'd been . . . guarding something.

Down I went.

The stairs clanked as I quick-stepped down them, turning, always turning, left, left, another left, encountering many landings, but no floors to exit to. Above me, I kept expecting to hear the clank of a third guard who'd found the other two unconscious and figured out where I'd gone. This fear spurred me on, but I literally had a sinking feeling that I had no chance in Helkunntanas down here. The light dimmed, and I had no time to make myself some light with my code card because I had to focus on my feet. God, if I *fell* . . .

At length, in almost utter darkness, I took what I assumed was the last flight of stairs and stepped onto a basement floor of hard concrete slick with water. I paused, wondering if an overhead, unrepaired sprinkler had done the damage. But, in a building as glossy as the Emirates Tower, that didn't make sense. Then I noticed the smell—strong and nose-wrinkingly identifiable as the scent of cinnamon. RuBy.

No footsteps on the stairs above me. I activated the code card's accessory node, found the light feature, and stretched the white, luminescent membrane. In an instant, the room revealed itself.

But not completely. It was vast, and my light didn't extend very far from my raised hand. The stairs had brought me to one corner, and near the far boundary of the light, probably the middle of the room, a broad pillar reached upward. I instinctively knew this to be an enclosed elevator shaft, which might ascend straight through the middle of the Emirates Tower.

The elevator might be my only way out.

With the area around me lit, I discovered why the floor seemed slick. At my feet lay thousands of red squares of RuBy. As I stepped gingerly toward the shaft, I saw even more of them coating the floor with a glistening blood red. I picked up a few papers. I'd not seen them this close since that unforget-table moment in the tent city. Back then—the Ultra plot still unknown—I'd done the same thing, checked out the RuBy as I was now doing, its cinnamon odor tantalizing me to use it myself.

What the hell was it doing in the Emirates Tower? What the hell was happening in the Tower, period? I'd received a cold reception—to say the least—from a place that should have welcomed me.

Forno, too, had noticed the anomalies. Abby Graff here. The mystery man who had probably been Alex Richards, kissing Terree, while also kissing up to Graff.

I put the RuBy squares in my pocket, duplicating my actions in that tent city in a way self-destructively alarming.

Before me, the elevator shaft—as I kept calling it—throbbed to life, as if it had suddenly powered up on its own. Diffused light coated its surface, but I couldn't tell where it came from. If this pillar was the only way out, so be it. I had to try because I might not have another chance.

I thought about calling Jennifer, if I could, but a door slammed shut somewhere up the stairwell, followed by the urgent clanking of multiple footsteps.

Run.

With enough code-card light to guide me now, I ran. I reached the pillar and stepped fast around it counter-clockwise looking for the opening. The RuBy-slick floor slid my feet out from under me as I rounded the corner, and I fell to my knees. With the pillar thrumming, I scrambled back up and kept going. I found the opening, light spilling extravagantly from a rectangular door of glass that protruded a foot or so from the pillar.

I froze in astonishment as Alex Richards smiled out at me from the other side of the door, one arm around my client, Terree, who seemed anything but happy.

Richards' brown eyes flickered crazily with more than the tic I'd noticed in the Memory. Wearing a brown jacket over a white T-shirt, he was definitely an older man than the one I'd chased in the warehouse. I was starting to remember him as a kid, and the sensation was more than a little troubling. I glared a warning at Richards, but he just gave me a mocking wave.

No sounds came from within the elevator cage.

Terree looked distressed. Was it an act? If she'd somehow been in cahoots with Richards, why would she fake dismay or terror? To throw me off? Because an unknowable integer in the equation linking them had recently changed? I had no idea. Terree's left arm, free from Richards' grasp, came up suddenly, and her hand awkwardly gestured near her throat. She mouthed a single word to me: *Father.* I had no trouble reading her lips. But why "Father"? And did she mean my father, or hers?

Then the glass opaqued. The light dimmed, the humming intensified, and when the glass lit up again, both Terree and Richards were gone.

"Goddamn it," I whispered to the empty elevator, my heart thumping and despair washing over me. I saw no way to get inside, but I tried, my hands all over the door's glass facade, feeling for cracks or hoping a hidden mechanism to spring it might open for me.

Instead, it opaqued again and plunged the entire vast room into darkness. The whine of blasters powered to life behind me. Footsteps shuffled to a stop on the RuBy-coated floor. Narrow-beam spotlights clicked on. Bathed in light now, an easy target, I turned to face four Emirates guards. Behind the spotlights attached to their weapons, their faces were nothing more than mask-like.

I didn't expect the guards to warn or arrest me. I expected them to shoot. They had no reason to spare me if this newest conspiracy was what I knew it to be. Ultras in control of the Emirates Tower. In control of the Envoys. Not like that news could get out.

It made sense now, knowing that the Envoy Greist Sahl-kla had done something traitorous—but maybe something necessary—to the Union long ago.

I raised my hands.

The four guards kept their weapons trained on me, but they soon sidestepped away, parting in the middle. Emerging slowly from the darkness between the paired guards came a solitary female figure:

Cara Landry stepped into the light.

Twenty-two

AFTER TEM FORNO LEFT THE MIRROR, HE TOOK SOME TIME TO SCAN the thoroughfare, curious if anyone had taken an interest in him. Knowing Juke was on the prowl for Qerral somewhere in the Square had him spooked. Forno knew nothing else about this Parr character, Rieser's supposed successor, so caution seemed a necessity.

Qerral's place was a few blocks behind The Mirror. He'd been there a few times before they declared to each other, a small studio home on the thoroughfare abutting nearly two dozen others. The interior he would've recognized with no trouble. Messy Qerral. It was why they'd moved into his own place. About the only room Qerral kept clean enough for Forno's taste was the bedroom.

Likely, Juke had been there already, so Forno wondered if he should check the place now. Or maybe Juke was watching, waiting for Qerral's return. In that case, only an idiot would go now.

Despite seeing no one, Forno had a palpable sense of being watched. Grasping his Helk-sized blaster in the pocket of his overcoat, he put some distance between himself and The Mirror, crossing the street and slinking into the shadows of a place called Helkify. Helk/Human fusion, equal opportunity cuisine. Putting his back to the restaurant's heavy wooden door, he scanned the thoroughfare. The dark, as always this time of year, was almost absolute. Most shops and establishments turned off all their signs and interior illumination when they closed, relying on state of the art hot zones and deterrents to keep their valuables safe. Power, after all, was at a premium here in Khrem. The Mirror was dark as well, Mayira having closed it up. Unless she she had a rear exit, she might still be inside.

Forno suddenly felt nervous for Mayira. She'd told him a few things that might not sit right with the Boss. If he found out about it . . .

A few heartbeats later, he left the shelter of Helkify, willing himself to the thoroughfare intersection and then around to the back of The Mirror. There, Forno was surprised to see Mayira standing in a circle of light on the blackrock, a solitary lamppost emitting a feeble glow. Hugging herself, she glanced at the door as if waiting for something to happen. Then a soft blue light seemed to irradiate the door, as its security hot zone took effect. When the blue vanished, Mayira, seemingly satisfied, turned to go.

Forno barely had to move for her to notice him.

She stopped, but was not visibly perturbed. "Well," she said, pulling her white vest tighter. "You back here to ask some follow-up questions?"

Forno, not wanting to encroach on her personal space in the near-dark, stood stock-still, his hand tight around his pocketed blaster. "Sorry. Doing that nosy thing again."

Mayira approached him. "That's okay. Mostly, I was out here waiting for you."

Well, that was not what he'd expected to hear. He self-consciously tugged at the fur on his chest. He forced a smile as he gazed down at her. "Because you remembered something you forgot to tell me?"

"You mean a hint?"

"Sure."

"I gave you plenty of hints."

"Maybe."

"Enough to warn you."

"About Rieser. And Parr."

"And Juke. You don't take hints too well. You shouldn't have come back."

"Uh, didn't you just say you were waiting for me?"

"I did."

"Did I tell you earlier I love a good mystery?"

"You did."

"So then," Forno drawled, "I shouldn't have come back to find you waiting for me?"

As she had done earlier, she twisted the black spikes of her hair. "That wasn't the plan. No."

Oh snot.

Forno spun, trying to get the blaster free of his pocket, and Juke was there, a few steps away. Like a badly cut virtual show, Juke seemed to magically spring forward. He struck Forno hard in the face. Once. Twice. Forno's blaster skittered off into the dark.

His vision clouded, pain raced through his head. He stumbled back as the

Second Clan struck a third time, but it took longer for Forno to fall than it had for Juke to throw the three punches that put him on the blackrock.

"Juke," Mayira's frightened voice said above him. "No! You said—"

Juke's furred arm did something Forno couldn't see, and Mayira stopped talking. A grunt escaped her, followed by the sound of her crumpling to the street.

Forno struggled to get up, but could not. He peered up in time to see Juke point his stunner at his head and fire.

You don't survive a point-blank stunner discharge. Muscles scramble, arteries and veins snap, and major organs harden like a mustard egg that rolls under the couch and stays there a week or more. Not a pretty sight—the egg or the stunned Helk—and nothing you can do to salvage either . . . and yet . . .

Why were these thoughts passing through Forno's head?

Alive?

Tash. There was just no way. No way to survive it and no way that Juke would miss at close range. Unless—

He'd missed on purpose. A slight graze, or even a bounce back from the blackrock, would have knocked him cold for a good half hour or so. The weapon *had* discharged, or he would have hopefully guessed that Mayira had deflected Juke's stunner somehow. But no, Juke had struck her, and she had fallen . . .

Groaning, he forced his unfocused eyes open. His face tingled from the punches Juke had thrown. He squinted. His cheeks hurt. He could neither raise his arms nor feel his face. Something bound his wrists. Ties so strong that his wrists ached when he attempted to struggle free.

He was not on the blackrock. No. Of course not. When he tried to move, he encountered a softness that shifted with his weight. A bed.

The room came into focus and he recognized it. Far more cluttered and dirty than he remembered, which was saying a lot. Qerral's bedroom in her studio. There stood her dresser, its top covered with clothes—dirty or clean, he couldn't tell—some of its drawers half open, clothes hanging from them. The cinnamon odor of RuBy seemed less pervasive here, probably because Qerral had taken to rolling hers at Forno's place.

Forno made a more strenuous effort to sit, wondering if the bonds would give him that much slack, but a firm hand grabbed his shoulder and pushed him down. He turned his head to the left, and Juke leaned forward, glowering.

"Stay there," Juke said, his voice raspy and low.

Forno stopped struggling, but kept his eyes on Juke's face. "Is that a new scar under your nose? Ugly."

"Scar?"

"Oh, nope, not a scar. It's your mouth. Confused me for a moment."

"Shut the fuck up." Juke slapped Forno's head with his open palm. It didn't hurt that much, just knocked the fuzziness from one side to the other and intensified his sense of helplessness.

"Good to see you're learning the lingo," Forno said, shaking it off. Juke never had to say much, but when he did, his English was halting. "Sort of."

"What you doing here, Forno?" Juke put a little space between them, but kept banging his stunner against his thigh.

It meant: Don't try anything snotty.

"You brought me here," Forno said. "You tell me."

"I mean to Khrem. You disappeared from district. We thought you dead. Now you here snooping Mirror, bothering help."

At least Forno could understand him. Juke rarely said that much at one time. "Not much help if she sets me up for you." In the back of his mind, though, he recalled that she'd said *something* to stop Juke from hurting him.

Juke growled a laugh. "Not her, me. She does what I say. She likes me."

"She likes you leaving her alone, maybe." *Or fears you.*

"She should remember and not answer questions."

"Where is she?" Forno asked, narrowing his eyes and straining visibly against his bonds, hoping to make Juke nervous.

Juke pointed his stunner across the room, and Forno turned his head. Mayira sat in a huge, overstuffed, Helk-sized chair with ugly green upholstery, what Qerral called her "thinking chair." Mayira was gagged with a transparent strip of sprayable polymer.

"Still alive," Juke said, making his way around the bed to Mayira's side. "Alive part not true much longer. Boss says she talked too much."

Forno said, "Which Boss? Rieser or Parr?"

The question surprised Juke, and his dark face crinkled in ambiguous response. "She told more than thought," Juke said, crouching beside Mayira, or trying to. "What else you tell, I wonder?"

Fear in her eyes, Mayira shook her head.

"I knew about them both," Forno lied.

"Please." Juke tapped his stunner lightly against Mayira's forehead. "No way you know. Rieser yes. Not Parr. Not unless you spent few years in Khrem.

You did not. I would know."

Forno kept quiet.

"So where you been, Forno?"

"Working for Graff."

Juke put the stunner against Mayira's head. "Try again."

"Honestly. I tried, and it didn't work out. I'm looking to come back to Khrem."

"You and Richards."

"Who?"

"Uh huh." The stunner whined when Juke disengaged the safety node, and a killing pulse ratcheted up inside.

Forno thought quickly. "I'm not with Richards, but I know he's trying to help Graff take over the Red. I can help you."

"Nothing new. Richards went to Graff. Something *new*, Forno." He pushed the stunner harder into Mayira's temple.

"Oscz's heart, Juke! What do you want?"

Juke raised his voice, something he rarely did, and every syllable was slow and distinct. "I want to know why you here."

"Before you kill me, you mean."

Juke pointed the stunner at Forno. "My orders are kill both. No matter who first. But could be willing to be kind. Say . . . to ex-mate."

Forno stared hard into Juke's eyes.

"Qerral, right?" the Second Clan said. "Tell me, she lives. I *will* find her. Her mate left big trail to follow."

Forno hesitated.

"Simple deal," Juke said. "Promise."

Qerral's life for information. It wouldn't happen.

"I feel . . . generous," Juke said. "Take time you need. I tell you when time is up."

"What are we waiting for?"

"Wait and see."

Forno didn't like the sound of that. On the clock. Something else was going to happen, and soon.

So *think*, already.

Forno glanced at Mayira's white face, but she regarded Juke determinedly, her hair still perfectly spiked, mouth a thin line beneath the polymer gag. Nothing either of them did now would make a difference. Juke didn't make promises, because no way in hell could he keep them when it came to the the district's hold on its RuBy trade. It *always* came down to the tashing RuBy.

The fact was, RuBy would be Qerral's undoing, just as it had been Shyler Frock's undoing. Juke had a nose for the Red. In a district filled with it, given time, he could find a single square stuck to a Helk's footpad.

If RuBy was Qerral's weakness, then so be it. Forno would give Juke all the RuBy he wanted. Enough to smother him, just as Thurston, the old Boss of Khrem, had once done to Forno, testing his loyalty. Thrown him into a crate full of RuBy, covered him almost head to toe, and said "Don't fucking touch it. One square ruined, and you'll be more than Rubed out, you'll be stained for life."

The Kenn had thrown Forno into Thurston's district and told him to get cozy there, but only so he could figure a way to undo Abby Graff. That hadn't happened, because the Kenn had fallen prey to the Ultras and Forno had to run, find Dave Crowell, and force him to understand the Ultra threat, including the danger of the Ultra army, fueled by RuBy, at the tent city of New Venasaille.

Helk's breath, he thought.

He tried to figure it out, to understand Abby Graff. Why hadn't he found a way to get deep enough into her district to satisfy the Kenn?

Forno thought back to Graff meeting Richards outside the Emirates Tower. A run on Baren Rieser's district? Now he wasn't too sure, particularly in light of his kiss with Terree. How in the wide Union did she know Richards well enough for him to *kiss* her? Even if he'd forced it on her?

Dave Crowell had taken on Terree's case to find her father, hoping it might help him locate his own. Crowell had a history with Rieser, who had a connection with Richards, who had some sort of deal with Graff over the RuBy trade, RuBy tied to the the Ultras' attempt to subdue the refugees at New Venasaille for their Thin Man plot. It stood to reason that much of that RuBy had come from Helkuntannas, and probably from the districts controlled by Rieser and Graff.

A sobering thought came to him: What if an Ultra was here, on Helkuntannas? What if the Ultras had worked both sides of the RuBy trade against each other? Their machinations would destabilize the districts, wreak havoc with the supply chain to other planets of the Union. Unrest and a crippling backlash would result, causing more damage than Plenko's ultimately failed Movement could ever have hoped to accomplish.

If that was the case, Baren Rieser had a stake in the whole thing. Likely, he hadn't told his district the truth: the Boss hadn't been trying to take down

Swain, he'd been trying to take down *all* the districts, *including his own.*

Doing it for the Ultras. For a purpose unknown to everyone, except maybe Rieser. Maybe this Vanderberg Parr knew, too. And Juke.

Juke stood by the door, arms crossed, sweeping away Qerral's clothing with one foot. "Thinking there, Forno?"

"It's what I do when I'm bored."

"Excitement soon, I promise."

"Who are we waiting for? Rieser?"

Juke shook his head. "Just shut up, Forno."

Plenko's ass, he had to hear that from Juke, too? "A hint?"

"From beyond mirror," Juke added, unconcerned, probably thinking he'd said something too enigmatic for him to understand.

Forno's pulse beat harder, because he did know a little about the phrase beyond the mirror, having been right in the line of fire the first time he'd heard something like it.

One of us has already gone beyond the mirror, the Ultra Joseph had said at the mortaline vault on Ribon, just before he self-immolated. *We can not hold.*

Beyond the Mirror. . . . the RuBy bar? Forno couldn't imagine anything of worth being beyond a snotty bar in Khrem.

An Ultra still in the Union, pulling more threads together? Maybe. Jennifer had told Crowell about rumors. It was an intriguing thought. Landry had blown up on Heron Station, her antimatter explosion taking her out, along with a good chunk of Heron Station. But maybe one had managed to escape the effect of the antimatter detonation. Maybe, somehow, that other Ultra hadn't been anywhere in the Union during their purge. Maybe they'd been "beyond the mirror." Had there been another Landry copy fused with an Ultra's genetic makeup? Had another Landry/Ultra waited offstage somewhere with easy access back?

Mayira looked Forno's way now, a question in her eyes. Forno sent a question back: What? She had no way to verbalize whatever she wanted to say.

Did she know something more? Something that might get them out of Qerral's place alive?

"Can't you take off her gag?" he asked Juke. "It's not like she's going to scream and bring Authority running in."

"No."

"Juke, seriously."

"Think small word, has 'n' and 'o' in it."

"Oh, you mean 'snot.'"

Juke glared at him hard, so he shut up, battle lost. Forno made a quick inventory of Qerral's bedroom, searching his memory for anything here that might help him. Mayira was his best chance to get some sort of drop on Juke.

Wait.

Qerral had a zip gun, a Helk mini-stunner designed for self-defense, hidden in this room, right under the ugly green cushion Mayira sat on.

A second later, someone pounded on the door, interrupting Forno's thoughts. He hadn't been quick enough. Too late.

Juke opened the door, and Forno felt despair building. Helpless, unable to act. He decided the zip gun couldn't possibly still be there after all this time. But maybe. Maybe.

Juke's bulk shielded the newcomer from view, and Forno simply closed his eyes.

"Both here?" said the newcomer.

Juke said nothing, but had probably nodded. Forno heard the clicks and whirrs of a portable cooler.

"Good," the voice said. "Did you find the Helkette?"

Now Juke did talk. "No."

Pause.

"*Can* you find her?" the voice said.

"Of course," Juke said.

Forno closed his eyes tighter, willing Qerral to stay put and be invisible. He tried to visualize the bedroom and what else he might use. His heart, beating painfully, kept time with the countdown, like Crowell's antique Rolex: nothing fancy or high-tech, just steady and reliable. Where the snot *was* Crowell?

"Fine," the voice said, the word drawn out in a sigh. "Khrem's had enough of them. Kill them both." Another pause. More whirrs. Clicks. A moment of indecision? "Do it now. Right here, and clean things up before you find the Helkette."

"Not have to tell me," Juke said.

"I know. Just—" Whirr. Click. "Do it."

Hesitation.

"Parr," Forno said, opening his eyes. This was Rieser's new man. The cooler gave him away as human, and orders for Juke could only come from Rieser or his lead sniffer. Juke looked at Forno quizzically, Parr still out of sight behind him. Forno took a chance. "You don't want to do this. I can tell you don't want to."

The door snapped shut, and the cooler wound down as Parr shut it off, its inner workings struggling to interpret the command.

"Shut up," Juke said, raising his stunner, ready to carry out Parr's order before anything else could happen.

"No," Parr said. "Wait."

"Vander," Juke said, "let me, quick. You not trust him."

"Wait." Parr's hand appeared to the right of Juke's bulk. "Get out of the way."

Juke edged away, and Vanderberg Parr moved into Forno's field of vision. His thin gray shirt, blotched with perspiration and wrinkled around his shoulders and chest from the cooler, fit his body like a glove, accentuating ripped muscle. But he had obviously not changed that shirt in a while.

Parr had his own blaster, which hummed to life as he came deeper into the room. Forno recognized the power-up and the shape. Jesus, a Wesson particle.

"And why the fuck wouldn't I want to kill you?" Parr said. His voice held a dark edge, but also a hint of doubt. He glanced over at Mayira. "Both of you."

The miracle presented itself in Parr's conflicted face. Forno hadn't expected this, couldn't have believed it possible in a million years.

His face.

"Because," Forno said, "I know who you are." To make sure Parr understood, he added, "Who you *really* are."

Twenty-three

CARA LANDRY. FROM MY PAST, A LOST LOVE AND A CONSTANT demon. She stood between the guards like a monument, erected not to honor any memory of her, but to warn of a past horror. She lived on in the memories of the Union, even though most citizens had never seen her. Only heard of her.

I had seen her.

She was more than a memory to me. My god, she *lived*.

It didn't take me long to know it was an Ultra and not a Thin Man copy of her. A *Landry*. I had blasted the Landry on Heron Station, then run like hell to escape her antimatter detonation.

The woman I'd loved, *Cara*, was dead. The good memories of her on Aryell—after we'd first met, after we'd fallen to the dance floor of the Flaming Sea Tavern, laughing at our efforts to stay on our feet during the world famous Limbo, after the all-night diner and spiced coffee—all those memories meant nothing anymore.

"Crowell," she said, "you must go."

Four words. It was more than she'd ever said to me in that form, and her ethereal voice made my skin crawl. The first time I'd met her she hadn't spoken at all. Even Jennifer's "One" had stayed quiet before lighting up her fingers with glow. On Heron, it had been the same, although it had seemed that the Landry *wanted* to say something. There, I'd been able to get the drop on her and her Helk guards, but I had no chance now, with the Emirates guards' weapons trained on me. Code card in my pocket, but useless to me. Not like I could call for help. My only chance would be to somehow startle the Ultra or the guards.

I thought of the perfect thing.

"What happened to my dad?" I asked.

She didn't startle. Didn't even seem to register the phrase. A couple guards glanced her way, but their weapons never moved.

"What happened to Greist Sahl-kla?" I asked.

A hint of white luminescence crossed her features. Glow. Like the glow that had enveloped her on Heron. Like the glow from Joseph on Ribon. Her eyes perceptibly twitched. That was something. I hadn't thought she knew how to control eyes or eyebrows enough to show emotion. She'd given a hint of a smile once, on Aryell outside the tent city, a slight twitching of her mouth.

"Where is he?" I said, pressing what I hoped might be an advantage.

"No," she said.

"No? What does that mean?"

You cannot know. Her words came to me in my mind now, as Joseph's had at the mortaline vault. Easier for her to do than force the human mouth to move. If I could hear it, so could the guards. They continued to sneak glances at her. Maybe, just maybe, I could get one of them to falter. Lower his guard just enough . . .

"Why not?" I asked.

You cannot know.

A shift in her head voice made me understand. She didn't mean I was forbidden to know where he was. I had *surprised* her. She couldn't believe I knew anything about Greist Sahl-kla at all.

"I know because of Terree, his daughter."

She cannot know.

"You saw her leave just moments ago."

She . . . can . . . not . . . know.

Concern in her voice. What might prove my secret weapon, the reason that I *did* know, could be my savior now. "She didn't know. Greist told me himself."

She murmured, "Memory . . ."

Her fingers glowed. Mouth slightly downturned. The Emirates guards stepped back together, surprised. Their weapons lowered slightly, the light from them no longer half-blinding me. They'd likely never seen this glow trick before. I'd seen it, and I didn't want to see it. I wondered if I'd made a big mistake. But then—what choice did I have?

The Landry glided forward. "You must go," she said aloud, fingers brightening.

She meant to kill me.

Or did she?

"Where?" I asked.

"To sleep."

I shivered. To sleep. As before, when she'd put me out cold near the tent city. Why now? To find out what I knew, maybe. Or maybe she actually meant to kill me. What good would any knowledge I had of Greist be if I were dead?

I retreated as she advanced, but I kept my eyes on her, even when I backed into the pillar, which had started to hum. The guards' spotlights lowered, and the light bathed the RuBy in a reddish glow.

Fingers, awash in glow, halted just inches from my forehead. I felt, or imagined, a slight heat on my brow. It was unnerving that I couldn't hear anything caused by that pulsing glow, and only heard the ragged beating of my heart. The Landry's skin looked yellowed, the texture rough, almost wrinkled, as if the Ultra inside had tried to smooth it out, but failed.

Light came from behind me—dim, but definitely there. No longer opaque, the elevator had engaged. The Landry's fingers brushed my eyebrows, and I relived that moment in the clearing, like déjà vu in reverse. I almost verbally begged for her to stop and snap out of it. I didn't lose consciousness, but vertigo seized me. I wondered if the Ultras had the same ability as the Memors, a talent to bring others into the Memory. Was that what the sleep was? A Memory-induced state?

As I fought to stay alert, what I'd wanted to happen earlier—but couldn't figure out how to do—occurred with little warning.

The door to the pillar whooshed open.

Shouts filled the room. The guards reacted, coming to attention and lifting their weapons. The Landry withdrew, all the glow and glamor of her dissipating. A blast of energy slashed past me, two guards fell, and someone screamed at me.

What?

"Jesus, Crowell, get the fuck *in!*"

When I turned, Jennifer Lisle grabbed me around the neck and pulled while two NIO hounds on either side of her fired past me at the Emirates guards. Inside the elevator, I stood helplessly as Jennifer fired again and palmed a sensor near the door.

One of the hounds cried out and fell just before the outer and inner doors slid shut. Only a few seconds had passed during the exchange of weapons, but it seemed like an eternity. Beyond the glass, two Emirates guards were down, and the others rushed the pillar. The Landry? I couldn't see her. Had she somehow fled unharmed?

No. She'd only retreated.

She reappeared from the darkness, the faint remnants of glow pulsing in her skin like insertion codes embedding into jump-slot plastic. The guards pounded on the door, but couldn't access the elevator from the outside.

The Landry banished all emotion from her face. I couldn't hear her, aloud or in my head, but I read her lips as she said *Cro-well* with two syllables.

Then the door opaqued, and she was out of sight, as if a jump slot had swallowed her. Jennifer's labored breathing sounded in my ears, and the NIO man's urgent commands to the fallen hound to stay with him seemed unnaturally loud.

As I leaned back against its inner door, the elevator rose.

"Tom," Jennifer said to the man working on his partner.

Tom, his NIO-issued blaster on the floor, had started compressions on his partner's chest. "C'mon, c'mon," he said through gritted teeth.

Jennifer reached down to touch his shoulder. "Tom, he's gone." Tom looked up at her, his eyes clouded with confusion. "I need you now," she said. "Grab your weapon, and Ethan's, and stand. Be ready."

The man's training took over, his eyes hardened, and he did as Jennifer directed. He grabbed the blasters, stood, and held firm, his gaze glued to the door.

Jennifer held out her hand for Ethan's blaster.

I almost asked her how she knew to come looking for me at the Emirates Tower. But I already knew. Amanda Hoban had known about Jennifer's efforts to get me on an Emirates transport to Helkunntanas, and when the director of Envoys accessed my code card, something had pinged Jennifer.

"Seems you've got some explaining to do," she said, glaring at me.

Yep, I did.

"But not now." She gave me the dead man's blaster. "Not until we get clear of here. A team's waiting on the roof, but be prepared to use that thing."

I stared at the blaster. "Locked?"

"No. I did an executive override."

"Did you see anybody leave before you came down?" I asked. "A Memor?"

"Not *now*," she said. She was not happy.

I pointed the blaster at the closed door. Our movement had stopped, and for several agonizing seconds, the three of us stood poised and alert.

We relaxed when the door opened to the Tower roof. Half a dozen NIO agents stood there in poses of readiness. Assistant Director Steven Hardy had accompanied them. He wasn't happy either.

The Landry was below us somewhere, and that fact alone demanded a fair degree of urgency. I doubted any of them knew about her being here, even if they'd had reports of her being alive, but they moved as if they realized *something* was amiss.

"Clear," Hardy said as a transport shuttle grumbled out of standby mode. "Move." Several agents entered the elevator to help Tom with Ethan's body while Hardy coaxed everyone toward the transport.

He glared at me as I walked past. I'd never even met Steven Hardy, who'd taken over Aaron Bardsley's assistant position when Bardsley became director, but he had a reputation as a hard-nosed by-the-book administrator. I couldn't begrudge him his displeasure in this instance, particularly since he had come on this extraction personally.

I kept my mouth shut and entered the transport, Jennifer at my elbow. When I sat, she sat across from me. I flashed back to Cara Landry sitting opposite me on the transport near the tent city, her fingers starting to glow.

For the rest of the trip I said nothing. I expected Jennifer to read me the riot act right then. Or for Steve Hardy to do so. They *would*, of course, but for now they punished me with silence, the whisper of the transport's engines more white noise than distraction. Even the agents on board stayed mute, staring out the windows at the Seattle skyline, now coated with the gloom of dusk.

I glanced at Jennifer sitting next to me, but, keeping her eyes forward, she ignored me.

It was going to be a long night. And where *was* that Temonus whiskey when I needed it?

We didn't fly back to the NIO's temporary HQ at the county morgue. Instead, the transport sped downtown and settled right in the middle of Madison Street, Eighth Avenue, a few blocks north of old Interstate 5. The transport engaged its hot zones in flight, immediately warning folks to stay away. Powered down to stand-by, the transport idled while the doors opened and the NIO agents climbed out.

I noticed the Eighth Avenue Apartments on the corner of the intersection, and knew why we were here. Liz Richards. She'd hired me to catch Alex Richards in the act with his lover, and to make sure I waved it in his face. *That* had turned out well.

Assistant Director Hardy said, "Go get her, standard protocols," and his team fanned out and took up positions. I lost track of them as they either entered the building or disappeared around it.

"She won't be there," I said.

Jennifer glared.

Hardy asked, "Why not?"

"She's a plant." This I said even as the details began to come together in my head. "Alex Richards was an Emirates page long ago, and might still have been except for the fact that Ultras got to him."

"Ultras," Hardy said.

Jennifer still said nothing.

"Liz Richards hired me to tail her husband and find out about his affair, but she didn't care about that at all. Neither did Alex."

"Why didn't they care, then?" Hardy asked.

"They were just trying to get my attention."

"Your attention. That's all? Really."

"I'm a celebrity."

"Knock it off, Crowell." Clearly, Hardy's patience was wearing thin.

I glanced at Jennifer across from me and said, "Someone's trying to get into my memories. Steal information. It was a setup."

Hardy slid over to me on the seat. "You did a good thing for the NIO, Crowell, but you took yourself out of it, if you recall. *Out* of it. And now here you are again, in the middle of everything. The Alex Richards body, his tattoo." He grumbled as he sat back. "Ultras again, for Christ's sake."

His grouching briefly silenced me. The hum of the transport seemed to grow louder, but nothing had changed; the pilot continued holding it in stand-by mode.

"It's true," I said, "and you know it. You authorized Jennifer to let me go to Helkunntanas because of Alex Richards and the tattoo. Because of the tip from one of Baren Rieser's men about Cara Landry. Because of the RuBy districts."

"Yeah, how's that trip worked out for you?" Jennifer finally said across from me.

It was my turn to glare at her.

"What, back already?" she asked, feigning surprise.

Hardy shook his head. "You've just had your ass saved by the NIO after an unauthorized visit to the Emirates Tower. *And*, you've asked after a Memor— what's her name?"

"Terree." Why hide it now?

"What else are you playing at, Crowell?" Hardy asked.

"Terree hired me."

"I thought Liz Richards hired you."

"This was later."

"You were supposed to be tracking Rieser. See what the connection was."

Jennifer continued to glare at me, and her hostility was beginning to freak me out. She looked away, staring out the transport window. "You kept that information secret from me."

I nodded, but she didn't see.

When she turned back, she said, "Terree was your third person for a travel visa, wasn't she?"

"Yes."

Hardy grunted and abruptly left the transport. He stood near the door, his hand atop the frame. Some of the NIO agents had appeared on the street.

"But not anymore," I said. "She left the Emirates Tower just ahead of me. With Alex Richards."

"Richards?" she asked.

"The older one. A copy. This one must have worked for Rieser, but now he seems to be on Abby Graff's side."

"Wait, Crowell. Graff? You just said Graff."

"You talk about Rieser, you talk about RuBy, you have to talk about Graff."

Jennifer's hostility level dropped appreciably. She loved this little mystery. Yeah, I could tell.

Steven Hardy poked his head back into the transport. "You were wrong, Crowell. Liz Richards is there."

"She is?"

"Yeah, but she's dead. Blaster to the head. Someone decided they didn't need her. We're tearing the place apart now. More teams are on their way to help."

Liz and Alex, together again, somewhere in death. At least one each of them.

Hardy said, "Lisle, go back with Crowell and find out everything he knows. Director Bardsley's waiting."

"What about the Alex Richards corpse?" I asked.

Jennifer shook her head. "It's still a corpse."

"No new developments?"

"Nothing. The marble camera in there hasn't recorded anything unusual."

"Autopsy?"

She shook her head apologetically. "We were waiting to hear from Liz."

"Jesus."

Hardy knocked hard on the top of the transport. "Go!" he yelled up front at the pilot.

"Seems like everyone we need to talk to is conveniently out of the picture," I said.

"Except Graff," Jennifer said.

"What do you mean, except Graff?"

"We caught her on an illegal underground shuttle near the Seattle port. Abigail Graff is in custody at the county morgue."

Now we were getting somewhere.

"And I'm still mad at you," Jennifer said, as the transport, whining, lifted off from Madison Street.

Director Aaron Bardlsey met us in Jennifer Lisle's temporary office at the morgue. When I'd contracted for the NIO with Brindos, I'd never stepped foot inside Director Timothy James's office. Close as I'd come had been then Assistant Director Bardsley's office. Now, as Director, Bardsley had made a special trip to Seattle, only to be relegated to a small corner of the gutted old church.

Jennifer waved me over to Bardlsey, giving me a look that said "Way to fuck up, Crowell."

The desk, less cluttered now than when I'd first seen it, seemed smaller. I had barely sat in one of the wobbly plastic chairs when Bardsley spoke: "Start at the top," he said, "and tell us everything."

Jennifer sat in a chair next to mine. Any moment now she'd become my staunch supporter again. I could tell.

Bardsley pulled out the chair from the desk, positioned it in front of us, took a seat, and waited.

I took a deep breath and began. For nearly half an hour I told them almost everything. About the incident with Alex Richards, about my watch, the ticking, and the passing out, the arrival of Terree and how she hired Forno and me to search for her father. How she helped me understand the Memory. How I decided going to Helkunntanas might help me understand what had really happened to my dad. About him being an Envoy until his disappearance, rather than a marina owner. About Tilson Hammond and the cover story. About knowing Greist Sahl-kla. The Emirates conference in Chicago. Forno's discovery of Graff and Richards together. About Richards once having worked as my Emirates page. About Joe and the Restaurant. About my search of the Emirates Tower and my frantic attempt to escape. About RuBy. Forno's connections with Khrem, Swain, and both Rieser and Graff.

As far as knowing about Greist betraying the Union in some way, I said nothing. It seemed wise to hold that back, because I didn't really know what Greist had done, good or bad.

And lastly, I told them about a copy of Cara Landry appearing to me in the basement of the Emirates Tower.

Bardsley and Jennifer listened intently, and I felt their stares boring into me—looking, no doubt, for signs that I'd been taken over by Ultras. But Jennifer, at least, knew me better than that. As angry as she was with me, she knew I wouldn't arbitrarily invent stuff in this context. Moreover, she'd learned the truth of many of my assertions from our earlier conversations.

"Now what?" she asked.

"Even if all this is true," Bardsley said, "we don't have enough to go on."

"That means no Arks," I said.

"Where would I tell President Nguyen to send them?" Bardsley asked. "Helkunntanas, perhaps, but *where* on Helkunntanas? Who would we target?"

"The RuBy districts?" Jennifer asked. "Khrem? Swain? To get Rieser?"

"We're just going to blow holes in those places and hope we get lucky?" Bardsley said.

"Nguyen tried that on Temonus looking for Plenko, tearing apart the Helk district," Jennifer said. "That's not going to work here. The ties between Helkunnanas's provincial government and ours are tenuous at best."

"You need to talk to Graff," I said.

They both glanced my way, and Bardsley shook his head. "We've tried. So far she's not talking to us. But we've just started. She's still in holding, locked in a side lab, still in her street clothes. She'll talk soon enough."

"She won't," I said. How had she let herself get captured? On Earth of all places? That's what I wanted to know.

"She might," Jennifer said.

"She'll talk to me," I said, my voice hollow in the director's office. Tension crept into my shoulders and neck.

Bardsley paused a moment. "Why would she talk to you?"

Jennifer said, "Forno worked for her. Undercover for the Kenn. Crowell knows Forno, so maybe she'll listen, considering Forno's poking around on Helkunntanas."

It's starting again, I thought. Somehow, it was all coming around. "This can't happen," I said. "Not this time."

Bardsley frowned. "What're you talking about?"

Jennifer gave the director a look that said *careful*. She knew what I meant. We'd discussed this phenomenon the first time we'd met here to talk about Alex Richards' body.

Stop beating yourself up about it. When she had quizzed me about Forno's trustworthiness, she had brought up the larger issue: Alan Brindos's death. I'd put him in harm's way, sending him ahead of me to snoop around Temonus, and then I pulled the trigger, killing him. True, Plenko, Joseph, and the Ultras forced me into it. Here we were again: Forno out of reach, cut off, and his old Boss, Abby Graff, here in custody.

Graff and Rieser involved in a RuBy war, and on the margins, something very wrong at the Emirates Tower. The Ultras had an interest in it all, including involvement of the RuBy districts and the long-sought-after Thin Men still hiding from the eyes of the Union.

"I'm sure Forno is safe," Jennifer said. "We'll get to him and work it all out. As far as I'm concerned, Graff can rot here."

I should've insisted on a code card for Forno to keep from having to rig mine to connect a two-way ping just to talk to him. And now, we'd lost that connection.

"Alerts have already been sent through the slot," Bardsley said.

Which is what had happened when Brindos and I had been on the run.

"We've got a few agents on the ground near Khrem," Bardsley said, "and some favors to call in with the Kenn. Get inside the districts and find Forno. Smoke out Rieser."

The Kenn? With all the drama happening there, and here, tensions between the two worlds at an all-time high? After years of failing to break Khrem and Swain, they were suddenly going to roll in there and do damage? They already had Abby Graff in custody. It wasn't likely they'd have a better chance than now to figure something out.

Why had Abby Graff risked coming to Earth? With the Ultras back and playing us with their newest secret war, I wondered why she had inserted herself into the chaos. Had she had a choice?

"Please, let me talk to her," I said.

Bardsley said, "No," emphatically.

"Dave," Jennifer said, "seriously, that's not going to work—"

"She must know who I am, and I bet she knows Forno works for me. I've met Landry. Joseph. Alex Richards, Lorway. Hell, even Rieser. A different lifetime, it seems, but we also have a history. I'm in the middle of everything."

Hell, I *was* a celebrity. "We can use everything I've just told you against her."

Jennifer said, "Then the NIO will use it—"

"It has to be me," I said. "It has to be."

"Director, tell him he can't."

Bardsley said, "Damn it," frowning at Jennifer.

Oh, so that was it. Bardsley all around the edge, finding out what he could about my intentions. I'd been right. He'd been sounding me out, wondering if I could handle a confrontation with Graff.

Jennifer shook her head. "What?"

"Graff asked for him."

"Gods," Jennifer said. "Why didn't you tell me?"

To protect you, I thought. If Graff knew Forno, if she knew Rieser, she probably knew what was brewing on a larger scale. If my lack of stability bothered Bardsley, Jennifer could've remained blissfully ignorant.

Some thoughts about Graff still nagged at me. Forno had seen her on Earth with Richards, but then she'd disappeared, supposedly on a stealth TWT flight to Helkunntanas. Maybe, maybe not. I'd get a good look at her, and then maybe I'd figure out something brilliant.

I stood. I would confront Abby Graff and get her to talk.

"I'm going in with you," Jennifer said, also standing.

"No, alone."

"That's unreasonable."

"That's the deal."

"What do you have to deal?" Bardsley said. "You don't work for the NIO anymore."

"I have more information."

"About what?"

About me. About Greist. "It's a mystery."

"Who's Graff working for?"

"That seems to be even more of a mystery."

"Another reason why we should sit in on your interrogation."

"No. Alone."

"And then what?"

"And then Jennifer and I take the slot to Helkunntanas. Visas all arranged. We do what the NIO and Kenn can't."

"What's that?"

"Get Forno, find Rieser and whoever else is pulling the strings in Khrem. Then to Swain."

"Like you'll get in there. What do you need in Swain?"

"Terree and Alex Richards."

"And how do they help?"

"Terree was under duress when I saw her in the elevator. She said something."

Frustrated, Jennifer sighed. "Dave, what did she tell you?"

"She said *father*."

"Hers or yours?" she asked.

"I didn't know at first, but I figured it out. She meant mine. She made a sign with her fingers, near her throat. The Emirates sign for Earth. I'd just seen the signs of most of the Union worlds in the holo-windows inside the Emirates entryway, including Earth's. A hearth."

Jennifer knew it. She made the sign with her right hand.

"Keep the home fires burning," I said.

Jennifer raised an eyebrow. Maybe my knowing the sign or the poem had awed her.

"I'll try and find Terree's dad, and mine, in Swain."

"You can't find anything but RuBy in Swain," Jennifer said.

"Graff will tell me," I said.

If Alex and Liz Richards didn't care about what happened to them, Graff might not either. She might be desperate, particularly since she'd spent so much time trying to get into Baren Rieser's business.

"She'll talk," I said, "and I'll see if I can find out what you need to know."

Bardsley thought a moment, then nodded at Jennifer. "Okay. Take him to her."

Twenty-four

DO YOU KNOW WHO I AM?

How long had Parr asked himself that question? Hell, not just himself. Others in the Boss's district, some known, some random, like Officer Kash Neviya, who hadn't known what the question even meant. Officer Neviya, who looked on in horror when Parr took his digipad with all that information about where he and his family lived.

At the House, Cara had done her glowing trick, and soon enough, the Quarry once again had confused guests, confused servants, and piles of Ruby. But no Rieser. He'd given Parr the keys, so to speak. Do your job. Take care of our problems.

I know who you are, the Second Clan Helk, Tem Forno, told him. *Who you really are.*

"Don't listen," Juke said, and before Parr knew it, Juke covered the distance to the bed and jabbed his stunner into Forno's temple.

Goddamn, Juke had moved fast. "Juke," Parr said, "I told you to *wait*."

The pressure of Juke's stunner turned Forno's head slightly, but Forno kept his eyes locked on Parr. Odd, Parr thought, how calm the Helk seemed. He was only moments from death, but Parr gave him no chance to get comfortable. He stiffened his arm, extending the Wesson particle blaster. He almost willed Forno to say "Vander, hey now," just so he could shoot the son of a bitch. But no. Not even that. *You know who I am?*

"Untie him."

"Vander."

"Do what I say."

Flustered, Juke said, "Nothing to know, Vander. Does not make difference."

"Untie him."

Juke grumbled, but roughly removed the bonds holding Forno down.

Parr watched, pain dulling his thoughts. Damn, he'd forgotten to pop Red before coming in. He fumbled in his pockets for a square of RuBy.

"He knows nothing." Juke dragged Forno off the foot of the bed to a standing position. He bumped into Qerral's dresser, swore, and slammed the open drawer shut.

Parr mentally sized Forno up for a coffin. He rolled the RuBy one-handed, paused, stared up at the Helk's sweaty, leathery face, and put the drug on his tongue. He closed his eyes only a moment to acknowledge the diminishing aches. "That true, Tem Forno?"

"Dead Helk, no matter," Juke said. "He is desperate."

Parr sighted down his blaster. "Is that *true*, Forno?"

Forno massaged his wrists and laughed. "Is it true that I'm desperate?"

Parr sighed. "That you know who I am."

Juke pleaded, "Vander—"

"Shut *up*, Juke," Parr said.

"It's true." Forno grimaced when Juke pushed his stunner harder into his head.

"Vanderberg Parr," Juke said. "No one else."

"The new Boss of Khrem," Forno said.

Parr took a step closer to Forno. "Yes, and you're my first bit of official business."

Forno laughed again. "When you find out who you really are, will you kill me? Once I tell you, what use will you have for me?"

"None I can think of."

"If I tell you, if you believe it, you might need to keep me alive. To find out more."

Juke whacked Forno on the head with the stunner. Forno fell, then tried to get up,.

"King of Khrem? Hell, you can't even control your lackey," Forno said, staying down.

Parr figured Forno as one tough Second Clan, but also smart, not blurting out the name. Trying to play Juke, get under his skin. Stalling. Juke hadn't listened too well, so now Parr had to show Forno who he was: The Boss. The only thing Juke knew that he didn't, was a fucking *name*.

"You willing to find out how much control I have over him?" Parr asked Forno, who was now inching toward Mayira on his hands and knees. "Where you going?"

The stupid Hulk kept crawling toward Mayira.

"You okay?" Forno asked her. Mayira nodded, but tried to disappear into the stupid chair's green upholstery.

"Just shoot her," Parr told Juke. It'd be one less problem to deal with.

"My pleasure," Juke muttered.

Forno said, "You kill her, I tell you nothing."

"Then I shoot *you*," Parr said, "and I'm none the wiser."

"You won't."

Parr glanced impatiently at Juke. "Do you work for me, Juke?"

"Of course," Juke said.

"Then tell me who I am. You tell me, and then I can shoot this son of a bitch." He waved his blaster at Forno. "Him and Miss Mayira here."

"Nothing to say, Vander."

"You can't? Or won't?"

Juke was silent.

Tem Forno pulled himself up on the chair, and still had to look down to give her a reassuring look.

"Tell me now, Juke."

"Vanderberg Parr."

"Goddamn it, Juke, you fucking tell me." Parr turned and pointed his blaster at Juke.

Juke pointed his at Parr. "What? You shoot me?"

"Don't forget who you're talking to."

"Not Rieser."

"Rieser's as good as gone. Done."

Juke said nothing, and Parr gripped his blaster tighter, not willing to show a moment's weakness.

"You're thinking he'll be back," Parr said. "If he does come back, he won't be Rieser anymore, not as you remember."

Juke's gaze faltered. He blinked and chanced a look at the green chair. Parr followed his gaze. Tem Forno remained on the floor before it, his right arm behind Mayira, moving behind her as if supporting her while she edged forward on the chair's cushion.

"An interesting standoff," Forno said. "Someone should take bets on how this goes down."

"There's only one way this is going down," Parr said, his blaster still pointed at Juke. "You'll tell me who you think I am, and Juke will do as I say."

Parr had given his full attention to Juke. Would he have to kill him? He was ready to. More than ready, because he knew things Juke did not. In the end, Juke did not matter. Not even to find out his name. Not if Tem Forno could be believed.

"Juke," he said. "Put . . . your weapon . . . down."

Juke stared at Parr, his stunner motionless. Then he faltered and slowly lowered the weapon. Parr thought, Good decision, Juke. Give him a second to understand why this was the right move, then get this asshole Forno to talk.

For a moment they regarded each other in silence, the tension dissipating. *But then—*

Parr lowered his own weapon and turned to Forno, and the door to the apartment opened. Startled, Parr whirled and instinctively aimed his weapon.

A female Helk stumbled through the door, looking like snot warmed over. Goddamn Shyler Frock's Helkette, Qerral. She nearly ran into Parr, glanced about wildly, saw Tem Forno, and whimpered pathetically. In stumbling forward to get past Parr, she jarred his weapon.

The thing about a Wesson particle blaster, especially one as valuable as the one he owned, was that it had a few quirks. Rieser was right about its sentimental value. Slight design flaws serious collectors overlooked. Because it had no DNA lock and a wide, slightly unstable particle beam that tended to fry unintended objects at a distance, when Qerral jarred it, it discharged.

Qerral screamed and slew sideways, struck by the blast; the Wesson blaster fell to the ground.

Tem Forno cried, "Qerral!" and stood awkwardly.

Juke swung his stunner around toward Forno.

As Qerral fell in slow motion, Parr was half aware of Forno coming toward him. He tripped over his cooler on the floor and reached out for something to steady himself. Juke's arm.

Juke's shot, intended for Forno, went wide. Juke swore and, aiming again, moved toward Forno. His sudden movement kept Parr from catching his balance, and he pinwheeled, falling back hard against the dresser. The sharp edge of the front corner jabbed him in the small of his back and he slumped forward, landing on his knees.

Juke positioned himself for another shot, aiming at Forno, who froze, nowhere to go.

No! Parr tried to say, but the moment was gone. The sizzle of a weapon's discharge burned the air.

It wasn't from Juke's stunner.

Juke made a strangled noise, grasping at his throat, and his stunner clattered to the floor. He sat down hard on his butt.

In that moment, Parr had a straight-on view of Mayira, her black spiked hair still perfectly in place, some sort of zip gun in her hand. Where had that come from? Hardly lethal against a Helk, but powerful enough to incapacitate one.

But not for long. Juke shook off the zip gun's effects and looked for his weapon as Forno crouched down next to Qerral.

Parr saw the stunner. Closer to him than to Juke. *No more of this shit.* As the Boss, he made the decisions now. He grabbed the stunner, fumbled with its size, the awkward position of the trigger, and glared at Juke, whose eyes registered first surprise, then resignation.

"Vander," he said. He tried to say more, but the charge from Mayira's zip gun had hit him near the throat and he couldn't quite get his mouth to work. The black skin around his mouth puckered as he tried to speak. "I . . ."

Parr pulled the trigger.

The whole sequence of events, from Qerral opening the door to Parr shooting Juke, had taken less than a minute.

"Jesus," someone said.

Parr stared at Juke's gigantic body wedged between the bed and the dresser. A slight flicker crossed Juke's face, a last breath maybe. Juke's right arm rested heavily on Parr's leg.

When he finally looked up, certain Juke was really dead, Tem Forno towered over him, pointing the Wesson particle that looked tiny in his hand. He looked like he might go berserk any moment and rip Parr to shreds. Mayira still had the zip gun; she edged toward the bed and kept the weapon trained on him.

Parr saw the Helkette on the floor. Dead. Shyler Frock's mate dead, and, hey, that was what the old Boss of Khrem had wanted, wasn't it? But now he had this angry Helk before him. What was he so pissed off about?

Parr thought: *The shortest reign ever for a King of Khrem.* But he showed them, right? Showed Juke. Showed this mysterious Hulk, Forno. This upstart human girl with the bad hairdo.

No. Hell, he hadn't shown them snot.

Heat seeped in through the open door, and Parr looked at his cooler, wondering if they'd let him wear it.

Forno wouldn't shoot him. Forno needed information too. Forno wanted to know about the Ultras.

Sure, he'd give him Ultras. Hell, he'd take him right to them. See how far that got the Hulk when he realized the truth. The truth and peace of the

Ultras that continued to come to him, like a U-One download.

"Forno?" Mayira said, breaking the silence.

"Yeah," Forno said.

"Is she—?"

"Yeah. Gone."

Waiting for Parr to give up. Fine, he would. Parr tossed Juke's stunner at Forno's feet. "There you go." He realized what had happened. What Forno had done to get him in this position.

"No worries now," Parr said. "Nice ploy with Juke. Man, you goddamn rode him like a virtual thrill ride." He couldn't help it; he laughed. "Put on the immersion specs, boys. Play the Juke box."

"What the hell you talking about?" Forno asked.

"All made up, man. You gambled and won. Oh, Juke knew all right. He knew who I was. Even if you didn't, it bothered the shit out of him that I might find out." He put his back up more firmly against the dresser. "It doesn't matter. You're more interested in the Ultras, aren't you?"

"Qerral was my ex-mate," Forno said in a low voice.

Parr jerked his head back, as if he'd been hit. Oh fuck. Forno and Qerral had been declared?

"She did nothing wrong except leave my place looking for her new mate," Forno said.

"Shyler Frock."

"She didn't deserve this."

"Rieser killed him," Parr said. "I was supposed to, but I failed to do it."

"Because you didn't want to."

"No."

"You're better than Rieser."

"Worse. I'm not even—" He was going to say *real*. Not completely human.

Forno inclined his head but said nothing. Dark sky was visible behind him through the open door.

"I can give you Ultras," Parr said. "I can bring you to where you can find them." Not that it would help Forno any.

Forno pointed the blaster with renewed urgency. "You do that. But first, we exchange information."

"Isn't that what I'm offering you?"

"My terms. Before we leave here. I'll tell you who you really are, and you'll tell me where to find who I'm looking for. If Ultras are part of the deal, I'll take it."

Parr sat up straighter, his heart beating faster, the encroaching heat forgotten. "You mean you really know who I am? You weren't just shitting me? Playing with Juke?"

"Do we have a deal?"

"You really know?"

"Yes."

Droplets of sweat ran down Parr's face. One caught in the corner of his eye and he blinked it away. "Who are you looking for?"

"A Memor by the name of Greist Sahl-kla."

The Donor. Baren Rieser had just told him that Greist was somewhere unknowable.

He didn't want to say anything to Forno. The Ultras would not be happy, and the peace they offered would be harder to achieve. But Rieser wasn't the Boss anymore, and it was his decision. It didn't matter as much as it once did, this fanatical worship of Rieser, and Cara Landry. The Ultras were more important. *He* was more important. He was going to find out who the fuck he was. *A special creature.* How much more special could he be?

"Griest. Sure, I'll tell you," Parr said.

"Good." Forno waved the blaster, indicating Parr should get up.

Parr stood, eyeing the weapon. The last thing he wanted was that Wesson discharging again accidentally, particularly when Forno could barely get his big mitt around it. "Fuck, hold that thing still. Do you remember what just happened?"

"I remember."

Forno glared down with his dark, distrusting eyes and Parr wondered, again, if the Helk really knew. Really, really knew. Did he know *what* he was? A Thin Man? He must, if he had a different name to give him. Would he make Parr tell him about Greist first, since he had the weapon? Then afterward tell him, I'm sorry, just kidding, you're Vanderberg Parr without a past. That's it. A nobody. Rieser took you in and trusted you, and *now* look what you've done.

He stared at Juke's body sprawled between them. At Qerral on her back by Mayira's green chair. At Mayira herself, who still held the zip gun.

"You want to know about Greist first, I imagine," Parr said.

Forno shrugged. "Naw, I can tell you're suspended."

"What?"

"In suspense," Mayira said.

Stupid Hulk, Parr thought. "You'll tell me first?"

Forno wagged his free hand at him. "But don't change your brain on this, or you'll join Juke . . . beyond the mirror."

Parr wondered if Forno really understood what that phrase meant. "So tell me already."

"You're a Thin Man."

Parr snorted his contempt. "That goddamn doesn't count."

"You're the only Thin Man that matters."

Chills crept down his spine. Jesus, he had to hear that phrase from this Helk, too?

Forno said, "The only one who matters to us."

"Us. Who's us? You and Mayira?"

"No, me and my partner. Especially my partner."

"Goddamn it, tell me."

"Your name," Forno said, "is Alan Brindos."

Vanderberg Parr blinked. Frowned. Tilted his head to the side and let that sink in. "Who?"

"Alan Brindos."

"Alan. Brindos."

"Yes."

"Who the fuck is Alan Brindos?"

Twenty-five

THE COUNTY MORGUE HAD A SMALL INTERROGATION ROOM, surprisingly enough. An exam room, actually, with a holo-window configured for viewing anonymously from the outside.

I had insisted on seeing Abigail Graff alone, and now I insisted on zero surveillance. No vid, no audio, no autoscripts, and no entrance to the interrogation room at any time by NIO personnel. No restraints while she was in the room. Nothing on her except the clothes she wore. She was not to know I would be in there with her. Jennifer objected. This was a morgue, not NIO headquarters, and security was minimal. But Graff wasn't allowed to breathe funny without alerting the agents around her, and the body of Alex Richards had remained secure, hadn't it?

Bardlsey, however, demanded at least vid.

"No," I said. "I'm alone in every way. Trust me on this one."

We debated what the word trust meant in this case, but eventually they agreed, as long as I had my code card with me in case of an emergency. That was just what I'd hoped for: I *needed* my code card in there.

Bardsley escorted us downstairs. I stood outside the makeshift interrogation room and stared through the large holo-window, waiting for them to haul in Graff. A rectangular room with a white tiled floor and gray wall panels housed a wide translucent table—usually reserved for dead people—three chairs, inset holo-cameras near the ceiling, and nothing else. Jennifer stood next to me while Bardsley left to assist with Graff's transfer from a holding room.

"Who has doubts now?" I asked her, still looking through the window at the room's interior.

"Our doubts are traitors."

I stared at her; she turned to me a moment later. I shrugged. "Shakespeare didn't know everything."

"Certainly didn't know about aliens," she said. "Or drug lords."

"Not so sure about the drug lords. RuBy by any other name would smell as sweet."

"Abby Graff is desperate. Desperate to get on top the RuBy pile. Don't underestimate her."

"I'll be careful. What can happen?"

She didn't answer. I turned back to the window and waited.

Five minutes later, NIO agents brought Graff into the room. A large woman indeed, as Forno had once told me. She had on a dark green jumpsuit, the material scrunched up around her waist where a black leather corset belt encircled her. It appeared that she'd been stuck in her outfit for a while. The braids of her light brown hair, streaked with gray, bobbed at her nape, and other braids—those that hadn't come loose—were coiled high atop her head.

As I'd requested, her hands were free. The agents sat her at the table and left. She stared at the mirror. At me.

Bardsley returned a moment later. "She's all yours."

"No sound or vid."

"Of course not."

"Have her say something."

Bardsley tweaked a sensor near the window. "For the record, state your name and Union affiliation."

Graff sighed inaudibly, then leaned back and spoke. I heard nothing, although I could read her lips well enough when she said *Abigail Graff.* I wasn't sure what else she said after that, except for *Helkunntanas.*

I pointed at the transmission sensor. "Not even one-way for sound."

Bardlsey swiped at it a few more times.

"Now the vid. Holo-recorders, this window, everything."

"This isn't NIO headquarters, you know," he said. "It doesn't feature a quarter of the surveillance equipment we normally use."

"Everything."

He sighed and flicked the sensor a few more times, and a few seconds later, the window opaqued.

"Good," I said. "How do I know for sure this won't be recorded in some way?"

"You're the one big on trust."

Trust.

Jennifer touched my shoulder, reassuring me, and I walked to the door connecting the observation room to the hallway and let myself out. A few steps later, I stood by the door separating me from the Queen of Swain, Abigail Graff.

During the race to capture Rieser, a few years before joining the NIO to look for Terl Plenko, I'd met a woman on Temonus who volunteered information about the data forger's background and past travels. Or maybe I forced it out of her. April Collings, her name was, a SeaGal at the Flaming Sea Tavern on Aryell. She'd hooked up with an ex-soldier named Bobby Song at the tavern, a guy with one arm. He'd lost the other in the Third Korean Conflict, then left Korea so he could retire in West City. April started working days at the Flaming Sea Tavern, Song became a regular, and she waited on him. Got to know him. When she wasn't working tables, they'd get together after hours. He stopped seeing the other girls, and stuck with her.

April Collings told me years earlier Song had led a small squad of enlisted troops and Authority cops to arrest a young Baren Rieser, who'd threatened some sort of heist using DataNet pods, which he'd invented. They were designed to siphon off credits from personal financial accounts with a touch of a membrane to any user's comm card.

Song traced him to a three-story storage facility nestled amid the upper reaches of the North River Han, east of Seoul. Song never spoke to Rieser and, in fact, never once saw him in person. Song sent in his squad, which stormed the facility through the doors and first-floor windows. Moments later, the building blew, killing twenty men and women. Rieser was nowhere to be found.

In the debris, however, they'd found traces of thin, waxy paper. Uncut, the formula not perfected yet, the paper was a precursor to the paper now used for RuBy. Song suspected that if Rieser had anything to do with this, he'd eventually end up on Helkunntanas, where it was manufactured. Call in favors from his underground contacts and get in on the action.

But during an extensive DNA sweep, Song's people found no traces of Baren Rieser. Instead, they found small but quantifiable DNA evidence of a fairly well-known drug lord from the west side of Chicago named Abigail Graff. I'd heard she'd fled to Helkunntanas herself after that, and she started pulling strings to take control of the RuBy trade. Brindos and I even investigated a RuBy-related murder she'd had a hand in, although she had remained untouchable in Swain.

At the time, Brindos and I hadn't thought much about this business. Maybe Rieser had tricked Graff, but the truth was now out about her. Back then, we lost Rieser's trail. April Collings was right: Rieser had fled to Helkunntanas, a place we were not able to get to. We stayed for a while on Aryell. We met Cara at the Flaming Sea. We later joined the NIO.

Rieser got in on the action, all right. The Boss of Khrem. The year before the Ultra scare, he and Abigail Graff both landed on a list of possible terrorists working for the Movement. They'd never cleared.

After that? RuBy ran in the streets of Khrem and Swain like blood.

The Movement, along with Terl Plenko and the Ultras, vanished. The Union government banned the manufacture, sale, and possession of RuBy anywhere but on Helkunntanas. Not that I believed anyone dependent on the drug kept to that.

Now, on the other side of the door, in the antiseptic interrogation room, sat Abigail Graff, who represented nearly half the RuBy trade in the Union. Was she in competition with Baren Rieser, attempting some kind of takeover of Khrem, or were she and Rieser in on it together?

I entered the room.

Graff looked up at me, glowering, but immediately, her face relaxed, and she smiled like a kid who, although grounded, has just won a big argument with strict parents. "David Crowell," she said, her voice as husky as her body. She leaned back, looking entirely too comfortable.

"That's me." Closer, the deep lines around her eyes, the pockmarks in her cheeks, and a ragged ugly scar across her chin and jawline were all conspicuous. "You asked for me. Something you hoping for?"

"Getting out of here, for one thing." She pointed to the mirrored holo-window. "They listening?"

I shook my head. "They agreed to squelch all surveillance." I pulled the code card from my pocket and let my fingers glide along its surface, fingerprint memory finding the hidden nodes. "Not that I trust they'll honor that promise."

I found the freesource prog I'd downloaded from the DataNet basement, the electromagnetic transblocker for all the NIO comm and recording devices, and activated it with a simple brush of a subnode.

A brief squeal sounded in the room, which was soon quiet again except for a slight ventilator hum.

"Transblocker," Graff said, her eyes crinkling with amusement.

I put the code card on the table, sat down, and leaned back, mimicking her. "We're just empty shells now."

"They'll come in demanding you deactivate that."

"No. They'll let it stand. The comm node is on standby, though. A quick flick of my finger and they're in here." It was also recording everything, for my sake. And, if matters went awry, also for the NIO.

Graff raised an eyebrow. "Why would they give in to you?"

"Because of who I am."

She grinned. "Dave Crowell, Ultra Slayer." She laughed, but suddenly turned serious, as if someone had palmed a switch. "Hulk Killer."

I let Graff's last comment slide past me, showing her nothing, but inside, I cringed. Hitting me with the Brindos card, goddamn it. Pretending she knew the extent of what happened on Ribon. Or maybe she did.

"Oh, *now* I did it," Graff said in a teasing voice. "Hurt your feelings."

I said, "No, I just wish I had a drink to accompany your lame story. Let's talk about *your* feelings."

"Mine?"

"Or whatever feelings you have left. Are you the Queen of Swain or the Jackshit of Earth?"

"Shut up," she muttered.

"You show up on Earth, infiltrate the Emirates Tower. You meet with Richards. One of them, anyway. Arrange for him to kidnap Terree. You sic Alex and his wife Liz on me. You probably killed Liz. Probably hand-picked the girl for him to have sex with. No one special, probably from an escort service. Paid her a lot of money."

She leaned forward, and I wondered if I should've been less demanding about leaving her hands free. Forno was right: she was scary. Big, scary, and likely able to take down just about anyone who wasn't a Second or a First Clan Helk.

I pressed on. "You're working with the Ultras, aren't you?"

"You don't know what you're talking about, asshole," she said, shifting back again. The scar on her chin jumped a little when she spoke.

"It's goddamn easy to say I don't know what I'm talking about," I said. "Prove it."

Graff said nothing.

"I'm looking for some people, and everything's pointing to Helkunntanas. My partner's already there. Forno. You know who he is?"

She nodded. "He's a spy for the Kenn."

"Was. He's with me now."

Crossing her arms, Graff leaned back even more, a too casual attitude.

I said, "Abby Graff would never let herself be cornered."

"They tricked me into coming here, you piece of shit! To meet someone in my organization who had information about the Emirates Building."

"Alex Richards."

"Yeah."

"Why? So you could leverage the Envoys against Rieser?"

"Pretty much. Richards *is* a Thin Man. The copy belonged to Rieser. The original Richards came to me in Swain. Anyway, I was stuck here. I tried to escape, but Richards ratted me out."

I tapped the table lightly, uncertain about her story. "I don't know. You were around and deep into RuBy when the Ultras first became known. What about the tent city where they readied the inhabitants for the copy procedure? The RuBy had to come from somewhere."

She glanced at the mirror again. Then at my code card. She seemed to wilt, and maybe the transblocker induced her say more: "The Ultras never picked me up, Crowell. No need to. They had Rieser."

"Rieser worked for the Ultras."

"Yes."

"You're not working with Rieser?"

"No. Rieser wants to bring down the whole RuBy distribution system. Take over *every* aspect of the drug. Have it all. It's true that for years, I've wanted to expand my influence outside Swain. That hasn't changed, and I'll do what I have to do to survive this and emerge stronger. But what Rieser's doing . . . well. No way."

"And you can prove these assertions how?"

"I'm not sure you'll like it."

"Try me. I'm involved, and have been for a long time."

The muscles in her bolded arms flexed, and they were as impressive as Tilson's had been. I pretended not to notice hers.

"Rieser's spent the last year rounding up whatever Thin Men he could find," she said, "getting them to work for him. Playing them. The Alex Richards copy, for example, which mostly has his full memories. He cozied up to the Memor woman, Terree. Promised her information about her father."

"That's what she hired *me* for. He's one of the ones I'm looking for. Why hire me if she already had a possible lead?"

"She couldn't figure it out alone. Rieser had already installed some Thin Men at the Emirates Tower."

"Yeah. I spoke to a few."

"You were chased by a few, more likely."

"That too."

"I told Richards fuck you and left."

"Tried to leave Earth."

"Not at first. Once I found out all this shit about Rieser, I did some looking around." She peered at the mirror again.

"Looking for someone? For something?"

"I ran out of time," Graff said. "I did all I could to route through underground channels. Get on a transport and off Earth, but no deal. Now, it really doesn't matter."

"Why not?"

"I'll find out what I need to know from you."

"Is this the part where I won't like how you validate your story?"

A smile lifted the corners of her mouth.

"Why did Richards take Terree to Helkunntanas?"

"To get her close to Rieser."

"What about the original Richards?"

Graff put her hands flat on the table. "Can't be certain, but Rieser probably got rid of him because of me."

"You kept Richards on, didn't you? You sent him back to Rieser with a promise you'd set him up for life if he could find out what the Boss was doing."

"Was that a guess?"

"Yep."

"I figured Rieser wouldn't take long to catch on to him, but you never know. Maybe he'd have some luck. Slimeball did all right sometimes."

I was getting the flow of this now. "So Rieser sends Richards—the copy— to Earth, he pretends he's the real one, and he entices you over for a meeting. Tells you he's had a breakthrough with the Emirates. With the Envoys. Something that might help with the RuBy trade."

She nodded.

"Do you know where Terree's father is?"

"No."

"But Rieser does."

"Richards seemed to think so."

"Is Rieser working with the Ultras now?" I believed him to be, but I wanted to hear her say it.

"Yes."

"He's with the Landry copy, isn't he?"

She nodded.

"And you know this how?"

"Richards."

"Original Richards."

"Yeah. He tried to get me what I needed on Rieser's operation. Said Rieser had a patron. An Ultra."

"Landry."

"Yeah. Richards was supposed to meet her at the Boss's house. Big reveal. Not too long ago, but I don't know for sure. I've lost track of time on this rock."

Alex Richards. One on the slab, who I thought might actually be the *real* original. Then there was the Richards who took Terree. And a third Richards, the one Graff said Rieser probably killed, thinking he was the traitor. Jesus, there were way too many Thin Men still walking around. Rieser had protected them. Kept them quiet.

"That's how I knew about you," Graff said, suddenly looking skittish. Her own skin actually reddened.

"What about me?" I asked.

"Rieser set you up with Alex Richards."

"I figured that out. How did *you* figure it out?"

"I followed you."

Oh Christ. The blood rushed in my ears, like the ocean in a shell, and I stood. "You. It was you?"

Graff didn't speak, but there was a kind of confession in the way she stared at me.

"You followed me from the warehouse. You—" I shook my head, amazed. All the bells and whistles in my head went off, warning me about Abby Graff and her motivations. "*You* put me in the Memory. Right outside my place."

"Tried to."

"You speak Memorese?"

"Some."

I had it now. She'd tried to put me in the Memory, was unsuccessful, and then she'd tried again in Montana.

"You put me into the Memory out at the lake," I said.

"Couldn't get off planet, but found a private shuttle. I got there ahead of you."

"You attacked me. Goddamn *shot* me." The wound in my side, previously almost forgotten, twinged in sympathy.

"An accident. Barely grazed you, big baby."

"I wrestled the blaster away, couldn't shoot back."

She looked smug. "You passed out."

"You didn't try again to get more information?"

"Doesn't work well when you're actually unconscious. Besides, I knew Tilson might be around."

"You knew about Tilson?"

"I knew it was someone. I got the name from you."

"When I was in the Memory?"

Another nod.

So the big question was—

"Why did you need that information? About my past?"

"To stop Rieser. To figure out how to get the Kenn onto him. And to get the fuck off this rock."

I did not want to think about where her story was leading. "Terree was helping me with the Memory stuff."

"Sure. She *prepared* you, took you into the Memory the first time. Afterward, she put you to work looking for her father."

"You're working together?"

"No. But you're looking for your dad, and that helps me. Richards could tell me only so much. Now he's probably dead, and the copy, which has Terree, is headed back to Helkunntanas with her."

I didn't like that Abby Graff had knowledge of my dad. More evidence that he'd been involved in doings not altogether on the level. Had Greist pulled him into all this, or had my dad done the pulling?

"Jesus." I sat down and put my head in my hands.

"If you find Rieser," Graff said, "that asshole gets gone, and you might find out what happened to your dad. And if you find your dad, you'll probably find Greist. And if you find Greist, you find the Ultras. That's *my* theory, anyway."

I looked up, suddenly tired. "Find them? There's one of them, my goddamn ex-girlfriend, here on Earth right now!"

"We can find the Ultras that matter, here, in the Union."

A shiver uncoiled my spine. "You think there are more?"

"We can travel right to them."

I snickered. "And how do we do that?"

"Sleep." Abby Graff reached out with her left arm and grasped my upper arm—a strange action for the RuBy queen of Swain to carry out. "And not the sleep of the Memory, Crowell. The sleep of the Ultras."

The sleep when they made the Thin Men. When they'd tried to take over the Union by replacing key people with copies. *Glow*. Complaints about missing time. Even I had succumbed to the alien Landry's illuminated fingers.

Graff's hand was on my elbow now. "It's the way the Ultras work. Somehow, they can *travel*."

"But we can't? Travel?"

"Not exactly."

"But you think there's a way to do it. To where they might be."

"I know there is. There's a place. A place of Rieser's, a house on Helkunntanas."

"How do you know this?"

"Because Rieser's done it, a number of times. That's what the Richards working for me said. I bet at least one of those Richards copies did, too."

Alex Richards, who might have been watching me, in one way or another, all my life.

"Greist traveled this way too," she added.

I sat in silence, the room dead to me. The code card had been recording, but how much of our talk would Bardsley and Jennifer believe if I played it back to them? Would they come to the same conclusion I had? That not only had Greist, Alex Richards, and Rieser used the sleep of the Ultras to travel, but . . .

"My dad?"

"Maybe. But I won't know until you tell me."

I frowned. "Tell you? How am I going to tell you?"

She slipped her hand from my elbow and grabbed my wrist, her fingers fanned out over my Rolex watch. "The same way as before."

With her other hand she pulled at one of her braids, which fell loose. Suddenly, a paper was in her hand.

"AmBer," I whispered, staring at the Earth-made drug in Graff's palm. It was sickly yellow, and now that she'd removed it from her hair, its tainted medicinal candle-wax smell pervaded the room. No wonder everyone hated it.

She brought the paper closer, and I briefly fuzzed out.

"Christ," I said. "My Rolex."

"Freelund gave it back to you, after they found it outside the warehouse. But I'd already altered it. DNA-tracker, and a somatic trigger tuned into your peripheral nervous system."

"A *tracker*?"

"Triggered by AmBer. Giving me control of your body movements. Skeletal muscles."

"So you could put me in the Memory . . ."

"Tried to, that first time. The AmBer was nearby, but not close enough. I was successful in Montana because I followed you and made a go at you. The third time you entered it yourself, but I put a square of AmBer in your pocket."

That's how it got there. I'd found it, puzzled over it, then discarded it. "But the Memory is a Memor thing. Shared memory between—"

"I've had some training in it," she said. "Someone taught me, but I needed some help with the AmBer and the trigger."

"A Memor helped you."

"You need to go in the Memory *now*," she said. "Here. While they're not watching. It helps you. It helps me." She raised her palm again. "Everyone wins."

"If I let this happen, what happens to you?"

She leaned back, pulling the AmBer away. "I get a ride home. I'm still a prisoner as far as the NIO is concerned. They can get me for any number of infractions related to the RuBy trade off Helkunntanas."

"Just tell them what you've told me."

"Yeah, right."

"Jennifer will listen."

She shook her head. "No NIO. There's too much at stake."

"Christ, it's of Union importance. Why not?"

"It'll spook Rieser, and I lose my chance. You can bring them in later, after I figure out what you know, and after I get to his people in Khrem."

"Which people?"

"His muscle, and his lead sniffer."

"And who's that?"

"Bar owner named Juke is Rieser's go-to for those he needs to disappear. His lead sniffer's name is Vanderberg Parr."

"I've heard his name from Forno, but I don't know him."

She pulled another face. "Well, you sort of *do* know him."

I shrugged. "Do I or don't I?"

"He's a Thin Man, but his past-life memories are gone. He's a RuBy addict, a changed man, but he's searching."

The flow of memories came erratically fast: the old private eye biz, the search for Rieser, the NIO commission, the desperate run from Earth, the Flaming Sea Tavern, Cara, Forno, the tent city, the ski resort—

I'm just a copy. A pattern in the buffer. They got to your partner, scanned his pattern . . .

The Brindos copy.

They could change him from a dozen captured patterns. His pattern is there . . .

"Alan Brindos," I heard myself whisper.

"Your old partner," Graff said. "I don't give a shit about him, personally, if he's in with Rieser, but he meant something to you, even if he has no recollection of his life before this. But maybe that's enough to convince you to get me out of here."

My moment of reckoning was short. An easy decision.

"Put me in the Memory," I said.

Abby Graff grinned—a bit too eagerly, maybe.

"A tiny data-stud in the Rolex will record everything you remember," Graff said.

"And then what?"

"Then I turn the data over to the Kenn. With Rieser gone, I get free rein over the Swain and Khrem districts. Either that, or I get my chance to kill him."

I gathered my resolve. *Brindos is out there somewhere.*

She touched the square of AmBer to my Rolex. "Don't fight it."

With the actual contact of AmBer to the glass face and the DNA trigger, the ticking had barely begun before my head spun and I lost my focus on Abby Graff.

She phased out.

My dad appeared and screamed at me to run.

Twenty-six

THE ROOM STANK OF CHARRED FLESH, RuBy, AND SWEAT. TEM FORNO stared hard at Vanderberg Parr. He'd never met the real Brindos, but recognized Parr for who he was pretty quickly. Crowell would have a hard time dealing with this wrinkle. His partner hadn't talked about Alan Brindos much since the funeral, a sentimental human ritual. Forno had only seen Brindos in his Plenko form, and now here Brindos was . . . but really, still not the true Brindos.

Ignoring Parr, Forno turned his attention to Qerral's lifeless body near the door. Mayira had Parr covered with Qerral's zip gun, so Forno turned his back to the sniffer and crouched again. Let the man fret a little longer.

Ah, Qerral. He ran his hand over her shoulder, feeling her bones through the matted fur, still shocked by how frail she had become during his absence. Now she was dead, a victim of Parr's stupidity. Or maybe it was Qerral's stupidity. Or his own.

I declare for you now. May the dust of Helkunntanas pass us by and the blackrock support our union.

That had been the extent of the declaring to Qerral, other than the small fee for administrative services rendered. No til-death-do-us-part garbage.

Ah, Qerral.

He kissed her forehead, stared at her open eyes a moment, and tenderly closed them.

"Goddamn it, I need more than a name," Parr grumbled from behind him. "Who was Alan Brindos?"

Forno stood, turned, and stared down angrily at Parr. The sniffer gulped. "Your name in exchange for your information about Greist. Wasn't that the deal?"

"A name tells me nothing," Parr said, softening. "Please. You implied I mattered to your partner. I need to know."

"You weren't meant to know. Otherwise, the Ultras or Movement scrubs would've given you more memories."

"Things are different now."

"Are they?"

"That was several years ago."

"Seems to me the Ultras are still here, Rieser's involved, and you're Rieser's main man."

"Please," Parr said. "Give me something to anchor myself to."

"You still have your beginning of the bargain to keep."

"Beginning?"

"Your end," Mayira corrected Forno, who smiled. She was getting into it now.

"Greist," Parr said. "Yes. I can help you. I can take you to him."

That was too easy, Forno knew. But it was something, a direction. He inched nearer Parr, causing the sniffer to crane his neck upward even more. But he declined to retreat, to show any more weakness.

Forno asked, "Where?"

"West of Khrem. Out in the blackrock. Rieser's place."

"The Olsare Outcrop?"

"That's it."

Right into the King of Khrem's lair, huh? Forno couldn't waste any more time. He needed to work out what had happened here on Helkunntanas, and if that meant going to where Rieser was?

"Fine," Forno said, giving in. "You want to know who you were? Brindos and my partner were friends. They worked together for the NIO, and before that, they had their own private detective agency. They spent a good while, in fact, looking for your Boss. Brindos was an unsung hero of the Ultra scare a year ago."

Parr blanched. "Crowell?"

"So you know him."

Parr barely nodded. "Heard of him."

"Through Rieser, no doubt."

"An Ultra is looking for him."

"I'd figured there might be one back in the Union. Who?"

"Cara Landry."

"That's what we figured."

"Rieser said she traveled to find Crowell. To get rid of him. She did so right before I came here looking for you."

"Well, we'd better hurry," Forno said, waving the blaster at the door. The outward calm he revealed to Parr barely masked his alarm at the possibility of Crowell in serious trouble with the Landry.

"Okay, okay," Parr said, hands up. Then he bent toward his cooler.

"Leave it."

"It's hot, man. The sun's coming up."

"Leave the cooler." Forno waved the blaster again. "You have a flier, I assume?"

Parr nodded.

"We all fit?" Forno held his free hand over his head to indicate his height.

"We'll fit. And it's not far."

"Rieser's place."

"I can take you right to him."

"To Greist?"

"He's not there, but Rieser is. He's the one who knows."

"Why would he tell us? He wanted us dead. He sent you to kill us."

"That was before you mentioned Greist. Before you told me who I was."

"I don't understand why all that would change his mind."

"When we get nearer the House, you'll understand."

The sun had come up all right. Forno had lost complete track of time while tied down in Qerral's apartment, Juke hovering like a carrion bird, waiting for Parr to show up.

Forno had Juke's stunner now, as well as Parr's Wesson blaster. Mayira had the zip gun. Three weapons to none. He liked the odds.

A search of the apartment hadn't turned up his own weapon or comm card. No way for Crowell to contact him now, even with the two-way ping. Forno hoped Crowell's visit to the Emirates Tower had yielded something useful.

Helk's breath, Crowell needed to get his ass here.

Forno thought about calling in a few favors with the Kenn, but that rock had crumbled. He'd need a lot of help from the NIO's end to clean that up.

They left behind Qerral's body for now. Juke's body in the apartment too. Forno would be back for Qerral, he promised himself. While he couldn't quite blame Parr for what happened, he could blame Baren Rieser, whose jeweler's hands had manipulated the chain of events leading to her death.

Rieser would pay.

Parr's flier sped out of Khrem, heading west, into the sun, at a bearing

Forno figured put them on an intersecting path with the Olsare Outcrop, a literal no-Helk land consisting of miles and miles of jagged blackrock spires, and sheer, impassable cliffs that even transports skirted.

Forno did not like the idea of the flier heading into that mess. The flier was quite nice, even if it presented a challenge wedging himself inside. Mayira, settled into the back, kept the zip gun aimed at Parr. One of her hair spikes had fluffed out like a leafy tree. Forno, his head brushing the top of the flier, even as he bent forward uncomfortably, made sure the sniffer saw both weapons he was holding: Juke's stunner in his right hand, aimed at Parr's head, and the blaster in his lap. He stared hard at Parr, but his brain kept showing him Brindos, a disorienting three-dimensional, live version of the images he'd come across.

Parr fumbled in his pocket and Forno tensed until he saw the square of RuBy. Parr rolled it expertly, with one hand, and put it on his tongue. The man's fingers were stained red from the constant use. Forno had never seen fingertips that red from the drug's dye.

He stared out at the approaching blackrock. The Outcrop. The house was there somewhere.

When the Outcrop appeared ahead of them, the flier dipped lower. Forno thought they might need to go higher, but Parr kept them on a straight line toward the blackrock, not slowing to search for a house that would be next to impossible to spot amid the crags and spires. Parr was the new Boss, apparently, so he must know his way around.

In fact, the flier seemed on some predetermined course. Forno willed himself to act in an instant, because he didn't trust Parr, even if the sniffer had seemed in earnest to keep the promise he'd made in exchange for his original name. But Rieser was involved, and he trusted that man even less.

Why had Rieser given up Khrem to Parr? Forno had to believe the Ultras had made Rieser a better offer.

"You on autopilot?" Forno asked.

Parr nodded again. "There's a breach, completely invisible until we're right on top of it. This is the only way to find it."

In the distance, Forno made out a shimmer of white. He squinted at it, a vague recollection forming in his mind, and before long colors flickered within the light, and he knew what he was seeing.

"He's got a tashing datascreen," Forno told Parr.

Parr looked taken aback. "You know what a datascreen is?"

"Oh yeah." He'd been through the one on Aryell guarding New Venasaille. He'd gone through a second time with Crowell and discovered the true purpose of the drugged refugees.

Ever-shifting patterns sliced through the light.

"The tent city," Parr said.

"That's the one."

"What's a datascreen?" Mayira asked from the back.

"Virtual deterrent," Forno said. "Very unpleasant to traverse."

"*Unpleasant?*" Mayira said.

"Light, colors, shapes, sounds, all bombarding you. Bumpy, that's for sure. It's alien tech."

"Alien as in—"

"Ultras. A gift from Cara, right, Parr?" He refused to call him Brindos.

The flier angled sideways and slowed, edging toward the middle of the light show. A preprogrammed course.

"There's a virtual breach," Parr said, ignoring the question. "The flier's course will line up perfectly with the insertion point."

Insertion point. Like a jump slot? Forno doubted it, but he didn't like the reference.

"Don't worry," Parr said. "It's fucking brilliant." He managed a weak smile, leaning toward the windshield and giving the datascreen a close look-see. "This flier has high tech repulsors that dampen some of the discomfort."

The datascreen came upon them quickly, its light intensifying, and a high-pitched whine rose as the flier flirted with the edge of the screen.

"Top-of-the-line noise suppressors," Parr said, leaning back again. He closed his eyes, unconcerned.

When the flier hit the breach, the bumps and shakes started.

"Good shielding, too," Parr said, and the flier's windows went dark. Only its interior lights illuminated the cabin.

"Yeah, I had a flier with similar shielding," Forno said, bracing himself against the successive jolts.

"If you could deal with the wild lights and constant screen," Parr said, "you'd get a goddamn crazy view of the House. That's a capital H, by the way. The place deserves it. One of a kind." He opened his eyes. "The blackrock is intimidating as hell and a little nerve-wracking."

Tell me about it, Forno thought.

"It *is* Ultra tech," Parr said, finally answering Forno's question about the datascreen's origins. "It's what the Boss has over all the other districts. One of the crown jewels of the king of the jewelers."

Parr nodded rhythmically for a long time. Forno attributed the tic to his RuBy high, because the sniffer kept talking, nodding. Still, Parr's behavior bothered him.

A sharp drop jarred Forno and he steadied himself with his left arm against the front panel. The stunner in his hand clunked hard against it.

"Oops," Parr said, and his nodding stopped. "No worries. No worries." He clicked his tongue in a rhythm similar to that of his earlier nodding.

Click click click

Like a countdown. Forno felt a tinge of panic as his vision blurred and his limbs suddenly jellied. In fact, he started to lose his grip on Juke's stunner.

"I could turn off the neural destabilizer," Parr said, "since it's now my right to do so, but in this case it's better if I don't."

Forno concentrated on Parr, forcing his hands to tighten around his weapon. He did not like the sound of *neural destabilizer*.

"Forno?" Mayira said from the back. "I feel funny. I can't move . . . I can't *move* right."

"Ultras, Ultras," Parr said. He popped more RuBy.

"Parr," Forno said . . . or tried to say. It came out sounding like *Purrrrr.* He wanted to warn Mayira to keep the zip gun steady, but his whole body slumped in his chair and he slipped left toward Parr.

"Now, now," Parr said, pushing him away, "I hardly know you."

But Parr's words had a strange timbre. He, too, was succumbing to this odd phenomenon. Forno thought: *Tash, I should've known.*

"*My* House now." Parr struggled to get the words out. "I know who I am now, but not who I *am*. Brindos. What kind of name is Brindos? Better than Frock, I guess."

Mayira hadn't spoken for a while. Forno managed, just barely, to twist his head enough to see that she was no longer visible in the back.

"Mayira?"

"She's already . . . gone," Parr said.

"Gone?" *The neural destabilizer.*

Parr said, "Hard to get used to . . . even now."

"What're . . . you doing?" Forno said.

"We're going in on even terms," Parr said clearly, and then he fell forward against the console.

Forno lasted a few seconds longer, but eventually he too gave in to the mounting destabilization and fell away to sleep.

Twenty-seven

MY DAD APPEARED AND SCREAMED AT ME TO RUN.

But there was something I'd forgotten.

And what I'd forgotten happened to be why my dad yelled at me to leave the Emirates conference and stay away.

No. I needed to back up. I had learned how to use some of the control Terree had told me about. How to focus well enough to sift through the thoughts of those I'd interacted with in this room.

The Memory took me full force, and I remembered.

Six figures were seated at the oblong conference table. I stood at the foot of the table, the door behind me, nervous because, for the first time, Dad had invited me to one of his sessions. He'd decided to do so on a whim, and had told me not to worry. If anyone made a fuss, he would smooth things over.

On the holo-window embedded in the front wall, arcane symbols scrolled in a repetitive pattern in all four corners. Memor symbols. Some unfamiliar Helk words scrolled there too, and a few recognizable human math symbols in equations that I didn't understand. The middle of the holo-window contained a number of diagrams and three-dimensional graphics. They seemed instructional, like schematics an architectural firm might present to a client.

One of the images, a thick, ominous black spire, labeled with more undecipherable symbols, looped in a bottom-to-top approximation of how it would be constructed, its 3D representation slowly roating to show all the angles. When the diagram finished building to the top of the tower, an antennae-like spindle appeared. Then a thin line erupted from it and flew away from the image, the perspective changing as it disappeared into a distant background, where another spire emerged. The complete image held for a few seconds, at which point the entire image sequence repeated.

My chest heaved, frightened by the implications of what one of the Memors had said earlier about these towers.

"Excuse me," said my dad from the seat to my right. "Why does Temonus need a weather control device?"

"The Transcontinental Conduit will fill a long-term need for meteorological stability, particularly in Ghal's larger cities," the Memor said.

This was Lorway.

I remembered my dad talking about her. Around the table, other than my dad and Lorway, sat four others, two humans and two Helks. Neither Lorway nor these four were Envoys. They were scientists and members of the newly formed Science Consortium. I knew a little about all of them, for they were famous on their own worlds, recognized geniuses in applied mathematics and science.

"I have no doubt it's a technological breakthrough," said Cerm Knol, the Helk sitting across from my dad. She was one of the brightest minds in the Union. My dad had helped her during a mediation with the lower Clans. The Clans had requested more oversight in all things related to Helkunntanas's attempt to convert to human measurements and standards.

Cerm Knol sat in one of the few Helk-sized chairs in the room. "I'm with Mr. Crowell. It seems like overkill." She twisted the gold circlet around her neck. "And you must understand how difficult it'll be to obtain enough mortaline from Coral Moon to construct that wire, even with the help of the NIO."

"Let alone getting it from there to Temonus economically," the human Bernice Talley said. "Lorway, where did you come upon some of this theoretical technology?"

Lorway paused and lowered her gaze, and her short ponytail swung over her shoulder to the front.

My dad looked at me, and I saw his concern.

Finally, Lorway said, "I understand your reservations, Ms. Talley, but we have a powerful sponsor. Greist Sahl-kla tells me that there will be a period of indoctrination at the retreat after this conference."

"The conference is a sham," Talley said. "Knol, tell them."

The Helk stood, making her presence felt as she glared at everyone in turn, her ornamental bracelets jangling. I gulped at her size. A First Clan female could still cause unease. The male Helk next to her also glared, but remained silent. I didn't know much about this Second Clan Helk, Fon Blensko.

"Seventy-five percent of the sessions have been cancelled," Cerm Knol said. "The few remaining ones were postponed and rescheduled for tomorrow."

"Half the Envoys have already left," Bernice Talley added. "There are more aides, pages, and family members inside the Knightley Tower than actual Envoys or administrative conflict instructors."

"Then," Lorway said, "you won't mind leaving today for the retreat so we can rest before trying to add the Conduit to Temonus Provincial's next session. We already have the blessing of President Nguyen."

"Bah." Knol backed away from the table while tugging on a calza ring encircling one of her fingers.

The other human, a small man with graying hair who had yet to speak, raised his hand. He wore a brown suit jacket, neatly pressed.

"Speak for Christ's sake," Talley said. "You don't have to raise your hand, Michael."

"Mr. Stanko?" Lorway said.

The older man arose now, dwarfed by the Helk standing next to him. "Perhaps everything set in motion by this Chicago conference was for the purpose of bringing us together."

Lorway looked down again.

"You've pulled us into this Consortium, and we're all thankful," Stanko continued. "It's an honor to participate. But the fact that you needed us here, and have offered us a trained Envoy to oversee the meeting—" he bowed politely to my dad "—speaks to the highly sensitive nature of this Conduit project. And if the conference is a sham, as Ms. Talley says, then perhaps someone can tell us who's behind it all. Mr. Crowell?"

Stanko sat down and braced his chin on both fists. My dad rose and smiled in turn at everyone at the table. Everyone except me, for I was not an official participant.

"Please," he said quietly. "If you respect my status as an Envoy, please take the time to think a moment." Everyone regarded him attentively. Then, my dad said, "You are all most brilliant individuals, and I highly respect your learning." His voice had a lyrical quality I'd never heard before, certainly not at home. "Greist is my friend," he continued. "I cannot imagine he would do anything to put the Consortium's ability to work on this project at risk. You all know Greist Sahl-kla as an Envoy of great standing, do you not?"

Every person nodded, mysteriously entranced.

"Then let him give you this opportunity," Dad said. "Even if he has somehow manipulated this conference to do so, you are all here now, and that—" He pointed at the endlessly scrolling data on the holo-window. "—seems to have undeniable potential to do Temonus some good." He laughed quietly and reassurringly. "I don't pretend to understand any of the science behind this thing, but I do understand each of you and respect the knowledge you possess."

He circumnavigated the table, giving each member of the Consortium plenty of space and sensibly avoiding making them wonder if he meant to stop behind them. When he did stop, he did so in front of the holo-window, his back to everyone as he studied the data.

Lorway cleared her throat. Talley sniffed loudly.

At length, he turned and spoke thoughtfully. "Cerm, do you believe in the science behind this tower?"

Cerm Knol took only a moment before nodding. "I do," she said. "The science behind it is impressive in design, scope and potential function."

Fon Blensko also nodded. "Impressive indeed," he rumbled.

"Ms. Talley," Dad said, smiling. "Is this something that can benefit Temonus? Perhaps all of the Union?"

Talley, fidgeting, spoke deliberately. "We would need to take great care with the wetlands in particular. Our impact studies could possibly delay construction for years, but it would be worth it in the long run. I'm not altogether sure Temonus, particularly the continent of Ghal, is the right venue for this project—other regions on Temonus, and indeed other Union worlds like Orgon and Aryell, would perhaps benefit more from it. But I do believe it would be a better testing ground owing to its relatively easy access to the jump slot from Coral, and Ribon itself is too big and too sparsely populated to expect measurable results."

"This fact does not suddenly make it economical," Stanko added. "But it seems we should take Greist Sahl-kla's patrons at face value and approve work on this project."

Cerm Knol sat back in her Helk seat. Bernice Talley sat taller, and Michael Stanko put his hands flat on the table. Fon Blensko grunted.

I regarded my dad in awe. Swiftly, he'd erased the scientists' feelings of unease and brought them to trust in Greist and to accept the Conduit. Having achieved his purpose, my dad calmly returned to his chair and sat.

Lorway stood. "Very well," she said. "I've had my own doubts, of course, and a few of the details concerning the ultrafast x-ray specs' applicableness to weather control data needs clarification before we go much further, but we can attend to these issues once we arrive in Montana." She looked at Dad. "We're all looking forward to seeing your beautiful lake."

"My pleasure," Dad said, and he finally turned and grinned at me. "David will be happy not to travel for once."

I smiled back, full of a newfound respect for my dad and his skills.

"Does anyone object to moving forward?" Lorway asked.

No one did.

"I'm calling in Greist's assistant for a briefing on the backers of this project," Lorway said, flicking a sensor near her on the table. "Greist, as it turns out, does have to work at one of the remaining sessions today."

Dad paused and scowled. "No, he should be available. He didn't mention any session today."

"This is what I was told," Lorway said.

The door clicked open behind me, and Dad stood. The Science Consortium also rose, the scrunch of chairs loud in the quiet following Lorway's remark. I turned.

My page Alex Richards stepped inside the room ahead of a tall, middle-aged, broad-shouldered man in a black pinstriped suit and white collared shirt, a narrow black tie barely visible. He had a full head of brown hair, and intense dark brown eyes that sparkled with amusement.

"Hello, my friends," the man said in a high-pitched voice. He moved past Alex, who also had a knowing smile on his face. I took a step back, and Dad gripped my shoulder.

"Allow me to introduce myself," the man said, spreading his arms. He seemed surprised to see me, but recovered and addressed the room: "My name is Wesley Baren Rieser, and I am your liason to the powers behind this project. A fine start to a new era of peace."

From behind me, Dad said, "What do you mean, peace?"

"To new beginnings!" Rieser shouted, ignoring him. "All the data in the world couldn't sway me from this path. The world is data, my good friends. Filled with data and colored *red*. So prepare yourselves, will you? It's nearly time to travel."

"Now?" Cerm Knol said.

"Red?" Fon Blenko said.

Wesley Baren Rieser ignored them and focused on me again. "And who are you, my good man?" He came up so close I had to crane my neck to keep my eyes on him. I did my best to show no fear. "Are you Lucky's son? Hmmm?"

"His name is *David*," Dad said. "I didn't think it would be a problem if he attended this session. I'm sorry, but who are you, really? How do you know Greist Sahl-kla?"

Rieser tsked. "Oh, but your son *is* a problem, Mr. Crowell. He's not part of the agreement."

"What agreement?"

"He can't go with us."

"Montana's our home. The lake is—"

Rieser interrupted with a laugh. "*Montana?* Oh fuck no, not Montana. We're taking the Consortium straight to the source. Straight to Temonus, to begin work on the Conduit."

When Rieser ruffled my hair, I instinctively drew back into Dad.

Rieser said, "You will go with Alex, Mr. Crowell. David will stay. Sadly, he knows more than he should."

"Alex?" Dad said. "Why am I going with Alex?"

"For now, he's the only one who can take you." Rieser spoke more loudly to Alex. "Isn't that right, Alex? Are you prepared?"

Alex puffed up and leered at us. "Totally Ultrafied, Boss." He pulled down his Emirates page uniform from his neck. The word *Ultra* ran along his collarbone.

Lorway had worked her way around the table. "Just what is this? I agreed to no such thing. You said our families would not be harmed."

"Lorway?" Michael Stanko said. "What *are* you talking about?"

"She's talking about rebuilding the Union!" Rieser yelled. "Revolution. Peace."

Angry now, his face flushed, Stanko stared at Rieser, and then Lorway. "Revolution?"

"Oh," Rieser said, his voice falling. "Oh, I see. You've not told them everything have you, Lorway? Well." He edged nearer the table. "You all belong to *them* now. Greist has given you to us, in exchange for your cooperation." He stretched out his arms again. "We're going to have an Ultra good time!"

Cerm Knol stood, threw back her chair, and growled at Rieser.

Wesley Baren Rieser held out a hand, as if warning her back. The Helk stopped, but continued snarling at Rieser. A second passed, then Rieser's hand glowed white.

The brightness of it, the unexpectedness of it, shocked me. "Dad?"

The room erupted with the indignant voices of the Science Consortium as all the others stood as one. My dad positioned me behind him. Everyone else surged forward. My page, Alex, had a blaster I hadn't noticed, and he squeezed the trigger, splashing beams over our heads and stopping everyone's momentum. Rieser moved. Wearing a serene smile, he strode forward with his hand a-glow.

Touched by Rieser's hand, Cerm Knol fell. The Helk's dead weight shook the floor. Michael Stanko yelled something about treason, but a moment later froze mid-sentence and slumped to the floor. Rieser kept moving between the remaining members of the Consortium.

My thoughts started to unravel. Dad grabbed my shoulders and turned me to him. He murmured, "Get out of here."

"I—I can't."

"You can!"

Lorway fell next. The glow around Rieser's hand spread and brightened.

I focused on the door, and Alex Richards smiled and dared me to do something. His blaster held us right where we were.

Bernice Talley fell.

My dad's hands slipped from my shoulders, but he surprised me by rushing Alex Richards before Alex could react. Dad knocked him backward, and the blaster discharged, its beam sizzling harmlessly past both Dad and me and disrupting the holo-window. The window melted and went dark. I turned back just as Dad slammed Alex's head into the edge of the open door. Alex grunted and fell.

Wesley Baren Rieser came toward Dad, who had landed on top of Alex. The fog of unconsciousness overcame me.

"David! Leave! Just leave!"

Dad's voice.

"Get away from here," he pleaded. "Stay away from us. We'll meet later!"

I stumbled, caught my balance, and fought my way to Dad, who had braced his forearm across Alex's neck. Alex couldn't breathe, could barely resist my dad. I crouched, and Dad's unfocused gaze darted back and forth.

"Dad," I said. Blinding tears came to my eyes, and I tried to blink them away.

Rieser had come up behind me, his hand hovering within inches of my shoulder. The glow from that hand bathed Dad's face in light.

"Run!" he screamed.

His eyes closed. I darted under Rieser's outstretched arm and out through the door.

I did not look back.

Twenty-eight

ABIGAIL GRAFF'S FACE CAME INTO FOCUS AS I LEFT THE MEMORY. When she grinned, I turned my head, not comfortable with that at all. Somehow, I had fallen from the chair and now lay flat on my back on the observation room's tiled floor.

Graff ground her foot into my chest. "Stay down," she said.

"What the hell?"

"This is on my terms, Crowell. You and I are going to Helkunntanas."

"The travel visas," I wheezed.

She increased the pressure on my chest. "Visas. Really."

I struggled to speak. "Jennifer won't let you have the visas. Anyway, no one will accept a visa not coded to you. Even then, you're Abby Graff. Everyone's looking for you. Everyone knows you."

"I have my own way out."

"No one is going to just let you walk out."

Graff regarded me. I squirmed under her gaze. And her foot. "Crowell, please. This is the county morgue. Temporary digs. How many NIO personnel do you think are actually here?"

"More than you can handle."

"If it was just me, maybe."

"I'm not helping you get out."

"Sure you are. Eventually. But I've got a partner." She leered down at me and pointed to her ear. "Notified the moment I activated the data-stud."

She waved my code card in my face, pleased that she had it and I didn't. "Simple transfer from here, and not traceable thanks to your freesource prog."

As if on cue, the door opened. I half expected to see Jennifer walk through. Or a copy of her. She'd been copied before. Maybe Graff had won this Jennifer over, like the Landry Ultra had done a year earlier. It would make sense—if Jennifer was a copy. Who else would have the correct visas, coded and ready?

But it wasn't Jennifer, and I scolded myself for even thinking that way. Nothing Jennifer had done today suggested a betrayal.

A Memor entered the room.

"Goddamn," I muttered. "Lorway." This was who Graff had meant when she said she'd had some training with the Memory.

"Maybe you should've killed her when you had the chance," Graff said, finally taking her knee off my chest. She stood straight. "Instead of letting her flee the mortaline vault on Ribon."

Lorway's lips thinned into a wide smile. I'd just seen the original Lorway in the Memory. This copy barely looked like her. Her orange hair, nearly faded to white, hung loose on her back, neither washed nor oiled for some time. She wore human clothes, blue trousers, and a black tunic that flowed past her hips.

"How did you get in here?" I asked, incredulous. I sat up, rubbing my chest. Lorway didn't have a weapon. Had she somehow incapacitated Jennifer? Were Bardsley and the other NIO agents still in the building?

"You have to ask?" Lorway chided.

Rieser had put down everyone in the room at the Chicago conference with the glow of the Ultras, and he wasn't an Ultra. He'd acquired some part of their power, but not all of it. I suspected Lorway had done the same to the NIO personnel in the building. Was it a different power because she was a Thin Man?

Graff held out her hand. When I grabbed it, she pulled me up. "Don't worry, they're all alive. They'll wake up eventually. Like I said, everyone wins. You know more about your dad, and Rieser, and the Ultras. I know enough to take down Rieser. I get to go home."

Honestly, I wanted to get to Helkunntanas, too. I might find this Vanderberg Parr and Forno. I might see Alan Brindos again. Find Terree. Find Griest. *Find Dad.*

"You might get out of the building, and even Seattle," I said, "but we still don't have the right documents to get to Helkunntanas. Unless Lorway's figured out a way to get you to some underground transport."

"We've figured out a way." Graff smiled, brushed past Lorway, and peeked out the door. Satisfied, she turned back to me and raised an eyebrow.

I couldn't resist edging past her and taking my own look at the hallway. Jennifer Lisle, Aaron Bardsley, and two agents lay on the hard floor.

"Our way does not involve travel visas," Graff said, slipping past me. She crouched, and fumbled around one of the NIO agents. When she straightened, she held his blaster.

"Let me guess," I said. "Does your way involve sleep?"

Graff grunted. "Wow. On your first guess, even."

"Sometimes it happens. But I still don't understand how the glowing sleepy-bye trick will help. You said we can't do it."

Lorway said, "You're not thinking like an Ultra."

I stared at her. "Maybe because I'm *not* an Ultra?"

"We *can* travel, Mr. Crowell," Graff said. "We just need a little help. And help is just a room away."

A room away? I puzzled it over, reminding myself of the church's layout: the worship area, the Nave, the north and south wings. The autopsy room—

And then I had the answer. "Alex Richards?"

Graff nodded and laughed, happy with my confusion, her laugh much too loud in the makeshift interrogation room.

"You mean dead-on-the-slab Alex Richards?" I asked.

She said, "I mean asleep-on-the-slab Alex Richards."

I felt my eyes go wide.

Graff laughed again. "Shall we go wake him up?"

The coroner had moved Alex Richards' body into one of the coolers. I'd relieved the second agent of his weapon as we left the holding cell, even though, like the weapon Graff had found, it would be DNA-locked to that agent. We entered a square concrete room which could have been a freezer if it had been set up that way. Instead, the morgue had rolled in an ancient portable fridge system. It was actually on casters. The brushed stainless steel box stood about as tall as me. Atop it, a noisy compressor chugged away.

Hell, I thought it was a pretty impressive antique. Not that I would be ordering my own anytime soon. Just another example of state-of-the-art junk from planet Earth, slowly devolving into a backwater planet. The irony wasn't lost on me: all the help from the Memors we'd initially received in the first place, and here we were. If the Ultras ever succeeded in whatever they hoped to do, they'd probably ignore Earth in favor of the other colony planets.

Graff opened the heavy door and revealed two body trays on telescoping racks, a covered body on the top one. She rolled it out and unceremoniously pulled off the sheet. Alex Richards' naked body looked almost normal. I figured it had lost some color, but if, as Graff had suggested, he was really alive, then the blood somehow had not congealed and might actually be flowing.

"Time to hurry." Graff turned and glared at Lorway. "How much longer?"

"Possibly another ten minutes," Lorway said, moving to the side of the table directly across from Graff. "But likely less."

Graff stared at Lorway over the body. "You *can* do this?"

She nodded.

"Crowell," Graff said without looking at me, "get over here."

Get over here. I could do something else if I wanted. Find some advantage. Slam Graff into the bottom body rack. Take my code card back from her. Get to Lorway before she did her magic trick.

That is, if I'd wanted to fuck up Graff's escape plan or to stall long enough to allow the NIO agents to recover. But no. I *wanted* to help. I needed to get out of here. Forno could be in serious trouble. Terree could be in serious trouble. Hell, *every*one was in serious trouble. Goddamn Ultras.

I paused only a moment longer, then approached Graff. In this case, despite an overwhelming need to release the tension in the room, I said nothing.

Graff pulled Alex Richards' head back, exposing his throat and the dark *Ultra* tattoo on his collarbone. She inclined her head toward Lorway. "You're on." To me, she said, "It hasn't been easy learning about this. Lorway's the key, of course."

"Learning what?" I wondered.

Lorway closed her eyes and held her hand near Richards' neck. A faint glow licked at her fingers.

"This is how Rieser does it," Graff said. "How he travels."

"Tattoos infused with a nano ink that transforms the energy of an Ultra," Lorway said, "causing a barely contained antimatter reaction. It's like a nuclear bomb wrapped in an impenetrable shell, except potentially more destructive, because the whole mass of the atom is converted into energy. As long as nothing breaks the shell, all is good."

"And if the shell's broken?" I asked.

Graff pulled a face. "If it had ever happened before, we wouldn't be having this conversation."

Matter and antimatter. There had to be a barrier. Collision of the two on a large scale would mean annihilation on a scale beyond comprehension.

Lorway's fingers glowed brighter.

"The process with Richards' tattoo isn't quite the same," Graff said. "When I saw your memories of the meeting with the Science Consortium, when I saw Alex Richardsshow his tattoo, I knew we had a chance to get out of here."

"But is he really alive? Right now?"

"Close enough," Graff said. "The Ultras put him in a very deep sleep of sorts."

I stared at the Ultra tattoo. "Quantum sleep," I said, remembering Terree's explanation when she first put me into the Memory. "You've tested this theory?"

Graff inclined her head toward Lorway. "She's the expert."

Lorway opened her eyes. Her hand, now enveloped in glow, inched toward the tattoo. She touched her pointer finger to the letter U, and a sliver of light outlined the letter. "Non-locality," she said, her finger now on the L. "Instantaneous transfer from one place to another without any physical apparatus. At the quantum level it's something similar to—" She paused, searching for a comparison. "—to telepathy and precognitive dreaming."

"The Memory," I said.

"The Memory is like it on a *very* small scale," Lorway explained. The L received its outline, and the U now pulsed all the way through with light. "We're very lucky. Alex Richards has power in these letters. I suppose Rieser had him save some of it to travel."

She kept multi-tasking and lighting up the tattoo while talking about the theory behind everything.

"If you silence the mind enough," she said, "information comes to you. If you lucid dream, you are in effect quantum traveling to other dimensions of being. Frequencies shift, alternate possibilities line up, and you access the vibrations of other beings you've had contact with. It's a connectivity with your past. And with others. Your body is relaxed, but your memories are not."

When the letter T received light, the previous letters took on more glow. Lorway touched the R.

"The Ultras have somehow harnessed this idea, and on a quantum level can cause a *physical* movement through space."

"But how?" I whispered.

"You'll have to ask them." She touched the letter A. "Almost ready."

"What's next?" Graff asked.

Lorway closed her eyes again. "I'm looking for Rieser's memories. Or someone interconnected to him. Then I can determine location on Helkunntanas."

"Try Vanderberg Parr," Graff said.

My mouth very dry, I swallowed. Parr. *Brindos.*

"Very confusing," Lorway said, her brow creasing with concern. All five letters glowed independently now. She lifted her finger from the A and placed her hand on Alex Richards' forehead. Her eyes closed again.

"What's wrong?" Graff asked. "Can you find them?

"Multiple possibilities," Lorway mumbled. "A number of entitites. Three, I think. Near Khrem. Slightly blocked. I think it might be because of the black-rock. Or maybe some sort of enclosed safe room, some place biometrically out of phase. This is extremely strange."

"Blackrock," Graff mused. "It's the House. I swear it's the fucking House. I knew it was out there somewhere, but we could never find it."

"Rieser?" I asked. "Can you—" I wasn't sure how to say it. "*See* him?"

Lorway shook her head. "I can't tell if he's one of them."

Graff put her weapon away, motioned me to pocket mine, then grabbed my hand. She held our hands to the Ultra tattoo. "Cover it completely."

"What about Alex?" I asked. "Will he . . . wake up?"

Lorway smiled sadly. "Alex will be with you. He'll get you two through, but because of the nature of this sleep state, there's no telling if he'll wake up. I have no way of knowing what this process will do to him."

"And what about you?"

"I'll be incapacitated for a long while, but I'll live."

"You won't travel?"

"No."

Left behind and damaged, she would have to contend with the NIO in the building.

Lorway's glow intensified, and I experienced the same fuzziness I felt when entering the Memory. Would it feel *exactly* the same? Graff's eyes were already closed. I closed mine.

The morgue unfocused around me.

Then I heard frantic footsteps and the whine of a blaster powering up.

"Crowell! Stop!"

Jennifer.

I mustered focus to open my eyes and turn my head toward her. "Don't," I whispered, shaking my head.

"I don't know what the hell you think you're doing," she said, "but you need to move away from the body now. *All* of you. Away and down on the floor."

Bardsley, still looking dazed, staggered into the room behind her, his own weapon ready. The NIO agents followed, looking naked without their blasters.

"I have to do this," I said, "and you have to let me do it. Please."

"No way."

I was fuzzing out. Lorway couldn't stop now, I figured, or everything would be lost.

She confirmed it by saying, loud enough for everyone to hear, "I won't be able to contain any reactions with the antimatter and nano-ink if we stop now. Keep your hands over the tattoo!"

"Jennifer," I said, conscious of the light of Lorway's hand, the light haloing my hand and Graff's. "You heard what she said."

"That's Lorway," Jennifer said, aiming the weapon at the Memor. "A Thin Man. Don't believe her. And *gods*, Crowell. You're doing this with Graff, too?"

"I can get the answers I need." What I meant was that I hoped to find out what I needed *personally*, but to Jennifer I said, "To stop the Ultras. You have to trust me."

She scoffed. "Trust. You throw that word around so much it doesn't mean anything anymore."

Bardsley kept his weapon leveled.

"Please," I said, and the room briefly phased out again like a virtual thrill ride dissolving into reality. "Too . . . important."

"Let it go, Dave." She lowered her weapon, but Bardsley kept his level.

"Let it go?" I laughed weakly.

Lorway and Graff barely moved. They were lost. Interconnected now, and here I was, holding out for all of us. I kept forcing back a tangible strand of *another place* fighting to break through the quantum state between us. Observed and observer. Awake and asleep. It seemed very, very far away.

"You can't bring him back," Jennifer said. "Let it go."

Bring him *back*? Oh no. It was still about *him*, after all this? Well, I could use it to my advantage.

"I can!" I yelled. "He's alive."

"What did you say?"

"Brindos is alive."

A black fissure from the other place shimmered in front of me. What *was* that? I looked away, doing my best to keep Jennifer in the middle of my vision.

She laughed, but it seemed forced. "You're joking."

"It's a copy, Jennifer, but he's alive. He doesn't even know who he is. Not really. But I'm certain he's the answer to everything Ultra."

Jennifer frowned. She was wavering, and I was leaving soon.

Now Bardsley spoke. "Crowell."

"Wait," Jennifer said to Bardsley. "Just . . . wait." She looked at me, eyes narrowed. "Can you really get there and fetch him back?"

"That's enough, Lisle," Bardsley said.

I nodded at her, ignoring Bardsley. I was coming ungrounded and had to try twice as hard to keep my hand on Graff's. "And maybe Rieser, and maybe my dad."

She nodded. "And save the Union."

"Something like that."

"I can come after you. I still have a visa."

"Good. Do it. Khrem. Rieser's House somewhere in the Olsare Outcrop. Bring the Kenn. Big party."

"What're you talking about?"

We locked eyes for several incredibly long seconds. I heard Bardsley's labored breathing next to her.

Jennifer's body language and demeanor changed. She was calming down even as I grew tense fighting the transition to—I hoped—Helkunntanas. The dark fissure—the portal or whatever it was—misted around me again. I saw a tunnel, a door. I'd seen these before.

I *felt* a transition. In fact, nausea signaled my imminent translation to this place.

"Gotta go," I said.

"If you're sure . . ."

"I'm sure."

Jennifer blew out air and said, "Then go get them."

Bardsley had enough. "I can't risk it." With three quick steps, he shoved past Jennifer. "Forget it, Crowell, you're done."

"No!" Jennifer yelled.

Bardsley aimed his blaster at me, low, probably to cause a leg wound that wouldn't prove fatal. Jennifer yelled something, and I sensed her insubstantial form rushing Bardsley, reaching out for his arm.

The blaster discharged.

Beside me, Abby Graff grunted just before the black fissure snapped back into place, and the outlines of a square room with deep blackrock walls immediately solidified around me. *A flash.*

And then I gave in to the sleep of the Ultras.

Twenty-nine

VANDERBERG PARR WOKE IN THE POOL ROOM.

He gathered his wits, hoping he hadn't lost his advantage. That is, the advantage he'd hoped to gain over Tem Forno when the deterrents of the datascreen took effect. Parr might be more experienced with the procedure, but Forno was a goddamn *Helk*; his kind tended to recover quickly.

The rock walls came into focus, as did the cots and the steel door. Luckily, Forno and Mayira still slept on the floor. Parr took a moment to check Forno for weapons, but knew he wouldn't find any. The Wesson blaster lay somewhere in the abandoned shuttle, along with the stunner and zip gun. He thought about moving the girl to a cot, but he didn't want to risk waking her.

The body of Alex Richards had vanished from the Pool Room.

He knew now how the room worked, that information suddenly lighting up his brain, passed on to him during the neural sleep. Rieser had given him control now, allowing access to the House on his own.

The room was a hub, a buffer of sorts, a holding cell for those invited to the House. The neural sleep—a product of Memor ingenuity, quantum aspects of the Memory, and Ultra tech—transported the occupants of vehicles approaching the House into the room. The vehicles continued on without them, autopiloted to the hidden hangar within the blackrock near the House. The neural sleep, a less destructive variety than the Ultra sleep, allowed the aliens to *travel*. It worked well enough for the short jaunt to the Pool Room.

Parr hated coming to the House, but now he had control of it. He could have ignored the datascreen procedure. Neutralized the neural sleep. Entered the House from the hangar. But he'd needed to get the jump on Tem Forno.

Forno, the partner of Dave Crowell.

Crowell, who had once called a version of Parr a partner. Alan Brindos.

A revelation. Hell, it's what he'd wanted, wasn't it? *Do you know who I am?* Now that he knew, he didn't feel any different. A big reveal, fallen flat. Was there any part of the real Alan Brindos still inside him, buried deep within the memories—or their absence—the Ultras had given him? Had the nanomaterials done the work, and that was that?

His head hurt as usual. He pulled out three RuBy squares—his last ones—rolled two of them, and placed them on his tongue to dull the edge of the pain. Thought: Fuck it, and rolled and took the third one. A glance at the steel door that connected to the Quarry reminded him of the DNA lock sensor there, underneath the buzzer.

Rieser had keyed the House to him. Touching that sensor would enable him to exit the Pool Room and leave these two wondering what the hell had happened.

In the main house, he would find Rieser waiting. Probably the other Alex Richards and the Memor woman, Terree. Parr shivered. He would have to explain what had happened down in Khrem. At the Helkette's place. *Goddamn it.* Forno's arrival had thrown everything into a jumbled mess. Turned a simple job into both a nightmare and a mystery.

Alan Brindos.

Doubt steeped in his RuBy-numbed brain. Maybe he'd taken too much, even for him. Maybe the haze derived from something else. Something trying to break free, escape his nano-fused memory.

Some*one.*

He glanced again at Forno and Mayira, still out cold.

Before he altogether lost his advantage, he made a decision and slapped the door sensor. Time to face the Boss.

The door opened, and the overwhelming smell of RuBy hit him. He stepped into the Quarry and registered not only the entire room but also the door thunking shut behind him.

Piles of RuBy lay scattered everywhere, but all of Rieser's guests had long since gone home.

Parr sensed Rieser's presence but instead, spotted Terree on the massive couch in the middle of the room. She lay on her back, her orange hair loose, her hands bound before her with a wide strip of dark plastic. She stared at him with alert wide eyes. *Alive.*

Alex Richards entered from the hall leading to the kitchen, where the serving girl had worked, bringing out plates of mustard eggs and red rice balls. This Alex, who leaned back into the door jamb, was older, with gray hair. He held a blaster.

Richards shouldn't have any weapons. Rieser allowed only his own in the

House. Just as he didn't allow RuBy to come in from the outside. *Goddamn it, this is supposed to be* my *House now.* But here was Richards with a blaster. Richards stopped at the threshold into the Quarry and glanced Parr's way.

"Come on in, Alex," Rieser's voice said.

The Boss had slipped in behind Parr. *Shit.* Parr started to turn, but something cold wedged into his neck. A blaster.

"Eyes forward, Vanderberg," Rieser said.

With Rieser's blaster firm against his skin, Parr nodded. His confidence wavered. He'd expected to have some time. Keep his distance from the Boss. Be allowed to explain gradually.

Rieser spoke into Parr's ear. "You've brought visitors."

Parr started to explain, but Rieser pushed the blaster so forcefully into his nape that he stumbled forward. Rieser followed, keeping the pressure constant. Parr regained his balance and watched as Richards entered the Quarry and stood next to Terree.

"Looks like everyone's here," Rieser said. "You were supposed to kill them, not invite them to the House."

"It wasn't my original plan."

"I *gave* you a plan. Now we've got everyone queued up in the Pool Room. Except—" Rieser grabbed Parr by the shoulder and spun him around, repositioning the blaster directly under his chin.

Rieser's eyes, wild with anger, searched Parr's. In the middle of his forehead, the number 9 seemed to flicker. Flicker on or off? Was it his imagination, or was Rieser about to use his last number?

"Vander," he whispered, almost amiably. He pushed harder on the blaster, and his tone changed, all pleasantries gone. "Where the fuck is Juke?"

Parr said nothing.

The blaster whined as Rieser stared him down.

Thirty

THE FLASH DIED, AND I BLINKED AWAY THE ACHE BEHIND MY EYES, fighting back a wave of nausea. I found myself standing in the room I'd witnessed in the morgue. The wall before me was made of blackrock, smooth and unfissured, polished to a sheen.

I tried to steady myself on the telescoping table Alex Richards had rested on, but of course it wasn't there. I stumbled, caught myself, and looked down. Richards lay on the floor, motionless, Abby Graff beside him, flat on her back. I'd heard her grunt as Bardsley's blaster had discharged, and now I knew why. She'd been hit.

She wasn't dead, though. Her eyes fluttered open, and her expression held no menance as she struggled with her pain. When she grit her teeth, the scar along her chin appeared to jump. Also, a festering slash across her neck shone with blood, as did her shoulder above her green jumpsuit's neckline. How much blood had she lost crossing the quantum portal? The wound had closed, partly cauterized by the blast itself, or from some effect of the traveling, but it looked ugly and needed attention.

I pulled the NIO agent's blaster from my coat pocket, readying it for anything, before recalling that it was useless to me. I put it away. "Graff?" I bent down to help her.

She waved me away, eyes still closed. "I'm fine." She touched her neck gingerly and sucked in a breath.

"You don't seem fine."

"Give me some fucking space, will you?" She opened her eyes and stared at the ceiling. "Just check the room."

I obeyed and saw a series of cots, all of them empty. Four black walls and a single steel door. I saw no other way out.

Being stuck in here made me real nervous, because Lorway had sensed, through Richards' power, that there were likely others close by.

"No Rieser," I said. "No Vanderberg Parr." *Brindos.*

"Just you and me and Richards," Graff said, grimacing as she turned her head.

I had hoped Tem Forno might've managed to work his way here. I had lots to tell him about what I'd learned from the Memory.

"Quantum sleep," Graff said. "I still have a hard time believing it's even possible."

"It's possible because the Ultras are *im*possible."

"Beats travel through the jump slot, I suppose," she said. "And no travel visas."

"Small comfort."

Graff had perched herself against one of the cots, arms folded on her chest, legs outstretched. We locked eyes, and in that moment we both realized what had happened to us during the process of traveling here.

Graff was hurt, certainly, but . . . Oh, Jesus. She was *older*. And that wound on her neck looked infected, disgustingly so. I knew what had happened, and the implications staggered me. It explained a lot. About Alex Richards. About my dad, and probably Terree's.

Graff gasped, pulling away. "Oh my god. You're—"

"Older. Well, sort of. So are you."

She touched her face, trying, no doubt, to feel the age there, the wrinkles. I didn't know her well enough to zero in on all the differences.

Like Alex Richards in the warehouse, I thought. Younger than the one I'd been chasing.

"You look ten years older at least," Graff said.

"You too."

Graff examined her hands and apprehended the difference. "How does that happen?" she half-whispered. She glared at me. "It's not *rational.*"

"Give it welcome," I murmured. "There are more things in heaven and earth than are dreamt of in your philosophy."

Graff stared at me. "What the hell are you talking about?"

"*Hamlet,*" I said. Graff glared at me. I thought about the one line of *Hamlet* Forno did know. *To be. Or? Not to be.*

I tried not to think too long about what had happened. We had traveled, all right. But not exactly to where Graff thought.

"I'm guessing Rieser or Parr's in there," I said, pointing at the door. "Wherever there is." I *had* glimpsed this place on the way here, and earlier, in the Memory, but I hadn't understood what it meant. Now a new idea sent a shiver eeling up my spine.

"Rieser's House," Graff said, standing, a finger on the wound in her neck. She gave Alex Richards' body a wide berth as she moved to the door.

"You know about this?" I asked as she studied a sensor pad and some type of signal box inset into the door. "This room?" *This cell.*

"Not a thing," she said. She touched the sensor.

"Wait a sec—" I warned, certain we shouldn't just barge haphazardly through this door, but she shook her head, putting her palm hard against the sensor.

"DNA lock. We're trapped."

"Shit." A hell of a long way to come and be stuck on the wrong side of a door.

"What the hell are we going to do?" Graff asked. "About what happened to us?"

I thought about the scenario Forno and I had used against Joseph on Ribon, pretending that I was Forno's prisoner so we could get close enough to do some damage to those guarding the mortaline vault.

Nodding at Richards, I asked, "What about him?"

Graff shook her head, and it made her wince. "Hell no, he's gone. Tapped. And even if he *could* give us that Ultra power, we don't have Lorway to focus it."

"Nice plan coming in on this side of the bars," I grumbled.

"It's not like I take the Ultra Express every day of the week," Graff said.

Alex Richards. Dead now for sure. I had seen him in the Memory several times, at the Lake House, and at the Knightley Tower in Chicago, at that fateful meeting with the Science Consortium and Baren Rieser. Richards had been a player early on. He'd known Rieser longer than anyone. It seemed he might be tight with the King of Khrem, maybe with some perks related to the House. Getting out of here couldn't be that easy, could it?

"Hold him up."

Graff looked at me. "Hold Richards up?"

"We'll grab him, and hold him up to the door."

When Graff scratched her forehead, she winced again. "You think he has access?"

"He's solid with Rieser," I said. "I think he might."

With great effort, the two of us picked up Richards and, balancing him upright between us, hauled him to the door. All the way there, Graff grumbled and hissed in pain.

"We don't really know what's on the other side of the door," I said. Not this time, I thought, thinking back to the Ribon vault.

"But we have to take the chance," Graff said.

I nodded. "I bet they have no clue we're in here. Might be an advantage."

"Element of surprise," Graff said.

"So I stand him up in front of me."

"A shield?" Graff asked.

"You have a better idea?"

"Works for me." She took out the blaster. "We can keep up appearances, though."

I took out mine and we jostled Richards some more, until I had him before me, with Graff propping him up on my left. "Stay close. I'll have my blaster pointed at his head."

We positioned ourselves in front of the door, and when ready, I took Richards' hand and raised it to the touch pad.

I paused, uncertain.

"Let's go, already," Graff said, blaster held out in front of her. She looked pale, and the blaster wavered a bit. I hoped she could hang on.

"We need to wait," I said, and she stared at me hard, probably wondering if I'd lost my nerve.

I felt like a clock ticked inside me, a feeling similar to what I'd felt on the way through the Ultra sleep to this House. Lorway had mentioned a buffer, a place out of phase, and I believed I'd glimpsed it within this House, outside this door, during my forays into the Memory.

"Crowell?" Graff asked.

"Wait." I squinted at the door. "There's a moment coming. An important . . . moment."

"You're not talking sense."

I waved her off and waited for the moment. A lightness. *A passage.*

Power vibrated in the room.

Although I believed Graff could feel it, I concentrated on *the moment.* I pulled at the sensation and my internal countdown, grasping for a hold, light imminent, light similar to what I'd experienced the instant I'd left the morgue and arrived here. Nausea.

It was the moment between life and death on the other side of the door.

I pointed the blaster at Richards' head with my right hand and, with my left, tapped his fingers against the sensor.

Thirty-one

Juke's dead," Parr mumbled, staring down at Rieser's blaster, which hummed with deadly potential. Tell the truth and get to the bottom of this quickly. Accidents happened. Surely the Boss understood that.

"Guessed as much," Rieser said. He took a step back and aimed the blaster higher. "Dead how?"

"Forno got him."

So much for the truth.

"Juke had said he was secure." Rieser squinted at him. "Until you arrived, it seems."

"Qerral had a zip gun, hidden. She got to it, distracted everyone, weapons were fired, Qerral went down, and in the confusion . . ." He trailed off and shrugged.

"So Qerral is dead."

"Yes. Forno forced us here, but he didn't know about the datascreen."

"And you went through it with the deterrents on." Rieser nodded, and the blaster lowered a notch. "Good thinking, Vanderberg."

Parr shrugged. "What're you going to do with those two?"

"Leave them. They're not going anywhere. You can kill them when you get back."

"Kill them?"

"It's a delicate situation," he said. "A request from Cara. They get taken out of the queue once and for all." He nodded at Richards. "He'll be here, too."

"And Terree?"

"She'll come with us. She'll not be the same after this, but we need her."

"Not the same?"

He pointed to his head. "No protection."

Parr swallowed hard. "Where is Cara?"

"I'm going to explain things to you," Rieser said. "Since you haven't figured it out yet." He lowered the blaster, letting the weapon graze Parr's hip. "Let's take a walk. A little fresh air might clear things up for you."

Fresh air. They would leave the House. It seemed the right plan of action.

Rieser patted Parr on the shoulder. "This way." He gestured at Terree. "Well, c'mon." As if he were calling to a pet. She managed to rise and shuffle their way. Rieser then angled toward what Parr had thought was the kitchen, since the serving girl had come from there during Rieser's . . . party. Alex Richards nodded at Rieser as he approached. Rieser gave him his blaster.

"Are you sure, Boss?"

"I won't need it where I'm going. You might have more use for it."

Richards nodded, Rieser slid past Richards, and Terree and Parr followed.

The side room looked like a pantry, but Parr would have expected to see more goods in here if that were true. A few boxes lined a few of the shelves, and those might contain some packaged foods. He could definitely smell *helksa*, a Helk spice he didn't much care for. Scattered along the shelves were some serving utensils, platters, and metal skewers. Wait, no: they were Helk toothpicks.

He'd never been this way in the House. Odd, considering it was adjacent to the Quarry, where he spent most of his time when he'd visited. Looking at the shelves, overly large and spaced too far apart for their contents, Parr had a moment of foreboding, as if the room had once held a warehouse's treasures, every shelf overflowing with Helk foods, spices, delicacies, and drinks, as well as human foods and supplies. Gone, like the RuBy that had disappeared on his previous visit.

Gone, like the bodies in the Quarry.

He followed Terree, keeping her directly before him in case she fell. Her orange braid bobbed as she stepped almost drunkenly through the hallway.

Parr concentrated on Baren Rieser's bald head, the numbers almost daring him to figure out the math behind this, but he couldn't see the number 8 from where he was behind the Boss. Not having its tangible shape front and center unnerved him, as if that 8 had utterly disappeared from Rieser's head. *It can't,* he thought. *It's my* number.

The pantry led to a dimly lit, wide hallway. Although it was spacious with high ceilings, like every other room in the House, Parr, feeling claustrophobic, kept to the center of the hall. He didn't have to touch them to know that the walls were natural blackrock.

A light at the end shone through a small window near the top of the door. It was daylight, he realized. The sun had already come up. This was an exit, a bona fide exit, a means to pass through a back alley into a lighted street. More than that, Parr could not believe this entry and exit in Baren Rieser's blackrock House had been so close to the Quarry.

Cara Landry stood to the left of the door, near the wall. Her sudden appearance surprised him, as it had the first time. She hardly moved, barely breathed—if she even *did* breathe—as she stared him down.

She raised her hand, and glow arced between its fingers.

Rieser turned, and Parr could see his face now. He closed his eyes, concentrated, and soon, in the middle of his forehead, the number 9, already glowing dimly, slowly brightened as if a switch had turned on. Parr's body hummed with electricity, a feeling of displacement—a somewhat unpleasant sensation—similar to what he'd felt when the party-goers had collapsed a day ago.

Terree fell. Parr quickly went to her, crouched, and found her out cold. He tried to rouse her, but she didn't respond.

Rieser reached the door, turned, and placed his back against it. Parr looked up. A few moments passed, and the number 9 on Rieser's forehead began to dim. The Boss smiled wide, excited about his big reveal.

"Pick her up," he told Parr.

After a struggle, Parr lifted the Memor and held her against his chest.

"So open the door already," Parr said, although he feared coming out among the cragged spires and crevices of blackrock.

Rieser gave Parr that familiar look of disappointment he had directed at Shyler Frock in The Mirror before killing him. Then his face softened, and he said, "I understand your impatience. Really, I don't blame you. But—" His face again changing, his eyes stern and full of warning. "—you will soon understand your place. Soon understand who you are."

Alan Brindos. *I know who I am. I'm a copy of Brindos, but who was I before?*

"You belong here, Vanderberg," Rieser said, stepping toward him. "You're a Thin Man, among the most hunted in the Union, and of all of them, the most important. Don't forget."

Parr nodded. He was Rieser's right hand, and Cara was to be his One. He was a special creature. He was the only Thin Man who mattered, and apparently it mattered a hell of a lot to Forno and his partner Dave Crowell.

Terree's unconscious weight pulled at him. *Open the fucking door already.*

Baren Rieser opened it, as if he'd heard Parr's silent request, and light filled the hall.

Rieser exited through the door and vanished in a flash of daylight, and not until Parr awkwardly followed him out did the Boss come into focus again. Without a cooler, Parr thought, stepping outside the House would be terribly unpleasant.

Cara Landry slipped out behind. To catch him if he lost his footing on the blackrock? To push and send him spiraling into a crevice? He glanced back at Landry, who wore an unsettled and faraway look on her face.

But there was no blackrock.

Parr's eyes adjusted, and looking beyond the foreground, he saw not only a total absence of blackrock, but also a total absence of, well, everything. He'd never used this exit before or viewed the House from this side. How could it be so different from this vantage point? Beyond the Olsare Outcrop, the land stretched toward Swain, and indeed the landscape flattened out, but he had never ventured into Graff's district, so he wasn't certain.

"Put her down, Vanderberg," Rieser said.

Parr carefully placed Terree on the ground. Her hands were still bound. Without asking Rieser, he removed the dark plastic ring around them by flicking a release node that appeared when he massaged the space with his finger.

Confused, he glanced about. The surface was as flat as flash paper, but hard and firm. It stretched for miles in every direction. The ground seemed continuous, with no breaks, rocks, pebbles, or sand. Almost gray. There was light. Yes, but very little, and he couldn't tell where it came from.

He stood. Behind him, the House. Ironically, its alien aesthetic felt familiar and reassuring, even though he'd never seen the House from this side, this close up. To his left, a quarter of the House appeared incomplete, the blackrock torn, as if workers had been attempting to tame the material and press it into shape. Within the jagged clumps ran veins of a smoother stone of highly polished black that reflected the dim light outside. "I'm not sure I understand," he said.

Cara replied in her ethereal brain talk: *I will be your One.*

Parr snapped, "I don't know what that means."

"She'll be your One," Rieser said behind him.

"Fuck!" Parr said. "That's *not* helping." He pivoted to face the Boss again. "You're the only Thin Man—"

"—that matters, I *know*. But—"

Rieser interrupted. "She means you're the only one the Ultras deem worthy of this opportunity. Remember when all the others were in the Quarry, you were the only one who remained conscious inside."

"Hard not to notice *or* to remember."

"You were chosen, no one else."

"And you, too."

"Yes, I'm here. That was decided long ago, Vanderberg."

Parr decided to wait until the Boss stopped playing games and told him what was going on.

Rieser gestured at the House, and Parr turned again to study it. Cara, now just to his left, did not look at the House, but at Parr, her eyes never leaving his face.

"Parr," Cara Landry said. He shivered, and this time not because of the cold air. She had said his name more distinctly this time, as if she had gained confidence speaking aloud only a few human sentences.

"It's a second House," Rieser said. "Surely you noticed. *This* House has no bodies in the Quarry, and no RuBy. The only constant, the only thing in common, is the Pool Room, where you found Richards dead."

"You built two of these?"

"I didn't build either of them. A Helk built both."

"Terl Plenko," Parr said, knowing he was right.

"Yes. The first Thin Man. The copy of the original DNA expert married to Dorie Senall."

"Where's this House?"

"I don't know."

"It's the Ultra's world, isn't it?"

"Well. It's a place of theirs. But I call it Rook."

"But we got here, to Rook, because of the House. From one—place—to the other. Does it have to do with the blackrock?"

"In a way."

"We're here through—what? A portal?"

"It's much more than that."

More mystery. Vanderberg Parr—a Thin Man who mattered, someone or something special in the eyes of the Ultras, coerced and manipulated by Baren Rieser—asked, in a steady voice, "Does the blackrock power it?"

"No."

"Then what does?"

Rieser clucked at him. "You know this, too, Vanderberg."

Parr stole a glance at the Boss's bald head. The tattooed numbers were dark and faded, including the 9 on his forehead, which had recently darkened like the others.

"*You* power it," Parr said.

"Very inefficiently. Nine times. A very finite, dead-end job, let me tell you. But a necessity."

"And after you're . . . done. If this is your ninth trip?"

"My lead sniffer Vanderberg Parr takes over."

Parr ran a hand through his hair. How might he look with a bald head and tattoos?

Rieser surprised him by saying, "No numbers for you, Vanderberg. You won't need them."

"Why not?"

"Because you're unique. Listen to me. Understand. The Ultras gave me the ability to do what I did, but it's burned me out. I'm a human being, not built for that kind of power."

"But I'm different?"

"You're a Thin Man. Not completely human. You will do what I can not."

"How do I do that?"

"The Ultras will teach you."

Parr looked Cara's way. Did Rieser mean her? "Teach me what?"

"The secrets of the House. Of the Pool Room. You have access to the House now. DNA locks keyed to you. She'll teach you of the Ultras and their plight. Of the next stage in the remaking of the Union."

Parr's pulse pounded in his throat. "The next stage?"

"They admit to making mistakes, and regret their small setback last year, but that's all irrelevant. Their plan has been long in the making, is still ongoing, and nothing the Union does will stop it."

Parr wanted to ask his favorite question, now that he knew the answer: *Do you know who I am?* But Rieser would merely answer he had to be who he was, Vanderberg Parr.

Forno had told him, and the Boss knew who Brindos was. For now he let that go. "You received your power from the Ultras," Parr said, "however damaging it is to you. So how will I be different?"

"Because you don't need all that power."

"What power do I have?"

"Again, you *know* this, Vanderberg. It's exactly what powers you now."

Without warning, Cara Landry moved uncomfortably close to Parr, gliding around the unconscious Memor at his feet. She lifted her hand. He thought she meant to touch him, a caress, a gesture of acceptance, but she stopped inches from his face.

Something was in her hand.

She said, "RuBy," and placed the red square of paper lovingly on his tongue.

Thirty-two

THE PEACE THAT CAME TO PARR RAN DEEP AND CLEAR.
He closed his eyes in deference to it. It wasn't the RuBy by itself that calmed him. The hell of it was, he rarely felt the euphoric after-effects anymore, taking the drug more to keep himself pain-free than for any blissful escape. Cara's presence somehow radiated warmth, granting this moment despite her cold eyes and impassive features, as if enveloping him in a bubble, protecting him from the dangers of this place, a foreign landscape outside the second House.

Fuck, now he was talking about peace as if it were a bubble. If, as Rieser had hinted, he was actually on a world outside the known planets of the Union, then maybe he should be grateful for the small comfort of Cara's presence. He had no idea how long he'd be able to maintain this quiet calm.

A special creature. Someone who mattered. Just needed to remember that, just needed to give in to Cara's peace. The Ultra's peace. That was it, wasn't it?

The Ultras wanted that peace. Just wanted to understand humans. Figure them out. Make them better. Better was good, right?

Did humans really matter in the collective consciousness of the cosmos?

Seriously. *Collective consciousness of the cosmos.* Where the hell did *that* come from?

Doubt.

Couldn't he just go back to the moment he gave Shyler Frock his ultimatum? Shoot the son of a bitch when he should have, before Rieser showed up and did it for him? Zip the stupid Fourth Clan, then tell Juke he was going out for some air. Crank his cooler to high and just fucking disappear.

Fuck, no.

He had to be who he was.

A Thin Man. A Trademark with a special quality, a sniffer practically composed of pure RuBy. Without it, he might as well be dead. Who else could he be? He had no place in the Union of Worlds. If the Union government found him out, he'd be detained and torn apart as they attempted to find out what made him special. Fuck that.

"Are you still with us then?" Rieser asked, as if sensing Parr's new resolve.

He shook off his remaining doubt and opened his eyes. Cara's own eyes, dead gray, were only inches away. Rieser stood next to her. While staring at Cara Landry, Parr let the RuBy dissolve on his tongue. "What do I need to do?" he finally asked.

"Learn," Cara said.

"When do I start?"

"Now," she said. "I will be your One."

She was practically a chatterbox, all these words coming from her. Complete sentences even. He took notice of Terree's presence, her unconscious body sprawled on the ground.

Cara's presence, however, was almost too intense. It made Parr back up a step, to regain some of his personal space. She seemed to shimmer, releasing some of the light inside her. Maybe it was that antimatter core he'd heard about, a potentially dangerous source coiled within like a live wire.

Even her hands pulsed with that white light.

Rieser said, "Ah. Looks like it's beginning."

"My learning," Parr said.

"This is the way the world ends," Rieser said.

"Ends?"

"With a whimper *and* a bang. But you are a Thin Man. You have crossed to this other kingdom. Remember us, Vanderberg. Here on this dead land. Here, under the fading light."

This dead land Rieser had named Rook.

Rieser stretched out his arms to indicate the world around him. "You can see. You can move us, you can act, and we will have hope."

Maybe Baren Rieser had finally gone over the edge. Those nine glowing numbers knocking something loose. Spouting more nonsense than usual. Or maybe he was quoting something.

Cara's hands glowed brighter.

"How does this work?" Parr asked. "How do I learn?"

Rieser slid in behind Cara. "That's the easy part," he said, and Cara reached out to Parr, her hand wrapped in white light. "You just have to sleep."

*

His life had started with RuBy, and his education began the same way. He had entered a state of reality few had ever experienced, as if he were in two places, hinged on the margin of light and shadow.

And now he found out a little about what Rieser had known for a long time, what the Ultras had offered, and why they came to him.

Cara had put him under, but kept him aware, pliable and ready to learn. A kind of sleep teaching. His brain sucked in data streaming from her very being, as if she functioned as a conduit for it all. A node. Like sentient flash-paper, spilling in a heartbeat all the secrets about the RuBy trade Rieser had kept from him.

An alien drug made on Helkunntanas, but not a uniquely Helk drug. The Ultras had offered an ingredient.

No such ingredient, no such element, natural or synthesized, existed in the known Union of Worlds. The active ingredient was a component of RuBy designed to produce the pharmacological activity that brought about the unique high in the bodies of humans and Memors, with varying degrees of potency. Varying degrees of addictiveness, too, depending on the chemical changes and modifications brought on by body chemistry.

This much he knew from this first immersion into the Ultra's sleep state, the wider picture downloading into his consciousness.

A representative node that Parr took to be Cara's *essence*—for lack of a better word—morphed into a humanoid figure to guide him through the complex details. The digital node beat like a heart with that same white light as it mushroomed into a crude representation of the body of Cara. Everything else, in the background, foreground, above and below, flickered with a sickly light, as if U-One had suddenly stopped broadcasting, going dead save for the grayish blue default vid-screen display, an expanse big enough to completely backlight any object in front of it.

The drug took advantage of new-found research on microemulsions and their efficacy, the 3D node "verbalized" to him, a crude representation of Cara's human voice.

Human words, and Cara's digital form seemed to have no trouble communicating this way. Big words, but he had the gist of it. "Sure. The oral delivery of the drug via the thin membranes of the RuBy paper became possible because of improvements in drug delivery systems," Parr felt himself saying. Did he say that aloud? Could Rieser and Cara—if they were even there, wherever *there* was—hear him? It was akin to engaging a set of immersion specs or implants and having them play with such intensity that you couldn't tell when you were shouting too loud at someone.

Yes, the microemulsions revolutionized drug delivery, the node said. *They are stable and do not require much energy. The paper contains a merged system of water, oil, and other thermodynamically stable and isotropic liquids.*

"Uh, in English? Isotropic?"

Meaning, identical in all ways. But we also needed a surfactant to facilitate the dispersion process, and since most of them had long been banned throughout the Union because of their toxicity to flora and fauna, and because none of the correct chemicals needed to synthesize them existed to do what we required, even biosurfactants, we turned to someone who could help in the process.

Parr blinked in confusion as Cara's image shimmered, parts of it going translucent and then transparent before again solidifying into digital coherence.

"Rieser? How could he help?"

Once more, he wondered if Rieser waited nearby and could hear him. Did it matter? Rieser's time was nearly up. Parr would have to do what the Ultras required to get the Union to understand the new order of the universe and the peace that it brought. More and more, he "sensed" that this outcome was the only outcome that mattered.

This had to be right.

Not Baren Rieser, Cara said. *A Memor.*

Of course. A Memor. From a smart and technologically superior race. Memors gave the Union jump slots, yes. But a Memor scientist had belonged to the Science Consortium that helped the Ultras build the Transcontinental Conduit on Temonus.

"Lorway?" he asked, remembering the Memor's name.

She would not help us. She served her purpose with the Conduit, but after that she refused to do more. In the end she betrayed us, sabotaging it.

Sabotage, Parr knew, that had occurred because the Ultras had eliminated her, setting off a chain of events concluding with the *Exeter* carrier's steering into the Conduit and dragging it through Midwest City.

"So there was someone else?"

There was someone else.

"You mean the Donor."

Yes. You know him as Griest Sahl-kla. We had Memors, humans and Helks at our disposal. Griest gave them to us.

"What do you mean, gave them to you?"

Donated them. There was no choice. They had no choice.

Hearing Cara's image talk about more traitors to the Union took Parr aback. "No choice, why?"

RuBy came to be, she continued, ignoring his question, *created on Helkunnta-nas, with an ingredient from the Ultras, modified by a Memor.*

"Okay. Let's see if I have this down. You worked out how to advance the delivery system so the drug could be administered quick and easy. You sold it to the districts. You made it a commodity. It became everything to places like Khrem and Swain. And then you turned to Rieser. He became a part of the plan and worked his contacts to ferry the drug to Aryell. Used it on the refugees in the camp, to placate them, to prepare them to be copied into Thin Men."

Yes.

"But it's more than that, isn't it? The drug has a secondary purpose. Drugging the new creations, drugging the drugged. That active ingredient. It works artificially, a substitute for the power you Ultras already have."

Cara was silent.

"You gave Rieser your power, but he couldn't wield it for long. You created just enough Thin Men to destroy the Union from within, but you needed one of us to lead the way from there."

He took Cara's continued silence as confirmation. The digital node barely pulsed. He knew he was right about this, too. The Ultra's fingerprints, or whatever they had, were all over Parr. The nanomaterials altered his memory, maybe even *giving* him a special personality, the transformations taking place as matter stayed uniform. He'd been specially designed to act as his own conduit, powered with RuBy. He was a type of microemulsion system himself.

He was thinking this through, and he didn't know how the hell he was doing it.

"I'm able to slip through without the phases—" He hesitated, figuring out a way to verbalize his learning "—*mixing.* Two phases, like oil and water. I can go back and forth somehow."

Your scientists call that surface tension.

"Yeah, I'm not remembering or understanding that science lesson."

Contact between your Union and the Ultras generates an extreme accumulation of energy. Two phases. If we're mixing, the results could be disastrous.

Parr understood. "Antimatter. The Ultras, the ones who'd come to the Union and taken over key roles, had anti-matter cores—"

We could not hold. When my other human body broke, the rest of us did also. We had to release them or face annihilation of the spheres. The antimatter cores destabi-

lized and the resulting collisons caused only minimal damage.

Certainly, few humans would have called the destruction caused by the Ultras *minimal.* Parr still didn't know what made the Ultras *Ultras,* or where they were, but that lesson was probably on its way. He did, however, realize his importance in facilitating the Ultra goal, the goal Rieser said embodied the peace of the Ultras. It simply had not changed from a year ago just because Terl Plenko had fallen, or because the Conduits were destroyed, and most of the Thin Men rounded up.

The Ultras had planned the takeover long ago. RuBy a part of it, the Thin Men a part of it, the House of Baren Rieser and this duplicate House a part of it, and *this* place. Part of it.

A setback.

But Parr had a job to do. A job just for him now, and far more important than roughing up sniffers behind on their tithes.

The end result will be the same, digital-Cara said. *We have not stopped. We were only delayed.*

The truth came to him. Whether from his own brain, or information fed to him from Cara, it became obvious. "You don't have enough Thin Men."

No. Not enough, but we can make more.

"There's no way. The conduits and towers have fallen, the mortaline is gone. Everyone has caught on to you now."

They know only a fraction of what we plan. You and Rieser know more than the Union government and the intelligence organizations ever will.

"You still can't make Thin Men."

We will make the Thin Men here, in this place.

Oh, what the *hell?* He shivered. He couldn't *see* this place at the moment, with Cara's image controlling his consciousness. Rook. Before, he'd seen only flat land in all directions. *This is a place of theirs,* Rieser had said. But *where* was it?

"There's no mortaline here."

There is now.

The Cara-node brightened a moment, then collapsed into a vertical line and shrank down and out of sight.

Rieser snapped back into existence as Parr woke, still standing behind Cara. Terree had never moved from her spot on the ground.

"Too hard to maintain that interface, I'm told," Rieser said. "But you know enough to understand what's happening here."

"I *don't* understand. Making Thin Men. Here?"

Rieser pointed back to the House, at its incomplete-looking corner. Or as if something huge had taken a bite out of it.

"Terl Plenko built this house out of blackrock, but it's not just blackrock. Underneath the surface layer? Those smooth veins of black? What do you suppose it is?"

Parr could hardly breathe. "Mortaline."

Rieser nodded. "It's not that the House on this side isn't finished. They've been doing some . . . remodeling. To boost the mortaline's efficiency."

"But . . . there can't possibly be enough mortaline, even here, to recreate the conduit."

"The Ultras expected to retrieve the stockpile on Ribon. But *before* then, just before Terl Plenko's copy instigated the Movement, they mined out the remaining mortaline on Coral. That's when the real Plenko went missing, you realize. At the Rock Dome on Coral."

"Plenko built his two Houses before his Movement?"

"Yes. Then they determined to use Ribon refugees to make the Thin Men and infiltrate the Union. Then, when the timing was right, the Ultras could come back en masse to the Union and join with them. Alter their consciousness so as to take control."

"Ultras like Cara. Or Joseph."

"Well, not quite. But for now, let's just say, close enough. But then the problem of consciousness rejection arose. Instability with their antimatter 'cores' as we called them. The Houses and the mortaline existed as a kind of contingency plan."

"Contigency plan? Seriously?"

"Or call it Phase Two. The difficulty lies in the fact that the Ultras exist in a form different than all other life as we know it."

Union scientists had spent the past several years studying the intricacies of Ultras and what they might be. Conveniently for the Ultras, nothing had remained to study. The Ultra copies detonated after the destruction of the Cara Landry copy.

Parr accessed his own consciousness and found knowledge left there from Cara's digital node. Even now, thousands of lifetimes of data were downloading into his brain, but he couldn't access them all. Not yet. But he soon grasped the larger encompassing picture. Such knowledge could change the very fabric of human life. Indeed, both Helk and Memor existence, virtually all of it.

"Oh *hell*, Parr said, almost reverently. "The Ultras have quantum consciousness."

"A consciousness that lives outside any physical form, and represents itself, well, digitally."

"Like the Cara-node." Parr glanced over at the Ultra, but she had not moved since he'd emerged from the quantum sleep.

Rieser said, "Yes, like her Cara-node. But like any consciousness, it seeks to make *life*."

"Theirs is made of antimatter."

"And ours of matter, and the two don't play well unless contained within each other. Creating the Thin Men gave the Ultras a way to merge with them."

"You lost me."

"We are their nearest target. If they can *get* to us, they can merge with our brains and so with our consciousness—merge with our neurons and with the very microtubules *within* the neurons."

"You're talking about consciousness outside of life forms. And all the quantum effects." Parr still had trouble dealing with his newfound intelligence, the knowledge the Ultras were passing on to him.

Rieser smiled. "It's almost spiritual, isn't it?"

"The Ultra's sleep is a quantum byproduct of their attempts to merge with us?"

"It's a kind of mini-death. Theories about quantum physics and consciousness have been around a long time, but this is unprecedented. Once that merger is complete, they can *remake* us. They understand the quantum effects of space and time. The effects of gravity. The purity of motion. Even our own conscious and unconscious actions."

Cara remained silent. Still.

Parr tried to quantify all the data: from Cara's instructions, from Rieser's explanations, and from the Ultra consciousness downloaded directly into his own brain.

"It's just one of those things, Vanderberg. *Consciousness* creates the universe. It creates *life*. Space is an endless amalgamation of universes, spherically enclosed, but none of them is aware of the others. Once in a while, though, universes come close to one another. There are dark recesses. Gaps." He smiled. "Holes."

"There are holes?"

"There are always holes." Rieser pointed at the House. "This is one of them."

Parr glanced again at the unfinished corner of the House and also at the landscape around him. "If this is their universe, how do you and I manage to exist here?"

"There's a bubble."

"A safe zone?"

"Call it the Ultra's Pool Room, if you will. The House on either end anchors both bubbles well enough, but the gap between . . . fluctuates."

"That doesn't sound good."

"It's a constant struggle to keep the gaps correctly aligned. Think about the forces involved for the Union to maintain the equilibrium needed for jump-slot technology. That's nothing compared to aligning the gaps."

"And if it isn't aligned?"

"Three things could happen. The equilibrium is maintained, or the spheres are knocked away from each other. Or—" He paused a moment. "They collide and both spheres are annihilated."

Parr's pulse pounded in his neck, and his legs wobbled under him. "Why do the Ultras even take that chance?"

"Because," Rieser said, "they're dying."

Thirty-three

THE DOOR SLID OPEN.

I scanned the room, taking in its towering walls and impossibly high ceiling. Built for Helks. It was deserted. A gigantic couch blocked me, but an opening to my right led to a side room. There was another room to the left.

Graff limped wearily toward the couch. Yes, she was hurt, but she definitely looked older.

I'd expected to find Terree here. I willed her to be alive somewhere close by.

I lay Alex Richards' body down, but remained vigilant. Bits and pieces began coming together. The trips in the Memory started adding up. Lorway had knocked some bits loose, somehow. We were somewhere else, some *place* else outside the Union, and I was certain Graff hadn't figured it out.

Antimatter. It would never play nice with humans—in any way that we understood it. A thought formed, and I wondered how much I could believe it. Had we truly *traveled* somewhere else? Not just to Helkunntanas?

I didn't have to tell Graff that. She could just think we traveled within the Union.

"So where's Rieser?" Graff asked.

"And Parr?" I added. "Richards. Terree."

Graff pointed toward a long, wide space. "You think they went this way?" She pointed back the other direction." Or—"

"It's that way," I said, nodding in the first direction. I'd seen this. The random images of the House, slowly stitched together, had taken shape in my head. "I'm checking it out."

Graff frowned, her scar stretching unnaturally. "I want Rieser," she said.

"You'll get your chance."

I wasn't certain of that. I thought it might be best to let Graff stew a bit.

I could hardly care less about her and what she wanted. She wasn't much better than Rieser, even though she had helped me get me here through Lorway.

On the other hand, she was big and mean, even injured, and older, and I'd probably be better off if she came along.

"Rear guard." I held out my hand. "And I get my code card back. Now."

She shrugged, dug it out from her jumpsuit and handed it to me. "Fair enough."

A check of the code card revealed that its communication membranes were inoperable, due, I assumed, to our location. Still, it made me feel better having it, and I *did* have access to some of its other progs.

I entered the hallway, which was large and nearly empty, save for some shelving with a few boxes and supplies. Intimidating blackrock walls towered on both sides, ceiling far out of reach. Graff followed.

A moment later, I heard Graff poking through one of the boxes behind me, still grumbling about Rieser.

"Huh," she said, as utensils clinked.

I looked back. "What?"

"Nothing," she said, fumbling with her hair. "Just junk. Keep going."

Through this room, into a dark hallway. I moved forward with purpose. Time was important now. I couldn't worry about what we might come across. Wherever we were.

The door at the end of the hall was ajar, and a pale yellow light seeped through from the other side. I stepped forward. Easy does it. Nothing to gain by rushing through it now, not after everything I'd gone through to get here. I touched the door's smooth, cold black surface. I turned my head, putting one ear close to the line of light. Listening for what?

Nothing.

"Give me some room," I told Graff. She cursed, but retreated a few steps.

I expected to find Terree here. I expected to find her dad.

I *hoped* to find mine. But, really, I didn't know what to think.

My expectations drove me forward, though, and I pushed the door wide open with my foot, Graff hanging back. I raised my blaster, the one I couldn't even shoot, and prepared to step into an alien world.

Thirty-four

THE GRAVITAS OF RIESER'S STATEMENT HIT PARR LIKE THE DEATH OF a child. *The Ultras, dying.* He suspected most of this knowledge had already downloaded into his consciousness, but, frustratingly, he couldn't yet access it himself.

Rieser said, "They're dying out after millennia of formless existence. They needed us to help them. We had their technology and the know-how of the Memors and from that we could create the Thin Men. A new species, able to contain their antimatter consciousness."

"This is why they took the Donor. Griest Sahl-kla."

"The Ultras gave him no choice. He had to do it."

Parr glanced at the motionless Cara, and understood the ultimatum presented to the Donor. "Because if he didn't agree to help the Ultras," Parr said, "and to provide them the scientists and the physical help *they* couldn't supply, it would have been option number three: annihalate both universes."

"They were dying already."

"But—"

"The Ultras have nothing to lose. We have *every*thing to lose. So we help them. We let them understand us, merge with us, and remake us. Ultras like Cara are only prototypes. They've got most of it figured out now. New creatures. We couldn't do it without Greist and Lorway. The Memors. The Science Consortium." He paused a moment. "The Envoys."

Parr didn't know anything about the Envoys. He rubbed his eyes, suddenly tired. "And what about me?"

"You'll soon take over, the Thin Man with unlimited power." Rieser winked. "As long as the RuBy shines. And it will, now more than ever. You can pass through without any negative effect. Anyone else who does is damaged, sometimes killed. The spheres may be close, and there may be a hole, but the gap is big enough—and the residual antimatter and gamma rays intense enough—to cause premature aging. Radiation sickness, DNA damage and cell death. Mutations."

"You're staying here," Parr said, pointing to the dark numbers on Rieser's head. "Without your power, you would most likely die. Or be sick and old and of no use to the district."

"It has robbed me of what I hold most dear, Vanderberg. Money, power. Life." Rieser slid his foot left to right, making an arc in the dust. "But this is my path. I won't complete the circle. I'll stay to do what I can for Cara. She was my One."

"Your One? But you're not a Thin Man."

"No, but she gave me these, long before she became your One." He pointed to the numbers. "And this." He pulled at his shirt collar. The word Ultra was tattooed there, but it seemed smudged. Dark, like the numbers on his head.

Parr raised an eyebrow. "Ultra. Like a Trademark."

Rieser laughed. "Good one. But yes, to mark me, and to initialize my ability to pass between here and the Ultra place. I had one, Alex Richards had one. The Donor. A few others. But I had more power. The numbers. You, however, will be able to do this on your own."

"They gave this power to you, Boss, and you knew what the limitations were."

"Yes. It's okay. I've done my best to help bring about the Ultra's peace." Rieser patted Parr's cheek good-naturedly. "And now I answer your question, the one you've never stopped asking me, who you really are."

Parr thought: *But I already know who I am.* "I'm Alan Brindos," he said.

The Boss stared at Parr with an almost sympathetic understanding. "Forno told you, did he?"

"Why Brindos? Why choose me?"

Rieser smiled wide. "Oh, it was a beautiful subterfuge. Totally appropriate, too. The Brindos pattern was in the buffer, still, when you were copied. You were one of the last. The original Brindos had become a Plenko copy. Crowell shot another copy of Brindos on Aryell. *You,* however, were brought to Khrem."

"But with no memories."

"That's how your copy was made, yes. You have to be who you are."

"Who was Vanderberg Parr, then? Because I have no memories that permit me to understand him or to know who *I* am."

Cara Landry came out of her vegetative state and approached. Surprised, Rieser stepped back. Landry, face to face with Parr, struggled to speak aloud.

The Ultras had a long way to go, Parr thought, if they were going to make this merger something other than downright *creepy*.

"Parr," she said, clearly enough.

"Who *am* I?"

She managed a slight nod, but said nothing.

Behind him, Terree groaned, and Parr shot her a look. She had managed to sit up. Yes, she was changed. Aged. A side-effect of the travel between the Houses.

"Vanderberg," Rieser said, "do you not understand the pain you've been through? The RuBy you constantly take to counteract it?"

His questions reminded Parr that he needed more of the drug, but he bit back a twinge of pain and replied, "Because I wasn't human before, was I?"

"Oh, you were human. You were Vanderberg Parr, a lowlife who worked for me, who was getting nowhere in my district until we turned you into—"

"A Thin Man," Parr concluded for Rieser. "Alan Brindos."

"A copy of Alan Brindos we hoped could sway Crowell to the Ultra point of view. Or if not that, get close enough to kill him, since that little experiment has gone quite sour on us."

"You tried before?"

"Yeah, and that didn't work, did it? And Forno knows now, anyway. No matter."

"If I'm a human copy of a human, then why do I have so much pain?"

Rieser deliberately blocked his view of Cara Landry. "Because you've been ultrafied."

"I've been *what*?"

"I told you. You're truly a special creature. You can think and talk and breathe," Rieser said. "Cara can talk to you digitally, for God's sake! But you. You're learning who you are, and how to interact in our world. You're creating your own fresh memories, uncovering your antimatter consciousness as a new physical being in our world of matter."

Oh, but it made sense to him. Why he'd known so much. Why the peace offered by the Ultras rang true.

Rieser smiled. "Do you understand now, Vanderberg?"

Parr lifted a hand and held it to his own cheek. "I'm an Ultra."

Thirty-five

WHEN I OPENED THE HALLWAY DOOR AND LET IN THE LIGHT, THE first thing I heard was Baren Rieser say, "Yes, an Ultra. But a *hybrid.*"

As I came out of the House, Graff behind me, I wondered what he meant. While taking in the surreal scene of an alien landscape, I kept my weapon trained on the group before me: Landry, Rieser, Terree, and—

Brindos.

No, it was Vanderberg Parr. The splitting image of Brindos, though, upright and conscious and looking as if nothing had happened to him a year ago. Looking exactly as I'd last seen him, in the NIO office while synching his TWT ticket and mission intinerary to his code card before shipping him to Temonus to search for Tony Koch and Terl Plenko. Before—

I froze, barely able to keep my blaster level.

Those inflatable Plenko Halloween costumes are real lifelike, and I've got one that's just your size.

I felt the weight of it again, but I had to focus.

Goddamn it, Alan, none of that should've happened to you.

Terree sat on the ground, alive, but barely moving. Was she okay? What had they done to her? She held her head, obviously in pain.

They'd seen us.

Rieser squared to face me. He wore one of his infamous pinstripe suits, a dark red one that seemed completely out of place here. Graff had come through the door, opening it wide and slamming it into the blackrock.

"What the hell?" she said. "This looks nothing like the Outcrop."

She didn't know or understand what had happened inside the House. I checked my code card again, but nothing had resurrected its dead communication protocols. *No signal.*

I hadn't had a drink for several days it seemed, but I was nevertheless doing okay, no longer craving bottled courage, probably because real adrenaline had sublimated my need for it.

None of Rieser's group was armed, but, then again, they had the Landry. I knew what she could do if given the chance. Parr—the Brindos—was there, too, and in some ways, he represented another offensive weapon for them. I'd shot a Brindos at the ski resort on Aryell, when I hadn't been a hundred percent sure that I could. Could I do it now? Maybe I should just think of him as Parr, and not a Brindos copy. Parr. *Parr.*

At last Terree saw me, and when she realized who I was, she immediately stood and ran to me. None of their group attempted to stop her.

"Crowell," Rieser said, his voice conveying both amusement and surprise. He had never expected to find me here in his secret place beyond the boundary of human life. "How *did* you get here?" he asked. "I'm more than impressed. And lookee here: Abigail Graff, my exasperating competitor from the Swain."

"Fuck you, too, Rieser," Graff said.

Terree stopped beside me, and I put my free arm around her to steady her. "Are you okay?"

She nodded even as she searched my older face. Her own face was older, too. Her hair's color washed out, the strands frayed. Being Memor—or being Greist's daughter—had not immunized her against the inevitable effects of travel between worlds.

Between universes, I thought, for now I was pretty sure of that. All the clues from the Memory, the interactions with Tilson, my mom, Graff, Lorway, Landry, the Ultra sleep . . .

"I thought I'd finally got you out of my hair," Rieser said.

"You don't have any hair," I told him, guiding Terree to a spot behind me, towards Graff. "Not any more."

Rieser sneered. "I had something much better," he said, indicating the numbers on his head. "Amazingly, you surived getting here, but now what? The depradations of interdimensional travel have turned you into an old man. Fifty, at least, I'd say."

"Fifty isn't old. And so what?"

"Imagine how dilapidated you'll be if you contrive a way to get back? Hmm? As if we'd ever *let* you do so. Think that's going to happen?"

"We'll see," I said.

"What's he talking about?" Graff said.

I ignored her and studied Rieser and his group, specifically the Landry and the Brindos. None of them had moved or said a word. Of course, Landry rarely spoke. No part of her was glowing, either. Always a good thing.

Rieser stepped toward me without hurry or menace. I kept my weapon aimed, useless as it was, because I couldn't be sure he didn't have *some*thing. Graff rustled behind me.

The King of Khrem—if that title still applied—approached near enough that I could've slapped him, and I really wanted to.

Now, the Brindos . . . damn it, *Parr* . . . also stepped forward.

"Rieser," Parr warned.

Rieser motioned Parr closer, as if Parr were a friend he'd just noticed. Parr grudgingly obeyed, but didn't get too close. Rieser smiled and leaned toward me, as if daring me to use my blaster.

"Have you come for your old friend?" Rieser asked. "You obviously want my personal copy of Alan Brindos. Such a shame you lost yours."

"You son of a bitch." I resisted the urge to shoot him.

"You've come a long way for nothing," Rieser said. He looked over my shoulder. "You hear me, Graff? Future's already been written. You're done for, and my man Parr here is taking over Khrem, the Swain, and the rest of the RuBy trade. And the Ultras are taking over everything else."

"Yeah, fuck you, Baren," Graff said. She seemed unable to say much else to him.

"I'm not here for Parr," I said.

"Well, you won't find Lucky Lawrence here, if that's who you were expecting," Rieser said.

I gritted my teeth, but didn't take his bait. Rieser wasn't lying. During our passage to this place I'd understood my father wouldn't be here. The truth was clear to me now: he was somewhere else. Not the Union, not this place, but in the other universe, the Ultra's universe. I had no idea how he could exist there, but my trip into the Memory had conveyed the message that he did. Still, I had no intention to forcefully tell Rieser what I knew about that.

"You've got someone else I'm looking for," I said.

"Griest. And why do you think Griest is here?" Rieser swept one arm in an arc to indicate their surroundings, but kept his other arm tight around Parr.

"I saw him."

Rieser smirked. "Really."

"I may not have seen him here, but I saw him. I've seen a lot, actually, thanks to Terree and Memor know-how. Even the Ultras helped, through one of your Alex Richards copies and their quantum-sleep travel, which seems to open up whole new pathways to the brain and collective memory."

"Convenient," Rieser said, but without much edge. He looked more than worried now.

"I remember what happened at the conference," I said, "when you entered and took everyone down. Lorway, the Consortium, my dad—"

He paled, but recovered. "I didn't take *you*, did I?"

"Not for lack of trying."

"But Griest betrayed everyone. And put the memory block on you."

"I've learned almost everything."

"But not enough."

No, not enough. Not yet. "Enough to solve the mystery," I lied.

Rieser shook his bald head and pulled self-consciously at his thin tie. "You'll never solve it. Never find him. And your father is lost to you forever."

"Let me kill him," Graff said.

With what? I thought. Your bare hands? Given the chance, she *could* undoubtedly do some damage. But two others stood there, an Ultra and a Thin Man, and none of the group seemed too worried about where this was going. Landry didn't glow. She'd been so altogether intent on killing me the last time we'd met at the Emirates Building, and now she seemed . . . weaker. Less sure of herself. "You can't kill him," I told Graff. "I need him."

"Aww, nice to be needed," Rieser said.

Graff came up beside me, flicking her blaster up and down as if in time to a dance rhythm. "No one needs him."

"Step back, Graff." I waved my blaster at her, but that meant nothing to Graff, who knew the truth about its DNA lock.

"Can't do it, Crowell," she said. "I don't expect you to understand, but this is where I take over."

"That's not your call, and you don't even have . . ." I frowned, my thoughts abruptly muddled and . . . wrong . . .

"It's my time," Graff said. She had grabbed my wrist. "I'm going to kill Rieser, and you can't stop me."

A ticking grew loud in my ears. When I looked down, I realized the truth. *My Rolex.* She still had AmBer. Goddamn it, goddamn it, she was putting me out. I grabbed at her jumpsuit, its geometric shapes resembling handholds, but she twisted away from me. I was losing control of my body because of the somatic trigger . . . muscles . . . letting loose. "Graff. *No . . .*"

With the butt of her blaster on my forehead, Graff pushed me back. I fell, unable to do anything but lie there stunned. I lifted my head, trying to resist this violation, but I couldn't, and my head fell back against the ground.

Above me, Terree's concerned face swam into focus.

She could have put me in the Memory whenever she chose, but Graff had forced matters, taking this chance to destroy Rieser, and the issue had reached this pass too goddamn early.

"Don't fight it," Terree whispered.

Good advice. If I managed to survive this moment, I still had a chance to learn something useful in the Memory, as unlikely as that alternative now seemed.

"You can manipulate it," she said. "You have a link to my father. Whether you were with him or not, you can learn from him."

I'd learned to control my access to the Memory to an extent. I could return to where I needed to go—to that fateful conference—and find out what had happened to Griest.

The Ultra dimension wavered around me, its outlines indistinct. The vast flatness gave way to walls, a large foyer, an escalator bathed in light. *The conference.* No, still on Rook. The woman—Terree?—disappeared, walked away maybe, and God, there stood my partner, my long lost partner whom I'd killed. He was backing up while the Ultra near him flashed with light. An older, decidedly large woman faced off with a bald man.

Simultaneously, another man—the Memory!—this one with hair, approached me. This man also wore a pinstriped suit, but a neatly pressed black one. I stared at him as the Ultra place completely disappeared.

I asked, "But am I done?"

He answered, "You will never be done."

Thirty-six

PARR DIDN'T HAVE LONG TO THINK ABOUT RIESER'S REVELATION.
He was a hybrid. One third Parr, one third Brindos, one third Ultra,
a creature trying to exist in the universe of the Union. But Rieser had said
Vanderberg Parr had been scum. Lowlife. So maybe he was more Brindos
than Parr. But he didn't know what Brindos knew, obviously. No, he suspected
his personality was more Parr than Brindos.

But the Ultra part of him understood what he really was. A guinea pig
to test a theory. The test was over, and the Ultras could, before they died out
completely, finish with the Thin Men here, introduce them to a glut of RuBy
and the glow of an Ultra presence, and send them out one by one. Ten by ten.
Hundreds. Thousands.

The truth rattled him. Millions. *Billions.* They might be dying out, but the
Ultras still had many souls to save. Parr might indeed have been the test case,
but he also would lead the others beyond the convergence of universes, the
consummation that the Ultras had hoped for.

This is what we have hoped for.

Then Dave Crowell showed up with Abigal Graff, the Queen of Swain,
and things got awfully confusing, fast. He could do nothing but stand there,
almost amused by this turn of events. How had they managed to find them?
They should be dead. As dead as Forno and Mayira would be after they were
taken out of the Pool Room on the other side.

Rieser toyed with them, and Parr warned the Boss, but nothing mattered
to Rieser now. He was dangerous, taunting Crowell and Graff, hinting about
the Donor, about Crowell's father. No, no, Rieser himself had told him why
the Donor could never be found, and now he knew why.

There are always holes.

Then Graff did something strange—grabbed the protesting Crowell's
wrist. But soon the man who'd been Parr's partner in another lifetime could

do nothing but fall over. Parr sensed that he had gone somewhere. Taken a little sleep, not the big sleep of the Ultras.

Interesting.

Next to him, Cara began to glow. Graff spun away from Crowell and threatened Rieser with her blaster, and Parr believed she would blow the Boss's head off before anyone could stop her.

But Rieser was one of those slippery, deceptively quick men who acted on impulse rather than training, surviving on instinct on Khrem's streets. If any situation ever got out of hand, well, there was always Juke.

Except not anymore.

Rieser widened his stance and, taking Graff totally by surprise, knocked the blaster from her grip, swiveled aside, and shoved his foot into her belly. Graff staggered back, but did not go down.

She smiled. "Goddamn thing doesn't work anyway." She nodded toward the blaster. "Neither of those damn blasters work." She raised her fists. "Fucking Rieser, I'm so tired of you and your crew. You've never played fair. Not since that first shit move you pulled in Korea with the RuBy and my DNA."

"You're welcome," Rieser said.

Graff lowered her center of gravity, taking a street fighter's stance and almost inviting Rieser to come at her. Rieser, grinning, started to square off, but Graff immediately lunged to keep him from doing so. Rieser drew back his fist, but Graff lashed out with her foot and hit him in the kneecap. Rieser blanched and pulled back, but kept both feet on the ground and swung his fist again. Graff ducked and struck him in the same knee, harder. As Rieser started to fall, she delivered a blow to the side of his head.

Parr pursed his lips. Interesting. He expected Rieser to recover quickly and get up, but instead he grimaced and tried to roll over enough to gain some leverage. Graff did not let him get that far. She pounced on him, rolled him back, and straddled his torso.

Glowing from her hands and arms, Cara stepped forward, but Parr surprised even himself, briefly at least, by saying, "No. Let them be."

And Cara the Ultra, an alien broken inside her human host, pulled back, her glow conspicuously diminishing.

I am the King of Khrem, Parr thought. *And I am the Ultra in charge here now.* Fuck yeah.

It was harder to think like Parr, but he could still work up a convincing curse.

Graff had a small needle in her hands, an adornment from her hair with a noticeably sharp end. No, it was a *Helk* thing. A toothpick. A toothpick that Parr had seen Marko Zantz use at the party, like the ones in the pantry on his way out here. But to a human like Graff or him, it was a skewer. It was a *weapon*. Worry captured Rieser's face as Graff ground her knees into the dirt and immobilized him.

"Fuck you," she said, jabbing the skewer into Rieser's neck.

Rieser grunted, grew alert to what had happened, and screamed, swiping desperately at Graff's face. She blocked him with one arm, and applied even more pressure to his neck. Rieser screamed again, a short and pleading cry, and dissolved into whimpers while trying fruitlessly to seize her with his hands. Blood seeped from the wound in his neck.

"This is the Red you've deserved for a long time." Graff yanked at the embedded skewer.

Parr blinked. Given the pivotal nature of the moment and the fact that the outcome of everything happening here on Rook could hinge on this face-off, Parr should have moved to stop Graff. But then again . . .

A strange mewling came from Cara. "Ries-er," she said in a wobbly voice.

"No." It no longer mattered what happened to Rieser. Cara's head swiveled toward him in three abrupt jerks. He let her know that Rieser was inconsequential by declaring, "His number is up."

Graff twisted the skewer deeper into Rieser's neck, and his blood gurgled as if in a blocked drain, his eyes now enormous in both disbelief and fear.

Then came his last labored breaths, Graff hunched over him like a predator impatient for a long-sought warm meal. Meanwhile, Parr experienced again the full price of his merger with his Ultra, pain and more pain. Damn. His hands shook uncontrollably. He dug into his pockets, but they were empty.

Near the House, outstretched on the gray dirt, David Crowell lay asleep, the Memor kneeling beside him.

"Come here," Parr said to Terree. "Get away from him."

Terree shook her head.

"Now, Terree."

She hesitated, yes, but soon rose and walked away from Crowell.

Parr wondered if Crowell had planned this chain of events to get himself into the Memory. Well, no matter. The Memory would not help him find the Donor.

Now. Where was he going to find more RuBy? He looked longingly over at Cara.

Thirty-seven

YOU WILL NEVER BE DONE.

I remembered what I had never known.

The man in the suit jacket walked swiftly away. In my hand rested the squares of RuBy he had given me. I rolled one, placed it on my tongue, and waited.

Finally, the man turned. Baren Rieser raised an eyebrow. "Well, Griest, let's go already."

"Where's my daughter? I'm not going until I find out—"

"As agreed upon," Rieser said, "she is ignorant of all this. Unlike that asshole Lawrence Crowell, who brought his son to the meeting room. So now we've had to deal with the boy, and we really didn't want to."

"He's already been processed?"

"Just moments ago. His new life will begin with no knowledge of this day."

"But Terree?"

"She's being sent home with a good excuse. Relax, Griest. Your family is safe. Rest easy knowing you betrayed the Union without a single black mark on your name."

"She'll eventually figure it out," I said.

"When it's too late."

But maybe not, I thought. I'd had the chance to prepare David Crowell. A slim chance. A way to break through the block if he and Terree ever achieved mutual understanding. As long as Tilson did what I'd asked him to do—watch David and his mother, understand their new reality, and remain ignorant of everything else until the block could be removed.

Baren Rieser continued forward, out of the foyer, and I followed. A few moments later, we pushed through a door into a side meeting room altogether unremarkable but for a single gray padded table in its center. The table looked like something one might see in an asylum, in an exam room. Someone had stacked the room's conference tables and chairs into a far corner.

"Right there," Rieser said, pointing at the table. "Now."

I sat on the table, knees up to my chest. Rieser fixed his patient gaze on the door we'd come through, until it opened and another man in a gray suit came in.

"Do you get it?" Rieser said. "Do you know who this is?"

"One of them. An Ultra."

"Well, this is a human named Joseph Sando. An Ultra inhabits him the best it can. He has just prepared the boy, Crowell's son. You know the truth about the Ultras and their plight. You know what's at stake for your own universe. Your donation today helps the Ultras, and keeps the Union alive."

As I stared at the Ultra, a lump formed in my throat.

"Don't try to talk to it. In this form, it cannot breathe or verbalize. That's something for another day, a better match with humans, an improvement on this crude approximation. And beyond that lies an ultimate goal of the Ultras to create the perfect hybrid creature. For now, the Ultra can do nothing other than help you travel. It will travel with you, but Joseph will remain behind."

"Dead?"

"Alive, with a crazy headache. But with no memory of what happened to him. He'll be useful in the future. Once the Consortium has completed the Conduit and the device's true purpose for existing goes live, the Ultras will begin their en masse migration to our worlds."

"And what about me? Where am I going?" I'd understood the choice to keep the spheres of the universes apart. To effect the best for all involved, right? The Consortium would go to Temonus to build the Conduit. But Lawrence Crowell and Alex Richards? Where were they going?

The Ultra, Joseph, shuffled to the table, his awkward steps causing him to stumble. He put a hand out and gripped the table's padding.

Rieser said, "Oh no, that's not for you to know. Do not play your Memor tricks on me, Griest. That's one memory you will never understand. You'll not hear that from me or anyone here, and no one will ever be able to see those memories. The Ultra will see to that."

"What can *he* do?"

Rieser laughed. "He can alter your very DNA, my good Memor. He can burn out your memory the very moment you travel. It's just one of those things, you know." He paused for effect, a half smile forming. "Ah, existence. So temporary. Everything resets. DNA resets. Everything unlocks. The old patterns never quite line up. Those genetic blueprints you Memors crow about. Don't you all preach about adjusting that stuff from time to time?"

What good was consciousness, after all, I thought, if we couldn't live with its altered states? I had altered David's. I had altered Tilson's. I didn't think those alterations would be enough.

"Why not kill me?" I asked. "What am I good for if you have what you need to create the Conduit?"

"Insurance," Rieser said.

"For what?"

"A house divided cannot stand," Rieser said.

It was a human saying about family that meant little to Memors. Little to me. But maybe that was the fault of the Memors. Our idea of identity and sexuality was confusing to those who didn't belong. Bondmates and their children were inured to the patriarchal nature of Memor society, known for its technological prowess and memory "tricks," the intersexual bonding mostly a curiosity.

Ah, David. If you ever access these memories, remember where Terree came from, for she will one day give her life for my bondmates, and all the children who have called me father.

"You're the Donor," Rieser said. "You gave the Ultras the Union's best minds, scientists and Envoys, and you get to keep on giving. And so . . . you travel." He wiggled his fingers at me. "Lie back."

I did so.

Joseph touched me with a glowing hand.

A house divided.

Thirty-eight

WHEN FORNO WOKE, HE LAY ON A HARD FLOOR. MAYIRA WAS tucked into a ball near him, her spiked hair poking out in all directions. He rolled and crawled to her side, fearing the worst, but he soon discovered that she was okay. Alive, anyway. He searched frantically around him, hoping to find Parr asleep. That would've been perfect, getting a jump on him, regaining some meaningful advantage.

No Parr. The room was simply four blackrock walls and one steel door. Their weapons were gone.

"Mayira?" He patted her face tenderly.

Mayira stirred. Forno waited until she had gathered her senses, then reached over and placed his big hand gently on her arm.

She woke and saw him. Her eyes glazed while she tried to collect her thoughts. She must have remembered everything then, for she forced a smile and nodded at him. When he reached for her, she waved him off and sat up without help. "Oh God." She rubbed her head.

"Yeah," Forno muttered, recalling the datascreen. "Mirror's breath, that was something."

"What happened?"

"That neural destabilizer happened."

"Where's Parr?"

"Gone."

"Gone where?

Forno pointed at the steel door. "Likely through there."

He stood and tried the door and sensor, but nothing worked. They were locked in. He pressed a button above the sensor multiple times, but nothing happened. Probably a buzzer. Whoever was on the other side was likely having a good laugh about the Helk trying to buzz himself out.

"They'll probably kill us," Mayira said.

"Probably."

He wondered where Crowell was. How the hell would they get out of here, and how would they do so without dying in the process?

For ten minutes, he checked the room, every wall, every corner, every cot. He had just sat down on a Helk-sized cot when a dull thud caught his ear.

Mayira heard it too. "What was that?"

Another thud, louder now, and the room vibrated slightly. Forno shook his head. "I don't know."

"Did it come from the other side of the door?"

"No clue."

"What's that smell?"

Forno started to ask what smell, but a second later he caught a whiff. "Plenko's balls," he said, wrinkling his nose at an even stronger wave of the odor. The door thumped again.

"What?" Mayira asked.

"Explosive residue."

Silence opened between them as the smell threatened to overwhelm the room. Finally, Mayira said, "What do you mean? Residue?"

"Call it whatever you want."

"I want to call it something other than what I'm thinking it's called."

"Gas. Smoke."

A sound far stronger than a thud shook the room like an earthquake.

"That originated over there." Forno pointed at the wall opposite the steel door. As he pointed, another explosion rocked the room, and a jagged crack zigzagged left to right across the wall.

Mayira came to his side. "Forno . . ."

"Back up," he said, guiding her toward the steel door.

"What's happening?"

"Someone's blowing the place up."

Thirty-nine

I AWOKE TO BLOOD.

Terree! Where was Terree?

I lay on my side, knees up, my right arm across my stomach, my left arm stretched out and under my head. Across from me, Rieser lay unmistakably lifeless, spread-eagled on the ground with blood coating his throat and chest.

Goddamn it, Graff had killed him. I'd expected to learn more from him, but the Memory had told me enough, and I figured Parr held all the Ultra secrets now.

Graff stood over Rieser holding a bloody needle. I knew she'd found it in the pantry on the way out here. Casually stuck into her wild hair, probably. Her blaster, seemingly forgotten, rested on the ground a short distance away. Maybe she'd threatened them with it, but moved to Plan B with the needle because she knew the blaster wouldn't work for her.

I felt a twinge in my side from something grinding into it, a stone or an object from the gray, alien surface. Right on the wound where Graff had grazed me in Montana. But I didn't move. Either Graff hadn't seen me awake yet or had turned her attention to Parr and Cara—no, the *Landry*.

And there was Terree, standing passively near Parr. Landry glowed, but her light appeared to be dimming, as if she were coming down from whatever had prompted her to glow so bright initially. Prepared to protect Rieser, perhaps, but without her having gone through with the Ultra touch. Why not?

Because of Parr.

Rieser telling Parr, as we had come out into the light, about an Ultra. A *hybrid.* I thought of Joseph, in the room with Rieser, an early blending of Ultra and human, like Cara Landry, like Joseph later, when the aliens had come back to entice him to trap Brindos. *Something for another day*, Rieser had said in the Memory. *A better match with humans, an ultimate goal.*

I tried to find *my* blaster. It had to be nearby, lost when I fell and ignored like Graff's.

I couldn't ignore it now.

There it was, inches from my left hand.

Everything resets.

I'd have to stretch for it—uncurl, raise my head, reach out.

Everything unlocks.

To be honest, it hardly mattered if Graff or anyone else saw me. To them, I was helpless.

Old patterns. Genetic blueprints.

But I wasn't helpless.

I moved, stretched, and grabbed the blaster. Graff approached Parr. What could she hope to achieve now? Nothing. She'd got her wish and killed Rieser, but so what? Rieser no longer controlled the Red. She wasn't in any better position now than when she'd started. Rieser had already given Parr the job. The King of Khrem.

The King is dead. Long live the King.

I found that funny. In fact, I snickered while struggling to stand. Graff turned and frowned at me. Parr and Landry hadn't moved, or said anything, or reacted in any way to Graff's actions.

"The detective awakes." Graff held the needle high enough so I could see it. "You're too late, Crowell."

I stretched tall, feeling a few aches and pains from the effects of traveling to this Ultra place. Aged, damaged, changed. Left hand dangling at my side, blaster held loosely. A slow survey of the ground disclosed the stone I'd landed on—smaller than a clenched fist, white but streaked with red lines. It matched Rieser's face, now pale in death, drops of blood spattered across it like strown rose petals.

"*You're* too late," I repeated to Graff, still not looking at her.

"You're a confused detective too, I see."

Now I locked my eyes on Graff.

"I can take care of these two," Graff said of Parr and Landry.

No, you can't, I thought.

"I'm free of Rieser, and now I'll run the Red!" she yelled.

No, you won't.

"You understand me, Crowell?"

I said, "How do you plan to get home?"

"What do you mean?"

"Home. How do you get back to Helkunntanas?"

"What are you talking about? The House—"

She'd been so concerned with Lorway's magic trick, congratulating herself on figuring out a way to travel between *worlds* like the Ultras, that she'd never considered she might be able to travel between *universes*. "This isn't the same House we came to when we wound up in that blackrock room inside. You noticed that when we got out here, even if you now choose to ignore it. We traveled, and you understand that the Ultras know how to do it."

"So?"

"But this time, we aged. We were seriously eroded, damaged, compromised. This was not the lesser sleep used to travel within our Union. It was a bigger sleep, and we traveled farther than you could ever imagine."

"What the fuck, Crowell? Traveled where?" She looked, as if seeing our surroundings for the first time.

"Some place the Ultras control and maintain as a safe zone. A buffer between their worlds and ours. If you go back now, assuming you knew how to, it would most likely kill you."

Graff fell utterly silent, her bloody needle drooping, her scarred face etched with worry. Confused and angry, she said, "You're just saying that to lower my guard."

"Sure, Graff. I'm just saying that to lower your guard."

"It's impossible, what you're saying."

"There are more things in heaven and earth than are dreamt of—"

"Fucking *stop* it with the Hamlet shit."

"Of course." The Landry still had done nothing, and her glow had almost completely abandoned her body. Parr crossed his arms while Terree moved deliberately away from him and Landry.

"If that's true," Graff said, "you're a dead man too. If you go back. To . . . whatever you mean."

"That's a distinct possibility. But I'll at least have a chance to find a viable way home. Unlike you."

She raised the needle again. "You're not going to stop me, Crowell."

I pointed the blaster at her heart. "I *am* going to stop you, Graff."

She laughed. "Yours works no better than mine does." She inched forward, gripping the needle tighter. A drop of blood clung to its tip.

"Everything resets," I said.

"Resets?"

"DNA resets. Everything unlocks."

Her eyes went wide. She backed up.

I put pressure on the blaster's trigger, knowing that the DNA lock had reset the moment I'd traveled to this world on the edge of the buffer, escaping death there, and surviving the quantum sleep.

I squeezed the trigger and shot her dead.

Forty

Ⅰ LOOKED ON AS VANDERBERG PARR STEPPED TOWARD GRAFF'S BODY.

"This makes things interesting," Vanderberg Parr said.

The Brindos, I thought. The hybrid Ultra.

I tensed, but he just smiled, staring at Graff as if she were a puzzle piece from a completely different puzzle.

The Landry did not move.

Terree stepped cautiously around the bodies. With my weapon and a bit of an edge over Parr and Landry, I felt comfortable beckoning her toward me.

"Now things are even more interesting," I said, pointing the blaster at Parr and keeping a wary eye on the Landry, now totally free of her phantasmagoric aura.

"You surprised me," Parr said, nudging Graff with one leg. "Even I didn't think about the DNA reseting." He pointed to his head. "Things are downloading and taking root here, but I'm a little behind. I get it now, of course, and even understand it."

Terree stood next to me, and I was glad to have her there. I didn't look at her, but said, "You okay?"

"Still here."

Parr took all this in, his smile giving way to thin-lipped confusion. Soon, moving almost casually, he skirted the bodies as Terree had done, and halted directly before me. He studied my face intently, as if wondering if I would shoot him then and there. Or if I would shoot Landry first, before she could pull one of her Ultra tricks?

But *Parr* was an Ultra.

I fought the urge to spin the blaster once to show him I meant business.

"So," Parr said. "David Crowell. I guess we've met." He nodded, agreeing with himself. "In different circumstances. In a different lifetime."

"You're not Alan Brindos," I said, gritting my teeth.

He nodded. "I am and I'm not. I understand what you mean. I even register some of what you're feeling. The history between you and me? That's in my brain now, too."

"Step back," I said. The hell with history. No matter how much I wanted to believe any part of Brindos inhabited Parr, no matter how much I wanted to hug him and apologize for what had happened to him, now, more than ever, I had to assume that *this* Brindos could reveal everything I needed to know about both Terree's father and mine. I was in a position to do something. If I actually figured out what it *was*, that is, here on the edge of the Ultras' universe.

No matter the cost.

I raised the blaster's muzzle. "Step *back*, I said."

Parr spread his arms. "You won't shoot me."

"You eager to find out?"

"No. But you won't."

"Because?"

"You need a ride home."

"I care more about what's happening here."

"And what do you think is happening here?"

"You're an Ultra. A hybrid."

"You were listening."

"I caught a little."

Parr turned his back on me.

"Dave," Terree whispered.

I nodded and said, "I know." I pointed at Graff's weapon in the dirt. "Grab that."

Terree did as I said, but slowly.

Parr also moved slowly, back to the Landry. In response, I grasped the blaster tighter, but I wasn't willing to shoot him. Goddamn, he was right. I couldn't. Not because he looked like Brindos, but because he knew everything. He must. And I had to find out.

A hybrid. An Ultra more capable of walking and talking and interacting with members of the Union than the Ultra copies of Cara Landry or Joseph Sando ever could.

Terl Plenko, spouting gibberish in the shuttle on Ribon. The gist of that conversation came back to me now, and some of it made sense.

They are One with us, Plenko had said. *They mimic our thinking, understand us, and weed out the deficiencies.*

The Movement of Worlds leader had told me the Union would never know the Ultras, never find them. Never understand them.

They can rebuild themselves by tearing us down and re-creating us.

Parr finally turned and put his arm around the Landry's shoulder. His features grew strangely menacing. "Look how I turned out," he said. "*Better* than I was, actually. Better than Vanderberg Parr before I became Alan Brindos, and better yet before finding the peace of the Ultras."

"My idea of peace doesn't mesh with the monumental invasion the Ultras seem ready to carry out."

From the corner of my eye, I saw that Terree had picked up the blaster Graff had brought with her. Neither Parr nor Cara seemed concerned with her.

"The Ultras are dying," Parr said, "their digital consciousness disintegrating." For a few maddening minutes, he told me more than I could digest about the Ultras and their plight, and their plans to live in our universe. "What the hell, Crowell, it's a win-win situation."

I shook my head. "It's not. I like my identity just the way it is, and so will the huge majority of the Union. You can't do this. You don't have the right or the means to do it. Not anymore."

Parr laughed. "Oh please, Dave."

Dave.

I heard *Brindos* laughing, saw the twinkle in those bright eyes as he called me by my first name in Brindos's cynical voice. I winced.

"You don't have the Conduits," I said.

Terree held the blaster out before her now, pointed at Parr.

"We don't need the Conduits anymore," Parr said. "We have the Houses with mortaline as *anchors*. The portal, made possible by an antimatter reaction that manipulates dark matter, is connected with a thin, mortaline—hmmm, let's call it an *antennae*—acting as a different kind of accelerator. One that can now create the perfect Ultra hybrid, intensified and powered by the very thing Baren Rieser and Abigail Graff hoped to control: RuBy."

He spread his fingers, revealing the redness there. I'd never seen such RuBy-stained fingertips.

"And, of course, we have something else. We have the *Donor*." Parr edged so close to the Landry that I thought he meant to grasp her head with both hands and kiss her.

"What're you doing?"

"How did this go again?" he asked. "I'm trying to sort out how it went down at the Snowy Mountain ski resort. Still a little slow on the download."

I sighted Parr down the barrel of the blaster as he searched the Landry's face. She stared at Parr without expression, although she may have twitched an eyebrow. Without any doubt, she began to glow.

"Well," Parr said, "it's not *quite* the same. Not really. But it sort of went like this." Parr gave the Landry's head a violent twist, breaking her neck. She slumped to the ground and lay still.

I gasped, startled by the suddenness of her apparent death. Parr's act reminded me too much of the kind of thing Baren Rieser used to do. *What the Brindos did to my own Cara a year ago.*

"Memory's mercy," Terree said. She looked at me. "Is this a good thing or a bad thing?"

"Undecided." I fast-walked to within a foot of Parr, my blaster aimed at his head. His Brindos appearance unsettled me, but I had to keep thinking *Parr*.

"Hey, now." Parr actually laughed.

"What's so funny?"

"Just thinking of someone else who used to say 'Hey, now.' Key phrase 'used to.' I couldn't resist the irony."

I said, "Who will protect you with the Ultra dead?"

He raised his hand as if he had an answer to a question asked by a school teacher, and a white glow enveloped his fingers. "*This* Ultra is not dead," he said. "And this one is new and improved, remember? And getting stronger all the time."

"What about her antimatter core?"

"That could indeed be a problem," Parr agreed. "Of course, this Cara wasn't shot like the one on Heron Station was, so I'd suppose we have some additional time. And who knows how well things might hold together here in the buffer zone."

I kept the blaster trained on him.

Parr waved at it with his glowing hand. "You're not going to use that."

"I might."

"What do you want, Dave?"

"How do I get to Griest Sahl-kla?" I asked. "And explain to me how he's the answer to your original need for the Conduits."

"The Donor is here, but not quite here," Parr said.

"Yes, I know."

"You know? Then why did you ask?"

"Because I don't know yet how to reach him and keep you from using him."

"I'm afraid we've been using him for quite a while now. But you can't possibly know where he is."

Visions from my trips to the Memory bombarded me, and those tidbits I'd gleaned from Tilson, my mom, Terree, and Graff, as well as the information the infiltrators at the Emirates Building had provided me, started to coalesce into . . .

Well, a theory.

Griest Sahl-kla existed between universes. He was some place where he could manipulate both universes, between the Houses. Whatever the portal was, Griest needed to be there, to keep them aligned. I could think of only one thing that could do that, only one race with the know-how to manipulate it, and only one person who might understand the threat to our worlds so well that he would willingly sacrifice his way of life and "betray" the Union to keep the Union whole.

"I *do* know where he is," I said, hoping I was right. If I could startle a reaction out of Parr that would confirm my theory, maybe I could find a way out of this mess. Terree needed to be ready. I caught her eye. A nonverbal understanding passed between us.

"Do tell," Parr said, half smiling. "I don't think you can say anything to convince me you know where—"

"There are always holes."

Parr looked as if I'd slapped his face. His eyes widened, and a sudden tic pulsed in his left eyelid.

Oh yeah, I was right.

"Griest engineered and built a jump slot for you out in the void," I lectured him, "in the space between the Ultra universe and our own. Only the Memors could understand that, and Griest donated a host of Memors to accomplish that feat, as well as scientists, Envoys, and whoever else he could manipulate for you."

The glow diminished from Parr's hand in fits and starts. He looked vulnerable, and much more like Brindos now, albeit without the Parr persona and bravado. Goddamn it. Angry for thinking about Brindos, I thought instead about Parr's glowing hand.

I stood as tall as I could. "Griest was left there to anchor the holes, maintaining the distance all these years so as to avoid the annihilation of the spheres while you made your plans."

Parr stared at me hard, but kept quiet.

"Ultras took my father, too," I said, "and I think, for some reason, he's worth more to you than Griest is. So much so, that you decided to alter my life. You gave me a new one."

"The Ultra's . . . peace." Parr struggled with his words. "It—it is meant to be. I am . . . understanding it now, you see . . ." He seemed flustered.

I pressed on. "I don't know why you took my father, or why you manipulated me for so long, but I'll keep searching for him—after I find Greist and after we stop the Ultras from taking over our worlds."

Parr looked down, his arms at his sides. Then, inexorably, the glow around his hands fizzled, dimmed, and went out. That's when I hit the hybrid in the nose, as hard as I could, sending him to the ground. Terree rushed up, ready to help. Parr looked up at me from the ground, dazed.

I stepped on his right hand. Terree stepped on his left hand.

"That won't help—"

I hushed Parr by grinding my heel on his hand, causing him to groan. "You're a hybrid," I said, "so you understand human pain. You've experienced a lot of it, haven't you?"

"He doesn't like the heat of Helkunntanas, I imagine," Terree said. "Probably has a cooler back home."

"He's faced some discomfort," I said. "But also real pain." I put more pressure on Parr's hand and noticed the red fingertips again. "You've felt the kind of pain that RuBy keeps at bay."

The kind of pain Alan Brindos had endured at the very end.

Parr tried to rein in his agony by concentrating. His eyes were slits, and a weak glow flickered across his face, his neck, and down his arms, but his hands seemed incapable of hosting any of its light.

"When did you have RuBy last?" I asked. "Did Rieser give you some when you came here?"

Parr groaned.

"Or maybe the Landry gave you some." I looked at the Landry's body, half expecting to see her antimatter glow re-engage. It was hard enough seeing her lying there, looking more like the Cara I'd once known than the Ultra version of her, but causing this pain to Parr—seeing more Brindos than the Ultra as he suffered—

Parr cocked his head toward the Landry, such desperation in his eyes that Terree said, "I'm guessing she has some more."

Parr said, "Please. A square is all I need."

The request was so disgustingly pitiful that I took my code card, mostly forgotten since getting it back from Graff, and with a sweep of my finger on the membrane and a nudging of the prog node, activated the illegal image blender I'd downloaded there. I tracked the image of Parr on the ground, gave the code card a moment to process the data, and activated the distorter.

To those within ten feet of Parr, meaning Terree and me, and the bodies of the Landry, Rieser and Graff, Parr's face took on a visage that was a blend of all our faces and thereby became someone totally unrecognizable.

Terree said, "I just *have* to get one of those." She leaned forward to examine it more closely and forgot that she was standing on Parr's hand.

Parr screamed in agony.

I chose that moment to give Parr an ultimatum: "Greist is somewhere on a jump-slot station in the between place, and you'll take us there now."

Parr sputtered, "Can't. Need . . . Cara."

"You're stronger than she was, Parr," I said, gaining confidence, perhaps because I no longer saw Brindos staring at me. "You have the same powers she did, and more. You told me you were new and improved. You take us, and we get you RuBy. If you don't, you'll lie here in pain until Cara detonates and kills us all."

Parr shook his head. "No."

I squatted, taking my face closer to him. This put more weight on Parr's hand, bringing back his whimper. "Yes," I said. "Listen to Parr. To *Brindos*."

"We—the Ultras—will die."

"So? We'll be free of them. Nothing good has come from the Ultras."

"Please."

"The Ultras were smart enough to orchestrate this desperate plan and let it play out . . . for over a *decade*. If your kind wants to survive, figure it out without us."

Parr's new, unrecognizable face softened. "Maybe they can. But—"

"They can. And you don't have to worry about them."

"Send you to the jump slot?"

"All of us."

"That's too many. It would burn me out."

I wondered: Burn him out of the Brindos? Leaving only a Brindos shell? Or would Parr's ever-changing consciousness change things? The Ultras had opened him up, expanding those memories of Brindos, playing with that binary switching and adjusting the nano-materials. Would Parr the Thin Man become Brindos the human, when he awoke from the Ultra's big sleep?

"All of us," I repeated.

"I need RuBy to power it."

"You already have enough for that. You just want more for the pain."

Parr glanced at the Landry again. Longing for that RuBy, probably. But now a laminate of glow whitened her face. The wrong kind of glow. The glow of an antimatter core about to escape its shell. Not long now.

"You'll get the RuBy," I said.

Parr took a moment, but nodded in agreement.

"Any Ultra trick, anything I don't understand, and the deal's off. You'll find yourself in more human pain than ever."

"You'd let everyone here die?" Parr asked.

"I'm trying to *save* everyone here," I answered. "Including you."

I raised my foot from his hand. Terree stepped back, too. I extended my own hand and Parr reached out to take it.

He didn't try anything. He stood. Brushed himself off. Headed towards the House.

We followed.

Forty-one

VANDERBERG PARR FUMED. HE *WOULD* GET HIS RUBY.

In the gigantic Helk House of Terl Plenko, there were three of them: Parr, Terree, and Crowell. Earlier, as they worked their way back through the hallway from outside to the Quarry, Parr heard Terree warn Crowell, *Parr might betray us. He's an Ultra, desperate for life.* She wondered if Parr might take them all the way to Helkunntanas, which would kill them *and* keep the portal open.

It was true, Parr thought. He could do that easily enough. *I'm an Ultra.* He had reached out and killed Cara with barely a thought. The human part of him had not stopped him, had not interfered with his Ultrafied consciousness. She was weak, but she could have harmed the rest of them. Had he killed her because of that, too? She could've helped them travel, but now he could do that.

If he could push back the pain and concentrate.

He had knowingly started something he could not set aside. He was a special creature, the only one that mattered. What would that feel like, to be alone in a world without others like him? Sure, he could easily betray Crowell and Terree and lead them to their deaths. But why would he?

"No," Crowell had whispered back. "He wants to live."

Did they think Parr couldn't hear them? Hello! Enhanced hearing, thanks to the Ultras' upgrades.

Was Crowell right? *I want to live.* He wasn't so sure that sounded right to him. The push and pull between his hybrid parts left him unhinged and stuck between universes. This newest experiment of the Ultras would not end well. Although the alien side of him felt an almost dangerous desperation to salvage this larger mission, time ticked slowly for Ultras. Perhaps they'd find another way to live on, even in their own universe.

If I live, Parr thought, *I might finally be free of the connection to my creators.* Alone.

Now, inside the Quarry, they all waited for Parr.

Crowell explained to him that a code card program had distorted their perceptions of him, blending his features with those around him so that he no longer looked anything like Brindos. The irony wasn't lost on his human consciousness. Even now, he was many. A creature without a single dominant identity.

Do you know who I am?

Parr stood between Terree and Crowell. "I can get you to the jump slot," he said, "and the trip won't harm you. From there back home, however, I don't know. Crossing the brane into your own universe . . ."

"I don't care," Crowell interrupted. "Just get us to Griest. Together. No one gets left behind."

Crossing the brane would likely kill all of them. Parr might burn out on the way to the jump slot, but then he would be in the same predicament as the rest. He was his own conduit, powered by RuBy, keeping the energy at bay, keeping the universes from mixing.

Surface tension.

But how far would RuBy take him, when his body screamed for more and he could barely keep his pain from overwhelming him? He didn't know what shape Griest would be in when they arrived at the jump slot. But there would be RuBy, without a doubt. Would the Memor be able to help or would they all die there, in the middle, neither here nor there?

He wasn't sure he knew anything anymore.

"Any time," Crowell said.

Parr shook away his thoughts and let his power bleed through. "Stay close."

Nothing to it, really, barely requiring a conscious choice, even though he'd never attempted *traveling* on his own. He had this. This place, a buffer. Just a little sleep, not destructive, just focus on the portal at the other end of the conduit. Just focus like Cara did to get to and from the Emirates Building. As the Ultrafied Alex Richards did to get to the warehouse unharmed. Richards asleep, of course. Waiting for Crowell and Jennifer Lisle to pick him up and take him inside the NIO. Asleep, but unharmed.

Yeah, he could get them there; he had enough power. Cara had RuBy, but little time remained. He really did want to get them away from here unharmed. One less person to transport might make a big difference, but he wasn't certain he could pinpoint the travel that precisely.

Glow, he thought. *Glow like a hundred beautiful full moons.*

He closed his eyes, sensing that his travelers wanted to back away, afraid, seeing him light up, and he yelled at them to stand still, even as they hoped against all odds that he would not plunge them into a deep sleep and straight away to their deaths. They wanted to live. They were both insignificant Shyler Frocks, pleading for their lives.

Hey, now.

He sent them on their way, pretty certain they had reached the jump slot safely.

Parr, however, still stood in the middle of the Quarry. Alone. It had been too risky for three of them, and he couldn't keep one of *them* here. And so he had stayed behind.

He could still go in a moment. He just needed RuBy. Just a pick-me-up, a booster, a remedy for the pain, a quick fix for improved concentration. Around him towered the cavernous Quarry, but within it, he wouldn't find a single square. Not in *this* House. Never a paystick around when you needed one.

He really hated the House.

Parr sighed, then trotted out of the room, down the hall past the nearly empty pantry, and out the door to Rook. The Ultra world was a small planetoid they'd pushed to the edge of the gap in their universe.

Rook. Rieser had named the place. Dark and forbidding, like a rook—a crow—a symbol of death. In the game of chess, rooks were castles that had power to move great distances through unoccupied spaces.

The dark world, the dead world.

And yet there was more light.

Parr gazed out at the source of the light: Cara Landry, awash in glow. Dead, but alive with power, and what better proof did he need to understand the futility of merging one way of life with another when all that resulted was annihilation?

Parr walked, did not run, to Cara's side, and crouched. Searched her hands and her pockets until he found what he needed: three squares of RuBy. Still crouching, he rolled them and put them all on his tongue. He closed his eyes. Oh, this would be heavenly. An eternity later, he opened his eyes and noticed the bright glowing body next to him.

He didn't think he had enough time.

He craned his neck and looked back at the door to the House. Shit. So far away. If he ran now he could get there, and he might even make it to the

Quarry, and once there he might have the time necessary to let the room amplify and center his energy for travel.

The glow said otherwise.

Maybe he had made a mistake coming back out here. A very Ultra-like whimper escaped him, and that triggered a decision. This is how the world ends . . .

He clasped Cara's hand, stood, and dragged her body toward the door.

. . . with a whimper *and* a bang.

Take out the House. To be absolutely sure. Inside the House, Cara's detonation would more likely sever the connection from this side to the portal and jump slot. He still had to get her to the Quarry, to maximize the blast.

Parr was just one Ultra among millions. Special, yes, but alone on this side or the other. The Ultra half of him now understood, thanks to the human half, that individuality allowed choices and decisions a group consciousness could not always make.

A group consciousness could work together to figure out the next step toward survival. It just had to understand that taking over the Union was no longer an option. It no longer mattered.

The Ultras *did* have luck on their side. *Lucky Lawrence.* But that was not for Parr to worry about. He had only himself, now, and he had to worry only about helping the Union.

I will be your One.

He dragged her as fast as he could through the door and the long hallway, the Quarry seemingly miles away. The RuBy pushed him. It pulled him. Oil and water.

The heat from Cara's body started to test his nerves, cause him to hold on tighter. Was it really heat, or his perception of her immininent destruction?

Crowell and the others would wonder where he was. Wonder what had happened to him. Not knowing if he was alive or dead. They couldn't come back. He would see to that.

He crossed the threshold into the Quarry and he left Cara in the middle of the room. Only moments left now. She was so bright that he had to look away. When he did, he saw the Pool Room, and Rieser's mixing up of queue and cue made more sense now. He had *games* buffering both ends, pool and chess.

Okay. Maybe that was stretching things.

Parr stepped toward the room, gained some distance from Cara, then turned back to stare at her, hands in his pockets. He felt as if he were at a funeral, or attending a final viewing of the body, and he thought that, to be truly respectful, he should have placed her inside a coffin.

He thought about Rieser telling him he'd crossed to this other kingdom. The dead land. Even with Cara's body ravaged by death, her blistering light reminded him of the Ultra within him, her light pulling at his fading life.

As an Ultra, without a name to label his consciousness, he thought: *Yes, she is life.*

She was his One.

As Vanderberg Parr, he thought: *I know who I am.*

As Alan Brindos, he thought: *Union bright.*

And the world became bright.

He smiled and ran and said hello to life.

Forty-two

IT WAS A JUMP-SLOT STATION ALMOST LIKE ANY OTHER IN THE UNION, except smaller, no berths for ships, and the ragged tear of the jump slot itself lay dangerously close to the structure.

I woke and immediately got to my feet. I took in the station at a glance, saw Terree still asleep, and wondered how long I'd been out.

Parr was gone.

The room, cramped and dark, disoriented me, and the smells of antiseptic and old air struck me simultaneously. The low ceiling made me feel cold and claustrophobic, the walls too close. Shadows of the few crates and overhead ducts flickered in the low, green-tinted light of a nearby open door. A crate next to me begged for me to peek inside, and I opened it and caught the scent of cinnamon. RuBy. At least it hadn't been another Alex Richards copy.

On my way to the door, I stepped over Terree. She twitched once, and groaned. She was coming around. Good. But damn it, where was Parr?

Only one exit. I poked my head through the door and in the middle of the room was a spherical enclosure not unlike a flight bubble sheltering a slot pilot during a jump. This one was larger. My body vibrated from a heavy thrum coming from somewhere inside the bubble.

Inside the bubble.

A tall, lanky being, almost stick-like, stood in front of controls racing with wild white and blue lights. The being took a few seconds to adjust a toggle on the control board, his motions slow, as if at any moment the effort might cause him to overextend and fall. He wore frayed and threadbare clothes. White pale hair hung from his head all the way to the floor.

A moment later, I realized who it was.

"Griest."

Griest Sahl-kla stiffened, but did not immediately turn around. I marveled at his ability not to jump in fright and shock. After all, he was here alone.

Perhaps he had been expecting me. Perhaps he hadn't always been alone.

The Memor turned, and I saw his long, haggard face, framed by his ratty white hair. He was dangerously thin and frail. The Memory had shown a different Griest, but now that I thought about it, that image had gripped me twenty years ago. His physical appearance had nothing to do with any side-effects of traveling, but derived from being here for many years, abused and neglected. A nasty bruise along his arm and wrist might have led me to conclude he'd hurt himself, but I knew better. My experiences with both Alex Richards and Baren Rieser told me that the dark smudge was the world *Ultra*, Griest's protection and his ticket between universes.

I wondered if the tattoo on Griest had been rendered useless, as it had on the Alex Richards who lay dead at the House, the nano ink used up. Or did Griest still have the ability to travel without harm from here back to the Union? He seemed confused as he studied me. Or surprised. Or afraid. Obviously, I wasn't anyone he had expected.

"Who are you?" he asked, his voice weak from disuse.

His question took me aback for a moment. But of course he wouldn't recognize me. I was sixteen when last he saw me, and I now *looked* fifty after my Ultra sleep. "Griest," I said as calmly as I could. "It's David."

He looked at me, at the door behind me, twisted his neck to gaze at the control panel, then back at me. Maybe he wondered if I was alone. Maybe he could hear his daughter stirring, regaining consciousness in the other room.

I could tell he didn't understand. And why would he? A lot of time had passed. I couldn't possibly know what this place had done to his memory or his state of mind. Besides, how could he ever imagine a normal human arriving unannounced when he might have been visited previously only by an Ultra, or maybe Rieser with his numbers to protect him? For all intents and purposes, he'd lived here the last fifteen years alone.

"Who?" Griest whispered. "Who did you say?"

I paused, because now I *could* hear Terree waking up in the other room, and he could too.

"Lucky Lad," I said.

He visibly recoiled. "David . . . Crowell?"

I nodded. Griest's eyes went wide, and I gave him a reassuring smile. "I've remembered. I've fought through the block and I've been recovering much of my life before . . ." I trailed off.

"Before Chicago," Griest said, his chest heaving with the shock and surprise.

"Yeah. I've been in the Memory multiple times, and I've discovered the truth about the Ultras. I've been to the edge of their universe, and now I'm here. Long story. But it's going to end here if we don't do something soon."

"The Memory," Griest said. "You entered the Memory . . .?"

"I had help."

He stepped toward me expectantly. "Terree," he whispered.

I turned to the door. It was beautiful, of course. The timing so impeccable, I couldn't have orchestrated it better had I been in the wings giving an actor a cue. Terree came through the door. Her hand went to her trembling thick lips, and she rushed toward her father.

But she had to stop. The bubble kept her from getting to him, and the two Memors had to be content gazing at each other in a hard-to-bear silence. Although we couldn't wait long, I still granted them some time, and father and daughter talked in hushed whispers.

Again, I wondered about Parr. Had he stayed behind? Had he traveled somewhere else? After all the man had done to get us here, how could he abandon us now? We had no safe way off this station.

Griest also knew time was short, and soon he spoke to me. "Thank you, David."

Terree turned to me too and said, "Yes, thank you. That seems inadequate right now, saying thank you for a job no one ever imagined would be possible." She smiled. "I guess that means I owe you some more money. Case closed."

"Don't worry about it," I said. "And even if I've found your father, we're far from home, and far from safe."

"And you didn't find your own father," she added.

"He's out there somewhere. In the hands of the Ultras, in their universe. If there's a way to get to him, I'll do it."

Griest gestured at the control panel with his four-fingered hand. His arm shook. "The lockouts are in. I'm stuck in here, and there's no way to access the slot, even if a safe place existed. Baren Rieser took the lockout membrane. No insertion equations to morph, no countermeasures."

Damn it, worse and worse. "You can't break the coded gel? Reprogram the nodes?"

"No. We're locked to the anchors of each universe."

"The Houses of Terl Plenko," I said.

Griest pursed his thick, chapped lips. "You have indeed been busy. But if you're here, you must have found them and became aware of their purpose."

"That link is my ticket to return some day and find my dad, Lucky Lawrence."

Griest shook his head sadly. "No, David. 'A house divided cannot stand.' That link cannot remain. Only extreme forces I've harnessed and controlled from this station have lent a certain stability to the link, keeping our universes from meeting and annihilating each other."

I knew he was right, but I refused to listen to common sense. My father was out there. "Terree gave me your antique Tarot card," I said. "I'd had no interest in learning about it, and wondered why a Memor would have one to begin with, but the card . . . it's the Chariot."

"Yes."

"A knight sits in the chariot holding a round object. I think it's a mirror."

"It could be a mirror," Griest said.

"On Ribon, I remember Joseph saying they were going beyond the mirror after that first Landry detonated. 'We cannot hold,' he said." I smiled, feeling my bottom lip tremble. "Well, that chariot is my ride, Griest. My ride beyond the mirror."

Griest shook his head, and the resignation in that gesture made my heart gallop, as if to keep up with this latest act of futility.

"You have to let him go," he said.

No.

"Your father. You *have* to let him go."

I shook my head. "I can't."

"He's been lost to us since he was taken. He and a few other Envoys were singled out and sent for something larger."

"And what was that?"

"I never knew. But he's gone, and your path to him must also disappear."

"I can *not* leave him."

"Dave," Terree said, sounding sternly parental. "There's no way. You can't reach him. We don't even have a way out of *here*."

"So is that true?" I asked. "No escape without Parr?"

Griest cocked his head to one side. "Who is Parr?"

"A true human and Ultra hybrid," I said. "He sent us here, and he thought he could return us home, even though he wasn't sure we would survive. But he didn't come with us."

"So they've done it," Griest said in awe. "They figured it out . . ."

The station trembled.

"Did you feel that?" Terree asked.

Griest checked his slot controls. "Nothing seems to be—"

The station shook. The room rocked, and everyone fell to the deck. Now alarms sounded, and when I gazed up at Griest's control board, red lights flashed.

I got to my feet and pulled Terree up even as another wave hit the station. This time we all stayed upright, fighting the motion, and Griest frantically checked out his panel, his white hair a blur.

"Impossible," he muttered.

I asked, "What is it?"

"The station . . ."

"Damaged? What hit us?"

"Yes, damaged. It's depressurizing, probably through some fractures. But that's not what's impossible. The blast that hit us didn't come from here."

I immediately intuited the source. "The Landry. The Ultra. An antimatter detonation on Rook has damaged the House."

"That could be," Griest said, "if she was inside."

"She was outside," Terree said.

I realized the truth. Why Parr had not come with us. "Parr stayed behind and took her inside," I said. Jesus, he'd sacrificed himself to ensure that the portal closed. I tried not to think about Brindos, but he was there in my mind, no image blender rendering his face unfamiliar.

Gone again, Alan.

"We're disconnected from the portal!" Griest yelled.

A steady hum, a disturbing hiss, and dozens of aftershocks buffeted the station.

"What does that *mean*?" I asked.

Griest's diaphanous bubble shimmered now, brief pulses of color enveloping it. "The House on Rook is damaged severely, and the connection to the jump slot severed. I have no way to calculate the dimensions of this disaster, but the universes, aligned near the gaps for all this time, have come untethered."

Terree gasped. "If the two meet . . ."

Griest steadied himself on the control panel as another shockwave hit. Then he shook his head. "No. We would've already been dead." He turned to me, and his face softened. "The Parr hybrid must've been able to influence the direction. The Ultra universe has moved away."

"We're safe," Terree said.

"Not if this station falls apart, we're not," I said.

The lights in the room flickered, flashed, brightened, then winked out, sending the room into near-darkness. Blue safety lights in the angular recesses of the walls snapped on. In the low light, I watched, amazed, as the bubble surrounding Greist shimmered, expanded, shrank, then faded until it had utterly vanished.

"So much for the lockout," I said, as a new shockwave buffeted the station.

The bubble gone, Griest and Terree met where the outer layer had been and took a moment to greet each other properly, touching foreheads and then both cheeks. They held each others' faces before falling into a light embrace.

I smiled to see the two properly reunited, but the station was collapsing all around us, and we had no escape plan that didn't involve death.

"Griest?" I shouted, respectful, but louder than I intended.

"Yes," he said, returning to his panel, "the lockout is gone."

"Is that good news or bad?" I asked.

"Good."

I sighed in relief.

"But the chances of this station surviving that good news, is bad news."

The station shuddered again. I shook my head. *A house divided can not stand.* "Obviously. But can we get out of here before, uh, the station does not survive?"

Griest rubbed his Ultra tattoo. "I can safely transport myself, and *maybe* one other. But not all three of us. We'd need someone else who had the nano ink of the quantum sleep, or someone who could share the power and focus it."

The same difficulty Parr had. As a hybrid, he'd been strong enough to transport two of us here, particularly with the enhancements of the Quarry.

Griest Sahl-kla took a deep breath, and gave me an odd look. It reminded me of the time Griest had put his hand flat on my chest and made me look at him on the balcony at the Chicago conference. His purpose then had been to prepare me ahead of the memory block. Then he'd left me unconscious, and descended the stairway to meet with Baren Rieser in the foyer.

That memory surprised me. Why? Because it was *my memory*. I had made it my own, not recalling it solely because of my trip into the Memory. It came from my authentic childhood, now emerging from the edges of the fading memory block.

Ah, David . . . remember . . .

"Oh shit," I said, and it disclosed itself like a bomb with a long slow fuse. Terree frowned in response, but I turned my full attention to Griest. "The Memory. Bondmates."

Griest still wore his odd expression. "Yes."

"'Remember where Terree came from,' you said. You *thought* that to me, when Rieser and Joseph took you away."

The station jolted us again, sending me to my knees. Terree reached out to her father, fought to stay upright.

"Look," Terree said. "Can we get out of here or not?"

I stood. "Griest, you said that one day Terree would . . . give her life for your bondmates and your children."

Terree sucked in a breath and snatched her father's arm. "Father, *no*. I just found you!"

"Terree," he said, "we're all going to die here."

"*Not* what I'd hoped to hear," I said.

"We don't have to die," Griest said. "If we try this, maybe we survive."

I said, "You two will become bondmates."

Considering that the station should have been alive with sound, caught as it was in its irreversible death throes, the ensuing silence felt strange indeed.

"How would that work?" I said. "You're father and daughter."

"Don't draw analogies with human mating," Griest said. "I have seven bondmates and many children. It's just not the same for us. We have too much knowledge of our families with whom we share the greatest of bonds. Mating this way is not the taboo it is for humans, or Helks, with their traditional, monogamous sex roles." He embraced Terree again. "You understand this, Terree."

She again touched her forehead to his, put her hand on his chest, and stared at him tenderly.

The concept came clear to me, the trips in the Memory bearing it out. Terree shared Griest's DNA and memories, and Griest believed he could share his power with her and amplify the chance of sleep travel for all of us.

Death wasn't truly death, Griest had said during my first trip into the Memory. Not if the connections to your bondmates were strong. It was nothing more than a long, uneventful sleep.

Terree's name means sleep, Tilson had told me.

At the conference, when I'd asked Griest about his bondmates, he'd said one had been very ill. He would have given his life for her, if possible, but he could not. He was who he was: a male.

"It's why most Memor females morph male," Terree said to me. "Shared memory and procreation come only from male DNA."

The final piece fell into place. "You never morphed male because you never had the opportunity to procreate."

"Yes."

"You can still morph male," I said, picking my words carefully. "As a bond-mate in preparation for procreation, you can share with Griest everything he has within."

Griest could share his ability to travel, and together he and Terree could wield sufficient power to get all three of us out of there safely.

Another shockwave hit, not strong, but it was accompanied by a loud crash of metal and a terrifying whoosh of air escaping through a fatal rent in the station's hull. We were truly out of time.

The Memor bonding had already started, Terree and Griest touching hands and linking gazes. I wasn't sure whether I should look away or not, but I did, staring at the door separating us from life and death.

The aftershocks were no longer really aftershocks, but continual explosions of sound and movement, the floor sliding back and forth like a funhouse, cables and supply boxes shifting. Beyond that door, the hissing of air and the wrenching of metal grated at my nerves.

Then all the noise ceased, or seemed to, as if someone had pulled a grand cosmic plug. Transfixed, I found the door oddly graceful in its silent vibrations. But then a different but familiar sound entranced me: Griest Sahl-kla's voice, a dream voice that became a real voice, because I had awakened to find that the dream world and the real world had intersected.

"David! You must come to us!"

I turned, and two male Memors embraced, almost totally focused on each other in a bonding that defied my full comprehension. I reached out and touched one Memor's long hair. A white glow on Griest's wrist rendered the word *Ultra* in a strange incandescent calligraphy. I now had a sense of which Memor was which. White hair on one and orange hair on the other aided me in identifying them, for the orange-haired other had a glow about him, an inner brilliance from within that arose through his pores and laced his skin with webs of silver and yellow.

Then a bright gold and orange blossomed, reflecting from the Memor's skin, the result of an explosion inside the station, and this was it, finding ourselves on the cusp of two universes, death coming at us as we leaned urgently away into the darkness of space. We left behind a vacuum, hoping for an awakening, an alien birth amid the bright matter of Union.

But first: sleep.

*

When I awoke, sprawled on the floor of the Quarry next to Griest and Terree, I looked up into the face of NIO Special Ops Director Jennifer Lisle and four First Clan Helks dressed in the red and black leathers of the Kenn. The Helks all had their standard-issue stunners aimed at us.

The room smelled like a RuBy factory.

Jennifer stared down, shock in her eyes. "Crowell, Jesus, what the hell happened to you?"

For a moment I thought that although the Memors had returned us to Helkunntanas, the protection hadn't worked, and I had either sickened or aged another twenty years. At least I'd survived the trip. Tem Forno and some woman with black spiky hair stood close by. Forno's confused look duplicated Jennifer's. Neither of them had seen my aged self from the trip to the House on Rook.

Jennifer offered her hand.

"This is what happens working with Forno," I said as I took her hand, groaned, and let her pull me up. Jennifer and I helped Griest and Terree to their feet. "See all these gray hairs?"

Forno managed a smile. "He's now entering his dusk years."

"You mean twilight years," Jennifer said.

"Got you." Forno rubbed the top of his bald head. "Crowell, this is Mayira. Mayira, David Crowell."

I nodded and felt immediately dizzy. "Helk's breath. I'd almost say yes to a square of RuBy right now."

"There's plenty here," Jennifer said.

Indeed, piles of RuBy were scattered everywhere. To Jennifer, I said, "Thanks for letting me leave the morgue."

"Yeah, well, looks like I found Forno before you did."

"Blew up half the place to get to us," Forno said, "but we survived."

"Thanks for the tip about this place," Jennifer said. "We found it with some difficulty. Glad I was familiar with the virtual datascreen from our time infiltrating New Venasaille. I was able to keep these guys—" She pointed at her Kenn backup team "—calm and level-headed."

One of the Helks spoke briefly in Helk, and I raised an eyebrow at Forno.

"You don't want to know," he said. He didn't try to hide his smile.

"We found the older Alex Richards," Jennifer said. "He was in this room when we arrived, but he surrendered peacefully."

I didn't tell her about the body of the younger Richards we'd taken from the morgue, his body still on Rook, at the other House. There'd be time to explain everything later.

Now, in the calm of the House, I took a close look at the two Memors. Griest, who pulled his straggly white hair into some semblance of proper Memor style, and . . . Terree. He looked now almost the same as his earlier female self had looked. His skin, and Griest's, glowed an angry red, apparently an after-effect of their bonding.

Griest saw me looking and said, "May I introduce to you Terree Sahl-kla?"

Griest smiled proudly. Terree smiled. I smiled back. Terree could claim Griest's last name now. They were Memors, and they were happy, and they knew what they knew and understood what we could not, and that was fine. I also understood a lot about myself now, and very few could understand *that*. But Griest and Terree understood. Memory from the Memory. My past unknowable until I was able to examine it.

"I hope you'll be happy with your new life," I said.

"I hope you're happy with yours," Terree replied.

I nodded my thanks. "Oh. Griest, I have a gift for you. You did a lot of traveling, made sacrifices and knowingly gave yourself to the Ultras, ultimately saving the Union. A long time . . . asleep." I took off my Rolex watch and handed it to Griest. He examined it, curious about its significance. "It's a timepiece. A human antique."

He bowed ever so slightly. "Thank you, Lucky Lad."

I pointed at the Rolex. "And it's got an alarm."

"Oh?"

"No, I'm kidding. Rolex never made a watch with an alarm."

"Crowell, that's a treasure," Jennifer said. "You won't miss it?"

"A little. But the NIO will give me a new one, right? I can hear the speech now: 'Thanks again, Dave, for saving the Union.'"

"Dreamer."

"Maybe you'll be able to buy one with the money I owe you," Terree said.

And now I could finally say, "Case closed."

"Shall we go?" Jennifer pointed toward the blackrock room, a copy of the one Graff and I had been locked in, except it looked smokey in there. She said, "We had to blast our way in."

We walked into the room. Daylight poured into it. "Destroy the rest of the place when we're gone," I said. Another link to my father relegated only to memory.

Jennifer said, "Gladly. The Kenn will take you to their headquarters for debriefing. I'll join you after clearing things up here."

Beyond the breach, the jagged blackrock spires of the Outcrop looked menacing. The huge Helk scout ships of the Kenn waited, poised on a few flat surfaces. I might have to face the Helkunntanas weather after all.

"Any chance those Kenn-mobiles have air conditioning?"

The Kenn agents all stared at me.

"It's the heat," I said.

Epilogue

I TOLD THE KENN EVERYTHING, AND I TOLD THE NIO EVERYTHING. Okay, *almost* everything. I didn't talk about my father. About the memory block and the life I'd led before. I saw no need to bring undue attention to my mother or to her watcher, Tilson Hammond. Or to me, for that matter.

I would keep my mom ignorant of her own memory block. At her age, placing her in the Memory or having her undergo some radical surgical procedure to remove the block might not be a good idea. She was happy at the lake. She had long ago accepted the reality of her husband's death, and unless the situation warranted it in the future, why add any stress or doubt to her life? Tilson agreed to stay on, for reasons he had confessed to me that one day at Caroline Point. I felt a million times better knowing he would continue to do what he'd always done: watch over my mom.

The Ultra threat, in both my estimation and the minds of those in authority, had been thwarted for good. It took a lot of explaining to the Kenn and the NIO for them to grasp the idea of two universes—to understand portals, quantum sleep, and the alternate plans involving the Houses the Ultras had hoped to use to create more Thin Men.

I also told them what Parr had become. A hybrid human/Ultra who had just come into his powers when the connection to the universes was severed. I told them how, in the end, he'd helped us to escape Rook, sacrificing his own life to destroy the House there. I did not tell them in whose image Parr had been made. Brindos deserved to rest in peace.

True, there were still Thin Men out there, but fewer than before. Perhaps they would become future threats if they fell in with criminals, but this time, for real, they would have no more connections to the Ultras. When the NIO and Authority swept in to the Emirates Building in Seattle, they found a number of Thin Men who had infiltrated it and used it as a terminal to and from which Cara and the Ultras could travel safely. They had secretly replaced a number of Envoys and found ways to post them to locations around the Union to prepare the way for the coming of the Ultras. None of the Thin Man there shed any light on the significance of several Envoys, denying knowledge of those plans. Not that it mattered now, with the universes apart and drifting even farther away from each other.

Alex Richards—the remaining older version of him—was taken into custody by the NIO and charged with so many felonies and misdemeanors that they quite legitimately put him away for a good while. I never attended any of the trials, never attempted to talk to him, and, during my debriefing, said nothing of my connection to him. I'd never liked Richards as a kid, hadn't liked him during this whole mess, and saw no reason to interact with him now. All the memories of my life before the block were slowly returning, including details about my Emirates page. If he ever got out of prison while my mom was still alive, I would likely confront him, but until that day came, if it ever did, I was content to forget him. Lorway, still alive after using Alex Richards to transport me and Graff to Rook, was also taken into custody. She was, after all, a Thin Man. After I let her go on Ribon, she had escaped detection, but now she would face the scrutiny that the other discovered copies had brought upon themselves.

I cleared up with the Kenn what had happened to Juke and Qerral at her place. I blamed Parr for both deaths, but insisted Qerral's death was an accident. Baren Rieser received the blame for Shyler Frock's death. Mayira avoided any type of prosecution and returned to work for The Mirror under new management.

With Baren Rieser and Abigail Graff out of the RuBy trade, their districts fell into disarray, and the Kenn finally felt comfortable raiding Khrem and Swain. They cleaned things up by arresting the most troublesome sniffers and vendors. New RuBy laws went into effect, the League of City Councils going so far as to prohibit the mass production of the drug, making it illegal to own or sell it outside of licensed shops and vendors. Obtaining a license became a difficult process for anyone hoping to sell RuBy on Helkunntanas.

Griest and Terree Sahl-kla revoked their bonding. After all, the process had taken place as a life and death necessity. Terree could never go back to being female, but when I asked him about it a few days after the debriefings, he professed to have no regrets. Griest, now too old for active duty with the Emirates, decided to consult for them. He also took on a position educating and training aspiring Envoys. Terree chose to follow in his father's footsteps and entered the Envoy program. Because Griest had been an Envoy, Terree received a hefty discount on tuition and fees.

The NIO didn't give me a new Rolex. Instead, they took back my code card and confiscated Forno's altered comm card for security reasons. Earlier, however, I had managed to delete the less than legal progs on his card and mine. With her own money, Jennifer bought me a nice Tudor watch from Rolex's sister company. This one *did* have an alarm. When I talked to her last, a few weeks after I'd returned to my place in Seattle, she said she'd made a good case to Director Bardsley about promoting her to assistant director, since Hardy had given notice that he would retire from the NIO in a few months.

Before I left Helkunntanas, the Kenn gave me something even better than a Rolex *or* a Tudor for helping rid them of Rieser and Graff: free passage through the slot to Ribon.

Which was why—two days after Griest Sahl-kla safely transported us to Helkunntanas—I used my TWT voucher and slotted to Ribon. I found Dorie Senall in Ribon's north resettlement dome of New Coral, situated on land that had once been part of the original city of Venasaille. I'd managed to inform Dorie beforehand of my visit, and the first stop was to be New Venasaille, the south dome, and the Brindos Building, the site of her day office. I waited thirty minutes for the shuttle to pass through the domelock and undergo stringent security checks in the Shell, a transparent ring running under the outer skin of the dome for shuttles and other vessels not allowed in New Venasaille's airspace. Dorie's assistant, Tom Sakson, met me in the Shell and told me Dorie had been unexpectedly called away to New Coral, the north dome, and would I like a shuttle ride out there to see the dome and meet Dorie on site?

Our travel to the dome was uneventful, and I resisted the temptation to gaze out the windows at the damaged planet's surface. Instead, I focused on the excitement mounting inside me about seeing Dorie again. Making good on my promise to visit.

We arrived at New Coral, and after a ping from Sakson, Dorie Senall arranged to meet me at Tempest, one of the few bars under the dome. Buildings and other structures, as well as roads and thoroughfares, were few, but resettlement had indeed begun. Humans made up ninety percent of the planet's returning population. We took a self-powered skiff to the west arch, Fourth Thoroughfare, and Sakson allowed me to go in alone to meet Dorie.

She greeted me with a huge smile and an enthusiastic hug, and we sat at one of the modest tables along the back wall. The bar was small, as were most structures near the arches of the dome. A single flash panel, inset into the middle of the table, doubled as menu and order board. Dorie ordered a soft drink, and I chose water, ignoring the advertising from the flash panel pushing cold Ultra drinks and Temonus whiskey.

"Are we going to keep meeting like this every time you save the Union?" Dorie asked. She had cut her lustrous black hair short, and she looked awfully good. She sipped her drink through a straw, intently studying me.

"It's that private investigator domination I'm working on," I told her.

She leaned in close. "I'd prefer you don't overdo it."

"Not my fault. But I think I'm done with Union-wide plots and double-universe invasions."

"You think?" She reached out and touched my cheek, let her fingers trail back to my ear and my crewcut. "I like the new look."

When setting up this visit, I'd given her fair warning about the damage the Ultra sleep had done to me. "It was time for a change."

"It was brave of you, knowing what would happen."

"I didn't have much choice." I leaned back, chin up, and turned my head from side to side. "But it makes me look more distinguished, don't you think?"

"Always handsome, Crowell."

I swirled the water in my glass. "You're doing well."

She took another sip of her soda, then held out her arms. "RuBy free."

I nodded, happy to hear this news. Here I was drinking water in lieu of hard liquor, but my detox was nothing like the one Dorie had gone through.

We talked another thirty minutes. About the resettlement domes and the colonization schedule, about my mom, Forno, Griest and Terree Sahl-kla, Brindos, and lastly, my father. I told her more than I told any Union intelligence agency about where I believed he was, and how I had come to terms with losing him for good.

"Another universe," Dorie said. "It's hard to imagine your father there."

"The good in Parr—I really think it was Alan starting to emerge into his consciousness—helped me realize the larger scope of the Ultra threat to the Union. But it was Griest who made me understand that letting my father go was not only okay, but absolutely vital to the safety of the Union."

"Then you're ready to move on."

I stared at my water glass and shook my head. "Not really."

"Not really?"

"I want to find him, more than ever." I looked at her.

"Dave. You said it yourself. It's another universe. Closed to us and traveling away at unimaginable speeds."

"I know. It's impossible, and I understand that. I'll keep working with Forno on those cheating-spouse cases, say yes to the occasional missing-persons case, and keep living the lie."

"It's not a lie."

"Not exactly. I'll never be completely comfortable keeping this secret from my mom, but I can't tell her because . . ."

Again, she reached out and touched me. "I know."

"I'll be fine." I sipped my water.

We talked a little more, but eventually Dorie started checking her comm card, and I knew we'd run out of time.

"I have to go," she said. "Always busy, these days."

"Sure."

We stood and faced each other.

"When do you leave?" she asked.

"Later today."

"I wish I had more time. Next time you save the Union and come to see me, we'll arrange for a longer visit."

"That would be great."

"Say hi to Forno for me."

"Of course. He's still on Helkunntanas. He has lots of loose ends there, and he does indeed like being warm."

"Maybe he'll want to stay."

"No, he'll come back. I think he likes this P.I. stuff."

"So the jury's no longer out? He's a keeper?"

"As long as he doesn't wear a fedora? Yeah."

We hugged once more and said good-bye. I left without looking back.

It was nearly a month before Forno returned to Seattle.

I was sitting at my desk, feet up, when he entered the office. As soon as he closed the door, he complained about the weather. "We should've had Griest do a little extra push on that jump-slot station and move this planet closer to your sun."

"Welcome back to you, too. Get everything squared away?"

He plopped into his Helk chair by the dividing wall. "Yeah."

He offered me nothing about Qerral, her family, or any other dealings he might have had with his underworld contacts.

"What'd the Kenn give *you*?" I asked.

"A Rolex."

I blinked at him.

He laughed and bumped his head against the wall. The whole partition shook. "Just messing with you."

"No. Seriously."

"You really want to know?"

"Why wouldn't I?"

"An open visa to Helkunntanas."

I raised an eyebrow. "Nice gift."

"And full restoration of my retirement funds."

"Even better. You still want to work here, right?"

"For the Forno and Crowell Agency?"

"Not exactly the name on my business license."

"Helk snot. Okay, but only if you finally do something about this stupid wall."

"Fair enough."

He stood, rubbed his hands together briskly, and blew air into them. "So what's next?"

I swung my legs to the floor and grabbed Terree's Tarot card of the Chariot from its place on the corner of my desk. I chucked it at him. "Go find the rest of this Tarot deck."

He caught it with one hand, where it altogether disappeared. "Are you kidding?"

"It'll keep you busy. Keep you warm running around."

"No new cases?"

"Nope."

He gazed at the Tarot card. "New side occupation? Fortune teller?"

I shrugged. "Actually? Maybe."

He looked dubious. "As long as it doesn't take you to universes far away."

"Why's that?"

"I'd get lonely."

"Hulks don't get lonely."

"Shut up, Crowell."

Acknowledgements

It's typical for authors in their acknowledgements to point out that no writer works in isolation, and this is definitely true. Sometimes, however, authors are forced to be more solitary than they like, until that moment they burst forth screaming, hoping to find friends to lean on to make everything better. This book has definitely been a labor of love—a completely different experience for me than the first book—and many who know me understand the long, somewhat frustrating story behind it all. As such, there are people to thank.

First, I'd like to thank my good friend Mark Teppo, who gave moral support and plenty of expertise about the publication of this book, and listed all my options and the pros and cons of each. Along those lines, too, I'd like to thank my agent, Paul Lucas, who was also on board from the start. Other kind souls lent their wisdom in different ways: talking about process, reading early drafts of the novel, or taking the time to read and contribute wonderful blurbs. Some did all three! I apologize in advance for the names I'm sure to miss: Gordon Van Gelder, Sean Wallace, Gary Jonas, Michael Bishop, Risa Scranton, Tod McCoy, Ted Kosmatka, Brenda Cooper, Beth Cato, Fran Wilde, Barb & J.C. Hendee, Evelyn Schmit Nicholas, Kristene Perron, John Pitts, Amy Sundberg, Dave Bara, and James C. Glass. Also, I must thank Janna Silverstein, because I made a horrible error in leaving her off the list of writer group pals in the first book's acknowledgements!

Victor Mosquera provided the artwork for the cover of *The Ultra Thin Man* (it was wonderful!), and my heartfelt thanks goes out to him. I'm now indebted to Estonia artist Kuldar Leement for the beautiful cover for this book. Thanks, Kuldar!

This sequel goes down its own path, but I must again give a shout-out to my brother Paul for his imagination and vision that allowed us to write in this universe all those years ago. I also extend my love and admiration to my family, and of course my son Orion, whose accomplishments never cease to amaze me.

Last, I must save a moment to point out that the editor of my first novel, David G. Hartwell, passed away unexpectedly earlier this year. He is sorely missed, not only by me, but by many in the field. I wouldn't be here with this sequel now if it hadn't been for his faith in that first book. Rest in peace, David.

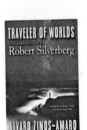